An Obvious Slam Dunk

A Novel

William T. Goodman

Oak Lee Publishing

OAK LEE PUBLISHING

www.oakleepublishing.com

AN OBVIOUS SLAM DUNK

Oak Lee Publishing
P.O. Box 2002
Bozeman, MT 59771

www.williamtgoodman.com

Printed in the United States of America

2017912654
ISBN 978-0-9862262-7-4

Cover Design by Oak Lee Publishing

ACKNOWLEDGEMENT

For a number of years I taught creative writing to groups of enthusiastic fifth graders. On the first day of class I handed out a sheet titled, "IMPORTANT THINGS TO KEEP IN MIND WHEN WRITING." Number one on this list was to *write about what you know*. I added that if you don't know about some aspect of a topic you wish to write about, *find out* before getting yourself into trouble! For this reason, I am indebted to my brother, Robert T. Goodman, for not only his legal expertise, but for his superb editorial instincts. Any mistakes in these areas are certainly mine and not his.

- William T. Goodman -

In a New York minute everything can change.
In a New York minute things can get pretty strange.

-Don Henley, singer-songwriter
(The End of Innocence)

ONE

Next to Christmas, Super Bowl Sunday was the quietest traffic day of the year. The white Ford Econoline delivery van meandered down Palm Drive well under the thirty mile an hour speed limit. The driver's window was open and Chester Bentley smiled as he drove. WDET played Motown hits 24/7 and he mouthed the words to "Let's Get It On" by Marvin Gaye. *If only they still made songs like this,* he thought, chuckling to himself. He remembered using this exact song years ago in high school. While the other boys played hip-hop and rap, Chester found the old rhythm and blues soul music worked magic on teenage girls. In their innocent minds it placed Chester in a separate category, a somehow more mature, sophisticated class from the rest. And not just the black girls – Chester laughed again reminiscing better, less complicated times.

In bold block lettering, STEINBERG'S DELICATSSEN AND CATERING, MIAMI, FT. LAUDERDALE AND PALM BEACH decorated the sides of the Ford. Chester had never received a parking ticket while leaving the van for even extended periods in restricted or illegal parking areas – a small perk that came with the job. It was still a few hours before kick-off. Now was the slow period, but orders would pick up before the pre-game show and again near half-time. For the present Chester enjoyed the lack of traffic and the old songs on the radio.

Effortlessly Chester pulled the van to the curb behind the sign stating DELIVERY VEHICLES ONLY. Not a car was parked along the entire block. He shut off the motor, reached behind into the cooler and retrieved the white paper bag marked Saltzman's Jewelry. Stepping down to the asphalt he realized how hot it was for a February afternoon. *Gotta be near ninety*, he thought walking to the store's front door, reinforced discreetly with steel security bars behind the glass. Thirty-one, black, bulked, six feet four inches tall and two hundred forty pounds, Chester looked more like a middle linebacker in today's Super Bowl game than as a delivery guy for a Jewish deli in South Florida. Entering through the door embossed with *Saltzman's Fine Jewelry and Watches, established 1973,* he welcomed the air-conditioned sanctuary from the humid Fort Lauderdale heat.

"And a fine good afternoon to you, Chester."

"Thanks, Mr. Saltzman, even if it is a hot one today!"

"Yes it is indeed."

Befitting his profession and regardless of the weather, Mr. Saltzman wore a three-piece navy pinstriped suit. White, slicked hair and a thin mustache gave the frail seventy-nine year old jeweler an air of gentility.

"Got a new one for me today?"

"An old one, but maybe a new one to you."

"Good! Let's hear it."

"Okay," Chester began, "see, this horse walks into a bar. The bartender looks at him and says, 'Why the long face?'"

Mr. Saltzman stared blankly at Chester a moment before his eyes squinted and the corners of his mouth upturned with glee. "I get it! Good one, Chester. I'll have to remember that!"

Chester grinned, playing along good-naturedly. In the year he'd been delivering to Saltzman's, he'd noticed a decline in the old proprietor. Not a serious one yet, but probably before long he'd need retirement.

"Are you going to watch the game today, Chester?"

"Not this time. Super Bowl's always a busy delivery day."

"Yes, I suppose it is. Too bad."

Chester placed the bag on the glass counter in front of Mr. Saltzman. "I have pastrami on pumpernickel for you and a turkey breast on wheat for Miss Silva."

"Excellent. I assume this was put on my tab?"

"Like it always is, Mr. Saltzman." Chester thought a moment before speaking again. "I got a question for you, if that's okay?"

"Sure, what it is it?"

"Why do you bother to stay open on Super Bowl Sunday when nobody's out?"

Laurie Silva emerged from the back office and walked to the showroom. "Oh, hi Chester," she said.

"Hi, Miss Silva."

Mr. Saltzman turned to his niece, "Perhaps you'd like to answer Chester's question?"

"Sure," she said to her uncle and turned to face the towering man standing before her wearing the white Miami Dolphins cap with the aqua and orange logo. "You see Chester, this was the first lesson my wise uncle taught me about this business. Much of our sales are derived from masculine guilt. It can be as horrific as a wife finding out about a dalliance with a secretary or some other woman – that's usually a big sale – diamonds, an expensive watch perhaps. Or it can be small guilt like a forgotten anniversary or maybe coming home a bit late or tipsy from an evening out with the boys – that might translate into simple gold earrings or a sterling key ring. Super Bowl alienates a lot of wives and girlfriends. So the guys get together and to ease their guilt, the women are sent out to shop... with *the men's* credit cards or cash. The game hasn't started yet, so things are quiet, but after the game begins, the wives and girlfriends drift in ready to buy."

As if for approval, Laurie looked over to Mr. Saltzman. He winked at her and smiled.

Shifting to Chester he added, "She's a smart cookie and a fast learner, too."

Unseen by the three in Saltzman's Fine Jewelry and Watches, a beige Toyota sedan eased to the curb behind the delivery van. Despite the heat, the man inside wore a black motorcycle jacket with the sleeves zipped past his wrists down to matching leather gloves. He was of medium height and build, short red hair and brown eyes. A hooked nose was his only remarkable attribute. He was not exactly handsome, but not unattractive either – just an average-looking thirty-something nobody. He turned off the motor leaving the keys in the ignition. Almost instantly the heat made sweat beads emerge on his forehead. The man opened the door, stepped into the hot street and quickly glanced up and down Palm Drive – empty as he'd expected. Good.

A few years ago, Mr. Saltzman would have been immediately suspicious of this leather jacketed and gloved customer on such an unusually muggy Florida afternoon, but the years had dulled his instincts. Nothing about the man registered an alarm. Laurie Silva was sorting the sandwiches from the bag in front of Chester and took no notice of the man. Chester's back was to the door, and he never heard him enter.

"May I be of some assistance?" Mr. Saltzman asked as he'd done thousands of times before.

There was no response. The man walked the few feet to Chester and tapped him on the back with his left hand while reaching around under his jacket with his right. Startled, Chester turned around and stared down at him.

Later, Laurie Silva would testify she saw Chester's jaw drop and a look of possible recognition appear on his face a moment before the man yelled, "SURPRISE, NIGGER!" shoved the barrel of a huge nickel plated revolver in Chester's mouth and pulled the trigger.

Contained within the walls of the shop, the muzzle blast from the .41 Magnum Smith & Wesson would have been deafening had it not been absorbed within the confines of Chester's mouth and throat. Performing precisely as it was designed, the high velocity hollow-pointed slug expanded as it plowed through the cranial cavity and exploded out the top of Chester's skull plastering his once white Miami Dolphins cap to the showroom ceiling of Saltzman's Fine Jewelry and Watches by a gluey mixture of blood and brains.

At the shot, the expanding gunpowder gases that propelled the bullet blew out his cheeks leaving equal gaping voids in both sides of Chester's face, exposing his smoldering tongue and molars in a hideous grin. Simultaneously, the fierce recoil drove the revolver skyward, shattering Chester's front teeth and imbedding the raised front sight blade on the end of the barrel solidly into the roof of his mouth. Thus anchored, the Smith & Wesson was jerked from the man's hand as Chester fell backward. There it remained protruding from his ruined mouth.

Hesitating for only a moment, the man reached inside the front of his jacket and withdrew an olive-drab military surplus laundry bag. He turned to Laurie Silva and Mr. Saltzman, who were both too stunned and shocked to respond in any way at all, and spoke in a calm voice, "I have another gun in my pocket. If you do as I say, nobody else will get hurt." Handing the cloth sack to Laurie, he said, "Now open these cases and dump everything in the bag."

Still, Laurie could not react. A short, sharp slap to the left side of her face by a gloved hand got her attention. "Do it now. Fill the bag. Start with the watches and work down the cases. If they aren't emptied into the bag in sixty seconds I pull the other gun."

Fifty-eight seconds later the man turned from Laurie Silva and Mr. Saltzman – who had barely moved since the shot was fired – and confidently exited the shop, opened the door to the Toyota, tossed the heavy laundry bag to the passenger seat and slowly drove away.

The face slap had the effect of bringing Laurie Silva to total awareness and mental acuity. As the man entered the Toyota she ran around the counter, stepped over the prostrate Chester and managed to see the last four numbers of the Florida license plate as well as noticing the broken taillight on the curb side of the car.

With no traffic to contend with, the Fort Lauderdale police cars arrived within minutes of Laurie Silva's frantic 911 call. She thought it strangely surreal that the officers cautiously entered the shop with guns drawn as if the man was still inside and posing a threat. They said nothing while walking the shop and back office with their black automatic pistols pointing and jerking during their short search. Mr. Saltzman slouched in a chair behind the now empty diamond engagement ring counter. Laurie was not certain when he'd taken the seat as her main concern had been writing the license plate number on a pad and calling the police. Obviously dead, Chester lay in a grotesque heap while Laurie avoided looking at the expanding pool encircling what remained of his head.

As guns were returned to their holsters, a welcome sense of calm settled over the shop. A short time later a tall man wearing a brown suit was asking Laurie if she was the 911 caller while another similarly dressed man tried to question Mr. Saltzman. Getting no coherent response, he told the just arriving paramedics to get the old gentleman to the hospital.

Laurie Silva nodded in affirmation that she was the 911 caller, and the brown suited man introduced himself as Detective

Hanson. Before leading Laurie Silva to the back office for questioning he glanced at the group of uniformed officers gathered around Chester's body, massive revolver still protruding from his mouth. "Jesus," one said to the group in an almost reverent tone looking first at Chester and then up to the Miami Dolphins cap stuck to the ceiling. "Been on the force over twenty years and never seen anything like this...Jesus," he softly repeated as Detective Hanson took Laurie Silva gently by the arm and walked her to the back office.

Three indoor security cameras ran full time in Saltzman's Fine Jewelry and Watches. One angled in from the left, one focused straight over the main jewelry counters in the center of the showroom, and one aimed from the right. A fourth camera with a wide-angle lens mounted outside the entrance filmed the sidewalk directly in front of the store. All were working perfectly when the leather-jacketed gunman pulled up in the Toyota, walked in, shot Chester, had the laundry bag filled, walked out and drove away. Even the Toyota's full license plate revealed Laurie Silva had correctly written down the last four numbers. Within an hour of the crime, the police had distinct front and side photographs of the killer and ID'd the Toyota as registered to a Roy Dillard whose Florida driver's license photo matched the security camera images perfectly. A S.W.A.T. team was already closing in on the small home off Broward Boulevard owned by one Roy Dillard.

From a vacant lot situated diagonally across the street from Roy Dillard's house, Detective Hanson watched through binoculars as the S.W.A.T. team surrounded the property. Amazingly, in plain sight the Toyota was parked in the driveway, broken tail light glinting in the afternoon sun. A body-armored officer called to the house through a megaphone, "You are surrounded by the Fort Lauderdale Police. Come out the front door with your hands above your head. Do not make any sudden moves."

Within seconds the front door slowly opened and a man wearing shorts, a t-shirt and flip-flops emerged with his arms raised high over his head. He nervously looked at the assault rifles pointed at him and weakly asked, "What's this all about?"

The megaphone blared, "On your face, spread your arms and legs. Now!"

When the ginger haired man complied, two officers ran at him from behind, grabbed his wrists, and in one swift movement had them cuffed behind his back.

"Identify yourself!" one of the officers demanded.

"I'm Roy Dillard," came the reply. "What did I do?"

Even from a distance, Detective Hanson could actually hear the laughter from some of the S.W.A.T. team members. Lowering his binoculars and walking to the house he passed two officers putting Roy Dillard into a patrol car. Stopping, he looked into the cuffed man's face and recognized him as the man in the security camera photos. Detective Hanson shook his head from side to side and under his breath mumbled to the two cops, "What a fucking moron. This case is an obvious slam dunk."

TWO

Ken Melzer was fairly sure he was taking the most direct route to the Broward County Courthouse. This was his third time navigating the way from his home in Imperial Point. He allowed himself forty minutes, but at six twenty in the morning that allowance was more than generous. Ken felt sure that in the coming weeks and months he'd eventually find the shortest, most direct route, and driving to work would be a mindless, rote activity. He knew it would become routine and perfunctory, but today the anticipation of his first day as an assistant public defender, his first day as a true lawyer, was exhilarating.

B.A. degree from Tulane at twenty-two, three years of law at the University of Florida, some time off to study for the Bar exam, and now, twelve days past his twenty-sixth birthday, an employed, licensed defender of the down-trodden, the less fortunate, the misunderstood, and yes, perhaps even some honest-to-goodness evil-doers. They all deserved representation – good, empathetic, perhaps even sympathetic, representation – and, of course, their day in court. Contrary to what he'd been told time and again, Ken Melzer didn't believe his clients were mostly a bunch of dishonest criminals, cheats, bums, thieves or, as he'd been shocked to hear his own wife say, "low-life scumbags." Charlene was upset when she'd said that. Ken knew she didn't mean it. When people get emotional and upset, they can say the cruelest things. While he didn't have the chance to verbally forgive her – she had stormed from their small living room and slammed the bedroom door after saying what she did – Ken thought he understood her frustration, and silently forgave her outburst. Neither of them mentioned the event again, and Ken felt certain Charlene was too ashamed of what she'd said to revisit it.

Ken Melzer, Assistant Public Defender, parked the faded metallic blue Honda Civic in the separate lot reserved for those with offices in the Broward County Courthouse. The car had been his high school graduation gift from his parents. Almost new, it was his pride and joy as a freshman at Tulane. Lots of adventures in the blue Honda. But, old and worn as it might be, the Civic was now the vehicle of a respected professional. Not a kid's car anymore, but the sedan belonging to an attorney. For exactly this day, he'd washed it and cleaned out all traces of the past. It might be the same trusted cruiser from his youth, but it was presently his conveyance to a world of justice and constitutional precedence – a transporter to his future.

From the trunk he removed a cardboard box containing a few necessities for his new office. Once inside, Ken Melzer passed a sleepy-eyed security guard manning the metal detector, who without a word nodded him through. The main hallway was deserted, and with doors open in a symbolic welcoming gesture, the elevator was waiting. A short ride and a few floors later Ken arrived at the office of the Public Defender, Broward County, State of Florida. He fumbled for the key he'd been issued and opened his office door. Flipping the light switch, he stood staring and realized smiling; this was *his* office, the office of Ken Melzer, attorney at law. The walls were painted a pale yellow – freshly applied with a hint of new paint smell. Bookshelves contained a few abandoned law volumes and a short stack of worn magazines – he'd peruse those later. A Steelcase desk under which sat a county owned computer and antiquated intercom box, with swivel chair behind and two mismatched oak straight back chairs in front, finished the milieu. Some decorating – maybe a sofa, a little personalizing – and this office would come alive.

He started on the cardboard box. First out was a silver framed wedding photo of Charlene and him taken the previous year at the Fort Lauderdale Yacht Club – his father-in-law's idea to be married at *The Club* just as her two older sisters had been. That was okay. Weddings were for the brides; the groom was simply along as a necessary accessory. It was not his idea or desire to be married there, in front of a hundred or more people he'd never met, but if that's what Charlene wanted, that was fine with him. He set the photo on the desk. His laptop went to the side along with a gold pen and pencil set standing at attention in an onyx stand – a combined law school graduation gift from his two brothers. A battery-powered brass clock in the shape of a ship's wheel – a gift from Charlene's father – and a few non-descript items were strategically placed.

Satisfied with his work, Ken sat behind his desk for the first time. He checked the clock in the brass ship's wheel. Seven on the button. An hour early. Exactly as he'd wanted. He needed the hour to acclimate, to get used to his office, the sense of his surroundings, the gravity of it all. This was serious business. He'd planned on this exact moment for nearly four years. Closing his eyes he caught himself beginning to pray – old habits die hard. He opened them, took a breath and closed his eyes again. A quiet, soul-cleansing meditation was what he needed. The prayers were in the past, in a different life. There'd be no more of that. Fine for his mom and dad, his two brothers, but not for him, not anymore. Ken blanked his mind and let himself drift in blackness.

A sharp knock on his door brought Ken Melzer out of his meditation and instantly to attention. Refreshed and alert, he glanced at his brass ship's wheel clock – precisely eight o'clock – and responded with a louder than he'd wanted, "Yes?"

The door opened a crack and a young woman's head peered in, "Oh, hi. I'm Tina, the receptionist. I'm sure we'll get to know each other."

"Hi, and I guess you know I'm Ken Melzer," he paused awkwardly and continued, "My first day."

He saw her glance at the brass ship's wheel clock before she answered with a big grin, "I know, welcome aboard! Hey listen, I have to run, but I just wanted to warn you that your first client is waiting." Stepping fully into the nearly empty office, she walked to his desk and handed him a folder. "You might want to review this. It would have prepared you for your client, but being your first day and all, there was no way to get it to you…"

Taking the folder, Ken cut her off saying, "Not a problem, Tina. Send him in. Or is it a her?"

"It's a him. If you need anything, just hit the button on the intercom."

"Got it."

The door closed. Ken quickly removed a yellow legal pad

from a desk drawer, pulled a gold pen from the onyx stand, and pretended to write. He was aware of the door opening and someone standing inside, but Ken didn't look up from his work for four seconds – he actually counted the seconds silently to himself. He needed his client to think he was busy and engaged. At least he thought the ruse would enhance his air of importance.

When he did put his pen down and peer over his desk, he hoped the shock on his face didn't register with his first client.

"Please..." Ken glanced at the papers he'd been handed, "please take a seat, Mr. Fudd."

"Thanks, no. I'll stand."

"Okay, if you are more comfortable that way. That's fine." Ken stared at the man in front of his desk. He was well over six feet tall and lean, probably mid-thirties. He wore some kind of exotic cowboy boots – lizard or snakeskin, Ken didn't know which. Faded, tight leg jeans were accented with a huge brass belt buckle in the shape of an armadillo. He wore a frayed yellow T-shirt with *TEXAS* printed across the front that was partially hidden by an open brown leather vest with buttons made of old silver Mexican coins. From under his sweat-stained tan cowboy hat streamed ringlets of dark brown hair that curled below his shoulders. He was clean-shaven – at least five days ago he had been. For a moment they locked eyes until Ken broke away and glanced down at the papers Tina had handed him.

"Mr. Fudd, I'm afraid I haven't had a chance to review your case-"

"And just why the hell not? Ain't I important enough for you?" He drawled in an obvious deep southern accent.

"No, of course not, it's just that... well, you see, Mr. Fudd-"

"The name's Hobart, Hobart Fudd. You can call me Hobart or Hoby like my friends do, but I don't like Bart and I don't cotton to 'Mr. Fudd' if it's all the same to you."

"Certainly, Mr.... ah, I mean Hobart. What I was saying is that this is my first day here, and I just now found out you were to be my client. I have to admit to being unprepared for your visit at the present."

"Your first day? Well, where'd you work before this?"

"This is my first job actually. Truth be told, you are my first client."

Hobart Fudd looked down at Ken sitting behind his desk, "Well, sheeit," he swore under his breath. "Are you at least a lawyer?"

"Yes, of course. I recently passed the Florida Bar Exam," Ken answered and immediately wished he'd left out the Bar exam part. "Let's start over. I'm Ken Melzer. I'm a public defender and I've been assigned to your case...to be your attorney. Wouldn't you rather have a seat so we can discuss your situation?"

Hobart paused a moment, appeared to ponder Ken's words, let out a sigh and said, "Sure, why not, Dr. Melzer."

"It's not 'Dr.' Melzer, Hobart. You can call me Mr. Melzer or just Ken would be fine."

"I thought lawyers were doctors."

"Technically, perhaps. I have a Doctor of Jurisprudence degree. Were I to teach on a college campus, for example, I might be called 'Dr. Melzer' because that is a title of respect reserved for academia-"

"So you are a doctor of whatever you just said, but I don't have to call you doctor?"

Ken heard noise coming from the reception area outside his office. Was it always this loud out there? "As I said, Mr. Fudd, just call me Ken if you are comfortable with that?"

"I am, Pardner, just so long as you call me Hobart or Hoby." He stood again and extended his hand across the desk. Ken also stood and they shook... and shook. Fudd's grip was firm, almost painful, and he increased the pressure for what seemed to Ken an eternity.

"My pappy, God rest his soul, used to say you can tell a lot about a man by his handshake."

"And what did you discern from mine?"

"I ain't sure yet."

Taking their seats, Ken began, "Mr. Fudd, I mean Hobart, rather than me read this report, why don't you explain in your own words what happened, and we can go on from there."

"Okay, but is everything I say here just between us? I mean, if I screw up and say something wrong, you ain't gonna tell the cops or get me into more trouble?"

The noise outside was distracting, but Ken smiled reassuringly and said, "No, of course not. There is a strict attorney/client privilege protocol all lawyers follow-"

"Stop all the high-fallutin' lawyer talk and just answer my question!"

Ken was keenly aware of his client's quick temper. At some point he'd need to address this, especially if Fudd was eventually to take the stand and testify. "In simple terms, Hoby, anything you say to me stays with me. It's private, just between us, nobody else."

"Okay then. You shudda just said that in the first place. It'd saved a lotta time."

"Sorry. Why don't you tell me what happened. And remember, what is said in this office goes no further than these four walls." Again, Ken was aware of voices and sounds beyond his closed door.

"Okay, Pard, here goes." Hobart took a deep, audible breath, let it out slowly and began. "See, I make my living runnin' a small circus. I guess you could call it a circus, maybe a carnival is better, but I don't have no rides for the kids or shootin' galleries 'n such. I ain't got no cotton candy or popcorn neither. Anyway, what I ain't got ain't as important as what I do got. And what I do got is pretty spectacular!" He paused here for effect.

"I'm all ears, Hobart. Please continue."

"Right. Well, my show – see it ain't really a circus or a carnival – it's just one act. And that act is my pig! His name is Bruno, and he ain't no ordinary, run-o'-the-mill boar. Bruno's special. Indeed he is." Again, Hobart paused and looked expectantly at Ken.

"Mr. Fudd, I mean, Hobart, please just tell me what happened. Give me the condensed version."

"What's that supposed to mean? I don't know all them fancy words."

"It means the short version. We can go over details later."

"Oh, okay. You mean, like, just the facts 'n such?"

"Precisely. I mean yes."

"Okay, so my boar, Bruno, is different from other boars. Hell, he's different from just about any animal I ever seen. You see,

Bruno has been given a special gift. To be factual, I think that's
the word, *factual*, the Lord done gave Bruno two dicks and sets of
balls, I mean penises and two scrotusses." Hobart looked at Ken,
"I don't want to give offense here, and I don't want to use no
dirty words or nothin', but I don't know any other way to
describe Bruno."

Ken's smile turned into a guffaw, "you're saying your pig has
two complete sets of anatomically correct genitalia?"

Hobart sat silently looking at Ken. Abruptly he was back on
his feet and said, "I don't like the way you're smirkin' over
Bruno's God-given gift, and I don't know what two sets of
'automatic generals' means, but I can tell you that I don't think
you're taking me serious! Look, Mr. New Fuckin' Lawyer, I'm in
a heap a deep shit here, and I sure as hell don't need you laughin'
at me and my pig!"

Shocked at this sudden outburst, Ken lost his smile and said,
"I'm sorry, Hobart. I wasn't laughing at you or your pig. Please
forgive me and please calm down...please."

Fudd stared down at Ken and remained standing for a few
moments longer than Ken found comfortable. *This crazy guy
might really come unhinged*, Ken thought. He was relieved when
the corners of Hobart's mouth turned slightly upward and he said,
"Okay, Ken, I'm sorry, too. See, I'm under a lot of stress here.
My whole livelihood is on the line! I'm a bit touchy. I'll try to
control my temper."

"How about taking your seat again. Try to relax a little...take a
deep breath maybe, and continue with your story."

Hobart slumped into the oak chair and, as Ken had suggested,
actually did take a deep breath before continuing.

"So, where was I?" Hobart paused in thought and then
continued, "So, I established the particulars, so to speak, of
Bruno, my boar. See, Dr. Melzer...Mr. Ken, I realized when
Bruno was born on my cousin's farm in Waco that he might be
my key to fame and fortune. I have a way of recognizin' an
opportunity when I see one – everybody says that 'bout me-"

Ken interrupted, "Hoby, I think you're getting sidetracked
again. I need the facts of your case now. Like I said before, you
can fill me in on the details later."

"Oh, sure. No problem. I'll skip to the part where I get busted by a bunch of fat, dick-head Broward Sheriff's Deputies!" Fudd started to raise his voice, and Ken noticed a vein begin to show on his forehead and disappear up under his hat.

"Them sons-a-bitches was rough with me, too! I got it in my mind to sue them bastards for what they done to me and Bruno-"

"Hobart, HOBART! Come on, man, you've got to calm down. If I'm going to help you, you have to settle down, control yourself, and just tell me what happened."

"I'm sorry again, Mr. Ken. I'm just so riled up I could spit!"

Ken was again conscious of all the commotion in the reception area outside his office. Could *all* the public defenders have crazies like this Fudd character in their offices?

"Please, Hobart, try to continue."

"Right. Mr. Ken, first let me say I take good care of Bruno. He only gets fed the best slop I can find. And sometimes that gets expensive. I make sure he eats before I do. I know, I know, you just want the facts, but that is a fact and you need to know it."

Ken nodded patiently.

"I'm sure you take excellent care of Bruno. Go on."

"So, you see, Dr. Melzer, I mean Dr. Ken, Bruno has a good appetite. And I ain't talking about slop, neither. Bruno is a young stud boar. He likes his sows! Whoowee, does he like his sows! 'Specially them big, round pot-belly variety! Let me tell you, he gets the scent of one of them juicy porkers and he starts to snortin' and ruttin' 'round somethin' fierce!"

"Hobart, Please! Can you just get on with what happened?"

"I am, Goddamnit!" Hobart stammered. "Sorry, again. You can see I'm like a hornet's nest that's had a stone chucked at it-"

"Settle down, Hoby. Take another breath. You can do this."

"You're right, Doctor. I can do this, and by God I will!" Hobart closed his eyes and breathed slowly for a few moments.

"When Bruno gets to ruttin' with a sow, he starts with his left… thing. I'm tryin' not to be offensive here."

"I appreciate that. Just continue."

"So, when he's finished up on the sow with his left pecker, he still has his right one to deal with. See, they don't work exactly together. Kinda like them old-fashioned sinks with a hot water and cold water faucet next to each other. When you turn one on, the other don't do nothin' till you turn it on, too. And when you turn one off, t'other one stays on till you shut it off irregardless of the first one-"

"I think I get what your saying, Hobart. Go on."

"So, once Bruno uses one spigot he still has to use the other spigot. And that's the whole point! He's a freak o' nature. He can do the same sow twice, or he can do one then another! Everybody's happy and I make money!"

"Hobart, I don't understand. Let me clarify that. I understand Bruno's peculiar attributes and needs, but how do you make money? And why are you here?"

"Well, shit Doc, can't you recognize the opportunity? I did! I thought you lawyers was smart."

"Just continue."

"I got me something here nobody else got. I knew right away folks would pay to see Bruno and then pay additional to see him in action! So, I set up a little roadside pen and tent with a sign sayin', 'SEE THE AMAZING BRUNO – THE WORLD'S ONLY DOUBLE STUD BOAR – $3.00,' and Mr. Ken, you can't believe all the people whose curiosity gets the best of 'em and they stop and pay three bucks to gawk at Bruno. Then I wait 'til I got a good crowd of folks. And don't worry; I don't do this with no kids around. I got scruples 'bout that. Yessir, I do. But anyway, when I get the right crowd circlin' 'round Ol' Double-Stud, I let the word slip that I got two sows in the tent and for three bucks more I can put Bruno in there with them!" Hobart chuckled. "Man, them rubes can't get their money out fast enough!"

"This is how you make a living?"

"Bet yo' ass I do! And a damn good livin' it is... *was* at least...'til last night."

"I'm thinking this is the part in which I should be the most interested."

"So here's the nasty part of my story. Nasty for me in a legal way, not to mention all the money I coulda made had them cops not showed up."

"Again, please, Hobart. Just tell me what happened."

"Okay, see I got this nice gathering of folks in the tent. Ol' Bruno's a snortin' and a ruttin' with Sally. Oh, I forgot to mention I travel around with two sows- Sally and Penny. They're both the big pot-belly variety Bruno favors-"

"Mr. Fudd! You need to tell me about the police, not the sows!"

"Hey, you just wait a damn minute here, Mr. High 'N Mighty!" Ken could see the temper flair once again. "I'm tellin' this here story as best I can, and if that ain't good 'nuf for you, than you can just go suck eggs-"

"No, please, Hobart… Hoby, I just want to help you. I'm not a cop. I'm not the enemy. I'm not trying to get you in trouble. I'm your attorney, your lawyer. I'm a public defender. You are the Defendant. I'm on your team. We're the team of Melzer and Fudd or Fudd and Melzer, if you prefer." Ken thought, *jeez, did I really say that last part? I should have been required to take acting classes in law school! And all that damn noise outside. Was that a scream I just heard?*

"I understand. Sorry. You gotta forgive my bad manners. I'm much obliged, Doc. I best get on with what happened 'fore you throw me out of your fine office here-"

"No, Hoby, you're doing fine. I'm not going to throw you out. Please, tell me the rest."

"And one last detail I gotta tell ya first, Doc. Ya gotta believe me when I tell ya I really do take good care of Bruno. For example, once when he seemed a little under the weather and was having, you know, some trouble performin', I mixed a little Viagra into his slop. And like that ad says on TV, and, Mr. Ken, I took it seriously enough to memorize, 'seek immediate medical attention for an erection lasting more than four hours.' So when Bruno did Sally and then did Penny and then did Sally and then Penny and then Sally again and then Penny again… and again and again, well I figured four hours for a one-dick pig was more like eight hours for a double-dicker, so I hustled him straight off to a vet. Cost me almost two hundred bucks, but they got him calmed down, if you know what I mean. Now he's back to his old self an' good as new. Ain't had no problems with the performin' part since, neither."

"I can see you have great concern for Bruno, and I'm sure you care for the sows equally. Now, please, Hobart... Hoby, tell me about the police."

"Oh, yeah, I almost forgot about that part. I mean, that's why I'm here, right?

"Right, that's why you're here, Hobart."

Hobart motioned over his shoulder with his thumb, "Man, it sure is loud out there. Always like this?"

"I wouldn't know, my first day on the job. Remember?"

"Oh yeah, that's right. I forgot about that."

"You were going to tell me about the police."

"Okay, okay. I'm getting to that. What was the last thing I told you?"

Ken wondered if this was merely insanity or advanced adult attention deficit disorder. "You said you had a crowd ready to see Bruno in the tent."

"Yeah, that's where I left off. Okay, so I take this bunch into the tent and Bruno gets a good whiff of Sally and Penny. First Ol' Lefty goes to attention, that's what I call his left one."

"I figured as much. Go on."

"So Bruno's doin' what Bruno does best. But there's this one woman in the crowd, and I guess she don't like the show, cuz she leaves and goes to sit in the car while her husband or boyfriend or whoever he was, stays in the tent – havin' a good time, I might add – certainly gettin' his three dollars worth as Bruno was feeling particularly frisky-"

"Hobart, the police... remember? You were going to tell me about the police?"

"Right, so I didn't know it at the time, but that bitch in the car called the cops on her damn cellphone and next thing I know them sheriff deputy fellers show up. They tell everyone to leave and they say I'm under arrest! I'm pissed at this and I say, 'what the hell for?' and one of them deputies says something like, 'a whole lotta things, Boy.' He actually called me 'Boy.' So I says, 'who you callin' *Boy*?' And I can tell you right now, I don't like nobody callin' me *Boy*. I won't stand for that shit! And he says, 'that's it, Boy,' he called me *Boy* again, 'you're goin' to jail!'"

Ken looked at Fudd who sat in front of his desk looking

confused. "The officer didn't explain the charges or complaints against you?"

"I'm not sure. Things happened pretty fast after that. Next thing I knew I had a lump on the back of my head and I was sitting in a damn cop car!" Hobart lifted the back of his cowboy hat and turned his head for Ken to see. He put his finger somewhere near the crown of his skull and said, "Got one hell of a lump right here. Them bastards musta walloped me good."

Ken couldn't see anything through all the hair, and he wasn't about to feel for a wound. "That's all you know?"

"I swear that's all I know. Do you think I can sue them assholes for roughin' me up for no good reason?"

"I think I better review this report that I didn't get a chance to read before you arrived."

Ken picked up one of the sheets of paper, skipped to the bottom and said, "It says here you are being charged with operating a circus without a license or permit; using unlicensed and unregistered performing animals for profit; allowing porcine sexual harassment on two sows by one boar; indecent use of animals in a cruel fashion for viewing and exploitation for money; and..." Ken stopped reading and looked up at Hobart before continuing, "And Hobart, it says here you are further charged with resisting arrest and physically assaulting two officers of the law. It states you punched one deputy in the nose, breaking it, and punched the other in the mouth, knocking out two front teeth!" Ken again looked at the expressionless Hobart. "Hobart, my God, why didn't you tell me this? Battery on a law enforcement officer is a serious violent offence. I don't even know how you are here in this office. These are violent offences. You should be in jail!"

"I should be in jail? Did you just say '*I should be in jail?*' You told me you were on my side. You told me we were a team, that you were here to help me! I knew you was a lyin' sack o' shit from your handshake. You're not here to help me. You're one of *them,* ain't you one of ...*them?*"

"Take it easy, Hobart. What exactly do you mean 'one of them?'"

"I mean *exactly* one of them government types who try to take away an innocent man's freedoms. I mean *exactly* one of them military types who fly around in black helicopters spyin' on folks just tryin' to make an honest livin'. I mean *exactly* one of them people who's been turned into an alien from a UFO! I'm talkin' evil here! I'm talkin' 'bout Satin here! I'm talkin' nasty, bad-ass, deviltry of the worst kind!"

Before Ken could digest this tirade, with amazing athleticism, in one smooth movement, Fudd let out a rebel yell, leapt to the desk top, and crouched into some semblance of a karate fighting stance. Ken saw Fudd's eyes roll for a moment and then refocus down on him.

In a low, controlled whisper Hobart hissed, "I ain't gonna let it happen. Not now. Not here. Not by you. Not never again!"

Ken's voice nearly left him. He managed to croak, "Hobart, for God's sake-"

"You called me *Bart*! I told you never to call me Bart. My Pappy used to call me Bart before he'd take me to the woodshed when I was a young'un and beat me. Well, I fixed him good for that! And now I'm gonna fix you, too!"

Mustering all his strength, Ken stammered, "I didn't call you Bart! I swear to God, I didn't! I called you Hobart. HO, HO, HO-BART! *Not* Bart!"

"Don't lie to me, you alien piece of shit!"

"I'm not an alien, Hobart. I swear. I'm an Earthling and a citizen of the United States of America!"

"You ain't none of them things!" Hobart seemed to calm and then smile down at Ken. In a throaty growl he said, "Now, I'm gonna open a can o' whup-ass on you the likes of which you ain't never knowed. I'm gonna make you pay, you sorry-ass little weasel."

Ken made a desperate lurch for the intercom box by Hobart's right foot. Grabbing it with both hands he pulled it in close and slammed his palm on the activation button, "Tina! Tina! I need help!" The ruckus from the reception room seemed even louder now. *What if she can't hear me?* He tried again, "Tina, TINA!"

From above, Ken heard, "It's too late for that, Melzer, or whoever you are."

Ken rolled out of his chair and curled on the floor clutching the intercom box to his chest, hand still holding down the button. "Tina!" he yelled again.

Finally a calm reply, "Yes, Mr. Melzer, what can I do for you?"

"I need help! He's gonna kill me!"

"What was that, Mr. Melzer? Sorry, it's kind of loud in here today and I couldn't hear you very well."

Then, from above again, "Your time's run out, Pard. Time to end the team of Fudd and Melzer. Time for the Grim Reaper-"

"For the love of Christ, show me some mercy!"

Suddenly, the door burst open. From the floor behind his desk Ken could not see what was happening, but the noise was almost deafening. He opened his eyes to find a hand extended down to him.

"Ken, it's okay. Let me help you up." He accepted the hand and was pulled to his feet, but Ken's legs shook and felt too weak to support his weight. He fell back into his chair. It was then he realized his office was jammed with screaming, shrieking, laughing people. Looking up, he recoiled at the sight of Hobart still standing on his desk, hands on his hips and a big smile on his stubbly face. Ken felt he was in a fog of confusion.

He was next aware of Tina leaning in front of him. She put her hands on his shoulders and asked, "Ken, are you all right? It really wasn't supposed to get so out of hand."

"What's going on? I...I don't understand."

"This was your first day initiation, Ken. It's sort of a tradition around here." Tina looked around at the hysterical faces, "Maybe a sick tradition."

Ken heard laughter again and someone yelled, "Let's hear it for Ken!"

The room erupted with applause while Ken slowly regained his senses. He looked up to see Hobart still standing on his desk. "So, who the heck are you?" he asked.

Tina answered, "Ken, let me introduce you to my brother, Ira Goldstein."

The former Hobart Fudd jumped down from the desk and held out his hand to Ken. "I hope that wasn't too intense for you, Ken. I just let the scene play out and things escalated... sort of turned into the theater of the absurd." Gone was the Texas drawl.

"Do you work here?"

More laughter around the room, "Not hardly. I teach at Broward College – theater department."

"Sounds like you're not from Texas either."

"Moved down from Brooklyn three years ago."

Two huge flats of doughnuts were placed on Ken's desk, along with a box wrapped in gold foil with a red ribbon. "This is for you, for being such a good sport, and for being so damn funny! Welcome to the Broward County Public Defender's Office."

A woman started repeating "Ho, Ho, Ho-bart! Ho, Ho, Ho-bart!" and the rest picked up the chant for a few moments until their laughter once again filled the room. Then someone else exclaimed, "For the love of Christ, show me some mercy!" and the room exploded in hoots and cheers. Ken saw two secretaries laugh so uncontrollably, they had to throw their arms around each other for support.

Tina said, "Open your gift, Ken."

Ken unwrapped his present and found a decorative walnut desk plaque incised in bold, block letters, KEN "HOBART" MELZER, ESQ.

Someone else said, "Too bad it doesn't say 'THE LEGAL TEAM OF MELZER AND FUDD', or was that supposed to be 'FUDD AND MELZER?'"

An older man in a pinstriped gray suit looked at his watch and spoke to the room, "Okay everyone, fun's over. Grab a last doughnut and let's get back to work. Tina, why don't you stay and show Ken around." Then, as an afterthought, he said, "But before we leave, how 'bout one last hand for Ken Melzer." He then walked to Ken, offered his hand in friendship and said, "I'm Hank Parnell. I'm sure we'll get to know each other over time." Releasing Ken's hand he added, "Well done and welcome to the team. My office is always open if there's anything I can help you with."

When the room had cleared, Tina said, "Sometimes I think this whole initiation thing should end. This one got a bit crazy. You shouldn't have had to endure that much trauma."

"Oh, that's okay, Tina. Now that I have a chance to reflect on the whole situation, it *was* pretty funny."

"This one's been planned for a long time. My brother, Ira, gets a kick out of role-playing. He's a trained actor."

"Yes, he mentioned teaching theater." Ken thought a moment and asked, "How were you all able to hear what was going on?"

"We rigged a wireless mike under your desk, and broadcast the whole show through a speaker in reception. That's what all the noise was about. I tried to hush everyone, but it was just too funny. We purposely made sure there were no clients or outsiders scheduled before nine o'clock today. It was also recorded. They all are. We have a collection of initiation CDs in a locked file cabinet. They'll burn a copy for you to keep. I've listened to all the initiations, and I gotta say, Ken, yours was the best."

"That's a comfort."

Tina chuckled and said, "Why don't you kick back and relax for fifteen minutes. I'll come back to show you around and introduce you to everyone."

THREE

Roy Dillard went through the standard booking process. He'd been read his Miranda rights by the arresting officers before being put in the back of the patrol car. Aside from acting confused, Roy Dillard remained evasive to any questions asked by the cops on the drive to the jail. He asked repeatedly why his house had been surrounded by the S.W.A.T. team, why he'd been made to lie spread eagle on the ground and why he was being taken away in a police car. Thinking their prisoner was probably off his rocker, the two cops in the front seats gave up asking questions after getting few coherent responses for their efforts.

At the jail, Roy Dillard was logged in, photographed, stripped of all personal property and clothing, issued a crisp orange jumpsuit, and placed in a holding cell. During this process he tried to tell anyone who would listen that there must be a mistake, that he was home alone getting ready to watch the Super Bowl. He became quiet when one of the officers said, "Sure, you're innocent just like everyone in this place. They all say they're innocent until they're found guilty or plea out and do some time. Now, shut up and save all the gab for your lawyer!"

Because Detective Hanson was one of the first on the scene of the crime, and later supervised the arrest of Roy Dillard, he filled out the Probable Cause Affidavit – known by both police and lawyers alike as the P.C. Sheet. In his sworn affidavit, Detective Hanson described the murder scene as he'd found it upon arriving at Saltzman's Fine Jewelry and Watches. He reported his conversation with Laurie Silva, specifically quoting her on the description she gave of the suspect and his vehicle. He also noted that Laurie Silva told him the gunman said, "Surprise, nigger" to the deceased before literally blowing his brains out, and then how the gunman slapped her in the face and threatened to pull a second gun if she didn't empty the display cases into a laundry bag. Detective Hanson further stated in the P.C. sheet that he had seen footage from all three of the inside security cameras plus the fourth curbside camera. He concluded his report stating that the cameras clearly captured images consistent with Laurie Silva's interview at the scene of the crime. The cameras also showed the suspect getting into a Toyota, including full and unmistakable license plate resolution. The DMV identified the car as being registered to Roy Dillard, and they also supplied a copy of his Florida driver's license photo, which perfectly matched the security camera images. Detective Hanson *wanted* to summarize his sworn affidavit by concluding that never before in his career had he seen such an open and shut case, and in his opinion Roy Dillard should be taken out into the Everglades, shot, and left for the 'gators to feed upon. But of course, he didn't.

On Super Bowl plus one, Monday morning, Roy Dillard and several other men were marched into a stark, windowless room where they were led to a row of benches. They were told to sit until their names were called, at which point they were to stand at the podium in front of the benches, watch the closed circuit monitor mounted on the wall in front, and speak into the microphone only if directed to do so. Three men were called prior to Roy Dillard. Each said little more than "yes" or "no" to the magistrate's brief questions before being led out of the room. Then the magistrate called Roy Dillard's name.

"Mr. Dillard, you are being held on a number of charges, the most serious of which are murder, robbery and assault. I have reviewed the Probable Cause Affidavit and I find there is ample probable cause to hold you without bond."

Roy Dillard could not contain himself and blurted into the microphone, "This is all a mistake! I didn't do anything! I was home watching-"

"Mr. Dillard!" the judge cut him off sternly. "You are not on trial here. My job is *only* to decide if there is sufficient probable cause to hold you in jail. And from this report, I have little choice but to do exactly that."

"But sir-"

"Mr. Dillard, by your vehemence I ascertain that you

understand the charges against you. There is nothing more for either of us to say."

Roy Dillard was moved back to the holding cell while his paperwork was moved to Felony Case Filing division of the Office of the State's Attorney for determination of formal charges to be filed against one Roy Dillard of Ft. Lauderdale, Florida.

FOUR

After his first day as a paid attorney, and having been duly initiated by the Office of the Public Defender in and for Broward County, Florida, Ken Melzer parked his Honda Civic in the driveway of his modest, two-bedroom Imperial Point home. Walking to the front entrance, Ken could see a faint light coming through the two narrow windows on each side of the door. He turned his key and walked in to find his wife, Charlene, standing a few feet beyond, waiting for him to enter.

"Well, hello Mr. Lawyer! How was your first day?"

Charlene was smiling broadly at her husband. He walked up and engulfed her in his arms. Ken detected the faint essence of citrus on her still slightly damp hair – *must be a new shampoo or conditioner*, he thought. In his mind he could envision her in their small shower, her long, honey-blonde hair in suds. He forced away the arousing thoughts and pushed back. "Not exactly what I expected," he chuckled.

Charlene took his hand, and leading him to their four-seat oak kitchen table said, "I want to hear all about it. You can tell me after dinner. I made your favorite."

Walking behind her, Ken was aware his wife had planned a special dinner. She wore one of her sleeveless, sheer and clingy, black dresses that accentuated her firm, gym workout physique. The stiletto heels had the effect of making the shortness of her hemline seem even higher to him. Around Charlene's neck, a pearl choker remained hidden from the back by her straight hair; but from the front, it created a sharp contrast with her tanned skin. All of which was accentuated by a plunging neckline. The ever-present gold Rolex wristwatch – an odd and inappropriate wedding gift from her father, Ken felt, but had never voiced – was the only part of her he found somehow un-alluring. Once again, he allowed the watch's presence to be ignored.

Charlene led Ken to his usual chair at one side of the small, square table, now covered by a lacy, cream-colored tablecloth. He sat while Charlene walked a few steps and opened the oven.

"Stuffed Cornish game hens," she announced over her shoulder, pulling a baking pan with the two sizzling, browned birds. She scooped them onto two simple, white plates containing creamed baby onions and asparagus tips. Turning, she carried the two dishes to the table, placed one at each opposing side, and sat down.

"This is a wonderful surprise, Honey," Ken said, scanning the dinner before him.

From a bottle whose label Ken didn't recognize, Charlene poured a white, French wine into two crystal glasses.

"I've been planning this for a while," she said while lighting a single candle set in a sterling holder centered on the table.

"This is great, but really, it wasn't necessary-"

"Nonsense! Don't be so modest. Today marks the culmination of all the law school classes, and work, and stress, and studying for the Bar exam. Today you're a real lawyer, Ken. And I'm so proud of you!" Charlene left her chair and moving behind her seated husband, wrapped her arms around him, planted a long kiss on his right cheek, and just as quickly returned to her seat. "This is only the first part of your celebration," she whispered with a playful leer. "The best comes later... But for now, eat up before it gets cold, and then you can tell me all about your first day."

After the Cornish game hens were reduced to thin bones and Ken's crème brulee devoured – Charlene was off desserts again – she cleared the table, refilled their wine glasses for the third time, and suggested they move to the sofa a few feet beyond in the cramped living room.

Settling next to her husband, Charlene said, "Okay, I'm ready. Tell me everything that happened today."

Ken let out a light laugh and still smiling said, "Rather than tell you, I'll let you *listen* to exactly what went on in my important office today."

"I don't understand. You record what goes on...what you say? What about attorney-client privilege? This can't be ethical. You can't play this for me-"

"I can this once." Ken left the sofa and searched his briefcase. Finding the CD, he placed it in the stereo. "This is an interesting case."

"Ken, you can't play-"

"Relax and let me bask in the glow of my first legal triumph."

Ken returned to the sofa next to Charlene and hit the play button on the remote. As the minutes rolled by and the Hobart Fudd case played out to its conclusion, Ken's initial placid demeanor had risen to a crescendo of giggles and hysterical laughter. He tried to stifle the volume of his mirth because he wanted Charlene to hear the full show uninterrupted. Because he had been so captivated by the dialogue from the speakers, Ken was unaware of the silence beside him. The recording ended with the deliberate fading out of laughter and final applause by Ken's new colleagues in the P.D.'s office. Within a few moments of the CD's end, Ken had control of himself again. He waited for Charlene's reaction to what he considered one of the funniest pranks ever devised. And to have it recorded for all time was priceless. Finally Charlene spoke.

"This was your first day?"

He laughed again, "Yeah, pretty unforgettable, huh?"

"These are the people you are going to work with?"

"Yes, of course. You know they are."

"*This* is the office you want to work in? *These* are the people you want to work with? *This* is your idea of a good first day practicing law? And you-"

"For goodness sake, Char, lighten up. They do this to all the new people-"

"I won't *lighten up*! This is all crap! I don't give a good goddamn if they do this to *all the new people!* You, Ken Melzer, are a lawyer, a professional. These people are clowns. They make a mockery of our legal system, our system of justice. This isn't funny. It's an insult!"

"C'mon, Char, there's no need to use language like that-"

"You have to be kidding! You are more upset with me saying *goddamn* than you are with the fact that you were made to be an ass in front of the whole Public Defender's Office! And you're okay with it being recorded! This could come back to bite you on the butt at some later date!"

Serious now, Ken said, "Charlene, Honey, you've got this all wrong. It was like an initiation... a right of passage... like when you joined Tri-Delta sorority at The University of Florida-"

"Are you out of your gourd? You're not pledging a fraternity! This is your *career*, your *life*! *Our* life!"

"Char, calm down. This has no affect on my career or our life. C'mon now, this just shows I'm going to be working with people who have senses of humor."

"Bullshit, Ken-"

"Charlene Please!"

"Please, nothing! This *IS* bullshit whether you like it or not, whether you admit it or not! And don't try to shut me up either! And before you say anything else, I'll use any damn language I want!"

"Honey, you have to control your temper-"

"What? Like that phony Elmer Fudd redneck?"

"It was *Hobart* Fudd, and he was an actor."

"Fine, like that Jewish actor, Ira Goldberg! Like him, I have to watch my temper?"

"Ira Goldstein."

"What?"

"His name is Ira Goldstein, not Goldberg."

"For Christ's sake! I don't care if he's Ira Goldberg or Ira Fucking Goldstein!"

"If you continue on in this way, I'll go into the study-"

"Now there's a big threat! Gonna go in there and throw yourself on the floor, practicing for your first real client? Gonna practice calling to Tina for help? Gonna practice asking your clients to show you some goddamn mercy?"

"That was pretty uncalled for."

Charlene sat staring into her husband's passive face.

"Sometimes I don't think I really even know you."

"Why, because I can take a joke?"

"No, because you refuse to see the real world."

"And how's that?"

"You turned down a job in my father's firm. Sure, you'd have worked long, hard hours like all lawyers do when they're fresh out of law school and have just passed the Bar. But that wouldn't last forever. Your starting salary would be two, maybe three times what you're making now – going to be making now. You'd have made partner while we're still young, and then we'd be on easy street. We'd have a big house, all the things we want, time to travel…"

Ken Melzer gazed intently into his wife's taut face. Calmly he spoke to her, "Charlene, we've discussed this. We discussed this *before* we got married, before we ever got engaged. I fully explained my intentions concerning my career in law. I made certain there were no illusions or misunderstandings regarding this. That discussion has come and gone. You can't throw all this in my face now. Not after our agreement."

For a few long moments Charlene sat quietly digesting Ken's words. "You're right, Ken. I'm sorry. I had no right to say those things." She thought a moment before continuing, "I just feel you have such potential, such a great legal mind, that I hate to see you throw it away at the PD's office."

"So, you are saying that some parts of the law, some parts of being a lawyer, are valued higher than others? Defending those who can't afford a private lawyer is less valuable than representing a person of wealth? If this is the only way you evaluate a legal career… if you only see it in terms of the dollars and cents put in an attorney's pocket…well, Charlene, I don't even know how to react to that."

"No, I'm saying if you are honest – and I know you are – you can be a fine lawyer, doing fine work, and still profit from your career. You don't have to choose to only be involved in the lowest paying, least prestigious, kind of practice. I know you feel a need to do good for mankind, and help those in need, and all that, but you can also use your talent, your skill, and your great mind to make some money! Do you want to live in this crummy house forever? Do you want to raise kids in this place? Are your kids, *our* kids, going to work summers, and then get student loans for college?"

Ken had carefully listened to his wife. "I don't know the future. I've only thought about the present. Until the last month or two, I couldn't think about anything but passing the Bar! Now, I've got my first job practicing law. I'm going to get experience with clients, with court procedure, and with other lawyers. I can't think beyond that."

"Okay, Ken. That part I *can* understand. That makes some sense to me. Just promise me you'll at least consider private practice some time in the not-too-distant future. Think about what I said about this house, and about having kids."

"I will," Ken Melzer said softly, contemplatively.

"Thank you."

Ken and Charlene sat motionless on the sofa. For fear of another argument, neither felt any more should be said. After a couple of awkward minutes, Charlene said, "I think all this talk, on top of the wine, has given me a headache. I'm going to bed."

Ken remained seated as Charlene slowly stood, rubbing her temples with her fingertips. She looked at the gold Rolex and said, "It's still early. Maybe you should do your work in the study, and sleep there tonight, so you don't wake me when you go to bed."

Without saying goodnight, Ken watched his wife walk into their bedroom and shut the door.

 FIVE

Winston Schneck waited alone at the curb in front of his simple, one story stucco home in Plantation, Florida. Unknown to him, Winston's mother stood watching by the living room window, mostly hidden by the heavy blackout drapes pulled to the side. She didn't want him to notice her, should he turn his gaze back toward the house. She needn't have worried. Without altering the direction of his watchfulness, Winston stared down their street, waiting for the kids who would walk with him on this first day of school.

When the weather was good Mrs. Schneck had walked with Winston to kindergarten. On inclement days, she'd driven him. That was last year when Winston was only five. Now at six and going into the first grade, he was a *big boy* and needed to walk the three blocks to school with the other kids – at least that's how Mr. Schneck viewed it. "Stop babying the boy, for Christ's sake," he'd said for the millionth time. "Do you want him to grow up to be a goddamn sissy?" And so with a strong sense of relief, Mrs. Schneck watched her son as a group of five older, bigger boys walked down the sidewalk passing her house. And the spot where Winston had stood, seconds before, was now deserted.

Unknown to Mr. and Mrs. Schneck, this same neighborhood gang picked on Winston – the youngest resident of Citrus Drive. They did not torment, terrorize, or even bully Winston. Rather, they ignored him when important boy-stuff was about. They laughed at Winston and ridiculed him for being the slowest runner. They blamed him for minor unwritten neighborhood infractions such as trampling through a carefully tended flower bed and crushing a mass of pansies to retrieve a poorly thrown ball that had never been intended for Winston in the first place. Winston wasn't going to tattle – even the most moronic kid knows that's the quickest route to real bullying and kid torture.

He'd keep his mouth shut, knowing he wouldn't always be the littlest, weakest kid on the block. He might be two years younger than the next smallest of the neighborhood bunch, but Winston knew he was probably the smartest. Even at that young age, this subtle knowledge was more an awareness, a self-actualization, which he accepted without much thought.

Last year in kindergarten, Winston was the first to grasp telling time, the first to learn the alphabet (without reciting it to that silly-sounding alphabet song), and the first to figure out small numbers could be made incredibly large by merely adding zeros and commas. It was not surprising that Winston was also his teacher's favorite, although she tried not to show it. But unfortunately, for all Winston's obvious potential, he was the smallest kindergartner and the least adept at playground activities. He arrived last in races, couldn't seem to master pumping his legs to keep momentum on the swing set, and called a spazz by the other more athletic kindergartners when it came to anything to do with throwing or catching. Even the kindergarten girls seated at the sidelines giggled at Winston's efforts.

But that was all last year, when he was a *really* little kid. Now Winston was walking to school without his mother as an escort. He was a year older now, six. There were actually kids younger than him in school, but still not many smaller. That was okay, he must be stronger by now, a little bigger, maybe even faster...

Such were Winston's hopeful thoughts as he walked that last block to school. Suddenly out of nowhere an arm came across his shoulder, and he was roughly pulled into Phil Margolis, a fifth grader. As he was manhandled off the sidewalk and onto the grass by this *really* big kid, a friendly voice spoke down to the stumbling Winston, "So, Schnecky my friend, how's it feel to be walking with the big kids this year, huh?"

"Ah, it feels good, I guess."

"You guess? *You guess*? C'mon Schnecky, you're with pals here! We'll be walking to school like this every day. You're one of us now! Hey, relax and enjoy the walk."

What Winston didn't realize given his lack of balance having been forced to walk awkwardly crushed against the side of Phil Margolis, was that his new pal had purposely marched him into a fresh, Florida-sun-warmed pile of stinking dog shit. Thinking this was the funniest joke any of them had ever seen, the other five boys ran the last way to school, laughing and looking back at the straggling Winston, who was desperately trying to scuff the dog shit off his right sneaker on the grass. Then, to make matters worse, Winston heard a door open to his right. A barefoot, heavyset man – recently transplanted from Staten Island – wearing plaid Bermuda shorts and a stained sleeveless white undershirt, pulled a huge, half-chewed cigar from his mouth, and in a thick New York accent yelled, "Hey Kid, waddaya doin' to my lawn, huh? Get atta heah, and stay on the damn sidewalk! Jeez..."

The teachers and administrators of Stephen Foster Elementary were scattered around the fenced grounds to guide the students to the gym on this first day of school. From there the students were herded, by grade, to separate "stations," where they would eventually be called by name for teacher and classroom assignments. Suddenly everyone was hushed by the voice of the principal speaking on a crackling, feedback interrupted microphone. "Welcome back to Stephen Foster Elementary, everyone!"

This was met mostly with groans and chuckles, but before the principal could continue, there came a child's protracted scream from the first grade station of the gym. Margaret Blanchard, after her initial howl, pushed Winston so hard he fell backward into a sitting position on the hard gym floor while yelling at the top of her first grade soprano voice, "He put dog-doo on me! Winston Schneck stepped on my new shoes, and got dog-doo all over them!" And that outburst was followed by loud sobbing until Mrs. Weis, the school librarian, hustled over to Margaret, and being very careful to not get her own shoes too close to those of the hysterical Margaret's, embraced her, patting her back. All eyes now turned to Winston, who was too stunned and humiliated to do anything but sit on his ass, his legs outstretched, offending sneaker prominently exposed for all of Stephen Foster Elementary School to see and smell, mumbling in a weak voice, "I didn't mean to step on her shoes..." Then, after a few more silent seconds, all eyes turned back to the partially consoled Margaret, where Mrs. Weis was heard to exclaim, "Oh my! That really is a terrible smell!"

As if the news had broken out that Winston Schneck had some horrible, contagious disease, all the gathered first graders jumped back with shouts of their own like, "Gross!" "He stinks!" "Ewe, that's awful!" "Oh yuck!" – and then it happened. Over from the fifth grade station Phil Margolis, the real culprit in this matter, called out, "He's not Winston Schneck! He's *Winnie the Pooh*!"

Even the principal speaking into the microphone saying, "Now children, please. Please be quiet. That will be quite enough..." couldn't stop the riotous, adolescent pandemonium and laughter in the Stephen Foster Elementary School gymnasium.

And for the following eight grade levels, Winston Schneck was known as "Winnie the Pooh."

By high school, if asked about the old Winnie the Pooh name, Winston would disinterestedly shrug, and respond with something like, "Stupid, immature stuff... I stepped in dog shit when I was a little kid and someone thought it clever to call me that name." It was the way Winston Schneck gave his answer, the intimidating, condescension of his attitude, his persona, that made the individual who asked the question feel he or she was relegated to shallowness, if not agreeing with Winston's apparent assessment of the inanity of the long-ago situation. Usually the follow-up by the questioner was something like, "Doesn't seem like such a big deal. When I was a kid I stepped in dog shit all the time..."

Whether kindergarten or eleventh grade in high school, some things seemed universal and timeless. The larger, athletic boys were the most popular. Toss in good looks and that popularity increased proportionally. Add to the equation a flashy car, the latest clothes, some swagger, spending cash, a little weed perhaps, and of course, a clique of similar friends – and one's status moved further skyward.

Winston's status was static. Actually, he had no status. He wasn't large, nor was he athletic. Whether he was good-looking was difficult to discern. If good looks existed at all they were hard to detect beneath a persistent veil of acne. He had no car of his own – occasionally driving the Ol' Man's Buick didn't count for much. His mother bought his clothes – consistently conservative, practical, and always on sale. As for spending cash, the small amount he saved from his summer jobs bagging groceries had to last all year. Friends and a social life never played a significant role in his existence. Winston did his schoolwork and spent much of his spare time reading non-fiction. Other kids his age bored him and struck him as superficial. Girls, while desired to distraction, were always at a distance. He learned early that what he wanted and what he could have rarely coincided. Yet, Winston's life was not without satisfactions, and he used a good portion of his time planning and plotting to those ends.

Little Margaret Blanchard never spoke to Winston after the gymnasium affair that first day of school so many years before. She ignored him, or perhaps he seemed too inconsequential for her to bother with. But he was aware of her. For years he continued to be aware of her. Winston created a skill for observing Margaret without her being aware of his spying. He knew sooner or later it would pay off, and eventually it did.

Eleventh grade at South Plantation High found Margaret fully plumed and ripened into young womanhood. Winston took a specific dislike to the broad, perfect, orthodontically enhanced smile she perpetually displayed. He bet she even smiled to herself when she was alone. She oozed self-confidence with every pose, whether around the other girls on the varsity cheerleading squad or with groups of admiring boys in the parking lot. He hated her for her startling good looks, that constant damn smile, and her feigned – or otherwise – happiness. He also hated her for the wealthy, successful parents he'd never met, the blue BMW she drove, and the circle of friends who seemed to revolve around her in some kind of celestial way that was too much for Winston to fathom, much less stomach.

Everyone knew about the beach parties. After victorious Friday night football games, the star junior and senior players, their acolytes, and of course, the cheerleaders all coalesced at a previously agreed upon Atlantic site for an unsupervised and well-deserved celebration. Rumors about the activities during these affairs were legend, if exaggerated.

Hiding unseen in the sea grape scrub with Mr. Schneck's Buick safely parked several blocks away from any South Plantation High cars, Winston felt a thrill course through his body he could only think of in sexual terms, even though he had no actual experience in that department beyond his frequent solo-projects. His breathing increased and he found his hands shaking as he raised the pawn shop purchased Konica 35mm camera with a cheap, battered telephoto lens. By the light of a small driftwood fire and a few Coleman lamps, he clearly saw his subject... with that damn unmistakable smile. Well, he'd see if he couldn't do something about that once and for all. Others were gathered in the glow too, but Winston had a clear view of Margaret.

First, he snapped a shot of her, face tilted high, silky blonde hair loose and swaying behind her back in the gentle sea breeze... and a half-empty Wild Turkey bottle in her mouth with the label fully visible – what a stroke of luck that was! With that photo he wanted to sneak away, take his camera and get the hell out of Dodge, but he decided to wait a little longer. He smiled to himself at the comparison with the commercials on TV hawking dopey products for kitchen or closet in which the announcer finally says, "...but wait, there's more!" And this time, at this place, indeed there *was* more!

Quarterback John Tabor, Margaret's boyfriend, suddenly grabbed a small lantern in his left hand and took Margaret's hand in his right. Pulling her up on wobbly legs, the two stumbled directly toward the bushes concealing Winston. A moment of panic struck, and Winston desperately searched for an escape. As a trickle of sweat rolled down his back and he was about to bolt, the now laughing, oblivious couple plopped down in the sand no more than twenty feet from Winston's cover.

John Tabor placed the lantern in the sand and then reached in his pocket. A moment later his hand reappeared holding a huge rolled joint. A flick of a lighter, and the unmistakable sweet, pungent aroma of pot was on the same breeze that only minutes before had caressed Margaret's hair. Snapping another photo, Winston caught John with the spliff between his lips in a lung-filling, glowing toke. A long breath hold, then an exhale of smoke framed the next photo with a dramatic flair. Then it was Margaret's turn, with similarly satisfying photographic results.

Winston was spellbound. He felt the power he wielded with his camera, the power over other people's lives. He didn't feel deceitful or even particularly sneaky. They were underage and drinking – and eventually driving. They were also breaking another law – smoking marijuana. You do the crime, you take the consequences.

Feeling the effects of both the Wild Turkey and the pot, Margaret let out a sigh and lay back on the sand. John Tabor understood and accepted the obvious invitation. He too reclined and covered her face with his. A few struggles and more sighs brought John's hand up under Margaret's short cheerleading skirt. Instead of protesting, pushing his hand away, or crossing her legs – as Winston thought she must – with a soft moan, Margaret spread her legs. Whether out of jealousy or some other indiscernible outrage in Winston's head, he took one last photo before silently backing out of the scrub brush and hurrying to his Buick escape vehicle.

The all night photo department at a local 24-hour pharmacy was Winston's destination and only stop on his way home from the beach. The photo guy, reading a car magazine behind the counter, appeared lazy and oblivious to any store regulations prohibiting technicians from developing film that might prove indecent or inappropriate. A five-dollar bill encouraged this loser to get the film developed and printed into eight by ten color enlargements, pronto.

By Monday after school, Winston was in a self-serve copy store. He was both surprised and proud of the clarity of the photos he'd taken at the beach party. Learning shutter speeds and light conditions had paid off big time. These photos would make decent enough copies for their intended purpose. Not as sharp as the originals, of course, the Xerox replicas on standard paper took on a hazy attitude that Winston thought had made them look even more lurid and candid, as if some cigar-smoking, cheap, gumshoe private detective had hastily snapped them.

A sophomore named Nathan – last name forgotten by Winston – was called. He would be the distribution guy. If caught, Winston would casually deny knowing the kid. A poor student with even more acne than Winston, for ten bucks Nathan would do as he was instructed, no questions asked. The job was simple. Sneak into the rear of the cafeteria through the delivery entrance, its lock having been jammed in the open position with some chewing gum and wet cardboard. Then thumbtack to each of the thirty-eight hallway bulletin boards the photos of Wild Turkey, the shared giant joint, and the *piece de resistance* – one quarterback's famous throwing arm half-hidden by a cheerleader's skirt.

The results were nearly instantaneous and predictable. John Tabor and Margaret Blanchard were suspended for two weeks. John had to turn in his football uniform and Margaret was dropped from the cheerleading squad. The parents of both forbade them to see each other, and on threats of lost cars, allowances, groundings etc., etc., etc., forced a breakup. Margaret's reputation plummeted to that of the promiscuous girls who were known to put-out for just about anyone; John had trouble dating any girl – except those who put-out for just about anyone. And on top of all that, the whole student body, faculty and staff were pissed. With Tabor gone from the football team, the quarterback spot fell to a second string sophomore who sucked.

Winston didn't give a shit. They got what they deserved and had no one to blame but themselves. Try smiling now, Margaret.

Harriman Grabalski, finally a name that challenged the tonal and syllabic quality of *Winston Schneck*, was the senior star wrestler for South Plantation High. At six feet four and two twenty-five, he was the undefeated team's heavyweight. Not only was he simply undefeated; his victories were all by pins – not even a single win on points. A full wrestling scholarship to Nebraska was his after graduation. Not a penny would be spent on Harry Grabalski's college degree.

Doesn't seem right, thought Winston. A scholarship should be for scholars, not oafs who bully opponents into submission to the hoots and hollers of idiots who actually watch and are attracted to this crap. Unbelievable, simply unbelievable. The guy's a doofus – and a dishonest doofus to boot. To put it in terms even the moronic Grabalski could comprehend, "what ain't right, shouldn't be right, and wouldn't be right."

Winston had made a habit of sitting in the back corner desk of all his classes. Better to observe classroom dynamics from that location. Front row students saw only the teacher, but a back corner spot saw everyone and everything without anyone seeing him. Pure strategic logic, nothing more complex than that.

U.S. History was Winston's only non-advanced placement class. This was for two reasons. First, he detested the old bitch teaching A.P. U.S. History, and second, he was interested in the subject and would rather discover its secrets by his own efforts – without bias, without any high school teacher's interpretation. He'd learn United States history, and it would stick with him better if he did it on his own. Quirky? Perhaps, but that was Winston. Being aware of his quirkiness made it okay. It's when you aren't aware of your quirkiness; you might be treading on thin ice. Winston was sure he was just fine.

For most of his junior year Winston had observed the goings-on of this class. And who just happened to be occupying a desk one seat diagonally in front of Winston? Why, none other than senior wrestling champ, Harriman Grabalski, taking the class for the second time after flunking it the year before. And who sat next to him directly in front of Winston? Jason Williams, a surprisingly bright student and wrestling teammate of Harry Grabalski. Winston saw Jason hand a crib-sheet to Dummy Grabalski before each quiz and test. Harry kept the long, narrow sheets with the tiny words and dates up the sleeve of his letter sweater. Throughout each test it would be pulled out for a moment's consultation, and then be shoved back out of sight.

Three days before the final exam, the teacher, Mr. Crenshaw, received a note in a girl's obviously rounded cursive:

Dear Mr. Crenshaw,
I first want to tell you how much I've enjoyed U.S. History this year! You are a great teacher and I learned a great deal from your class. I'll never forget you!

There is one thing I need to tell you. A number of times I've heard Jason Williams and Harry Grabalski brag how they cheat in your class. It seems Jason writes a long sheet with all the dates and names and stuff we need to know for the tests and gives it to Harry who keeps it up his sleeve and then he uses it during the tests. It's not fair that I have to study hard to pass your tests and Harry doesn't! I don't like to snitch, but this has gone on all year and someone needs to say something, so now I am!

I better not say who I am as I don't want everyone to know I'm the one who told on Jason and Harry. I hope you don't think I'm a coward.

Sincerely,
A Grateful Student in Your U.S. History Class

Winston prided himself on his handwriting skills. He could write like a girl, write like a young child, write like his mother – this came in handy forging notes for tardiness or an occasional cut class – and he could even write in a flowing Victorian Era hand, full of old fashioned swirls and flairs. The "Grateful Student" letter was a five-minute piece of cake. Little circle-dotted i's and some run on sentences with poor structure. Nobody would ever suspect straight-A student Winston Schneck of writing such a missive.

Final exam day came and Winston aced the test with ease and time to spare. In the first ten minutes, Harriman Grabalski and Jason Williams were plucked from the class. The evidence was found and both ratted on each other in the dean's office. Bye-bye Nebraska wrestling scholarship. Hello manual labor. To Winston, Jason Williams was simply collateral damage. He seemed like an okay sort, but Williams helped Dum-Dum cheat, so what happened to Jason Williams was inconsequential. In short, as usual, Winston really couldn't give a shit.

Winston Schneck graduated high school with a near perfect academic record. He also graduated with a substantial record of busts. Margaret Blanchard would always be his favorite, but there were many others. Varsity basketball players caught selling ecstasy behind the gym, the homecoming king and queen nabbed before the big homecoming dance on a *minors in possession of alcohol* charge – populars, jocks, class officers, rich kids, snobs, bitchy girls, bullying boys – lots of busts by anonymous tips to the right authorities at the right time. Parents and teachers alike were talking about the new "crime wave" at the school. Winston thought this ridiculous. Was everyone so out of touch that they thought this some new behavior pattern? This shit's been going on mostly undetected forever. Now there was simply someone blowing the whistle, someone unnoticed and lost in the crowd, someone getting a kick out of the whole thing, and someone experiencing power over others who break laws and rules – an empowerment that was engrossing and satisfying.

An academic scholarship to the University of South Florida in Tampa relaxed the financial concerns of Winston Schneck's college education. He kicked in a few extra bucks of his own to secure one of the smaller single dorm rooms, eliminating the annoyance of dealing with a roommate. Freshman year was spent taking the usual core courses required of all first year USF students. Winston's advanced placement high school classes conveniently earned him credit for a number of his core courses. So he relaxed his first year, pulled a perfect 4.0 grade point average, and had plenty of time to spare for his other hobby – anonymously busting wrongdoers.

Cheaters and petty drug busts were routine and became boring, but Winston persisted. He tried different techniques and strategies, but the results were always the same. Suspensions, a few expulsions, some minor criminal charges and never, not ever, an accusing finger pointed his way. As a spy and sleuth, Winston had honed his skills, but he knew he must never get lazy or sloppy. His victims were always angry, always trying to figure who ratted them out. He once witnessed a USF basketball player beat the holy crap out of his roommate who, he wrongly assumed, narked on him for selling a little cocaine. Moving the coke was bad enough, but assaulting his innocent roommate took away both his athletic and college careers as well as establish his place in the criminal system. He had obviously been a badass, and it was good that this had happened now. If he ever made the pros, there would be no telling the real trouble he would find. Sometimes *sooner rather than later* was better for all involved. At least, that's what Winston told himself. As for the roommate, well, that was out of his control. It just went to prove what a stupid piece of shit the jock was. In fact, Winston proved to himself over and over again, these idiots shouldn't be in college in the first place. Maybe they should all enroll in sports schools where nobody cared a good goddamn if they could read or add two and two, a place where they simply did what they did best – beat each other up in some asinine game (for the enjoyment of equally asinine spectators), being paid big bucks salaries until their bodies gave out, and they blew all their huge sports career earnings only to become low-life, broke bums with no futures. Fuck 'em all. They got what they deserved. They did it to themselves, stupid jerks.

Although it left him lightly scarred, Winston's high school acne had nearly disappeared by college. At barely five feet five inches tall, one hundred thirty-three pounds and myopic, he was physically almost invisible to the opposite sex. His intellect and superior knowledge might have made him slightly more attractive, but Winston kept that to himself, rarely participating in class discussions or debates. He took quiet satisfaction in knowing he had the intellectual acuity to dominate the other students, should he decide to enter the verbal jousting of the classroom. He was also confident that he could destroy the classroom arguments made by his professors, but he didn't. There was nothing to gain from it. Why expend the energy or bring attention to himself? Why piss off those in authority? Besides, they gave out the grades in the end. He knew what he could do, what he was capable of. His time would come. There was certainly plenty of time.

Perfect grades were always within his grasp. Popularity or friends he couldn't care less about. Cars were for transportation, not to impress. His eleven-year-old Mazda was easy on gas and got him where he needed to go. Books and a few classes supplied intellectual stimulation and entertainment. Food mattered little. While everyone else complained about the dorm cafeteria food, Winston found it acceptable, even palatable. But there was one thing he longed for, one thing that consumed him to the point of total distraction. Winston craved the physiological and psychological release gotten only from sex. He did not want a relationship, a girlfriend, or anything that would intrude for more than an occasional thirty minutes of time.

To fulfill his needs, Winston took a part time job in a nearby bookstore. When not helping or checking out customers, Winston could read or study. He worked enough hours to pay for sex once or twice every couple weeks. He found the time in between filled with anticipation that was almost as exciting as the purchase itself.

Downtown Tampa had its share of hookers, call girls, and massage parlors. From past experience, he ruled out call girls. Not only were they more expensive, he found they all sounded enticing and beautiful on the phone until he actually met them in person. More than once he had to pay return transportation for some drugged-out skag he wouldn't touch with a leather work glove. Street hookers could be okay, but there was always the possibility of being set up by vice cops. That left frequenting a number of massage parlors. These establishments provided private rooms, and he usually had a choice of girls – he learned quickly that mid-week afternoons afforded the best choices; weekend evenings, not so much. If he didn't like the selection at one establishment, he could try another. He enjoyed this sex-shopping that encouraged his imagination to run wild. Sometimes there were black girls – light skinned and dark – sometimes Asians, usually some Latinas, tall, short, blondes, brunettes, redheads, heavy, thin, young, older... Pay the money, get some action, leave with memories to last a week, and then begin again. It was a game, a hobby, an obsession – always the same, yet somehow always different; always the intrigue of the unknown, the exotic, the possibility of an erotic surprise.

Once, after catching a dose of the clap from a whore he had a bad feeling about, Winston did some elaborate planning. With an anonymous phone call and a brown envelope containing cash left behind a dumpster, the infected skank was busted in a University of South Florida parking lot giving head to the visiting fourteen-year-old brother of a guy in the dorm. It was worth the sacrifice of the money he'd set aside for his own pleasure to launch the vessel that carried the skank straight up shit-creek. Mission accomplished. Flag of victory at full staff. Time to move on.

The University of Florida Law School was more of a challenge than his B.A. history degree from USF had ever been. Classes couldn't be missed, and his full attention was required for everything, regardless of whether he found it interesting or relevant. This stuff he needed to know, regardless of any practical value, in order to pass the Florida Bar Exam.

From the time of his decision to study law, Winston knew if not for criminal law, he'd never have considered law school at all. Law was his calling, his path in life. Hell, in his own way, in his own mind, he'd been handing out justice and dealing with criminals since high school! Becoming a lawyer only made it official. No more anonymity. No more sneaking around. He'd get the criminals and engineer their fates. Right out in the open he'd investigate, he'd dig up the dirt, he'd find the juicy, bad shit all these assholes had in their closets. And he'd use it against them. He'd prosecute them. He'd prosecute them to the fullest extent the law allowed. And he'd know the law – inside and out. He'd be the most feared prosecutor the Florida criminal world would ever know. His reputation would grow and expand. And after he made his mark locally, who knew how far he could go? Attorney General of the State of Florida? Attorney General of the United States of America? Sure, why the hell not?

 SIX

At one minute before eight o'clock in the morning, Tina stopped Ken Melzer in reception on the way to his office. "Ken, Mr. Parnell left word he wants to see you as soon as you come in.

"Everything okay?"

"Far as I know. He didn't say more."

It was a cool, late February morning in Ft. Lauderdale, and Ken quickly entered his office to hang his coat before seeing Hank Parnell. A twinge of nervousness washed over him as he wondered if he'd done something wrong. His first two months in the public defender's office had gone well. At least, Ken thought they had. He'd been given easy cases to deal with, nothing complicated and certainly nothing serious – a few DUIs, a couple of shoplifting arrests, marijuana possession, vandalism of public property by graffiti artists – small stuff, but important for Ken because they afforded him opportunities to learn criminal procedure and get his feet wet in court.

At 54-years-old and senior member of the PD's office, Hank Parnell had outlasted most attorneys in the field of public defense. Many lawyers used the position for a couple of years to gain experience before opening their own private practices or joining an established law firm. Hank Parnell said he liked where he was, liked the folks in the office, felt he was doing a good service for Broward County, and was content to stay put. Judging by the Lexus he drove and the house he owned on the Intracoastal Waterway, there was merit to the persistent rumors that he'd either been born to wealth or married into money. None of that mattered to Ken; he had learned to respect the man regardless of his affluence or the lack of it. Hank Parnell had helped Ken during his first weeks on the job, and as he'd said on that first day after the Hobart Fudd initiation, his door was always open if Ken needed any help. And Ken had taken advantage of that on a number of occasions. But this was the first time Hank Parnell had summoned him.

"Come on in, Ken," Hank answered to the knock on his door.

"Mr. Parnell, Tina said you wanted to see me."

"For the hundredth time, it's perfectly all right to call me Hank. I prefer it."

"I know. Old habits die hard."

"Have a seat," he said gesturing to a worn leather sofa by his desk. With an expansive view of downtown Ft. Lauderdale, Hank Parnell had the largest office on the floor.

Ken sat awkwardly, waiting for whatever was to come.

Hank began, "Ken, you've been here a little over two months now. How do you like working here?"

Without thinking, he responded honestly, "I'm enjoying every day and learning a great deal in the process. It's all I'd hoped it would be. I'm also looking forward to handling bigger cases... that is, when you think I'm ready, of course."

"Good to hear. I've been with the PD's office twenty-seven, no, twenty-eight years now, and I agree with your sentiments. I feel it's practicing the most elemental kind of law, the kind of law the founding fathers of this great nation of ours intended."

"I suppose it is."

"Yes, indeed! Equal justice for all, regardless of their station in society. Same for everyone, whether they dropped out of the third grade or went to Harvard. Rich or poor, immigrant or blue-blood tracing ancestry back to the Mayflower, blind justice for all."

Ken didn't know what to say to this, so he sat silently and waited for Hank to continue.

"Sorry for the pontificating. I must sound like some idealistic professor on the first day of a first year constitutional law class."

"Not at all," Ken wanted to say more, but was truthfully lost for words.

"Anyway, enough of all that." He stared at Ken for a moment and continued, "I like what I see in you. In fact, I liked what I saw in you during the initiation on your first day. I know, I know, there are a lot of people around here who think that particular tradition should be abandoned, but I'm not one of them. It shows me whether the person being, shall we say 'tried' can show resilience and character. And to a lesser degree, and of lesser importance, can show a sense of humor. For what it's worth, I thought you came through the ordeal quite well. And since that time I've found you to be conscientious and hard working. I also see the rare quality of humility in you. A lot of young hot-shots right out of law school who come to work here seem to be looking for self-aggrandizement, some kind of ego enhancement that might later propel them into a high powered law firm." Hank stopped speaking, closed his eyes for the briefest of time before continuing, "But, like I said, I don't see that in you. I'm not saying you are not ambitious. Only you can answer that, but I do see someone who is trying to do the best he can – both for himself and his clients. Don't think I'm unaware of the hours you put in. I know you have spent more time than most on what a lot of people around here would consider trivial cases – the kids with the spray paint come to mind. I listened when you spoke to their parents. I saw the honesty and empathy in the way you dealt with them collectively, as well as in front of the judge. I see a great deal of potential in you. In some ways you remind me of myself as a young lawyer… Yes, yes, I know that sounds like a stupid cliché coming from an older attorney, but it's true. I hope you'll consider staying on at this office for at least a little longer than most who come to work here."

Ken didn't have to ponder his words, "I have no plans to leave at this time. I mean, I know I've only been here a couple of months, but I'm not just using this job as a quick stepping stone to something more lucrative. If that's what you meant."

"Glad to hear it. And yes, that is what I meant."

Ken did not know what this was all about, but at least he was now certain he hadn't done anything wrong. He knew there had to be more to this meeting than what he'd been presented with so far.

Hank said nothing for a moment. He reached into a drawer, pulled out a file, and placed it on his desk. "You've heard of the Super Bowl Murder?"

"Sure. It was in the papers and on the TV news a lot when it happened. I'm not hearing much about it now. I suppose these things have a certain media-life that grabs the headlines for a while until everyone gets saturated and bored of hearing about it."

"Yes, that pretty well sums up most of these sensational cases. Big news for a day or maybe a week, and then nothing."

"I was told the guy who did the killing and robbery was assigned here – to the PD's office. Pretty big case. I heard talk you got it."

"Unfortunately, I did."

"Unfortunately?" Ken asked.

"Yeah, unfortunately. Not much I or anyone can do for this guy. He's a strange one, too."

"How so?"

"Well, the grand jury looked at the evidence and indicted him on a murder one charge plus the robbery, assault, and other lesser charges. The evidence against this guy is overwhelming, to say the least. Four cameras from four different angles got him doing the shooting, slapping the girl who worked in the jewelry store, giving her the laundry bag to fill with loot from the glass showcases, carrying the bag out to his car, and then driving away. Cameras got the car and license plate, and all this corroborates everything said on the 911 call from the girl who got slapped. So we have an eyewitness; two if you count the old man who owned the store. The whole crime got filmed and the guy caught at his house with the getaway car parked in his driveway. And all within an hour! If ever there was a case for the Prosecution, this one is it."

"He's going to try to plead this out, isn't he? Not that he has much to bargain with."

"Well, that's the conundrum. I covered his arraignment, and of course we entered a not guilty plea and demanded a trial by jury. But the damnedest thing is, the guy actually wants to have the trial. I explained – and believe me when I say I explained – that with the evidence against him, and this being a capital murder with a hate-crime enhancement – the witness said Dillard called the victim a nigger before he shot him…" Hank seemed lost for a second and sat looking at Ken shaking his head back and forth. "Anyway, I explained to him that the State will definitely seek the death penalty, but that I might be able to have the death penalty taken off the table in exchange for a plea. I told him that under the circumstances even that would be a long shot, but I could argue to the State that it would look bad to spend a load of taxpayers' money on a trial, the automatic appeal on a death penalty verdict, and all the man hours that would be spent trying to get a stay of execution when they could accept a quick plea in exchange for life."

Taking all this in, Ken asked, "So why won't he take a plea? Do you think he has a death wish?"

"No, that's the odd part. I've known people who committed some wicked crimes and then try to kill themselves afterward rather than face prison or execution. I understand that. But this Dillard guy insists he's going to be acquitted and a trial will prove it."

"How does he figure that?"

"He won't say more than that he didn't do anything wrong and no jury will convict him."

"Is he nuts, I mean seriously psychotic or something?"

"No, at least he doesn't appear to be. He seems reasonably smart, too. Never been in trouble, had a good job managing a fast food chicken place. He'd held that job for several years and made more than enough money to get by without having to commit robbery. And then a couple of months ago he simply quit. Apparently he told the franchise owners it was time for him to move on, and he left."

"Does he have any assets?"

"Nope. He rents his house. His car isn't worth much and he's only got a couple hundred bucks in his checking account. That's how he got assigned to us."

"He has no savings, yet he quit his job?"

"Seems that way. Taken altogether, none of this makes much sense, yet he obviously did what he's shown doing on video."

Ken looked to Hank, "Okay, so why are you telling me all this?"

Anticipating this question, Hank smiled, shrugged his shoulders and replied, "Because he asked for you."

"What do you mean, 'he asked for me?'"

With a bewildered smile, Hank said, "Well, not exactly by name. He insisted he wanted to be represented by the youngest and freshest attorney in the office. He said, and this is almost verbatim, that he didn't want some old, burned-out lawyer who's worked for the PD's office for the last dozen years to yawn through his trial. He said he wanted someone with enthusiasm and energy."

"Mr. Parnell, that's ridiculous!"

"Hank."

"Sorry. *Hank,* this is crazy! Dillard needs someone with experience, someone who's handled this kind of case before, someone –"

"Ken, save your breath. We both agree on this. I discussed this with Dillard, but he wouldn't have any of it. I can't get through to him, and I can't get much useful information out of him either. So I made an informal deal with him."

"A deal?"

"Yes, sort of." Hank stopped speaking, waiting for Ken to reply.

"I'm assuming this is where I come into the picture."

"Precisely. You fit Dillard's request better than anyone else in the office. So, I assured him I'd assign you to the case, provided you remain second chair in the capacity as an assistant to me. I made him understand that the PD's office requires a death-penalty qualified attorney to first chair the case, and nothing he could say would change that policy. I emphatically left no room for doubt that I was in charge, and that you would be reporting to me."

"And he agreed to this?"

"Yup. Hook, line and sinker. Actually, this may work out better as I'm not able to get much information from him. Perhaps you two can build a rapport that will prove advantageous. Maybe he'll be more forthcoming with you than with me. If he rejects me and wants you, let's give him what he wants and see what develops. Maybe you can convince him to plead out. Unless there's more to this than we know, and considering the evidence against him, I don't see how that's possible – a jury trial will end with a conviction and probable death sentence.

"In a nutshell, Ken, this case is a loser. I don't want it, yet I have to take it. There's a first-degree murder charge, and it's high profile to boot. Experienced lawyers have to handle cases like this, and I'm the most senior guy in the office. I have other cases where I can actually do some good – help some people – and this Dillard case will prove a big waste of time for me, time much better spent elsewhere. The most I could hope for after a lengthy trial would be a life sentence instead of the death penalty. And I could accomplish that right now with a simple plea deal. You however, young bright lawyer that you are, and seeking bigger and more important cases than petty thefts and DUIs, might just benefit from the experience of a capital case. And since there are absolutely no expectations that you can do anything for Dillard, you have nothing to lose and a lot to gain. It'll be a great learning experience for you. You can research motions to suppress, motions to exclude, motions to challenge the technology, drafting special jury instructions, post-trial motions, the penalty phase... a whole course on criminal law and procedure in one case! The case will still be mine, but you'll be second chair at trial."

"How will that free you up?"

"I'll oversee the case and supervise your work. I'm here for you to consult with as much as you need and as often as you want. I'll be lead counsel at the trial with you, and we can share a hanky when the jury comes back after a ten minute deliberation with a guilty verdict, and they inevitably haul Dillard off to death row. So, to encapsulate, I'll be present for all to see, but you'll be doing the work."

"Whatever you say."

"Good. I've already reassigned the cases you currently have to others in the office. At arraignment, Dillard refused to waive his right to a speedy trial, so the judge set the case for trial on May 28th. You've only got ninety days to prepare!"

Apprehensively Ken asked, "So when do I begin?"

"You begin in fifteen minutes. I've got a lot on my plate right now, but you suddenly seem to have a clear schedule. Imagine that! Grab your coat; it's cold this morning. We're going to the jail. They've been called and will have your new best pal, Roy Dillard, waiting for you in an interview room. I'll go with you this time. Then you're on your own. Maybe you can get more out of him than I could."

"I'll do my best..."

"I'm sure you will. And Ken," Hank became very serious, "a couple things: first, he insists, and I mean really, adamantly insists, we not file a Notice of Discovery."

"Not file for discovery? That's almost automatic. Does he have any idea what discovery is?"

"Oh, he understands all right. He understands that unless we file for discovery we won't know what evidence or witnesses the Prosecution will present. I told him that without discovery, we'd be flying blind."

"So, what's his problem with that?"

"Believe it or not, he says, and I quote, 'we'll win this case without any *tricks or help* from legal loopholes.'"

"Loopholes? Is he nuts? Discovery isn't a loophole."

"You're preaching to the choir, Ken. You know that and I know that, but this guy Dillard doesn't know it or won't believe it."

"So what do we do?"

"We? No, *you* are going to follow your client's wishes and not file for discovery. He's been given excellent legal counsel in the matter and rejected it. That's his right. So be it. We do what he wants. Just be sure you get him to sign something that outlines what his right to discovery is, that he has consulted with counsel, and that against legal advice he has instructed us not to elect to participate in discovery. We'll need that in our file when he files a Motion for Post Conviction Relief on the grounds of ineffective assistance of counsel – the old Rule 3.850 Motion. So don't set us up for that."

"You ever have a client decline discovery before?"

"Only a couple times when we had an ace up our sleeves, but very rarely. Discovery is almost always to the advantage of the Defense. But in this case not having discovery shouldn't matter. We know what the evidence is going to be and who the main witnesses are. It's not like the Prosecution is going to surprise us with anything we're not already aware of."

"Okay..." Ken said and thoughtfully added, "You said there was something else?"

"Right, if you can get him to change his mind and agree to a plea, call me right away and I'll handle that aspect of this. He'll need someone with experience to cut the best deal with the state. And with what little I know of this guy, if he does agree to a deal, we better set a change of plea hearing quickly or he could change his mind on the eve of trial. Then we'd be even more screwed unless we could get a continuance, which Dillard probably wouldn't agree to.

"Okay, I'll do my best, Hank"

Hank and Ken signed in, showed their Bar cards to the jail deputy behind a glass window, and were buzzed through two heavy security doors. They emerged into a stark, gray, windowless attorney waiting area. Toward the center of the room several cheap chairs and a couple of tables were spaced sufficiently apart from each other to afford limited privacy. Along the length of the left side of the area were several tiny conference rooms with doors containing large glass windows that offered privacy only as to what was said between lawyer and client. To the left of the row of conference rooms was another security door separating the in-custody clients waiting in blue jumpsuits from the attorneys with whom they were scheduled to meet. After a ten-minute wait, the security door to the inmate holding area buzzed and opened, and a jailer announced, "Dillard. Who's here for Roy Dillard?" Hank and Ken stood up as Roy Dillard walked into the meeting area. Ken thought the guard glared at the two lawyers from the PD's office before he left saying, "Let the guys behind the window know when you're done, and they'll buzz you out after your client is returned to the holding area."

"Thank you. I'll be leaving in a few minutes, but Mr. Melzer will be here a while."

"Like I said, just let them know."

Ken and Hank escorted Roy Dillard to one of the unoccupied conference rooms and took seats on the opposite side of the table from Roy. Hank spoke first. "Mr. Dillard, this is Mr. Ken Melzer. He's going to be assisting me with your case. I'll still be in charge, but Mr. Melzer will be what's called 'second chair.' That means we'll be working as a team, but I'm lead counsel on this case. Mr. Melzer has cleared his entire schedule to work solely on your behalf. I strongly suggest you cooperate with him. I know you'll find him a highly intelligent and skilled attorney. He will be in constant contact with me, and between the two of us, we will provide the best legal defense we can. However, we will need your openness, honesty and cooperation if we are to represent effectively. Do you understand this, Mr. Dillard?"

"Yes, of course."

"Excellent. I have instructed Mr. Melzer to record your sessions so they can be evaluated and discussed by the two of us later. I assure you no one outside of us will be privy to these recorded meetings. Also, anything you say to Mr. Melzer, or to me for that matter, won't go any further than the three of us. We adhere to a strict policy of attorney-client privilege, which means any information you share with us, anything you say at all, will be held in the strictest confidence and cannot be revealed to anyone else. Do you understand that?"

"I do."

"Do you agree to have your meetings with Mr. Melzer recorded at his discretion?"

"Yes."

"That's all very good." Turning to Ken he conspicuously looked at his watch and added, "I have an important hearing in court and I'm running late. Mr. Dillard, I am leaving you in very competent hands." Hank left the conference room, stood in front of the glass window next to the security exit and waited a moment to be noticed and buzzed out.

Roy Dillard stared without expression at Ken Melzer who felt suddenly lost and alone in a vast legal ocean. He wanted to yell to Hank to wait, to not leave, to help… but of course he showed none of those emotions. Instead he placed his phone on the steel desk top, scrolled to an audio recording app, and began the interview.

"Let's start with a simple question."

"Okay."

"What would you like to be called? Mr. Dillard? Roy?"

"Roy's fine. And you?"

"Ken or Mr. Melzer, whichever you are most comfortable

with."

"Ken. If that's okay then."

"Great." Ken hesitated, not knowing what to say next, and suddenly felt uncomfortably hot. Roy Dillard rescued him.

"Ken, if you don't mind me saying, you look pretty young. How long you been a lawyer?"

"I'm 26. I've been a lawyer since passing the Bar a few months ago."

"Hmm, I see. So I'm your first case?"

"No, I've had a slew of cases before this one…"

"Anything big?"

"A few," Ken said reflexively, "Nothing as big as this. You've been all over the news… well, not you exactly, more the murder scene and all…"

"You're right. The murder scene and all, but not me. Know why?"

"Tell me."

"Because I won't be convicted."

"That's what Mr. Parnell told me. He said you are adamant that you won't be found guilty. Is that so?"

"Which part? Hank telling you I'm adamant or me being found not guilty?"

"Mr. Dillard, Roy, I'm on your side here. How 'bout just telling me why you insist you will not be found guilty."

"Sure, I won't be found guilty because on the day and time of the murder and robbery, the jury will be convinced I was in my home watching the Super Bowl."

"Okay, fine. And the witness that said you did the crime and the cameras that show you killing the delivery guy…"

"Like I said to Hank, give me the trial I'm entitled to and put me on the stand to testify. The justice system will work as it should, and I'll be found not guilty and be a free man."

"You're not giving me much to work with here. Why won't you answer my questions? Do you think I'm working for the police or for the Prosecution?"

"Don't be condescending. I'm not stupid. Do I think you're working for the police or the State's Attorney! Are you kidding me? What, you think I'm crazy or some kind of imbecile?"

"I never said that."

"That silly question implied it."

"If you took that from what I asked, I apologize."

"Good. Accepted. So, you gonna put me on the stand or what?"

"I'm going to give you the best legal representation I can. If that means putting you on the stand, then I will. If I think that won't help your case, I won't."

"Nice answer. But unless you put me on the stand, I'll refuse to talk, refuse to cooperate. You'll look pretty unprepared and dumb on that first day of court when you won't have an opening statement, won't know what witnesses to call or what questions to ask."

"Whether to take the stand is always the client's final decision. I can only make a strong recommendation. So in order for us to make the best decision down the line, I think you need to open up now."

"Why? Don't you believe me when I tell you a jury will agree I didn't do anything wrong? Don't you believe in the justice system like I do?"

"Oh sure, I believe in the justice system, and I believe if you take this attitude for much longer you'll find yourself on death row."

Roy Dillard went eyeball to eyeball with Ken Melzer. Neither blinked or showed any expression for a short time until a smirk appeared on Roy's face. Without speaking another word, Dillard suddenly stood up, left the conference room, signaled the jailer behind the window that he was finished, and was buzzed back into the inmate holding area. Trying to comprehend what had just happened, Ken found himself alone at the table, his phone chronicling nothing but silence.

SEVEN

"He's mine! That stupid little shit's all mine! Somebody get Raiford on the phone and tell them to start charging up Ole Sparky! Wet the sponges! Got 'em a payin' customer! Tell them I'll make sure the son-of-a-bitch is gonna fry! No doubt about it! He's mine, all mine, and I'm not gonna waste this opportunity! No-sir-ree, this fucker's as good as dead! Dead man walkin' everyone, you hear me, DEAD MAN WALKIN'!"

"Ah, Boss...I don't think they use the electric chair anymore..."

A lot of head shaking and laughter followed this remark innocently offered to Winston Schneck in the Office of the State's Attorney, Broward County, Florida.

"Glaston, you shit-for-brains, do you really think I don't know that?"

"Well, I was just going by what you were saying..."

"Jesus, can't a guy show some enthusiasm around here without being taken literally? C'mon Glaston, I know you haven't been here that long, but for Christ's sake, give me a little credit for knowing something about what I do."

"Sorry sir, I didn't mean to insinuate...or, or ah, spoil your-"

"It's okay. Don't worry about it. Really, I'm just blown away by that stupid Dillard moron they got at the jail." Winston Schneck spoke further to the prosecutors surrounding him. "McNally just called to say that dumb-fuck Dillard is demanding a jury trial. No plea, no admission of guilt. No sniveling, no..." and Winston Schneck continued in a falsetto, whiney voice, "'I'm sorry, I didn't mean to do it, please spare me...'" Then reverting back to his rich, baritone, courtroom voice he declared, "I'm taking him down!" On a roll now he spoke faster. "No wife, no kids, both parents dead and buried, no brothers, no sisters, no friends, not politically aligned, not an illegal alien... excuse me, an *undocumented immigrant*," still more chuckles, "not gay, not a minority – hell he's *white!* And he blew the brains out of an innocent *black* man! This guy is perfect! No agenda, no accusations of wrongful overzealous prosecution. He's a choice cut of meat, the cream of the crop, the top banana! Hell, he's manna from heaven! As I've heard said on the mean streets of our fair community, 'It don't get no bettah than this…'"

Alone in his office, Winston Schneck sat behind his desk and very slowly opened his eyes. Occasional mind-tripping fantasies were an indulgence he allowed himself when the staid dignity of the State's Attorney's Office forced him to keep his enthusiasm in check. In this way he could allow detailed conversations, debates, and situations to play out in his brain that could never be heard in public. It offered at least some relief from the façade of seriousness and respectability he was forced to maintain.

Fifteen years with the State's Attorney's Office put Winston Schneck, age forty-one, at the pinnacle of his career. Top dog in the office, he was actually known as the "Attack Dog" among defense attorneys. After his first few years of learning the ropes, being given the difficult cases and still proving himself a relentless and tenacious courtroom gladiator, Winston Schneck was looking beyond Broward County. He knew the right people – influential players – who could make or break careers. And he wanted his to be made. Schneck wanted to move up. His eight-year perfect conviction record spoke volumes about his dedication to law and justice. It was common knowledge around the courthouse that Schneck was a merciless crusader who believed in right and wrong. There was no gray area in between, no extenuating circumstances. You do the crime, and if serious enough, Winston "Attack Dog" Schneck was personally going to railroad your ass to Raiford Prison to do the time.

Schneck also collected information. He knew secrets, had informants – sometimes paid informants – who passed along documents, intercepted emails, texts and photos of the powerbrokers of South Florida business and politics. Prostitutes, bookies, ex-cons, junkies, dealers, snitches, private detectives, all knew dirty little secrets to pass on to Schneck in return for a trifling favor or two, bits of gossip that proved true and potentially useful, all live ammunition stockpiled for possible future skirmishes or battles – or perhaps used to avoid skirmishes or battles. Files, lots of files, each tucked neatly away... just in case. Not to be used lightly and kept from even his closest associates, his files just might hold the key to an advancement, perhaps under the right conditions, to the position of Attorney General for the State of Florida.

But not yet. Schneck needed more recognition. He needed his name and face in the papers and on the TV news. Attack Dog Schneck had to be on the lips of secretaries and office workers around countless water coolers and coffee machines. He needed a high profile case, a winner, a perfect courtroom drama to show South Florida and the rest of the state that Winston Schneck fought for the righteous citizens who believed in law and order, fairness, and an eye for an eye. The neighborhoods would be safer with Winston Schneck at the helm of the good ship *Justice*. He'd sail South Florida like a swashbuckler of old, boarding the pirate ships of evil and sending them down to Davy Jones' Locker, by God! And it was looking more and more like exactly the right case had dropped into Schneck's lap. The local news had even broken into the half-time show for a sixty-second special bulletin on the unfolding crime scene that eventful day. The brutal *Super Bowl Murder and Jewelry Heist* was known to everyone. It was custom made for Winston Schneck. If not karma, he thought, perhaps it was simply a matter of fate.

EIGHT

His office door closed, Ken Melzer sat at his desk. With both hands locked behind his head he closed his eyes, leaned back, and allowed a self-satisfied smile to creep across his lips. No more shoplifting cases, he thought. No more petty vandalism to deal with. DUIs? Not any more. Well, he realized, at least not for a while. A first-degree murder case. Not second-degree. Nope, a capital case. A big one. The real McCoy. He had arrived. Ken Melzer's train had pulled into the station. It was gonna be show time!

Absently he reached for the phone on his desk, pressed the button for an outside line and called Charlene.

"Honey, don't cook anything for dinner tonight."

"Ken you don't usually call during work hours. Everything okay?"

"More than okay!" Ken waited for a reaction, but after getting only silence he continued, "We're going to celebrate tonight. Make a reservation for dinner any place you like."

"What's going on, Ken?"

"Like I just said, we're going to celebrate."

"Celebrate what?"

"I'll tell you over dinner."

"Maybe you should tell me now. You know I'm not one for surprises."

"Nope, over dinner. I want to tell you face-to-face."

"Fine, whatever you say. Where do you want to eat?"

"How 'bout Antoine's? I know you like that place."

"Are you sure? It's kinda pricey."

"I'm sure. Make it for six. I'll meet you there."

"And you really can't tell me what this is all about?"

"I'll tell you everything tonight. I gotta run. Make the reservation. I'll see you at six. Love ya."

Ken arrived early at Antoine's and requested a table in the most private section of the dining room. He sat alone and looked at his watch; 5:50. The ten minutes until Charlene arrived would seem like an eternity, but somehow that added to his excitement.

At exactly six Charlene arrived. She wore a tight fitting cream color sleeveless dress with the hem several inches above her knees. A single strand of pearls, matching dangling earrings, and three-inch heels caused several men to glance in her direction as the maître d' led her to Ken's table.

Ken stood, walked to her side of the table, kissed her cheek, and held her chair. Wordlessly she sat and waited for him to retake his seat. They stared at each other with neither saying a word until a huge smile appeared on Ken's face and he said, "So, how was your day?"

Charlene returned his smile, "Fine. And yours?"

"Oh, you know. Just the usual."

"Okay Ken, cut the crap. What's going on?"

"Why ever would you ask such a question?"

Serious now, almost annoyed she said, "Enough of this. Tell me."

"All right. Actually, I've been dying to tell you all day. Great news."

"Please Ken, don't make me beg."

"Charlene, I got a real case today! I mean a big-time case. The kind of case that's going to be in the papers and on the news. And I've been chosen to handle it."

"If the case is that important, how could they give it to you? Don't big cases have to go to the most experienced attorneys in your office? No offense to you, Ken, I know how smart and competent you are, but you've only been on the job a few months."

"You're right. Technically the case belongs to Hank Parnell. He's assigned me second chair. He'll be there for support and advice, but I'm handling this one."

Charlene tilted her head and looked at him slightly askance.

"What kind of case is this?"

"First-degree murder, assault, robbery and some lesser

charges."

Almost incredulous she hesitantly replied, "Do I know of this case?"

Ken looked almost smug when he said, "Everyone knows this case."

"Ken, stop beating around the bush. What case did they give you?"

"None other than the Super Bowl Murder and Jewelry Heist!"

Charlene sat back in her chair and stared at her husband with disbelieving eyes. "I've been following this case in the papers. The cops got the guy within an hour of the crime. He's been recorded on video killing a black guy and stealing the jewelry. He even hit the girl behind the counter! They're calling this the biggest slam dunk murder case in Florida history! This guy's going to be executed if he doesn't plea it out."

"Well, we'll see if it's such a slam dunk..."

"Ken, how can you be so naïve? Don't you see what's happening here?"

"Charlene-"

"Nobody would want this case. It's a loser! Anyone involved in the Defense is gonna look foolish. This is the kind of case that sticks to a person's name and reputation."

"The Defendant is entitled to legal representation-"

"Are you out of your fucking mind?"

"Charlene! Please!"

"Fine, are you out of your f'ing mind? Is that better? I'll swear if I want to!"

They sat at an intimate table, their heads barely two feet apart. Ken stared at the white tablecloth while Charlene glared at him. Finally she hissed, "Now you listen to me, Ken Melzer."

He looked up as she continued, "Don't you take this case or have anything to do with it. If you are connected to this guy, this killer..." Momentarily distracted, she paused before continuing, "Isn't it going to be a hate crime? Anyway, if you are associated with him, it'll ruin your chances for any position in a decent firm later on. Reputations mean everything in this business. You're second chair because Parnell, that sleazy weasel, that son-of-a-bitch, wants as little to do with this case as possible. He knows how potentially damaging a case like this can be. He's pawning it off on you because you don't know any better; because you are young and green and idealistic and humble and..." she seemed to search for a word, "and pathetic."

Ken opened his mouth to say something, but Charlene cut him off, "Wise up, Ken. For Christ's sake, if not for you and your career, for me and our future!"

The waiter arrived out of nowhere and hovered over their table, "May I interest you in a cocktail before dinner?"

Charlene answered, "Thanks, no. Change of plans actually," before rising and walking briskly to the door.

Along with the men who had watched Charlene enter, Ken stared at the back of his wife striding out of the restaurant. Fortunately the waiter had sensed a major problem at their table and drifted away. Ken took a sip from his water glass, pulled a five-dollar bill from his wallet and placed it on the table. He knew that was a fraction of what he should leave, but too bad. Perhaps the entertainment value of Charlene's departure was worth a few extra bucks. He wouldn't be coming back to Antoine's anytime soon, or perhaps ever.

Aware of a few stares from other diners, Ken rose from the table, walked toward the restrooms as nonchalantly as he was able, and then made a long, circuitous stroll toward the exit. Leaving the parking lot, Ken's mind was a confused blank. He needed to think, to collect himself, to define his feelings. He was on an emotional rollercoaster and it was making him sick to his stomach. It was six-thirty and still heavy traffic surrounded the Honda. A BMW next to him blared a horn-warning as Ken began drifting out of his lane. He shouldn't be driving. An empty parking lot loomed to his right and he pulled in. Stopping his car he looked up to realize he was at a Methodist church. A few cars were parked close by the main double doors, and noticing the bumper sticker parking permits and assorted paraphernalia hanging from the rear view mirrors, Ken figured they must be high school kids, probably some kind of church youth group. He thought of driving elsewhere, but lacked the motivation. What difference did it make what parking lot he sat in? He simply needed a little quiet solitude to transform his swirling mind into something that made sense, something manageable.

Ken closed his eyes and forced himself to take a few deep breaths. Time to be calm, time to be smart, time to take stock of this situation. Was Charlene right? Was Parnell using him? As Charlene had insinuated, was he being a naïve and pathetic fool? Would this hurt his career as she'd said? Maybe. Maybe to all those questions, but maybe not. He was working as a public defender. His job description couldn't be more clear. He would represent clients who couldn't afford to hire a private attorney. Not all cases were winners; in fact, most of these clients were guilty. But, Ken fully understood, they still deserved the best legal representation he or any other lawyer working in the public defender's office could render. As an attorney fresh out of law school and a new hire in the public defender's office, he couldn't pick and choose his cases. If Hank Parnell wanted him on this case, he had no choice in the matter. Hank promised him experience, and experience is what he needed. Was he expected to blow this case wide open and somehow get Roy Dillard acquitted? No, of course not. But maybe he could convince him to plead out to life in prison; maybe even life with parole at some point, assuming the state would even offer a plea. Someone had to represent Dillard. Why shouldn't it be Ken Melzer? No reason at all. He was going to do the job required of him; there was no other option.

Ken was jarred from his thoughts by a gentle tapping on his car door window. Lowering it revealed the kindly wrinkled face of a minister. Quickly glancing toward the church doors, Ken saw the other cars had gone.

"Son, are you okay? I saw you sitting here when the others left. I didn't know if you were troubled."

Still half lost in his thinking, Ken was barely able to stammer, "Ah, no. I'm fine…"

"I've been pastor here for a lot of years, and I think I can tell a troubled soul when I see one. If you'd like to come inside and talk, I might be able to help. Got some leftover coffee and cookies…"

Ken stared into the pastor's liquid brown eyes, "Thanks, but really I'm okay. I just needed a few minutes to think some things through. I've got the answers I need, but thanks again anyway."

Ken drove slowly and carefully north to Imperial Point. The house was dark when he parked in the driveway. Entering, he turned on a few lights and walked to the fridge to get some bread, mustard, ham and cheese. Not exactly Antoine's, but at least it was a lot cheaper. Charlene obviously was still out somewhere, and that was more than a little disconcerting, but Ken tried to put the thought of her and their next meeting out of his mind. He ate standing up by the kitchen counter. When the sandwich was finished he placed his plate and half-full water glass in the sink. That was easy and fast – no more hunger, not much to wash – and no complications.

Ken realized he must have dozed on the sofa. The front door opening had awakened him. Instinctively he glanced at his watch: eight-twenty. Charlene was home.

Ken stood to face her as she closed the door and walked toward him. Wordlessly she gently placed her arms around his neck and pulled him close. Neither said a word for a long moment, and then in a soft, conciliatory tone Charlene whispered, "Oh Darling, I'm so, so sorry," and she pulled him even closer. Ken felt the arousing thrill that always excited him when she held him close enough that their thighs touched. Yet at this moment, he wished he could extinguish the sensation.

Pulling slightly away he asked, "Where have you been?"

"I stopped in to see my father."

Ken said nothing. Charlene had a close relationship with her father. If she needed to speak with him, well, he guessed that was okay, even though it irked him. He waited for her to speak.

Leading her husband to the sofa, she sat next to him, took his hand in hers and said, "I want to apologize for tonight. My behavior was awful and I hope you can forgive me."

This was about the last thing Ken had expected to hear from Charlene. He'd been dreading her arrival home and the inevitable confrontation that would ensue. Best to be quiet, not say anything, and let her play her hand.

"I was so confused and angry when I left the restaurant I didn't know what to do."

Ken still said nothing and she continued, "So, I called Daddy. He always seems to have good advice, and I figured if anyone could help me understand this, he could."

"And?"

"And I explained to him the whole situation of your involvement in the Super Bowl Murder and Jewelry Heist case."

"And?"

"And he said I was wrong to have reacted the way I did. He said you worked at the PD's office and this was your job. He told me that this early in your career, well, a big loser of a case like this didn't really matter all that much and it sorta goes with the territory."

Ken sat mulling this over without responding.

"Daddy also hinted that once you got the experience you were after, you know, the whole defender of the downtrodden thing," Charlene paused as if she might be on uncertain ground. "Look, what I mean is, you've explained your reasons for working for the state and I kinda get that, although not completely. But what I do know is that very few lawyers devote their whole lives to public defense. I mean, at some point they want more for themselves and their families. And we talked about eventually having kids, so I can use the word *family*. But what Daddy let me know was that at some point in the future, and hopefully the not too distant future, you'll want to move up the ladder. Basically, he told me that when that time came, he could find a place for you in his firm."

Ken leaned forward on the sofa and placed his hands on each side of his face. No, he thought, she didn't really understand him. But he couldn't deal with that now. At least this was better than the big blowout fight he was expecting. He got an apology instead of an altercation. He'd be an idiot not to take this offering. Tonight, this was a win. A big win.

Charlene leaned forward too and put her arms around his shoulders. She kissed his cheek. "I know how hard you work and I really do appreciate that in your own way you only want to do good for... for whoever needs your help. I think that is admirable, and I'm proud of you." She pulled him tighter and said, "I'm so terribly sorry I ruined your special dinner. I didn't mean to be such a bitch, but I've been straightened out now. Let me try to make it up to you."

Charlene stood and slowly, sensually walked to their bedroom while unbuttoning the top back clasp of her clinging, short dress.

NINE

The office door to State's Attorney Winston Schneck was open, and Detective Hanson tapped on it as he walked through.

Winston stood behind his desk. He reached across and offered his outstretched hand. "Good to see you, Detective. Have a seat."

"Thanks," he said, ending the brief shake and sitting in one of the two leather chairs facing Winston's broad, oak desk.

"I've been anxious to see you, Andy. Give me some good news."

Winston sat back in his recliner while Detective Hanson removed a small notepad from his shirt pocket. "First of all, we did everything by the book. After the arrest we made certain the house was clear. Then the place was sealed and nothing was touched. I posted two cops to yellow-tape the property and make sure no one went inside. And of course, I got the proper warrant before we returned and did our search."

"That's what I like to hear. Now tell me what you found."

Detective Hanson flipped through a few pages from his notepad and Winston felt certain he did this only to create some sense of self-important suspense. That was okay, Hanson was a hard worker, and now was a time he could shine a little. "We found a few interesting things in the house, and at the same time didn't find what we expected."

"Well, let's start with what you did find." Winston had learned to have patience with those he considered underlings. If this took a while, that was fine. Whatever kept his people and the police happy. It was important for him to be on good terms with them all, to be friends to everyone he might need at some time in the future.

"We found two other guns. One was a small, five shot .38 Special revolver and the other was an older Colt Python in mint condition. It's a .357 Magnum-"

"I'm familiar with the Colt Python, Detective. Magnificent

weapon, unfortunately no longer produced."

"Right. Well, we ran the serial number and found it was reported stolen from a doctor's house in Coral Ridge – big place on the golf course."

"I get the notion there is more to this."

"Yes. The Python was stolen a month ago along with a Smith & Wesson Model 57, .41 Magnum, nickel plated – same one used in the murder. We also found some jewelry. Nothing from the Saltzman store, just a few rings, some gold bracelets, necklaces, and a gold Cartier watch. All this stolen from the same doctor's house. Interestingly, we also found a box of cartridges for each of the guns. The .357 magnum box was full, but the .41 Magnum box was missing six. The five remaining unfired rounds and the one fired round from the murder weapon matched. Pretty obvious the guns, ammo, and jewelry were taken together."

"So, it looks like our man, Dillard, was active before this latest crime."

"Yeah, appears so."

"What else did you find?"

"Well, that's really about it."

Winston sat for a moment looking at Detective Andy Hanson. "What about the clothes from the heist? The leather jacket and gloves?"

"Not there."

"The laundry bag he put the jewelry in?"

"Nope. Missing, too."

"Just curious, was the TV on?"

"It was. The Super Bowl was on when we cleared the house after the suspect was taken in."

"Interesting," Winston leaned on his desk with both forearms. Detective Hanson noticed the old acne scars on his cheeks when the light from his window caught him at a certain angle. "Exactly where in the house did you find the Colt Python and the jewelry?"

"Yeah, that was kinda strange. They were wrapped in a big beach towel and stashed behind some gardening tools in the corner of the garage."

"That's not all that unusual. Anything else odd to you?"

"Nothing out of the ordinary in the house or garage. We checked the car for fingerprints and found only those matching Dillard. It seems he acted alone."

"Did you find evidence of anyone else in the house? Either living with him or visiting?"

"Nothing. According to neighbors, he lived alone and they didn't see anyone around except him. Quiet guy, they said. Kept to himself."

"No women's stuff in the house or bathroom? No pink razors or make-up? Condoms in the nightstand?"

"Nothing at all like that."

"So, we've got a guy who recently burglarized an upscale house, got some expensive guns and jewelry, but nothing else."

Detective Hanson sat silently.

"Okay, tell me about the car."

"Not much to tell. Just an average car with nothing in it except a few loose coins on the floor with some typical trash."

"Andy, you're not giving me much to go on here."

"Well shit, Winston, what more do you need? Hell, you got the guy on three indoor cameras saying something to the delivery guy before he shoves the .41 Mag in his mouth and blows the top of his head off. You got video of him slapping the counter girl and filling the laundry bag with jewelry and watches. Then you have the outside camera showing the car, and license plate, and him getting in with the loot and driving away! Three cameras, three different angles of the same guy doing the same nasty shit. Great facials of Dillard from each side and full front. Gross footage of the black dude getting blown away. Blood even sprayed the edge of one camera lens." Detective Hanson paused and smiled. "Even that movie director guy, Quentin Tarantino, couldn't have choreographed it better for dramatic effect!"

"All true, Detective, but I was hoping you'd find more direct physical evidence of the murder in the house."

"We found the Colt that was stolen along with the Smith & Wesson."

"True, but you know me. There's never enough evidence."

"I suppose, but he had nearly an hour to lose the leather jacket and gloves and stash the laundry bag."

"Did your boys search the dumpsters along the route from Saltzman's to Dillard's house?"

"Of course. But who knows where he drove after leaving the scene. Maybe he dropped the stuff off at a friend's, or at some hiding place he'd chosen earlier."

"Yes, lots of possibilities."

"Seems to me, Winston, you got all you need to fry this asshole."

"I couldn't agree more," Winston said as he stood up and again extended his hand to Detective Hanson. "I appreciate your thoroughness."

TEN

Alone, Ken Melzer showed the proper paperwork and IDs to enter the Broward County Jail. As he did the last time, he went through a metal detector, buzzed through several locked doors, and eventually ended up in the same concrete room where he'd first encountered his client, Roy Dillard.

Roy was seated behind the bolted-to-the-floor steel desk as before. He didn't stand or offer to shake hands when Ken took the seat on the opposite side. With a bored look on his face, the guard who had been standing by the door said, "Buzz when you want out," before leaving. Ken briefly wondered how many times he must have said those exact words. Who cares, time to get to work.

"Mr. Dillard, Roy?"

"None other. And before you ask and we have to go through all the same crap again, yes, you can call me Roy."

"That's good, Roy. And as before you can call me Ken." Both men looked at each other as if taking a measure of their individual masculinities, or some other such nonsense. Ken broke eye contact and bent down to remove the phone from his briefcase. "I assume I can record our meeting like last time?"

"I'd be honored."

"Great, but let's cut through the sarcasm, Roy, okay? We need to get something firmly established. I'm your lawyer, and I'm on your side. My job is to help you and to defend you against some pretty serious charges. We, you and me, together, are going to have to go against the State's Attorney who wants nothing less than to have you executed. They have a strong case against you, and truthfully, you need all the help and friends you can get."

A smile appeared on Roy's face. "Good speech. I'm feeling better now knowing that you are going to represent me, that you are on my side, and are now my friend."

"So you don't want to stop the sarcasm? Okay. Would you

rather I play a different tune? Want me to say your case is a loser? Want me to say the state has enough evidence to kill you? Want me to say you are a wise guy who obviously has every legal angle figured out and doesn't need my help? You tell me, Mr. Dillard. You tell me what you want or don't want from me. If I'm wasting my time, let me know now because I'm prepared to work my butt off on your behalf... but not if you don't want me to. So, say the word, and say it now. I can buzz that idiot guard and be out of here in a heartbeat."

Ken thought he saw the same smirky smile return. Roy looked down at the table in front of him and slowly shook his head from side to side. Ken felt the anger beginning to rise, but was surprised when his client, still looking down at the desk, said softly, "I'm sorry. You're right. I'm acting like a jerk. I want your help, and I very much appreciate anything you can do for me."

Ken's first thought was that this was an act, more sarcasm, but then Roy looked up and Ken saw his self-assuredness was shattered by a single tear that streaked his right cheek.

"Roy, I'm prepared to do everything humanly possible on this case. But you have to work with me, not against me. We have to be a team. Without your cooperation, I can do little for you. What do you say?"

"I'll do whatever you want. I'll tell you all I can. But you have to know right now, right from the beginning, that ultimately a jury will find me not guilty."

"And how can you be so sure of this?"

"Because I know."

"Because you know what?"

"I know the jury will find me not guilty."

"*How* do you know this?"

"This is where you are going to have to trust me."

A circle. Ken was reminded of a circle with no beginning and no end. Around and around you can go, but you get nowhere in a circle. Maybe, as Hank Parnell had said, Roy is truly nuts. Certainly, with the evidence against him, insanity will probably be the only defense option.

"Roy, I need to ask you some questions, and I need honest

answers."

"Anything."

"You understand the charges against you?"

"Yes."

"And you understand the most incriminating evidence right now is the film from four cameras showing you committing a truly heinous crime?"

"Yes."

"And you understand the cameras got clear footage of your car and license plate at the scene of the crime?"

"Yes."

"And you understand the person who committed the murder and robbery, who *the police have identified as you*, is captured on film getting into this car that is registered to you?"

"Yes."

"And you understand that this car, with the same license plate and broken tail light that was caught on video, was parked in plain sight in your driveway at your home where you were arrested an hour later?"

"Yes to all of that."

"And you understand that the girl behind the counter, a Miss Silva, is shown on the film being slapped by someone *who has been identified as you*?"

"Yes."

"And you understand she is a witness, a very credible witness, who says the person who shot the delivery man, and slapped her across the face, and stole the jewelry and watches was you."

"Yes."

"So, Roy, please tell me how a jury will view all of this evidence, and hear witnesses who will identify you as the person on the security video, and then find you not guilty?"

"Right now I prefer not to get into that."

"I thought you wanted me to help you."

"I do."

"If you prefer not to get into that, I think those were your words, how can I help you?"

"Just being my attorney is helping me."

Ken sat back in his chair and stared at the ceiling. His client sitting across from him was expressionless. Law school had not prepared him for something like this. He'd read countless case transcripts, appellate opinions and attended lectures on defense tactics and trial techniques, but nothing he'd read or heard from a professor could help him with a client like Roy Dillard. This man was intelligent. He was educated. Yet he seemed to have alarming attitude shifts. He remained a total enigma.

"Roy, you are a smart person."

"Thank you."

"Tell me how I can help you."

Roy leaned forward, "You can trust me, Ken. You can believe in me. And most of all, you can accept that a jury will find me not guilty."

"Okay. Let's assume I do trust you. Let's assume I believe in you. And let's even assume, which right now for the record I don't, that I accept a jury will find you not guilty. That's a long way from here. That's at the end of the trial you are demanding. That's the finality of your case. But Roy, we are at the *beginning* of your case. That is the goal at the *end*, a long time from now. Tell me what happens between *this beginning* and *that culmination* of your trial. Tell me what is going to transpire between us that will help me build a case that will make a jury declare you not guilty?"

"Well, that's what you are here for – to figure out a defense."

"This is double-talk. Don't play me for a fool."

"I'm not. What is your gut reaction to this meeting, Ken? Don't think too long on this. Here you are. You are a lawyer who is sent to defend me. Here I am. I'm a defendant who is facing the death penalty with overwhelming evidence against him. So go with what your gut tells you, Ken."

"My gut tells me you are crazy. Psychotic. That you can't grasp reality. While you understand the charges and evidence against you, you are in some kind of denial of your part in all of this. It seems like you know you are guilty of the charges, but refuse to believe you had anything to do with the crime. I'm not a psychologist or a psychiatrist, but what you are demonstrating isn't normal, isn't sane. There's a disconnect of some kind going on."

"Fair enough."

"I'm thinking you want me to pursue this course. I'm thinking you want me to prove you are mentally incompetent, that you cannot tell right from wrong, that you are not in control of your faculties… that you are insane."

"If you think that is the best course of action, I put my trust in you – just as I asked you to put your trust in me."

"All right, let's explore that as a possibility for your defense."

"Good. We're making progress now."

"Let me ask you some questions germane to the possibility of an insanity defense."

"Sure, ask me some germane questions."

Ken let the sarcasm go and asked, "Do you have a psychotic background?"

"Depends on what you call a psychotic background."

"Look, Roy, I don't want to go around and around with you. Just answer my questions. I'll try this one again, but from now on, don't make me ask the same question twice or ask me to restate it. Got that?"

"Yes."

"Good. Ever been to a psychologist or a psychiatrist?"

"Sort of."

"I'm warning you now. I'm playing this game with you because you wanted me to, but don't push me too far. What's 'sort of' mean?"

"Back in college, like maybe a dozen years ago, I saw one of the free counselors they offered on campus."

"Was this a licensed psychologist or psychiatrist?"

"How should I know? I was just a lonely kid having trouble with his course work, and I was depressed and confused. So I called social services on campus, and they arranged for me to speak to a counselor. I don't remember if this person, this woman, was licensed or what, but I had a number of sessions with her. Saw her once a week for most of my sophomore year."

"Remember her name?"

"Not fully. We were on a first name basis. I remember her as Rita. That's all."

"Were you prescribed any medication?"

"Yes."

"Then she must have been a psychiatrist. Only an MD can prescribe medication. Do you remember what the medication was?"

"No. It was an anti-depressant of some kind."

"Did it help?"

"It did. I was on it and off it for a year or so."

"And you don't know what it was?"

"No."

"Were you just depressed or was there more to it?"

"More to it. Hard to explain."

"Try."

"Okay. I haven't talked about this in a long time, so my memory is a little shaky. Basically, it's like this: I took an anthropology course – Cultural Anthropology. We had to read a lot of stuff about primitive tribes in third world countries. I found a common thread running through all these illiterate people regardless of where they were living. It became sort of an obsession for me. Seems they all had some kind of priest or holy man, or holy woman, who could connect with the spirit world. Actually, it's not all that different from some of the religious practices in our own country..." Roy seemed to lose himself in thought for a few moments before continuing, "anyway, I got into some meditations and shit, you know, trying to connect to what some call, 'the other side,' and that kinda screwed me up for a while."

"You're going to have to get specific without getting too detailed. Keep it to your mental condition at the time."

"Sure. No problem. To be blunt, I got into psychedelic drugs, mind-altering shit. I dropped a lot of acid, you know, LSD, did a ton of psilocybin 'shrooms and peyote – which by the way is pretty awful stuff that made me puke afterward every time. Some of the acid was mild and some powerful. I never knew where it came from or who made it. I just bought it on campus, and dropped it regardless. Anyhow, I had visions, experienced all kinds of weird stuff. To this day I don't know if it was real or just my inner-mind, my imagination and hallucinations at work. Fucked me up bad enough that I dropped out of college for a semester. I didn't get all Fs for my courses as I got Rita to sign off that I was ill and couldn't continue with my work. It was mostly bullshit, but I accepted it, and even got refunded for the classes I dropped."

"Is this when you started the medication?"

"Yeah, when I finally gave up on the dugs and metaphysical shit, I went into the depression I told you about. That's when I got on the meds."

"How'd all this end?"

"I took some time off. Got a job and a girlfriend for a while. Didn't do any drugs – not even pot or booze. As I said, I stopped the meditations and drugs, went back to college, and graduated a couple years later with a degree in business."

"And you've been fine since then?"

"I didn't say that."

"I'm asking, not assuming anything."

"I've been okay. Sometimes good, really good, where I feel I'm on top of the world, and then sometimes I sort of crash and get existential, you know, like thinking life is meaningless, and in the end we all die and are forgotten – that kind of shit."

"Are you still on any medication for the mood swings?"

"No. I told you I don't do drugs, any drugs. I mean, if I got sick and a doctor gave me some antibiotics that would be okay, but not mind or mood-altering drugs. Been there, done that. Never again. Not for me. No thank you."

"Roy, do you think you are psychotic?"

"I think everyone is a little psychotic."

"Wrong answer. Once more, do you think you are psychotic?"

"Maybe. That's the best I can do for now." Roy covered his eyes with his hands, "I'm feeling kinda drained, you know? Let's talk more about this next time."

Ken looked at his watch and couldn't believe how long he'd been alone with his client in this cell-of-a-room. He suddenly felt claustrophobic, and that he needed fresh air. It was a new and strange sensation that was hard for Ken to process. In fact, this whole scene was new and hard to process. "I think this has been constructive for our case. I'm out of time, but I'll arrange to meet with you again in the next few days."

Roy did not respond.

"If, and I mean *if* we choose to go down the insanity route, you'll need to be evaluated by a psychiatrist. You okay with that?"

"I guess so. If you say that's the best course of action, I go with whatever you think best."

"Before we proceed in that direction, and make no mistake, it is a tough road to travel and be convincing – in fact it rarely works – I want to talk to my co-chair. You met him briefly, Hank Parnell. He's had a lot more experience with this kind of defense, and he'll have final say. I'll get back to you soon. And thanks for your cooperation, Roy."

Ken picked up his briefcase and phone, buzzed for the guard, and in a few minutes was in the fresh, if humid, South Florida air.

ELEVEN

Roy Dillard was escorted back to his cell by the same silent guard who seemed just as bored walking with Roy as he appeared when standing motionless in the gray, concrete conference room waiting for yet another lawyer to confer with yet another crook-client. Roy's present home was a similar colorless room, but this one was smaller and contained a bolted-down steel desk and bunk with a thin mattress, a toilet, a sink and a flimsy folding chair. The cell was obviously decorated with suicide prevention a priority. No glass mirror, nothing with which to hang oneself, not even enough room to get a good running start for a lethal head-butt into the wall! That was all well and good, but inconsequential, as Roy Dillard had no intention of killing himself.

Instead he propped his meager pillow and sat on his cot. Roy stared blankly at the locked steel door with no inside handle and thought... and thought. How could he be managing a fast food chicken restaurant a couple of months ago and now be isolated here in the Broward County Jail? The franchise owners were certainly pissed when he left. And now they must be outraged – not only because they suddenly had no manager for the restaurant, but the bad publicity would be a long lasting nightmare. How could someone with no criminal record, not even a speeding ticket, be recorded brutally murdering a stranger, slapping an innocent counter girl, and stealing a load of expensive, high-end jewelry and watches? It was as if there were two of him, two Roy Dillards. One who was an average Joe, and another who was one badass criminal. Roy felt he only knew the former. The other guy was a stranger, someone else, not him – definitely not him. But there he was on that video. Not just *that* video, *those* videos, from three inside cameras with three angles plus an outside camera! He pondered the evidence, plus the two witnesses! Oh my God! Not only four distinct footages, but two eyewitnesses who heard him speak, saw him blow the top of that guy's head off, and saw exactly the same thing as the cameras recorded!

At least his lawyer seems a decent sort, a good man actually, even if he is inexperienced. Straight-laced with a strong work ethic, that was good. Hell, he said he'd *work his butt off* – his words – for Roy Dillard. At least he's got that. Roy thought about the things he'd revealed to Ken Melzer – the drugs, the counselor he saw a lifetime ago in college, the acid trips, the peyote and mescaline experiments, the breaks with reality and hallucinations – or maybe they weren't hallucinations at all. Melzer had listened to it all, and had focused on this aspect of his past. Roy knew Ken was looking for any kind of defense. This seemed like the only plausible reason for... Roy didn't even want to think about the images from the crime. Still photos taken after the event plus the actual real-time footage would be exhibited at his trial, and that might be difficult to endure, but the evidence has to be shown. Reliving those few minutes in Saltzman's Fine Jewelry and Watches again and again would be inevitable. But it's best not to ponder it all now. There would be time for that later.

Roy thought back on his childhood. Did everything with his family lead up to this point? Is he merely the product, the culmination, of awful events growing up in the Dillard household? Nope, not going to go there either, not right now. In fact, right now, the time for thinking should end. Leave things to Ken Melzer. He assured Roy they would be a team; that he was on Roy's side. He'd have to hold on to that, to have faith that Ken would pull him through this. Roy closed his eyes and let his mind go blank.

TWELVE

The door to Winston Schneck's office was uncharacteristically closed when his intercom announced that Evelyn Thompson was in the waiting room. It was 9:30 in the morning, and for the last two hours Winston had been meticulously viewing and reviewing the Saltzman jewelry store security camera recordings.

The guys in the tech department had put the images on a disc showing a three-part split screen. Each segment was comprised of a single camera video with each of them exactly synchronized in time. Dillard parked his car and walked into the store where the cameras simultaneously picked him up from three separate angles, plus of course, the fourth outside camera, which was unimportant at this moment. Winston was known as an evidence hound. If one piece of damning evidence would be sufficient, he demanded two, and three would be better. He crossed his t's and dotted his i's where evidence was concerned. No room for doubt, and no chance of spin from the Defense when it came to evidence. Maybe they could put some doubt in the jurors' minds on a single exhibit or testimony, but that became more difficult with multiple, even redundant exhibits and cumulative testimony.

Laurie Silva, the counter girl in Saltzman's, would testify she heard Dillard yell "Surprise, Nigger!" before shooting him. But that's only her best recollection. The old man, Saltzman, went into shock during the crime and remembers little of the shooting or theft. He's no good as a witness, but he might be worth putting on the stand for a sympathy nod from the jury; regardless, it's the "Surprise Nigger!" remark that Winston Schneck wanted the jury to remember. Couldn't be any doubt about Dillard yelling the slur. Can't have the defense lawyers finding ways to muddy the waters with doubts about Silva's memory during such a stressful time.

Winston opened the office door, smiled and introduced himself to Evelyn Thompson from the South Florida Hearing

Institute.

"Miss Thompson, I appreciate your coming in to help us out in this matter."

"Not at all. I'm glad to do what I can, you know, civic duty and all that."

"Exactly! I wish more Floridians had your sense of *civic duty*. It's both admirable and refreshing." Winston gestured to the leather sofa in front of a cleared mahogany coffee table, "please, Miss Thompson, have a seat."

Sitting she asked, "So, how can I help?"

Winston Schneck placed a laptop computer on the coffee table and sat beside her, "I would like to ask your opinion related to a critical piece of evidence in a case this office is prosecuting. Of course, you are entitled to an expert witness fee for the time that you spend with me reviewing evidence."

"Well," Evelyn hesitated, "I'm employed by the Institute on salary and don't work outside of my teaching job."

"I understand. So you haven't ever testified as an expert witness?" Schneck asked, confirming what he already knew.

"No, I haven't. I'm completely unfamiliar with how that works," Evelyn replied.

"What I need from you is very simple and I will have my office mail you a customary fee when we have finished today, if that's okay with you?"

"Yes, that's fine."

"Okay. So let's get down to the business at hand. Are you familiar with the Super Bowl Murder and Jewelry Heist, Ms. Thompson?"

"Well, a little, I guess. Just what I saw on the news. It sounded horrible."

"Yes, to say the least, it was horrible. And in order for you to help me seek justice in this case, I'm going to ask you to view a particularly awful film. I know this isn't something anyone would ever want to see, but it will be seen – by a number of lawyers, probably psychiatrists, some of the public, and of course by a jury. And, I hope by you."

Evelyn seemed visibly unsure for a moment and Winston felt he might lose her before he got the chance to use her. But then she relaxed, took a breath and said almost solemnly, "If I need to view this to help you get justice, I really don't feel I have a choice in the matter. Yes, I'll do whatever needs to be done."

"Thank you. Not only your civic duty, but your strength is to be admired." Winston knew this was crap, but she seemed to respond well to it. Best to keep her complimented and reinforced.

Evelyn blushed and was lost for words. Winston came to the rescue. "Before we begin, can you tell me exactly what you do at the Hearing Institute?" Winston knew more about her than she could have imagined, but she didn't need to know that.

"Sure. I teach lip reading to the deaf and hearing impaired. I also teach signing."

"How long have you been teaching?"

"Well, I interned during college, and they hired me when I graduated. That was nearly six years ago. I've been at the Institute full time since then."

"How did you get interested in this field?"

"My younger sister is hearing impaired. She was born with the condition, so my parents and I took classes with her and learned to sign. Lip reading was the next logical step."

"I see. Again, you are to be commended. First you help your little sister, and now you help others with the same disability. Remarkable."

"Thank you again, but how can I now help you?"

The shock of watching the split screen films was almost too much for Evelyn Thompson to absorb. At the blast of the revolver and the ensuing red mist, she closed her eyes and covered her mouth with her hands. It was a reflexive action and Winston was concerned she might vomit. Immediately he stopped the film and spoke softly, "I know this is difficult. If it weren't of the utmost importance, I never would have imposed this upon you. May I get you a glass of water?"

Evelyn opened her eyes and lowered her hands, "Yes, some water would be good. My mouth has gone dry."

A few moments later Winston returned from the water cooler and Evelyn took a few small sips. "Thank you. Give me a minute and I'll be ready to watch again. I'm sorry about that, I wasn't prepared for the shock of-"

"I completely understand, Miss Thompson. Take your time. Whenever you are ready, we can continue. And remember, I want you to concentrate on the middle film only, the full front angle. So watch only the middle footage on the screen, and I'll enlarge the image so you can see only the subject's face. That way you won't have to see the shooting. Sorry, that was thoughtless of me before. I should have done that in the first place to spare you the awful details."

"That's okay. I'm ready now. But let me ask you a couple of standard questions before we begin."

"Sure."

"Does this person speak standard English?"

"Yes."

"Any foreign accent?"

"No, not at all."

"Any speech impediments or facial paralysis?"

"None. He's just a regular American guy."

"Okay, that makes things easier. Let's see if I can read his lips and determine what he's saying."

Winston played the film several times, stopping when it was obvious any speaking was finished and only the shooting remained. Evelyn said, "From this front angle I can determine the two words that are spoken, or enunciated in anger, to be precise.

"How can you make such a characterization?"

"That's easy. Words personally directed to someone in anger or in a threatening manner are almost always articulated slowly. And in this case only two words are voiced."

"Well, that's very helpful indeed. How about we play it again and this time you can watch the left part of the split screen. This is the camera that caught the left side of his face. It may not be as clear as the first one because the camera is a little further away, but see what you can do."

"Sure. Play it."

Once more Evelyn carefully studied the film. "I see the same lip movement as the center shot. It's a little further away, like you said, but that's not a problem. It's very clear."

"And we have one more camera angle to view. This one

should be better as it's coming from the right side, and the subject was closer to this camera. Take a look."

Evelyn rested her forearms on her thighs and leaned in close to the monitor, watching intently. "Everything I see from this angle and the other supports what I was able to discern from the full front camera."

"I see," replied Winston, controlling any signs of elation. "So what two words do you think the subject said?"

"I don't like to use words like this, but the man on the screen clearly said, excuse me, not just said, but certainly yelled to some degree, '*Surprise, Nigger!* '"

"Are you absolutely sure this is what he said?"

"Yes, I'm sure."

"Is there any question in your mind that it could be something else?"

"No, none at all."

"Viewing only the side angles, could you still determine what was said?"

"That would be a little more difficult, but yes, the side recordings revealed the same two words."

"With no doubt whatsoever?"

"None."

"Absolutely positive?"

"Absolutely. This was easy. Only two words were involved and they were enunciated perfectly and even slowed down because they were enunciated in obvious anger."

"I see. Well, one last question. In your opinion, do you think there could be anyone in your field who might possibly disagree with your interpretation in any way?"

Evelyn Thompson shook her head and replied, "Not a chance. Like I said, this was easy and obvious. As awful as they are, those are the two words, and from these videos, no one could come to any other conclusion."

Standing, Winston closed the laptop and walked around his desk. Taking a seat in his swivel chair he said to Evelyn, "I think you have been a tremendous help. I can't tell you how pleased I am you agreed to assist us in this matter. If there is anything I can ever do to return the favor, please don't hesitate to call." And

Winston continued with a conspiratorial grin, "just don't ask me to fix any parking tickets!"

Evelyn laughed at this, "You're very welcome, Mr. Schneck. Like I said when I first got here, I'm glad to do my civic duty."

Winston stood and reached out his hand. "Thank you again, Miss Thompson. It was very nice meeting you."

Evelyn shook his hand gently and turned toward the door.

"Oh, I almost forgot," Winston interrupted her departure, "Who did you say you studied lip reading under? Whoever it was must have been a wonderful teacher as you are obviously an expert in this field."

"Well, thank you. I studied under Joan Landers. She's the best. In fact, she works at the Institute also."

"Really? I'm sure the two of you make a formidable team! It's good to know the hearing-impaired in our community are in such good hands. Thank you again for coming in."

The door closed and Winston put his hands on his hips, a huge smile spreading across his face. He knew Joan Landers was the foremost lip reading expert in the south. If her understudy was certain Dillard said "Surprise, Nigger!" well, Joan Landers would find the same result. One difference, she'd do it from the witness stand.

THIRTEEN

"Man, I really need this," Ken Melzer said after a long pull from his large size Starbucks coffee cup. "I'm not getting enough sleep. Dillard's ruining my life."

"Welcome to the world of capital punishment," Hank Parnell responded with a grin. "If you weren't tired, you wouldn't be giving it your all. This won't last forever."

They sat a few blocks from the courthouse at a typical small Starbucks table. Ken and Hank Parnell would make this a twice a week tradition for the next few months before the Dillard trial. Hank made it a point to encourage Ken to begin the conversations.

"Okay, so tell me your thoughts."

"Well, Hank, you've heard the last few recordings. I can't make head or tail out of this guy. He's smart; that's obvious. He tries to be controlling, yet he falls back almost into submission when I get annoyed or impatient with him. Sometimes I think we're working as a team, and sometimes it's like I'm dealing with a child who hasn't a clue."

"That seems apparent from the recordings. He's an odd duck, that's for sure, but what are your thoughts on a strategy?"

"A plea is out of the question. Each time I've brought up the subject I'm met with negativity on his part. Sometimes he even gets angry at the mere suggestion of a plea. Dillard insists a jury will find him not guilty. Doesn't make any sense as he never explains how this is going to happen."

"Go on..."

"When I broach the subject of either *how* or *why* a jury will find in his favor, he gets this goofy look on his face and tells me I need to have faith in him."

"And you think...?"

"And I think this guy is nuts, or delusional, or maybe has a death wish...or something."

"How 'bout when you bring up the whole murder and robbery to him? How does he react, physically I mean?"

"It's kinda strange. It doesn't seem to affect him. He doesn't really have much reaction. It's as if someone else did the crime, or as if he's in some sort of denial about the whole thing. I do know he doesn't like to talk about it."

"So what's your plan?"

"I see only one possible course of action. We have to prove insanity."

"You know how difficult that is – even under the most favorable conditions? It rarely works. Proving a person can't discern right from wrong, reality from fantasy, all that... well, good luck with proving that to a jury."

"What other choice do we have? I can't find a motive. He has no past criminal record. All I've got is a history of heavy drug use in college and him saying he saw a counselor after he dropped out for a while. That's it. There's nothing more. We're stuck with insanity."

"Then he'll need to be examined by a psychiatrist."

"Got anyone in mind?"

"Yeah, I do. He's an older gentleman, semi-retired, well, mostly retired, but works enough to qualify as an expert witness. We use him when we need a certain result. Let's just say he needs us as much as we need him. For lack of a better description, I'd categorize him as *compliant*."

Ken took another long swallow. "All right, so I can assume we have a psychiatrist in our corner?"

"Yup, I can arrange it, but let me ask you a few questions."

"Sure."

"You've interviewed the people he worked with at the fast food place, right?"

"Yes. Past and present employees as well as the owners."

"As a manager, how did his employees describe him?"

"They said he was fair and honest and patient – especially with new people. With minimum wage earners coming and going, turnover in that business is constant. Anyone who works there for more than six or eight months is considered an old timer."

"And the racial makeup of them?"

"Some Whites, mostly Blacks and Hispanics – Cubans and a few from Mexico and Latin America – and mostly fairly young."

"Any one of them say anything about a personal bias or prejudice from Dillard?"

"No. Not one."

"And the franchise owners?"

"They're of Cuban descent, I think, and nope, no prejudice. Actually they were shocked by the whole thing as Dillard had worked for them for several years with absolutely no problems. They said they own several fast food franchises, and Dillard was the best manager they'd ever had."

"So, how the hell are you going to claim he is or at least *was* legally insane at the time of the crime?"

"I'm not sure. I'll have to rely heavily on the psychiatrist's testimony." Ken thought a moment more, took another swallow of coffee and continued, "If there was no motive to kill the black delivery guy, and no obvious reason beyond greed to steal the jewelry and watches, then there must have been some deep-rooted, whacky psychological reason to do it. Plus, Dillard is smart. He must have known about the cameras. He must have *seen* the curbside camera and the three inside, yet he made no attempt to hide his face. No mask, no disguise. He could have grown a full beard and worn sunglasses with a ski cap, but he did none of those things. So, I ask myself why would a smart person not care that he was going to be videotaped killing a guy in cold blood and committing an armed robbery – *in full daylight and during business hours.*" Ken stared across the table at his expressionless mentor who said nothing. He raised the nearly empty cup again before continuing, "I ask myself this over and over – during the day, at dinner, in the shower, when I should be sleeping, I even dream it! And the only answer I come up with is that the guy is out of his gourd."

Hank considered what he'd just heard. "You might come to that conclusion, but you can't prove it. You can assume it, but that's not enough. You even said he might have a death wish. That doesn't make him legally insane. Maybe he simply wants to go out with some publicity and fanfare."

"Maybe. But like I said, Hank, that's all I've got."

The two finished their coffees and again silently looked at each other as if there was some answer that might miraculously emerge in the form of a spoken epiphany. But there was nothing. No *I've got it!* No *it's perfectly clear to me now!* Ken thought maybe there never would be an answer to the why of this case.

Hank spoke again, "Let's turn the table and make you the State's Attorney. You are the prosecutor. What would you say about an insanity defense?"

"I've been obsessing on this almost since Day One. From the standpoint of a prosecutor, I'd say he'll have an easier job showing Dillard isn't insane than I'll have trying to be convincing that he is insane. That's a given. The prosecutor will show the court he's held the same job for years with glowing evaluations time after time. He'll say Dillard's had a driver's license in the state of Florida since he arrived here, and never had even a parking ticket! He'll reveal that Dillard doesn't take any medications beyond an occasional aspirin or antacid and doesn't even have a primary physician, much less a psychiatrist! True, he doesn't seem to have any real friends, but he had been able to work six days a week from morning till night, earned more than enough money to put food on the table, and didn't have time for socializing. This guy worked all week, slept, and watched TV on Sunday... and started over again on Monday!" Ken looked exasperated, but went on. "The prosecutor will suggest that anyone who was this conscientious and successful at what he did couldn't be insane."

"You got it down pretty well, Ken."

"Thanks, but I wish I didn't."

"Look, I told you right from the start this was a good case for you because you'll get courtroom experience and will test your sea-legs before a jury. That doesn't mean anyone, and I mean *anyone,* expects you to do any more than go through the motions and give your client the representation to which he's entitled. I can't see any reason he won't go down for this. I fully expect him to get the death penalty. This is no reflection on you. It really has little to do with you. Dillard did this awful thing by himself, and got caught with enough supporting evidence to warrant execution. Do the best you can for him, but don't get too emotionally involved. This is your job, not your *life*. He's your client, not your *brother*. You will have to walk away from this after all is said and done knowing you gave it your all, did your job, and have a clear conscience. Then it'll be time to move on to the next case." Hank tossed a two dollar tip on the table and concluded, "And one more thing, Ken. Don't look back too much. That accomplishes nothing."

FOURTEEN

The first time he met Carla Christianson, Winston Schneck was in awe. She was a product of a Vietnamese grandmother and a Spanish/Indian mixed grandfather from Peru. Her other two grandparents were pure Nordic. In Carla the result was astounding – an athletic five feet ten inches tall, long and straight light brown hair, subdued Asian eyes with an alarming emerald hue, flawless skin that was easily and evenly tanned by the South Florida sun, a relaxed, seductive smile that seemed to communicate a hidden secret held in reserve, and all this entwined with an abundance of confidence. Carla's lineage could be traced from the villages of Southeast Asia to the Mayan Civilization; from the Spanish conquistadors to the Vikings. She managed to extract the best genetic features from each race, creating a single unique and stunning visage. At twenty-eight years of age, college educated with degrees in ancient history and anthropology, Carla was clearly in her prime. She spoke in a well-modulated, soft tone that oozed erudition and sophistication.

Their friendship began after a cop-friend called Winston informing him that a high-class hooker was brought in who said she had information she was willing to share in return for a deal. The cop said she would only speak to someone high up in the State's Attorney's Office. Meeting Carla nearly five years ago had left then Assistant State's Attorney, Winston Schneck, spellbound. He immediately ordered her handcuffs removed and had her brought to a private conference room instead of a holding cell. This was the first time Carla Christianson had been brought in. Winston had heard rumor of her, but until then, had never had the exquisite pleasure of being in her company. Since that initial introduction, they'd had occasional, mutually advantageous meetings each year.

Carla Christianson was one of South Florida's most expensive and desired call girls. Depending on her client's wealth, her fee could be anywhere from two thousand to ten thousand dollars an evening. Overnighters, short vacations on yachts, or time spent at luxurious chalets were negotiated on an individual basis. Often, Carla had been given as a gift. It could be a Saudi prince's sixteenth birthday present to a favorite son, a team's show of appreciation to a pro-basketball player for a winning hoop, or an offering to a politician for a favor. Many a government contract had been awarded through the influence of Carla Christianson.

On their first meeting those years ago, Winston realized Carla's value as an informant – not that she had much useful information to provide regarding criminal activity, but rather, the knowledge of *who* she spent time with could prove potentially valuable to Winston. A practical woman, Carla learned early on that her looks could secure advantages in various ways. Years before, a particularly difficult college class was further confounded because she missed classroom time resulting from the untimely death of a family member. When she tried to explain her situation during his office hours, her disagreeable professor was not interested in Carla's personal problems. She was headed for a D or perhaps a low C in his class. However, the professor intimated, there might be a way to raise her grade that could be discussed over dinner... Carla pulled an A for that class and never had to take the final exam.

Being a realist, Carla understood her window of opportunity would be relatively short. After graduating from college at twenty-two, she might have seven or eight years to rely on her youthfulness. For women in such careers – whether a model, an actress, or a prostitute – youth was everything. It was imperative to remain fit, and during business hours she'd always have be at her loveliest. Unless otherwise engaged, each morning Carla exercised strenuously under the guidance of a personal trainer and then napped two hours in the afternoon. She never touched hard alcohol or drugs of any kind. If she let herself go, even a little, her window would close. Sure, she would always be able to attract customers, but to be the best, the highest paid, and the most in demand would require real work. Carla spent her initial earnings on clothes, jewelry, and even took a course in cosmetology. These she considered necessary start-up business expenses. They would pay huge dividends after she brokered her own six-month deal with the most discrete and exclusive escort service in South Florida. By her business model, if she plied her skills and charms correctly, in six months she would collect the contacts she'd need to be an unencumbered independent contractor. By her early thirties, if she lived frugally and invested wisely, Carla calculated she could retire with independent wealth.

For Carla, the fly in the ointment was the law. Her profession was, of course, illegal. When she was arrested along with her underworld "date" that had been under police surveillance, Carla suffered much more than humiliation. She experienced a profound panic upon realizing that in that instant her plans for early retirement were crumbling. To Carla, Winston Schneck appeared like a messiah. Their initial meeting would set the standard for their relationship. Carla would supply names of her clients, and details concerning times, places and salient facts of their meetings. Carla rightly assumed this information was for Winston Schneck's own purposes. A little dirty laundry from someone's past could easily translate into a political endorsement or a much appreciated campaign donation. Yes, Carla's names and dates could prove valuable. In return, he would see to it that no charges would ever be filed against her. It was a simple and surprising *quid pro quo*. Simple, because it was a straightforward bargain – information for immunity. Surprising, because Winston Schneck didn't demand personal time with Carla, she wondered if he might be gay, but through her own intuition, she decided he was straight. Unusual, but certainly nothing to complain about.

For Winston, his alliance with Carla was similar to a lottery. The names Carla supplied were like a collection of lottery tickets that never expire, a small number of which might someday pay off. For nearly five years the tickets had been accumulating, and it appeared the big jackpot was about to materialize. Schneck was continually amazed at the sloppiness and lack of discretion exhibited by so many of the rich and powerful. While they were usually careful and meticulous in their professional lives, their personal lives were frequently left as an exploitable Achilles' heel.

Carla's phone call to Winston and their subsequent meeting in a quiet bar revealed she and a young man were to meet in a hotel room occupied by none other than the Governor of the great state of Florida. After being paid handsomely by a real estate development corporation needing a zoning variance for a strip mall and mobile home park in west Broward County, Carla and her companion would bestow a gift from the developer on the Governor. A small portion of the Everglades would need to be filled, but it shouldn't be too much of a hardship for a few alligators and water moccasins to relocate a little further west... Regardless of the usual "green arguments" against the project, the economic benefits to the county and state far outweighed any environmental concerns. The Governor had said he was on the fence about the matter and could see both sides of the situation. He had intimated that if the developers could convince him their project held additional benefits to the state, he could probably influence the zoning board to rule in their favor.

With his best poker face, Winston digested the information. The timing couldn't be better. The Attorney General for the State of Florida, an elected official, had announced he was stepping down for health reasons beginning in a few months. In such a situation, the Governor had the power to appoint a replacement to serve out the remaining term. If things worked according to the plan Winston was already concocting, the position would be his. He made one small request to Carla. "Carla, this young man who is to accompany you on your rendezvous with the Governor... Do you know him?"

"Sure, we've worked together a few times in the past."

"I see. Tell me, how old is he?"

"I'm not exactly sure. Early twenties, I'd say."

Winston thought a moment and then said, "I want you to find a replacement for him. Someone younger. In fact, I want you to show up with a boy no older than sixteen or seventeen, fourteen would be better. Can you do that?"

"Of course. South Florida is full of runaways. Being underage increases the risk, and costs more, but I can arrange it."

"Excellent. I'm sure your real estate backers will foot any additional costs."

"That's never a problem."

"Fine then, I'll let you get back to your business..." Winston felt suddenly awkward and embarrassed by the comment.

Carla smiled and covered his hand with hers, "Don't worry about a thing, Winston. I'll give you the details of time and place as soon as I know them. And one thing that I probably don't need to mention-"

"Sure, anything."

"I don't want the boy to get into any trouble."

Winston grinned, "Boy? What boy?"

"Thank you."

"There is one important point though. I will need his full name and address – his *real name and real address,* even if the address is temporary."

"I'll have that for you also."

"And you are positive the Governor won't change his plans, bring his wife... cancel his arrangement with you?"

Carla kept a straight face as she rose from her seat, "Not unless he flies her back from Paris."

Winston watched Carla leave the bar. He desired her more than any woman he'd ever seen. He also realized he could have her whenever he desired, but never had and never would. For Winston, Carla would be a *spoiler.* She was out of his league in every possible way. She was so far superior to any woman he might ever chance meeting socially, that being with Carla even once would ruin him for anyone else. He'd paid a few exceptional looking prostitutes in the past, but they showed themselves to be vacuous airheads with their first spoken utterances. One experience, one intimate interlude with Carla, would keep him dissatisfied with every woman he'd encountered – paid or otherwise – probably for the rest of his life. Perhaps, Winston once thought, if he were a multi-millionaire, he'd use half his wealth to lease her for a few years. But thinking along these lines was a foolish waste of time. No, he told himself time and again, Carla was for fantasy, not reality. She was a *spoiler.*

Gordon Little was an ex-cop and part time private detective. A year ago he'd accepted a job following a suspected cheating husband. The wife who hired him was considering a divorce and needed evidence of her husband's infidelity. On a Friday afternoon Little tailed the cheater and his younger, bleached-blonde friend. He followed them from a cheap bar to her apartment. Using a telephoto lens, he was able to photograph the two through partially pulled bedroom curtains.

Rather than turning the photos over to the wife, Gordon Little contacted the cheating husband and sold him the photos for five thousand dollars. He then told the wife who'd hired him that he wasn't able to come up with any evidence of cheating and collected his hourly fee. Job over... or so he thought.

For whatever reason, the idiot husband didn't destroy the photos Little had taken and his wife found them. In short order, the husband confessed everything, the wife forgave him, and together they called the police.

Winston Schneck recognized the potential in having an ally in someone with Gordon Little's skill set. He might be helpful some day and having him indebted to Schneck could be useful. So a generous deal was struck between the State's Attorney's Office and Little's attorney. Gordon Little's information was placed in one of Schneck's personal files.

According to Carla Christianson's message, Winston had three days to prepare before the Governor checked into the Gold Coast Sapphire Hotel on Ft. Lauderdale Beach.

Winston was relieved to know he wasn't staying in a penthouse suite. That would have made things more difficult. Instead, he was to stay in suite 1826. A call to the hotel confirmed that suites were available on floors sixteen to twenty-one and that they were all basically identical.

A meeting was arranged between Carla and Gordon Little. For the ex-cop private detective it was time to repay his debt. Carla gave Gordon the details with instructions that a video needed to be made and delivered to Schneck. She also gave him five hundred dollars expense money.

Wearing sunglasses and a fedora, Gordon Little arrived at the

Sapphire Hotel during housekeeping hours. He found a maid who barely spoke English cleaning rooms on the eighteenth floor and politely asked her in Spanish if he could get a look at room number 1826. Wiping a tear from his eye, Gordon told her he and his wife spent their wedding night in that suite three years ago. He then added that she had suddenly passed away the week before. Emotionally, he explained he wanted to see the room once again to relive a cherished memory. Gordon punctuated his tale with a proffered twenty-dollar bill. The maid said the couple staying in the suite was currently out, so if he could be quick, she'd allow him a fast look.

Gordon snapped a few photos with his phone, made note of window locations in the bedroom, and using a small tape measure took some measurements. He also studied the ceiling and was gratified to see there were no fans, lights or emergency sprinkler systems over the bed. He was out in less than three minutes.

Next he went to the main lobby to book a suite on the same date the Governor would be a guest. He used an assumed name with corresponding falsified identification. Gordon casually said he was planning to propose to his girlfriend on that particular night. He also just as casually requested suite 1926, explaining they had stayed there once before and that it was a special place for them. When he was informed suite number 1926 would be occupied that night, a fifty-dollar bill helped make it available. Gordon asked to view the room, to make sure it was the same, and that his memory hadn't deceived him. A bellhop was called and a few minutes later Gordon took satisfaction in knowing the location of everything in suite 1926 was identical in every way to suite 1826, one floor below. Gordon tipped a ten and left the Sapphire Hotel. Singing along to the radio in air-conditioned comfort while driving along A1A, Gordon couldn't seem to erase the smile from his face.

Gordon Little arranged an early afternoon check-in to the Gold Coast Sapphire Hotel. He knew the room had been occupied the night before, and housekeeping would not yet have made up and cleaned suite 1826. The Governor wasn't due until after a dinner engagement. Plenty of time.

From a small suitcase Gordon pulled a padded toolbox. Opening it, he withdrew an Exacto knife, a battery powered electric drill with an especially long half-inch diameter bit, and a separate zippered vinyl case. Entering the bedroom, he placed the items on one of the nightstands and slid the king size bed a few feet to one side. *So far so good*, he thought. Using the Exacto, he placed the blade on the carpet where the middle of the bed had been and cut a six-inch incision. Two more cuts at a 90-degree angle from the top and bottom of the first slice allowed him to pull a flap of the carpet to the side. He used the weight of his toolbox to hold the carpet out of the way. Next, Gordon turned the TV to a rock music video channel and upped the volume – always smart to take precautions, even when they weren't particularly needed. In some small way details like this added to the excitement of Gordon's preparations. The drill made little noise anyway as it easily bore through the floor in suite 1926 and emerged over the bed in suite 1826. Any dust from the hole would land on the unmade bed below and be whisked away unnoticed when the maid removed the sheets. This little precaution would avoid possible detection of the hole should someone find fresh plaster dust on the bedspread and look to the ceiling. All part of the fun of thorough planning!

Lastly, Gordon unzipped the vinyl case and removed the tiny camera lens affixed to the end of a 3/8 inch diameter cable. He fed it through the hole until he estimated it was flush with the ceiling and secured it. Hooking the other end of the cable to a recording monitor, Gordon switched on the device and was pleased to see a king size bed filling the screen. From the monitor he tested the wide angle and close-up adjustments and confirmed that the camera was flush with the ceiling. Even though the equipment was old and out of date, everything worked as it should. Child's play, really. Nothing particularly high tech about this. No need for any audio. The video would speak volumes.

Gordon lay on the bed staring at the ceiling. The hours passed slowly. He didn't dare leave the room for fear of being seen – not that someone recognizing him would make a difference anyway.

It was simply another part of doing the job correctly. Gordon had learned that in these operations being ultra careful paid off in ways that couldn't be realized at the time they took place. A chance meeting, a careless word spoken to a desk clerk – any number of things could come back to bite him at a later date. He lived by the old cliché *better safe than sorry*. He watched a little TV, read a People Magazine he found in the sitting room, stared at the ceiling some more, glanced at his watch for the hundredth time, and figured a few hours of boredom was a small price to pay for repaying an outstanding debt to Winston Schneck.

The Governor and his entourage arrived at nine o'clock. After fifteen minutes they left for their own rooms and the Governor removed his sport coat, tie and pants. He carefully hung these in the closet. He placed his shirt, underwear and socks in the hotel's complimentary plastic laundry bag. They'd be cleaned, folded and returned before checkout the next day. He took a long shower and emerged wearing a white terrycloth hotel bathrobe. It was nine forty-eight. Twelve minutes to lift off!

As planned, Carla and her young boy would arrive at ten. Carla would make sure adequate light would remain in the bedroom. She would also, at least initially, coax the Governor on his back. And, most importantly, it was agreed the recording would be edited to never show her face.

Gordon Little made a ten-minute video recording that Winston Schneck would later edit down to six. The thrill Gordon experienced watching Carla was quashed by his disgust at the Governor's actions with the boy – a pale, blonde-headed child who looked barely pubescent. In fact, the Governor seemed more fascinated with him than with Carla. Ten minutes was enough. Gordon shut down the monitor. Feeling suddenly unclean, he took a lengthy, steamy shower. After dressing, he watched cable news for twenty minutes and then flipped on the monitor. The bedroom in suite 1826 was dark. Gordon was relieved he could see that the Governor was alone, under the covers, and apparently asleep. He silently withdrew the camera, glued the carpet back in place, slid the bed to its original position, repacked his suitcase, and left the Gold Coast Sapphire Hotel unnoticed by a rear exit.

FIFTEEN

Roy Dillard sat in his usual chair in the gray concrete meeting room. The same bored guard buzzed Ken Melzer and another man through. "You know the drill," he said. "Let you out when you're done."

"Sure," said Ken, "But I'll be leaving in just a minute." He turned to Roy and said, "This is Dr. Conroy. He'll speak with you privately. He's been hired by the PD's office, so can I assume anything you two talk about can be shared with me?"

"Of course."

"Good, then I'll leave you two to get acquainted." Ken signaled the guard and was buzzed out through the security door.

With the bolted-to-the-floor steel desk between them, Dr. Conroy took the remaining chair in front of Roy Dillard. "I'm Dr. Conroy," he said extending his hand. "May I call you Roy?"

Roy ignored the hand, "Why do you introduce yourself as *Doctor* Conroy and then ask if you can call me by my first name? You doctors are all the same. You think you're some kind of special, better than everyone else. So, to answer your first question, hell no! You can afford me the same respect you seem to demand. Call me *Mister* Dillard."

"Fine then. I assure you I meant no disrespect. I was only asking how you liked to be addressed-"

"Bullshit! You were establishing a two-person pecking order here. You are the lord and I am the serf. You are the exalted one and I am the peon. I've had to deal with people like you my whole life."

"I see. Would you like to explain your feelings on this matter?"

"Oh please." Dillard laughed loudly and shook his head slowly from side to side. "So predictable, so fucking predictable. Can we please cut through this psychobabble crap? Are you really going to ask me to explain my *feelings* about every statement I make?" He stared at the doctor who sat expressionless and patient until finally he responded.

"Mr. Dillard, I'm here at the request of the Public Defender's office to examine you. As you know, I am a psychiatrist licensed in the state of Florida-"

Dillard cut him off, "No, *Doctor,* you're here not at the *request* of the Public Defender's office or the *request* of anyone for that matter. You are here because you are being paid to be here. I'm your patient and you are being *paid* to see me. The fucking Queen of England could *request* you do something, but unless the fucking Queen of England comes across with some dough, you'll be out playing golf somewhere."

"Mr. Dillard, you seem particularly agitated, even angry?"

"No shit! Should I be happy? I'm in a fucking jail cell waiting for a trial. And after that if the state gets its way, I'll be put to death. There's a shit-load of evidence against me, and I'm supposed to look to you like you are some kind of life boat or something sailing in to save my ass! Agitated? Angry? Are you kidding? I'm ready to fucking explode! To put it into psychological terms that *you* might prefer, I am completely self-actualized. And now you come waltzing in here treating me like I'm some piece of trash on the street you'd rather walk around than have to clean up!"

Smiling, Dr. Conroy said, "We seem to be off to a rather poor start."

"Is that a statement or a question?"

"Take your pick."

"If that's a statement, it's presumptuous. We are not started on anything yet. If it's a question, I'd say the same thing, but add that you arrived here with a bit of a disagreeable attitude toward me. Is that a fair assessment?"

"It is if you deem it fair."

Dillard laughed again. "Thanks for being non-judgmental. That certainly puts me at ease. I feel better now." Thinking momentarily he added, "And if you dare ask why I *feel* better about you being non-judgmental, I'll buzz that moron guard and be back in my cell before you can say 'Holy Fucking Freudian

Slip!'"

"May we begin again?"

"Let's."

Dr. Conroy paused for a few seconds as if collecting himself.

"Mr. Dillard, I'm Charles Conroy. You may call me Charles or Charlie or Dr. Conroy."

"Pleased to meet you, Dr. Conroy. You can call me Roy."

"Thank you, *Roy*. It's a pleasure to meet you."

"No, the pleasure is all mine, Doctor."

"So Roy, let me begin by saying I've spoken with your attorney, Ken Melzer. I first want to assure you that anything you said to him is in the strictest of attorney-client privilege. He only told me facts about you that could be found by anyone – your age, educational background, work history – things like that. Now, my job is to evaluate your mental state with regard to your case. Are you comfortable with that?"

"Yes, of course."

"Good. Let's start with some questions about you, and yes, about your feelings. Sound okay to you?"

"Sure, but you have me at a disadvantage." Dr. Conroy braced himself for a barrage of accusations. He needn't have. Roy continued calmly, "I would like to know a little more about you. May I ask a few questions?"

"Absolutely. Fire Away."

"If that was a joke, I can tell you have a good sense of humor, Doc – but poor timing."

"Please, Roy. I apologize. I simply meant you could ask me any – "

Roy's laughter stopped Dr. Conroy mid-sentence. "Of course, I know what you meant. Sometimes a little levity can be a good thing, a good ice breaker between two people trying to get to know one another."

"I agree. I should have said *ask* away."

"May I inquire how old you are?"

"I'm seventy-six."

"Are you retired from psychiatry?"

"Semi-retired."

"Wife? Kids? Grandchildren?"

"I have a wife, Ella. Two kids, boys – well, men now, of course – both married, five grandchildren."

"Close family?"

"Yes, very."

"Regardless of anything else, then you are a lucky man, Dr. Conroy."

"Thank you. That's exactly how I feel."

"Then, tell me about your feelings, Doc..."

"Well..."

Roy clapped his hands, tilted his head back and roared with laughter. "No, please! I was only kidding. I was making light of the whole *tell me about your feelings* thing that was kind of a stumbling block for us in the beginning. I'm sorry, sometimes I see the funny side of things and speak when I should keep my mouth shut."

Dr. Conroy chuckled along with his patient. "More questions for me?"

"Just one. Do you like being a psychiatrist? Was it a good life choice?"

"That's two questions."

"Forgive me, I-"

"Now I'm being facetious. I'll gladly answer your questions. Yes and yes. Every person is unique and interesting. I have tried to help my patients for almost fifty years. Some I succeeded with, and some I couldn't help. You asked if psychiatry was a good life choice. It was."

Roy nodded his head, "Thank you for being so candid with me. I'm ready to answer any questions you have."

Later that day Dr. Conroy stopped by the Public Defender's office. "Hello, Tina. Is Ken Melzer in?"

"Sure Charlie. I'll let him know you're here." Tina pressed the intercom and said, "Ken, Charlie Conroy is here to see you... Okay, I'll tell him." She turned back to the doctor, "He says the door's open."

"Thanks, Tina, and by the way, sharp dress."

"You're such a charmer..."

Dr. Conroy entered Ken Melzer's office and sat on the new leather sofa that had been delivered the day before. Feeling the leather with his hands he said, "This is nice. Looks new."

"It is. A present from Charlene, my wife."

"I like it. Goes well here."

"Thanks. Can I get you anything? Coffee?"

"Nope, I'm fine. I only have a few minutes."

"So, how'd you do with our boy today?"

"Well," Dr. Conroy began thoughtfully, "he's not what I expected – perplexing actually."

"How so?"

"This was my first session with him, so all I can offer at this time is a first impression. I'll be able to be more specific as I get to know him better, but we spent the first half of our time together arguing."

"Really? About what?"

"Formalities, names, a *pecking order* as he put it, everything and nothing. And then I suggested we start over, you know, begin with a sort of fresh slate, and he was totally different."

Ken chuckled softly, "Been there, done that."

"Okay, so what I'm saying isn't surprising to you?"

"No, he was like that the first time I met him. He's a weird duck."

"To be more clinical, I found him emotionally conflicted – as if he didn't know how to behave with an unknown person. He began as impulsive and truculent, definitely adversarial and threatening."

"Threatening?"

"Yes, but in a non-physical way. More like threatening to leave and go back to his cell. I took this as a threat to either behave in a manner acceptable to him or he would dismiss me."

Again, Ken smiled and nodded. "He pulled the same stunt with me at first, too."

"It was at the height of his animosity that I suggested we start over. I intimated some fault was mine and we'd begin again with me being more respectful and careful."

"How did that go?"

"Instantly he changed," Dr. Conroy explained. "Roy

transformed himself into an ultra polite and compliant patient absent of any bluster. Funny, he made a big issue over me being introduced as *Doctor* Conroy, but asking if I could call him by his first name. As if this were some sort of control move on my part, or maybe some kind of class distinction he thought I was trying to establish. And then when we started the session over, he wanted me to call him Roy and he referred to me as Doctor Conroy. So, in the end all the combativeness was for nothing, and we came full circle to where we began the session."

"Did you get into anything deep or disturbing?"

"Nothing deep yet, but disturbing, yes. The way he exhibits apparent mood swings – from overtly aggressive to controlled passivity – all in the course of a few seconds is unusual. I would have to wonder if this condition could escalate to violence, or perhaps did escalate to violence in the jewelry store." Dr. Conroy lifted his hands and eyebrows in a gesture of unknowing. "But, like I said, this was my first meeting with Roy. More will come out as our discussions probe into his life."

"When can you see him again?"

"My schedule is fairly open. I think about two times a week for the next two or three weeks should do it. I don't want too much time to transpire between my visits. He needs to get used to me, to be comfortable speaking with me – a routine of sorts. If he believes I am here to help him, he'll open up, and I can make an evaluation that should assist him in court."

"I appreciate that you want to help Dillard, but aren't you hired for the sole purpose of objectively evaluating him before trial?"

Conroy smiled warmly and said, "Well, of course. But I am still a medical doctor and I can't help but view everyone I evaluate as a patient of sorts. It's just who I am."

"And in court you'll be able to separate your role as an expert witness from acting as a practicing psychiatrist seeing a patient?"

"Yes, of course. In both roles I'll be able to help him."

Ken digested the last part of what Dr. Conroy had just said.

"You seem confident Dillard is off his rocker."

"I wouldn't put it that way exactly, but I am of the opinion that at least sometimes, everyone can be a little crazy…" Dr. Conroy abruptly stopped speaking, adjusted his glasses and looked deeply at Ken as he continued, "I want to be completely honest with you. I don't agree with the death penalty. I don't know if you are a religious man, Ken, but I am. And I truly believe there is both good and evil in all of us. Some keep it under control better than others. And some aren't capable of managing this control. I believe everyone can be saved, if not in this life then in the hereafter."

Ken was taken aback by what just transpired. Did he hear correctly what Conroy just said? Did his most important witness just blow his own credibility? If asked on the stand if he supports the death penalty, and Conroy answers he does *not*, in final argument the State could suggest to the jury that his testimony about Dillard being nuts was simply one old religious man's attempt to thwart another execution. *Good and evil in everyone? Some just lack control...?* Ken's face showed nothing when he responded, "I see. Well, for this trial and your testimony, I think it best we stick strictly to your observations and final evaluation of Roy Dillard."

Dr. Conroy smiled knowingly. "Don't worry. I've testified for the Defense in enough cases to handle myself appropriately in court."

"Have you ever testified for the State?"

"No, that would go against my Hippocratic Oath to do no harm and only try to help my patients. Locking someone away, or worse, goes against everything I believe."

"But he's not your patient-"

"We've been through this already," Dr. Conroy interrupted. "There's no point arguing over semantics. Don't worry, I can conduct myself appropriately on the stand."

"I see. Well," Ken said looking at his watch, "I have a meeting to get to. Tina can schedule your visits with Dillard. I look forward to discussing your findings."

They both stood and shook hands. When Dr. Conroy left and closed the office door behind, Ken closed his eyes, slumped back in his chair, and covered his face with his hands.

SIXTEEN

Calm and complacent, that was the mood Ken Melzer was trying to maintain. He sat at a simple oak desk in his home office, actually the unused second bedroom of their modest Imperial Point house. His pinstriped gray jacket and subtle red tie were long abandoned and draped over the back of the living room sofa. Ken's polished black shoes had been kicked off while tied and lay by his feet. Before him on the desk were yellow legal pads containing notes about the Dillard case – notes he'd scribbled to himself as ideas popped into his head, notes he'd written from conversations with Hank Parnell and notes from information he'd received from Dr. Conroy. Next to the loose pages and bound pads were dated recordings illuminated on his laptop screen compiled from his personal meetings with Dillard. Absently, Ken would select a recording, noting the time and date it was made, and play it for what seemed like the hundredth time. But nothing new came to him, no inspired ideas, no new possibilities. They were starting to seem like lines from a play, and he was learning them by heart.

Ken knew he had little to go with. Roy Dillard refused to discuss details of the murder and jewelry heist. He insisted he knew nothing about the stashed .357 magnum Colt Python and stolen goods from the Coral Ridge house the police found hidden in his garage. If pressed too hard Dillard would sit back and smile at Ken telling him to have faith in the justice system, to not worry, the jury would set him free. It was tiresome. It was frustrating. It was exhausting. Did Dillard have any clue to the hours Ken was putting in on his behalf? Did he even care? It all led to one conclusion. Dillard was out of his mind.

Still, Dillard seemed as if he were somehow in control. His confidence was almost convincing Ken that he *did need to have faith in the justice system.* But that was the problem, Ken truly did believe in the system. And that's why he was convinced

Dillard was going down for his crimes – and going down hard.

His one hope, Dr. Conroy, was hardly a place for much consolation. In his spare time Ken found himself role-playing as if he were the prosecutor with Conroy on the stand. It wasn't a pretty daydream. As Hank Parnell had pointed out, and Ken knew from studying countless cases in which the insanity defense was tried, under the most favorable of circumstances, it's a difficult way to win a case.

Resigned now to the almost certainty of a quick defeat in court, Ken told himself over and over that this is Dillard's doing, not his. He can only deal with the evidence and facts; he can't create or change either. Dillard is the hand he has been dealt, and he'll play it for all it is worth – which isn't much. Yet, Ken thought again for the thousandth time, judging from his contact with Dillard, it doesn't seem possible he could have been so wildly insane at the time of the crime, so incoherent and disconnected from reality that he didn't know right from wrong. The whole crime obviously took planning. It was purposely staged on Super Bowl Sunday at a time when hardly anybody would be on the streets. He brought a laundry bag for the loot and packed a huge revolver. Even the guy he shot, Bentley, wasn't addressed as "Hey, Fella…" or "Yo, Buddy…" He was called *nigger* before being shot in the mouth. To anyone that would indicate specific anger and hatred rather than the randomness of a lunatic caught in the midst of a murderous psychotic event. Everything seemed too deliberate, too planned. As for the cameras that were in plain sight, well, maybe at the time Dillard *had* a death wish, which he now denies. Maybe at the time he wanted to get caught. Mood swings and weirdness? Sure. But displaying some kind of temporary, fleeting, violent insanity at Saltzman's and not being able to discern right from wrong? Not very likely.

If Ken considered such an argument for insanity implausible and unconvincing, so would a jury. When he pondered all this he found himself becoming agitated and ill tempered. He had to sustain control, had to keep reinforcing to himself that he was a lawyer, not a miracle worker. *Calmness and complacency,* that's what Ken Melzer needed to maintain.

Charlene came in wearing yellow running shorts and a matching tank top. She walked up behind her seated husband and placed her hands on his shoulders, rubbing and kneading. "I was surprised to see your car in the driveway. Everything all right?"

Closing his eyes and leaning back Ken said, "Ooh, that feels good. Yes, everything is fine. I figured I could get the same work done here as I could at the office. I thought a change of environment would do me good, maybe even let me see this case in a new light or something... Anything."

"Honey, I know how hard you are working on this case. I only hope that Dillard creep appreciates all your efforts."

"Who knows? He's as much an enigma today as he was when I first met him. I still can't make head or tail out of him or his *alleged* crime."

Charlene worked her fingertips into the base of his neck and down to his upper arms. "When this case is over, you should ask for some time off. We could go on one of those three-day mini-cruises or spend a few days relaxing on the Gulf Coast – Sarasota or Long Boat Key maybe."

"That sounds nice. Or, maybe I could just sit here for three or four days while you do this."

"Slim chance of that, Buster."

Ken and Charlene laughed softly together. The closeness felt refreshing and soothing to him. Ken was worried their earlier rift over his accepting the Dillard case might drive a wedge between them. She admitted to being wrong after speaking to her father about the matter. Lately she'd told him she was having frequent lunch dates with him and that they both admired the fact that, as her father put it, "I have to admit, your husband should be commended. He's certainly not afraid to put in the work for his client." Charlene told him that her father started his law career as an Assistant State's Attorney in Palm Beach. He said it was a great way to "get your feet wet... learn the ropes." Ken had heard all this before.

Charlene didn't mention that her father also said he expected Ken to burn out as a public defender, probably within eighteen months or two years. He further said dealing with the low-life element of South Florida day after day would wear him thin, especially when drawing such a small paycheck for his efforts. Charlene hoped he was right. Perhaps, if she became pregnant about that time, he'd see the need to join a firm and make real use of his law degree and talent. Until then the best thing she could do would be to stay supportive of her husband. He needed to feel she was with him, beside him, his support team. She could do that. Being an adversary would only lead to unhappiness and possible disaster.

"How far did you run?"

"My usual three and a half mile course."

"Pretty hot out to run that far. I don't want you getting heat stroke."

"Don't worry about me. You're the one to worry about."

"And why's that?"

"Because you are working so hard and not sleeping enough."

"How do you know I'm not sleeping enough?"

Charlene stopped massaging and let her hands rest on Ken's shoulders. "Because sometimes I wake up in the night and see you sitting up in bed. You stare straight ahead and I know you're thinking about the case." Ken did not reply. Charlene began the massage again and said, "I'll be glad when this case is over and you can come back to me."

"I wasn't aware I ever left."

"You know what I mean. It's like Dillard has become your entire world and everything and everyone else has become secondary. I only want my husband back."

"I'm sorry, Char. I didn't realize I'd become so distant. This is my first big case and a man's life is on the line. It's hard for me to let go of that. I pretty much know the outcome of this trial, everybody does, but I have to live with it when everyone else can forget about it. I have to know I did my best, that I did all I could for my client."

"And that attitude reflects the man I fell in love with." Charlene leaned over and kissed the top of Ken's head. She wrapped her arms around him and put her still damp cheek against his. "I'm all hot and sweaty. I'm going to take a shower, and I think a nice long, warm shower might be just the thing to help *you* unwind. I'll get the water going and you can join me in a few minutes."

SEVENTEEN

Howard Schwartz had been with the State's Attorney's Office for slightly over two years. In his own mind he'd had enough of learning the ropes and finding his way. When Winston Schneck singled him out and asked him, ordered him actually, to take the deposition of Roy Dillard's psychiatrist, Dr. Charles Conroy, Howard was shocked. In disbelief he recalled saying, "I thought they didn't file for discovery. I don't have access to their witnesses."

"True, but in an insanity defense the Prosecution *does indeed* have the right to depose the Defense's expert witness." Schneck looked directly into Howard Schwartz's face and added, "That must have been one of the questions you missed on the bar exam."

"Sorry, I should have known that. But are you sure you want *me* to take the deposition? I mean, this is a big case – a death penalty case. Shouldn't *you* be the one taking the deposition...? Sure, of course I'll do it if that's what you want, but this is... like the biggest case to come into this office since... well, since I've been here. I don't want to make any mistakes or screw anything up."

Schwartz remembered Mr. Schneck's reply, "Yeah Schwartz, I want you to take the deposition. I'm busy and so is just about everyone else in this office. This guy, this Conroy character, is a patsy for the Defense. I know about him. I've thoroughly researched him. When I cross-examine him he'll be like butter and I'll be a hot knife. Even you, Schwartz, couldn't screw up with this guy."

"Okay, whatever you say."

"Good. Just find out what Conroy is going to testify about Dillard and lock him into his testimony."

Howard Schwartz was sitting in an unpadded chair outside Winston Schneck's office when through the closed door he heard the loud and gruff, "Schwartz, come in!"

Instantly he was sitting in another unpadded oak chair in front of Mr. Schneck's huge, cluttered desk.

Without looking up Schneck said, "I'm busy Howie, so make it fast. What have you got?" Schneck knew Howard Schwartz didn't like to be called "Howie," which was part of the reason he used the name. The other part was simply that he *could* use it. He'd call anyone in his office by whatever name he chose. It was a reminder to all of them who was in charge. Schneck did as he pleased. Screw everyone else. After fifteen years he'd earned the right. Names didn't mean shit so long as the jobs got done.

"Want me to read you my notes?" Schwartz asked.

"No, Howie! I can guess what you asked and probably what you should have asked but didn't! Just tell me what Conroy said."

Occasionally glancing at his notes, Howard Schwartz gave Winston the gist of the deposition. Schneck listened and said nothing until Schwartz finished. After a prolonged and awkward silence, Schneck said, "As I expected. No surprises there."

"Did I get what you wanted?"

"Yeah, you did fine." Then, considering out loud to himself, Schneck said, "I know this kid Melzer is inexperienced, but surely Parnell would have made certain he filed for discovery. I wonder what they've got up their sleeve..."

"That I couldn't say..."

As if still talking to himself, Schneck continued, seemingly unaware Howard Schwartz was still in his office, "Well, that's interesting but doesn't matter anyway. Hell, he could have Johnnie Cochran defending him and I wouldn't care."

"You mean O. J. Simpson's lawyer?"

"You know another Johnnie Cochran?"

"But Sir, Johnnie Cochran's dead."

"Christ, Howie! You think I don't know that?"

"Sorry, Sir."

"Anything else you want to add?"

Haltingly he began again, "Well, I... ah... also did some

research on this doctor. Seems he's testified for the Defense a few times."

"Like Cochran being dead, I think I also know that."

"Right. Well anyway, I read some transcripts from other trials he testified in and the psychological evaluations all seem pretty much the same... the subjects all had identity problems, schizophrenia, heard voices, can't tell right from wrong... all that stuff. Same as I got from him."

"You got that right. All the usual crap. And you know something, Howie?"

"What's that, Sir?"

"None of it makes a damn bit of difference. Sigmund Freud could testify on Dillard's behalf... and before you inform me that he too is dead, I know that... What I'm saying is that I've got Dillard by the balls, and the only time I'm gonna let go is when they take him to death row!"

"I believe you." Howard Schwartz hesitated before adding, "There is one thing that bothers me though."

"What's that?"

"Well, apparently Dillard is supposed to be pretty smart, college educated and had a decent job, you know, not your usual street punk. So, if he's sane, why would he go into a jewelry store not far from his own house, and in broad daylight knowing he was being filmed on several cameras, blow that black guy away and steal a load of jewelry? That sounds like something only an imbecile or a crazy person would do – and he's no imbecile. It somehow doesn't fit, you know?"

"Maybe you're right, Schwartz."

"Really?"

"Sure. Maybe Dillard is mentally impaired. It could be he is. But you know something?"

"No. What?"

"I don't honestly care whether the guy is sane or insane. It doesn't matter to me if he hears voices, or hallucinates, or thinks he gets psychic instructions from Adolph Hitler, Pol Pot, Jack the Ripper, Fidel Castro, John Wayne Gacy, John Wilkes Booth or Satan himself! I just don't really care! He blew away an innocent delivery guy and ripped off a ton of high-end bling! I've got no use for him and neither should society."

More than a little surprised by this outburst, almost meekly Schwartz asked, "What about our psychiatrist's evaluation? What if *he* thinks Dillard's nuts?"

"That's not likely. Our psychiatrist is top-notch and has testified for us before. I'm confident he'll produce the results we want. To tell you the truth, we don't even need our own psychiatrist. I've got enough evidence to fry this guy, and Dillard's shrink will work in our favor – and he doesn't even know it."

"Well, what about the hate-crime charge? I mean, from what our people found out Dillard worked with lots of Blacks and Hispanics – and I'm talking about workers in a fast food restaurant – you know, not exactly white collar types, and none said a bad word against him. They all insisted he was a great guy to work for, you know, treated everyone – regardless of color or ethnicity – really well. They all liked this guy... Black, Hispanic, Haitian, whatever."

Schneck glowered behind his desk as if appraising this underling. "Who knows and who cares? Maybe he just put on a front to keep his job. Maybe he got sick of working with a bunch of unreliable *minorities* and just flipped out. I don't know and, like I said before, I don't care. He's going down for what he did, and I'm going to see to it!"

Schwartz stared at Schneck and hid his gut reaction to this tirade. He suddenly felt glad of his recent decision to leave the State's Attorney's Office within the year and find a position in a private law firm. This was beginning to not feel right. "Whatever you say, Mr. Schneck."

"Good attitude." Schneck laughed lightly, and Howard was unsure of the intent when he concluded, "Now get out of here, Howie, and find something new I can use."

Already walking out of Schneck's office, Howard Schwartz said over his shoulder, "I'm on it, Sir."

EIGHTEEN

Flashing identification, emptying pockets and shuffling from locked door to locked door had become routine for Ken Melzer. The security staff all knew him and when Ken finally reached the windowless concrete meeting room, the guard no longer bothered to instruct him about signaling when he wanted to leave. Taking his usual seat across from his client, Ken placed his phone on the bolted-down steel desk and hit record.

"Well, good morning to you, Ken."

"Good morning, Roy. Everything okay with you?"

"As well as can be expected."

"Good."

Ken sat in silence while his phone recorded nothing. Roy Dillard held his slight smile and also said nothing. Finally, Roy broke the stalemate, "Everything okay with you, Ken? Charlene all right?"

"Yes. We're both fine."

"That's good."

Again, more staring and silence. Roy seemed perfectly contented to wait with that annoying little smirk that seemed permanently affixed to his face. Ken sat thinking the same thoughts he'd been thinking for several weeks now. Nothing new came to him. No insightful questions to ask, no overlooked information to glean from Roy.

Roy yawned and stretched. "Okay, I give up. What's on your mind?"

"You are on my mind. You are always on my mind. I think about you all day. I ponder this case when I eat. I agonize about every aspect of our relationship. I even dream about *us* at night! I feel lost. It's like you and I are on a long hike and I don't know where we are going, but you do… or at least you say you do. I'm ready to panic because I'm convinced we're lost, but you are always calm and confident."

"That's interesting, Ken. Nice analogy. Maybe you should look to me as a guide and comfort to you instead of someone to *agonize* over."

"This is exactly what I'm talking about. I'm trying to help you. I'm trying to save your life! And you do nothing to help me, to help *yourself.*"

"Ken, Ken Ken," Roy said tutting and smiling, "have a little faith."

"I don't know how to respond to that."

"Well," Roy began, "Do you believe in the justice system, the jury system?"

"Look, we've been through this before... Yes, of course I do. Please don't start all this again. This is exactly why I'm so troubled, no, *exasperated* with you. I could have more faith in you and this case if you'd give me something, anything, to work with. Don't talk about faith. Don't talk about trust in you. Just don't talk about that shit anymore!"

Smiling, Roy replied, "Why Ken, that's the first time I've heard you swear!"

"I'm sorry. I usually don't. In fact that is the first time I've used that kind of language in a very long time."

"It's okay. I don't mind."

"Well, I mind. I don't swear. It's part of my personal code, and now I'm breaking my own standards. If you knew me better, you'd know it takes a lot for me to get to this level of anxiety, and if you must know, *pain.*"

"Pain? Really?"

"Yes, really."

"Ken, you're my lawyer, my friend. I don't want to cause you pain. How can I help?"

"You know exactly how you can help. Give me something that will let me *help you!*" Ken closed his eyes and wiped perspiration from his forehead with his sleeve.

"Ask me anything you want. I'll do what I can. I hate the idea that I'm affecting your life this way."

"Thank you."

"You're welcome."

Ken seemed to take a few long breaths to regain his

composure. He'd been at this juncture before, "Okay, let me ask you this-"

"Sure, anything," Roy broke in.

"Okay, let's assume for a minute that the person depicted on the videos made at the jewelry store is an intelligent human being who knows where he is and what he's about. Can you imagine that?"

"Sure."

"Why would this person who is about to commit a crime, several crimes, walk into a store without trying to hide his identity, knowing cameras were running?"

"That would be hard to answer."

"Why? What motive would he have to stroll up to a supposed stranger and shoot him in a particularly horrible manner?"

"I can't say."

"And, why might this person steal a load of expensive jewelry from several glass display cases?"

"I don't know."

"And later, when the police search his house, why would they find stolen jewelry and another gun from a home burglary?"

"I guess someone stole those items and stashed them there."

"Who?"

"Someone."

"Listen, Roy, I'm at the point that if I ask another question I will probably swear again… and I don't want to do that."

"I'm sorry. I'm doing the best I can."

"No, you're not."

"Yes, I am."

"No."

"Yes."

"NO!"

"YES! I assure you I am helping you, Ken. You are simply incapable of understanding how!"

"This is insane!"

"Do you really think so?"

"Don't play games with me, Roy."

"I'm not. I merely asked if you think I'm insane." Ken gritted his teeth and hissed, "It really doesn't matter what I think."

"Oh, but it does, Ken."

Calming himself, Ken replied, "Fine. Do I think you are insane? Sometimes yes and sometimes no. A sane man would do everything in his power to help his attorney. You refuse to do that. So I think you must be nuts to not want to help yourself, unless you don't value your life or have some kind of death wish."

"I assure you I value my life and have no *death wish*. And I *am* helping you."

"No, you're not."

"But I am."

"How?"

"Put me on the stand and you'll see."

"See what? That you're insane? That you don't know right from wrong? That you don't know what is real from what is fantasy?"

"No, not at all."

"Then what?"

"You'll see how our justice system works. You'll see that an innocent man should be set free and a guilty man should be found guilty and sentenced to an appropriate punishment."

"And you wonder why I'm exasperated?"

"Actually, I don't. I understand your exasperation. If we reversed places, I'd feel the same as you."

Ken said nothing. He felt a slight burning in his stomach and reached for an antacid. Seeing him open the tube and pop one in his mouth, Roy asked, "Are you ill?"

"No. Just indigestion."

"That can be painful."

"Yes, it can."

More silence. Ken tried to compose himself and calm down. "I have no other defense but to claim you are insane. Dr. Conroy will testify to that, but truthfully, it rarely works."

"I know that."

"I have no witnesses to say you act crazy."

"I know that too."

"I called your old college and they said they don't keep

records of counseling sessions. It was all volunteer stuff with no fees or files or anything to show you ever sought help back then. And besides, it was a very long time ago."

"Yes, I can see how that could be problematic."

"So, all we have is Dr. Conroy's evaluation."

"That's not quite all you have, Ken."

"Please tell me I've missed something. Tell me you were committed to an insane asylum for two years that nobody knows about. Tell me you have a secret doctor who's been treating you since college. Just tell me *something*!"

"Okay, I will."

"I'm all ears."

"You have an ace in the hole, and you don't even know it. You have *ME!* You have one star witness, one saving grace. Put me on the stand. You'll see."

"I should leave. You're wasting my time, Roy."

"I'm only wasting your time if you think I'm wasting your time."

"That's exactly what I think."

"Then, think again."

"Explain."

"I'm all you've got. Let Dr. Conroy testify and be cross-examined. Then put me on the stand."

"And what exactly do I ask you?"

"Don't worry. When the time is right, I'll provide the questions you need to ask."

Ken blinked a few times as if bright light had suddenly poured into the room. "So let me get this straight. Conroy testifies as the main witness for the Defense-"

"No, not the *main* witness. You have me."

"Right. Conroy testifies and then I call you."

"Yes."

"And I have nothing to ask you, nothing prepared ahead of time."

"That's not so. I'll give you questions to ask."

"When?"

"Before you call me to the stand to testify, of course. I thought I made that clear."

"You did make that clear, but if you were me, how would you feel going to trial with maybe a couple of character witnesses, Dr. Conroy and you to put on the stand... and nothing else to present to the jury?"

"I'd feel exactly like you do now. I'd feel confused, and frustrated, and maybe even a little scared."

"Thank you for your empathy, Roy."

"You're welcome."

"So that's it then. This is your defense and you are happy with it?"

"I will be."

"When will you be?"

"When I testify."

"I can think of only one good thing to come from all this... this lack of preparedness and lack of... of... anything."

"And what's that?"

"When you are found guilty and eventually sentenced to death, you can appeal the verdict on the grounds of ineffective assistance of counsel. Then maybe you can get a new trial with a more experienced lawyer with whom you can work more effectively."

Roy exploded into laughter. He arched his back and threw his head back so fiercely that his chair nearly went over backwards.

"I'm glad you find that funny. At least if nothing else, I'm good for bringing some humor to your life."

"Oh, you are a scream," and Roy laughed again. "Please try to relax. Look, I know you are doing everything you can for me, and that you think I'm not being... shall we say, cooperative or forthcoming. I understand what you must be going through. But please, Ken, please have some faith and trust in your old pal, Roy Dillard."

Ken did all he could to keep emotion out of his glare. There were times, and this was one of them, that he actually hated his client. Again for the millionth time, he tried to tell himself that Roy Dillard was who he was, and there was no changing that. Ken was his appointed lawyer and he was trying, if in vain, to give him the best legal advice and representation of which he was capable. He needed to separate his emotions – his feelings of frustration – from his personal life. As Hank Parnell kept telling him, do the job as best you can, and at the end of the day close the office door behind you – and don't look back. Somehow, that was easier said than done. Maybe in a few years and a few hundred cases to his credit, he'd be able to master that, but for now it seemed impossible.

Ken grabbed at the phone with more force than he'd intended, and it nearly slid off the table. Placing it in his pocket as he rose, Ken waved for the guard to release him. A moment later he was briskly walking down the hallway toward the first set of locked doors while he thought he heard a new round of muffled laughter coming from the meeting room that contained Roy Dillard.

NINETEEN

Dr. Charles Conroy sat across from Roy Dillard for this, his last session with the accused murderer and jewelry thief. Roy had the same annoying smile on his face that he usually maintained when Dr. Conroy entered the windowless concrete meeting room.

Before Dr. Conroy could ask how Roy was holding up, he was met with, "So, Chuck-E-Boy, this is your last chance to determine if I'm out of my fucking head."

Nonplussed, Dr. Conroy responded, "Is that how you see yourself?"

"Christ on a crutch!" Dillard yelled at the doctor. "Are you going to play these fucking shrink games with me right to the end?" In a mocking tone he whined, *"Is that how you see yourself?* C'mon Doc, you can do better than that. Cut the crap and let's talk."

"Fine. What would you like to talk about?"

"Well, for starters, I need to know what you are going to say about me in court. I need to know if you are going to tell the jury that in your esteemed opinion based on years of psychiatric training and practice that I'm fucking nuts, or whether you are going to say there's not a goddamn thing wrong with me, and I should be sacrificed for my sins and for the good of society!"

"I see..."

"What the fuck does that mean, *I see*? I don't think you see shit. That's what I think. You're being paid by the state. And that's my tax dollars, Bud. I sure as hell want my money's worth! You better be ready to testify that I'm goofy as shit and that I don't know whether I'm in jail or whether I think I'm one of Santa's little helpers at the North Pole!"

"Roy, you seem particularly agitated today. Would you like to tell me what's on your mind?"

"Sure, Chucky, I'll tell you what's on my mind." Roy Dillard scowled at the emotionless man sitting before him and continued,

"I'm wondering about God. I'm wondering if there is a god and a heaven and a hell, or whether that's all a bunch of bullshit. I'm wondering if in a few short weeks I'm going to be scheduled to find this out for myself... like maybe fifty years prematurely. Frankly, I'm worried. I'm worried if you testify in a way that's, let's say, unconvincing on my behalf, that my puny life is over, that I'm fucked for all time. I'm worried I'll never see a sunrise or sunset again. I'm worried I'll never eat escargot again. I'm worried I'll never get laid again. I'm fucking worried I won't even have the means to kill myself if I feel I need to."

"Are you contemplating suicide, Roy?"

"Fuck you, Conroy!"

Roy Dillard fidgeted uneasily in his straight back chair while Dr. Conroy sat unmoving with his hands folded on the desk between them. The silence lasted a full minute before Dillard spoke. "So, what are you going to say in court?"

"I'm not through with my evaluation yet. I also have to review my notes from our previous sessions."

"Non-judgmental and non-committal 'til the very end, huh?" Dillard growled. "Thanks for putting my mind at ease."

"My job is not to put your mind at ease, Roy."

"Yeah, I know. Know how I know?"

"You are free to explain."

"I know, because every time you see me and then leave, I find myself worried and scared shitless."

"Why do you feel worried and scared?"

"Jesus Fucking Christ!" Roy instantly stood and yelled. "I just explained that! Are you fucking stupid or what?"

"Please sit back down, Roy. There's no need for anger and aggression."

Roy remained standing in defiance for a short moment, and then did as the doctor asked. "Sorry, I'll try to be more controlled."

"We've touched on this before. Is control an issue for you?"

"Yes, of course. Sometimes I act impulsively. Sometimes I act on something and afterward can't believe I did what I did. In fact, sometimes I don't even remember that I did what I did."

"Has it always been this way with you?"

"Yes."

"How long?"

"Like you've asked, and I've answered, *always.*"

"Since you were a boy?"

"Yes."

"How about at work?"

"I usually kept myself controlled there."

"Why is that?"

"I told myself I was being paid to be there, to do my job. I saw it as being owned for that amount of time, and I wasn't myself. That philosophy let me concentrate on only doing what was expected of me. I didn't allow myself to get upset, or angry, or frustrated because I wasn't me when I worked."

"Who were you at work?"

"Someone else."

"Who?"

"The guy who was hired to do the job. An actor playing the role expected of him. I didn't get emotionally involved with my job or the people who worked for me."

"How did you deal with the people who worked for you?"

"They didn't work for *me*, they worked for the guy doing my job, the guy hired to run the place. If they worked for *the me* who's sitting in front of you right now, I'd have fired all their asses and told them to grow some smarts before they try to get hired again."

"Were your employees not intelligent?"

"Intelligent and smart are two different things."

"Well put. Were they not smart then?"

"What the fuck do you think? They aspired to work in a fast food joint for not much more than minimum wage and no tips. These people were, *are,* the dregs of the potential worker pool. If they had half a brain, they'd at least try to get a job where they could either earn tips themselves or share in the tips earned by others. Shit, even dishwashers in restaurants share in some of the tips the serving staff earn. My people were too fucking stupid to realize this, and then they bitched about the low pay they got!"

"And this makes them stupid, in your opinion?"

"How 'bout in your opinion, Doctor? You think they're

smart?"

"Let me ask you this. Does race or ethnicity matter to you?"

"I prefer my own race."

"In what way?"

"I'm glad I'm white. Aren't you?"

"That's not what I meant. Do you look down on other races?"

"I look down on stupidity. Stupid is stupid. Being Black and stupid is no different than being White and stupid. I hate all stupid people."

"Hate is a strong word."

"Yes, it is."

"Do you act on this *hate*?"

"Not at work. I explained that before."

"How about outside of work?"

"Does that matter now? I may never be *outside* again. In jail I'm isolated. In death I'll either be in heaven or hell or just dead without a soul to go any place. And then none of this will matter, will it?"

"That's an interesting question."

"Care to answer it?"

"Actually, no."

Dr. Charles Conroy stood and held out his hand to Roy Dillard, who refused the gesture. Though their hands didn't meet, briefly their eyes did. The guard was signaled and Dr. Charles Conroy was gone.

TWENTY

Hank Parnell was already seated at their usual small table toward the back corner of Starbuck's. Resting on the table before him were two large paper cups of coffee. One still had the plastic cover fitted. Hank sipped at the other.

Glancing to the door, Hank caught a glimpse of Ken Melzer leaving his car and trotting to the entrance. He pushed open the door, spotted Hank, and with a deep sigh sat across from his friend and mentor.

"Sorry I'm late, Hank…"

"No worries. You okay?"

"Yeah, I'm okay. I just had a little trouble getting up this morning."

"A late one last night?"

"No, actually an early one. I'm not sleeping too well these days. No matter how tired I am when I hit the sack, as soon as my head touches the pillow my brain turns on. I want to sleep – believe me, I want to sleep in the worst way – but I can't seem to do it like I should."

"Worried?"

"Among other things, yeah I'm worried."

"So, talk to Uncle Hank."

They both laughed softly at this. Ken peeled away the lid from the steaming coffee cup and took a sip. "Just what I need."

"Tell me about this sleep thing."

"Not much to tell. Like I said, I go to bed and my mind gets active. Sometimes I lie there tossing from side to side for hours. Last night I know it was some time after four o'clock when I finally dozed off. Then the alarm went off at six-thirty and I must have fallen back to sleep for a few minutes – that's why I'm late."

"Are you keeping Charlene awake?"

"Not in the way I'd like," and they both chuckled again. "I'm sleeping on the guest cot in the spare bedroom. You know, the one I use as an office."

Hank said nothing and Ken continued, "It's not fair on Charlene to spoil her nights with my sleeping disorder."

"I suppose not, but you realize this isn't good for either of you or your marriage."

"Of course I know that. I keep telling myself and Charlene too, that as soon as this trial is over I'll get back to normal. This won't last."

"Hmm, well let's hope not. So, what do you think about when you should be sleeping?"

"C'mon, what do you think I'm thinking about?"

"Tell me."

Almost incredulously Ken shook his head from side to side. "I'm thinking about this case. I'm thinking about Dillard. I'm thinking about my opening statement. I'm thinking about the witnesses I don't have, and the evidence I wish the state didn't have, and the alibi I wish my client had, and on and on and so forth and so forth."

Hank listened intently and thoughtfully spoke, "Look, I've seen the evidence just like you, and I've listened to every recording you've made of your time with Dillard. I've also heard what Chuck Conroy has to say. So, to use one of Dillard's favorite questions, 'do you believe in the justice system?'"

Ken let out an exasperated breath, "Yes, of course I do."

"Good. Then let it work."

Ken closed his eyes and almost whispered, "And how is that going to help me proceed with this case and help my client?"

"It's not. It's a statement of fact. From everything I can tell, your *client* walked into Saltzman's Jewelry store, blew off the top of a black guy's head after calling him the N-word, and then stole something like a million-plus dollars worth of diamonds, emeralds, gold Rolex and Omega watches et cetera, et cetera, and drove away only to be positively ID'd and arrested an hour later."

"And your point?"

"My point, Ken, is that your *client* seems guilty of all the charges filed against him. He's a bad guy. He's going to get what he deserves. Your job, as we've discussed a number of times, and which you seem to not completely grasp, is to supply the legal counsel our system affords him. Period, that's it. That's the whole ball of wax."

Ken sipped some more of his coffee. "I know all that. But I feel his life is in my hands-"

"No!" Hank interrupted, "that's where you're wrong. His life is in *his own* hands. He made the choices that led him to where he is today. You tried to convince him, rightly of course, to plead guilty in return for a probable life sentence. But he refused your counsel and demanded a jury trial – which is his right, even though it was a misguided decision on his part. You did what you could in this regard, but he wouldn't have it. If he won't cooperate with you, that's *his* decision. You represent him whether he's guilty or innocent, cooperative or un-cooperative. As long as you are doing everything you can to represent his interests – which by the way, you are – then you should be sleeping like a baby and having sweet dreams to boot."

"I know you're right."

"Good, because I am right! Now, tell me this, if I'm not being too personal, everything all right with Charlene? This can't be easy for her."

"I think she's dealing with everything okay. At first she was upset I was offered this case-"

"Not *offered*," Hank interrupted again, "*assigned*."

Ken smiled weakly, "Okay, *assigned.* She thought it would make me look bad if I lost. *When I lose*, I should say. She seems better about it now."

"I know she talked it over with her father. In fact I talked to him before I gave you the case."

Ken sat up as if startled, "You know my father-in-law?"

"Sure. We even came up against each other a few times in court. I assume you know he started right out of law school with the State's Attorney's Office."

"Yes, but I had no idea you knew him..."

"It's not like we're best buddies, but we talk occasionally. I might add, he thinks very highly of you and wouldn't mind stealing you away from the PD's office to join his firm."

"Not a possibility. Even if I did leave, I wouldn't want to work for my father-in-law. He's an okay guy, but, well, would you go that route?"

Hank chuckled, took a swallow of his coffee and answered honestly, "Not in a million years!"

They shared a laugh over this and Ken turned serious. "Hank, I'm running out of time here. The trial date is only a week away and I have nothing much except Dr. Conroy's testimony. And we both know how weak that's going to be. I mean, I honestly don't know if Dillard is nuts or not. I do think he knows right from wrong at least *now* in the present time. How he was on Super Bowl Sunday I can't say. Maybe he flipped out and didn't know what he was doing, even though that seems remote. I don't know what his motive was. If he wanted to rip off a jewelry store, he could have worn a mask and broken in at night. At least that way he'd have had a chance of getting away with it. But going in like he did and shooting that delivery guy makes no sense. Part of me thinks that's why he must be insane and part of me thinks that's what makes him bad – evil actually." Ken looked directly into Hank's eyes and concluded, "So, after all is said and done, most of which we've hashed out before, I've got nowhere to go with this case."

"Sure you do."

Surprised, Ken said, "Hank, what are you talking about?"

"Do what your client wants you to do. Represent him by following his wishes."

"Which are what exactly?"

"Believe in the justice system."

"Now, don't *you* start with that! Help me out here!"

"I am. Pay attention to Dillard. It's all you can do. It's what he wants you to do."

"Go on."

"We'll put him on the stand after Conroy testifies. If it's all you've got and it's what Dillard wants you to do, well, then do it."

"Is that what you'd do?"

Hank thought a moment before speaking. "It's what I *will* do. Don't forget, this is technically *my* case. You are assisting me. A first year public defender is never entrusted with a case of this magnitude. It's *my* case. Let *me* lose sleep over it, not you. This is affecting you way too much. When I gave you this case, I had no idea it would get to you so profoundly and in such a negative way. I'm going to handle the trial. You're off the hook."

"Thanks, Hank. I know you're only trying to help me, but *you* are going to be at the defense table as a figurehead only. I'm going to be defending Roy Dillard because that's what he demands on no uncertain terms. He actually told me he'd fire you if you tried to *interfere*, as he put it, with the trial. C'mon, I've told him again and again that I lack the experience for a case like this. I've pleaded with him to consult with you personally. I've tried to persuade him to let you take his case to trial. But he won't have it. Not any of it. For the life of me, I don't know why, but he wants *me, and only me,* to represent him in court."

"Do you think maybe *I* could convince him otherwise?"

"Not a chance. He'd only get angry. And ultimately, it's not going to happen."

"Okay then. In that case, you've obviously been advising him correctly. You've given him excellent legal counsel. And that's your job. What I'm trying to tell you is that you've done everything right so far. You've knocked yourself out for this guy. That's all you can do, and all anyone expects from you." Hank shoved his napkin into his now empty coffee cup and stood. "And that goes for me, and I'm sure for Charlene and for your father-in-law, too."

TWENTY-ONE

Winston Schneck sat in the dark paneled waiting room. He glanced at his watch yet again and saw with chagrin that he'd been sitting alone for one hour and twenty-three minutes. Instead of allowing his anger to get the best of him, he actually smiled inwardly in anticipation of this meeting and silently assured himself that Winston Schneck would never be kept waiting in this office again. He'd overlook it this time, but never in the future. He'd be in control then.

His private thoughts were interrupted by an attractive black receptionist who put down a phone receiver and in a disinterested tone said, "Mr. Schneck, the Governor will see you now."

Winston did not respond. Picking up his expensive but worn canvas and leather valise, he rose from his chair, checked his watch one last time, and followed the slender woman through double doors into a spacious, richly decorated office. Once inside, she eased around him and closed the doors. Winston stood staring at the man seated behind an enormous walnut desk, either reading something or pretending to. Again, Winston let his annoyance slip into a neutral area of his brain. His time was almost at hand. He'd tolerate the officious behavior this once, but only this once.

Finally, the Governor looked up and appraised the man standing before him. "Mr. Schneck?"

"Yes, sir."

"Have a seat, please."

Winston sat in one of the matching brown leather chairs before the great desk. The Governor spoke again, "Mr. Schneck, have we met before?"

"No sir, we haven't."

"I didn't think so." He gazed at Winston, not bothering to stand or extend his hand. Winston took note of each little slight and took great satisfaction in knowing there would never again be even the remotest hint of this behavior.

"Normally I don't see people who refuse to tell my staff the nature of their business, but your persistence finally wore me down." Winston allowed the tiniest of smiles to emerge on his face, but said nothing. "So, I have to tell you I have a very busy schedule and haven't much time. I'd appreciate it if you'd get to the purpose of *needing to see me about a personal matter,* as I believe you told my people on the phone numerous times. And I'll add that if you weren't the Broward County State's Attorney, you'd not be seated in my office today."

"Well, thank you for making the time to see me, Governor."

"As I said, Mr. Schneck, I'm a little short on time..."

"I completely understand, sir. So I'll get right to the point."

"I appreciate that."

"I believe the Attorney General for the state of Florida is stepping down-"

"Mr. Schneck," the Governor broke in, "if you are looking to fill that position, the answer is no."

"Actually, that's exactly why I'm here."

"Sorry to waste your time, Schneck, but I'm going to run for re-election, and I need someone who can bring me some much needed support. Frankly, that ain't you."

"And why is that, Governor?"

"For starters, my polling shows Broward County is solidly in my camp. Appointing you Attorney General won't bring me any of the votes I need. Besides, I already have someone in mind – Hispanic, female, from Duval County."

"I'm sure if you hear what I have to say, you'll reconsider."

"I'm sure if you *heard what I just said* you'd realize you are wasting your own, and more importantly, *my* valuable time."

"Perhaps you need to listen to what I have to say."

The Governor stood and made an obvious show of communicating to Winston the meeting was over. With a smarmy smirk he added, "In case you haven't looked in the mirror lately, you are a white Anglo male. Not a very valuable commodity in the political realm of things these days. Sorry you traveled all the way to Tallahassee to hear that."

Undaunted, Winston remained in his seat. He slowly reached

down to his valise, unzipped a side compartment, and produced a DVD. Then he too stood and faced the Governor. "Sir, I think you should just have a quick look at this."

"If that's a resume or promo of some kind, you can leave it with my secretary on your way out. Good day, Mr. Schneck."

Instead of leaving, Winston surprised the Governor by retaking his seat, opening the plastic DVD case, and tossing the disk on the desk. "I'll tell you what, Governor. You stick that in your computer and view the first ten seconds. Then if you want me to give it to your secretary, I'll be glad to oblige your wishes." Before the Governor could respond, Winston growled menacingly, "Now, play the goddamn disk!"

Sensing an undefined primal danger, the Governor slid the disk into an open laptop. A few seconds later Winston watched the color drain from his face.

"Where did you get this, Schneck?"

"*Mister* Schneck."

"Excuse me. Where did you get this, Mr. Schneck?"

"I know a number of people in low places who owe me favors. This was made by a two-bit porn supplier," Winston lied.

"You know him?"

"I know a lot of people."

"How was it made?"

"This kind of thing goes on all the time. Small cameras are hidden in hotel rooms, and the perv waits and hopes for something good. Kinda like fishing. You drop your line in and hope a big one takes the hook. Recordings like this are sold online and in sex shops. They fall under the category of amateur porn or secret camera porn, you know, for people who don't like staged actors faking passion. This kind of thing attracts the voyeuristic types – peeping Toms, wannabe private detectives... that sort. Of course, it also appeals to a general audience of perverts and degenerates – especially those who like to see older men with young women or boys. I should add that a combination of an extremely attractive young woman and a very young, probably underage boy would be a *valuable commodity*, to use a term you seem familiar with, Governor."

The Governor slumped in his leather chair and shut his eyes as he reclined slightly. Without opening them he sighed, "So tell me exactly what you want for this recording, Mr. Schneck."

"You know *exactly* what I want."

"I see," he said thoughtfully, "and out of the blue, I simply announce I am appointing you the new Florida Attorney General?"

"Yes."

"And how the hell do I justify that?"

"Easy. Look Governor, in a couple of weeks I'm personally going to prosecute the Super Bowl Murder and Jewelry Heist case. I assume you've heard of it?"

"Of course. Everyone's heard of that."

"Well, I'm going to nail that murdering-son-of-a-bitch and put him on death row. I know people with most of the major newspapers around the state, and they've promised me full coverage – TV, too. Hell, everyone in Florida will know my name after this trial. The Blacks will love me for putting a cracker on death row for shooting a brother. Once this happens, you announce me for Attorney General. You could even pick up black votes you might have lost out on with that Latina broad from Jacksonville you were so sold on a few minutes ago."

"You're a persuasive man, Mr. Schneck."

"Not persuasive as much as ambitious. And one more thing Governor, I'll be one damn fine Attorney General. Banging that whore and kid might just turn out to be a good thing for you after all."

"If I do this-"

"*When* you do this," Winston corrected.

"*If* I do this," he barely maintained, "how will I get the original recording and copies?"

"You won't. I'll always retain the original unedited recording."

"In this way you can blackmail me forever?"

"No. I only want this job. Keeping the original recording is my life insurance."

"Explain."

"You're a powerful man with powerful connections. You could call in a favor and I'd disappear forever – that's a big ocean and a big gulf out there. But I have copies of this DVD in pre-addressed envelopes – for the Miami Herald and the Tampa Tribune, plus CNN and FOX News – all to be mailed should something unusual or untimely happen to yours truly. So, I think I'll be able to sleep soundly knowing nothing will ever go bump in the night."

"You've got this all figured out, haven't you?"

"Does it look like I've missed something, Governor?"

"No, it doesn't appear that you have."

"So we have an understanding?"

"What choice do I have? Win your trial. Put the bastard on death row, and I'll announce you for the new Florida Attorney General."

Winston zipped the empty pocket of his valise and stood. Over the massive walnut desk he offered his hand to the Governor who reluctantly gave a brief, weak shake. Then, removing the DVD from his laptop, the Governor asked, "I suppose you want this back."

"Nah, you can keep it. I got plenty more."

TWENTY-TWO

After she softly knocked on their spare bedroom door, Charlene opened it to find her husband, Ken, with elbows on his desk, staring into a stark glowing computer screen listing multiple dates of interviews with Roy Dillard. This was the only source of light in the room. Ken didn't hear his wife enter, and he continued to gaze into the monitor. Charlene watched her husband for several long moments before she whispered, "Honey, are you okay? It's three forty-five in the morning."

Startled, Ken turned in his chair to look at his wife. For a second Charlene thought he didn't recognize her, standing as she was, barefoot and encased in a light pink bathrobe. He appeared red eyed and dazed. Again Charlene coaxed, "Ken, Honey…?"

Ken blinked rapidly as if clearing his mind and mentally returning to his surroundings. "Charlene, oh… ah what are you doing up? Is it morning?"

"I woke up a little thirsty, and went to get some orange juice. I saw light under the door… Are you all right?"

"Yes, I guess I am. What time did you say it was?"

"It's late… or early, depending if you've been to sleep yet."

"It must be late then. I couldn't sleep. I thought I'd go over some of the recordings I made with Dillard, you know, in case I missed something."

"Honey, there's only a list of dates on your computer. Have you listened to any of the sessions?"

"I don't know," he mumbled unsure, "I've listened to each of them so many times I can almost recite them by heart – my questions, his answers, more questions and more answers. I can look at the dates and know what was said during that meeting. I think I'm looking for something that doesn't exist."

Charlene walked closer to Ken and wrapped her arms around his shoulders and put her cheek on his head. "I'm worried about you, Darling."

She could feel him slightly nod his head. "I'm worried about me, too," he said and stifled a sob.

Concerned, Charlene quickly moved to his front, sliding his chair back slightly on the hard plastic floor liner. She pushed away the monitor on the desk and sat on the edge facing him. She looked into the fatigued face of her husband and watched a single tear leave his left eye and track down to the corner of his mouth.

"Ken, Honey, talk to me."

"His... Dillard's life is in my hands." He wiped the tear and Charlene saw his lower lip quiver slightly. "He's going to be executed, and I can't save him." Ken raised both hands and again wiped his eyes. He looked down at his lap and then the floodgates opened. At first a muffled sob slipped from his lips through his fingers, but a moment later his shoulders convulsed, and he wept uncontrollably. Silently at first, then his anguish came out in long, protracted moans. "I... I can't save him, Char. I can't... help him."

Charlene leaned forward and again embraced her husband. She felt him shudder in her arms, and somehow deep inside it made her feel horribly insecure and vulnerable. It was not a feeling she was used to, and it wasn't a feeling she liked. Uncoiling her arms from her husband, Charlene walked to the door and flipped on the bright overhead ceiling light. "Ken, we have to talk."

Ken was quiet now, but Charlene could see he was still crying. She waited a few seconds and said she'd get him a glass of water. Purposely, she stood by the kitchen sink, full glass in her hand. She wanted to give him more time to pull himself together. She did not like what was happening, and it was time for it to end.

Accepting the glass of water from Charlene, Ken said, "I'm sorry, Char. You shouldn't have to see me like that."

"No, I shouldn't. But it's good I did. It shows me something is very, very wrong here."

Controlled now, Ken made one final wipe at his eyes, drank half the glass of water and said, "You're right. Something *is* wrong here."

Charlene waited for him to continue. "Something's wrong with this case. It doesn't make sense-"

"Ken! Stop! I'm not talking about the case. I'm talking about you!"

"But Char, I *am this case-*"

"No! You most certainly are *not* this case, this goddamn case!"

"Charlene please..." he pleaded.

"No! You listen to me, Ken Melzer. You are my husband. I love you. And I will not see this case, or any other damn case for that matter, bring you down like this." Still standing she looked down at her seated husband, "You are a lawyer. Your job is to defend your client. But that's all. You have a life to live. You have a wife to love and, I sincerely hope, a future family to grow and support. You absolutely cannot fall to pieces over a murderer and a thief who is probably going to get everything he deserves. You need to separate yourself from him before you become *a part* of him. You better realize, and realize quickly, that you are in the presence of evil when you are with that man. He's no good; he's bad news. I know you have to represent him, but don't get caught up with him. Do your job and close the door behind you when you are done. And I don't mean when the trial is over, I mean each day when you leave the office and come home. I don't want that kind of negativity following you into this house. This is my home too, you know. There should be peace here, not bad karma and the essence of that monster, Roy Dillard! Let go of him for God sake!"

Charlene had gone from concern and sympathy to a kind of anger and protectiveness she didn't know she possessed. She was convinced what she'd said was true and wise. Settling herself she continued, "Look, your dedication is admirable. But it's gone too far. You told me you discussed some of this with Hank Parnell. Didn't that sink in? Didn't you listen to him?"

"Char, leave it to you to say what needs to be said... Yes, you know Hank and I talked, but until now it didn't register. I needed you to hammer it home, and for that I thank you. You are right. I apologize..."

"I don't want your apology. I only want my husband back. I want him to return by himself without any clients clinging to him. I want him with me at meal times, and I want him with me on weekends, and I want him back in my bed." Now it was Charlene who felt a tear glide down her cheek.

Seeing this, Ken stood in front of his wife, and with the side of his little finger, gently erased her tear. She stepped closer, and his arms encircled her waist. With her lips inches from his ear she said, "Honey, there are other kinds of law – contracts, real estate, tax law... Maybe you should consider something like that."

Ken released his hold on his wife and backed up a step to face her. "I don't think so, Char. I'm where I'm supposed to be, where I have to be."

"Okay, fine. Then you need to control yourself and keep a distance between you and your cases... your clients."

"I will. I promise. This is my first big trial, and I let it get to me."

Charlene sat on the love seat next to Ken's desk. "Sit," she said. "We need to talk a little more, and then you are going to our bed, not this damn cot, and get a few hours sleep. I'll call your office and tell them you'll be late."

Ken swiveled his chair to face Charlene. "Okay. That sounds like a plan," and he smiled weakly.

"You've explained to me about your desire to help people, especially people who can't afford to pay for a lawyer. I know this is deep-seated in you and goes back to your family and all... But Honey, what you promised your brothers, or your father, or whoever – and that was years ago – wasn't a vow or a binding contract. You have a wife now. Someday we'll have a family and children. I, *and they,* need to be considered. You have to look to the future and do the right thing for yourself and for me...for *us.*"

"Char, I hear what you are saying, and I'm sure it makes sense. But right now I'm overwhelmed and emotionally drained. Nothing is making much sense. Nights are like that for me. Everything gets distorted at night. In the daylight things will become clearer. I know you are right, yet deep inside I feel such conflict. I can't explain it, but it's tearing me apart."

"That's what I'm talking about. Whatever is *conflicting* you and *tearing you apart* has to be let go, because if it is allowed to stay, it'll tear us both apart. And I don't think either of us wants that."

"Again, you're right. I don't want anything to pull us apart."

"Good. Now, turn that damn computer off."

Ken did as he was told. Charlene took his hand and led him to their bedroom. She had him sit on the edge of the bed. "I'm wide awake, and coffee is what I need," She said and smiled down at Ken. "Off with the clothes and get under the covers. That's an order!" she joked.

"Yes Ma'am."

When Ken was in bed, and she saw him roll on his side to sleep, Charlene quietly closed the door and did make herself a pot of coffee. She was too troubled to sleep. Instead, she sat in darkness at her usual kitchen chair, alone with her thoughts, until the first streaks of sunrise brought light to a new day.

TWENTY-THREE

It was part of a Psychology 101 class study group discussion that sophomore Ken Melzer couldn't shake from his memory. The students were reviewing a unit on early childhood development, and someone asked the rest of the group to reveal their earliest memories. One freshman girl recalled riding a pink tricycle, and another remembered eating birthday cake while seated in a highchair wearing a colorful bib. Ken's earliest recollection was sitting in a pew with a bunch of pre-kindergarten-age kids in Sunday school singing *Jesus loves me, this I know, for the Bible tells me so...* However, when it was his turn to relate this story, Ken made up something about twirling on a rope swing at a neighbor's backyard playground. He felt embarrassed about his Sunday school and church upbringing – embarrassed because he thought in some strange way it defined him. And Ken didn't like that definition. Let them envision him as a tot on a swing. That was fine. The truth was his business, and he'd just as soon keep it private.

Ken's father, Pastor Isaiah Melzer, worked diligently all week on the sermons he'd deliver to his Sunday flock. He took pride in his speaking ability – a mixture of rich and sonorous baritone combined with a clever wit. He tried to throw in just enough of the latter to keep his congregation alert and a touch further removed from sleep. A popular minister, Pastor Melzer seemed always welcome at the homes of his small-town Missouri parishioners. As he told his three sons, it was more effective being a role model to inspire his neighbors than being a verbose and preachy minister.

Mark and Matthew, a year apart in age, and several years and two miscarriages older than Ken, were destined to follow their father's lead. Like their father and grandfather before him, both aspired to graduate from divinity school and have future

148

congregations of their own. It was expected that Ken, too, would follow in similar fashion. When old enough, the two elder sons often sat with their father in his church office and let him practice his sermons on them. Sometimes they'd successfully beg him to omit a particularly corny joke or to change a phrase or word, but generally they listened and approved.

The tornado hit a neighboring town before Ken could occupy his brothers' vacated seats in their father's church office. At the time of the tragedy they were both attending college, and Ken was a sophomore in high school. His teachers found him an inquisitive and dedicated student. On back-to-school nights more than one teacher commented that Ken was a peacemaker and a fight stopper. His English teacher, Mr. Connor, told Pastor and Mrs. Melzer that he witnessed Ken insert himself between two older boys and a younger, smaller freshman about to be bullied in a hallway. He was able to diffuse the situation, much to the relief of the freshman, and all went their separate ways. Being mostly A's, Ken's grades were rarely an issue. Both Melzers were justly optimistic for their youngest son's future, at least until the Tornado.

For a long time after the Psych. 101 study group, Ken thought about his early life and memories. Frequently on his mind were the hours of Sunday school classes he attended year after year. This was before he was old enough to sit with his mother and brothers in the family pew while his father preached. He couldn't shake the fact that his family was so devout and convinced that everything about their faith could be accepted as fact. There were no discussions around the modest family dining table regarding their beliefs. They spoke of nearly everything else *but* their beliefs. Ken was sure that was because their faith was a given, a fact of their lives that left no room for doubt or discussion. The five Melzers were in agreement. There was no need for debate. So they spoke about local high school sports and some politics – they were right of center conservatives, town gossip – but not of the scandalous or hurtful sort, news of all kinds and church activities. Their conversations were full, and lively, and agreeable, that is, until the tornado hit.

Locked in Ken's mind was an image of himself, four, five, or maybe six years old, wearing pale green one-piece pajamas with the feet sewn in, kneeling at his bed with his father by his side as he said his nightly prayers before being safely tucked between warm covers. He thanked the Lord for his fine home and loving family, for the food they were blessed with, for his father's congregation of good neighbors, and for their collective health. He begged the Lord for the strength and will to help those in need, to always be honest and trustworthy, to do as his parents and teachers asked, and to obey the rules of school and home. Amen. Amen. Amen. Night after night, week after week, month after month, and year after year – until after the night the tornado struck.

Ken heard his two older brothers talk of the churches they'd like to lead when they were ordained, of where they might locate, even of the wives they hoped to find. Ken was impressed by their ambition, and looked forward to the day he'd have similar plans and aspirations. It had been a good life for their grandfather, and their father also seemed to thrive in the ministry. Mark and Matthew were on similar life paths, and theirs would no doubt be just as rewarding and satisfying. They'd break the ice and lead the way for Ken's own identical career. The future was a lock, a sure bet, carved in stone... at least until that damn tornado blasted its way through southern Missouri.

Ken had been an excellent student who learned his lessons, wrote his papers, studied diligently, and usually aced his quizzes, tests and exams. If he was supposed to know material from a textbook, he read it and knew it. If he was expected to understand his math, he reviewed it until he did. He performed all that was asked of him without questioning the wisdom or value of knowing what he was told to learn. In his Sunday school classes, and later sitting in the family pew, he accepted what he heard and made it a part of his knowledge and consciousness. He was studious in school and a true member of his father's devout congregation. Nobody found fault with him, not his teachers, or his parents, or his brothers. Ken was exactly what everyone wanted him to be. Other parents pointed Ken out to their own children as an example for them to follow. Ken was aware of this but pretended not to know. He was liked, and was polite, popular and respected. He'd become what everyone expected him to be, that is, until that monster tornado ripped houses, and barns, and trees, and livestock, and stores, and buildings, and families, and *lives* apart!

The Melzers watched little evening TV. Pastor Melzer worked on church business, the boys completed homework or read, and Mrs. Melzer finalized whatever never-ending work was required in and around their house. Yet, all over their town the TV broadcasts were interrupted with weather bulletins warning of probable tornados, and telling of recent funnel cloud touchdowns in surrounding areas. Viewers were told to seek storm shelters, or basements, or evacuate to designated safe areas. But in the unconcerned Melzer household, Ken said his nightly prayers and thanked God for their abundant life. An hour later Matthew and Mark, home from college for spring break, went to bed. And fifteen minutes after them, Pastor and Mrs. Melzer did the same.

Sounding like the coalescence of a buffalo stampede with a runaway freight train, the twister swirled past the Melzer house without so much as loosening a roof shingle, coursed a half mile swath through fields and forest, and smashed directly into the neighboring town of Singleton. It scored a direct strike on a mobile home park, which fortunately had been evacuated, and blew out the windows and removed the roofs of every brick-walled business along Main Street before turning the subdivisions into a vacant, unidentifiable wasteland. Between 1:18 and 1:24 in the morning, thirty-two people lost their lives on that pitch-black Missouri landscape.

Ken's father, mother and two brothers had converged at their kitchen table, held hands, and prayed while the storm passed them by, and the chaos invisible in the darkness faded to a stillness and an eerie quiet. In her neat hand, Mrs. Melzer left a note on the table for Ken explaining there had been a tornado that the radio said hit Singleton. The four had driven out to help where they could, and Ken should ride his bike to Singleton when he woke. Ken slept through it all and rose from his bed to an empty house. Reading the note, he immediately lost interest in breakfast, jumped on his old Schwinn, and headed for Singleton.

Ken peddled to a shortcut he knew that led through what used to be woods. He wound his way around windblown debris, and then nearing the first remnants of a farmhouse, he stopped suddenly, slowly got off his bike, fell to his knees, and vomited what little from his last meal remained in his stomach. Ken had never seen a dead body before. Caskets he'd viewed and watched lowered into pre-dug graves by suited and somber mourners, but this was new, and atrocious, and deeply disturbing. A blonde haired girl he judged to be four or five years old dangled nearly naked six feet off the ground, suspended by a sharp, broken tree branch that protruded from her thin, bare chest. Shreds of a blue nightgown were wrapped around her neck and under one arm. Urine and feces streaked the insides of her impossibly short, pale thighs. She'd been swept from her bed by the unimaginable wind and launched for god-only-knew-how-far until her trajectory was abruptly halted by the unyielding and steadfast broken oak limb. Recovering, he stood and walked to the child. She seemed to stare down at him with open, empty blue eyes. Ken started to reach up to her, but recoiled and pulled his arm back when he was unexpectedly assaulted by the ferocious stench of her death. He turned from the body, got back on his bike, and more slowly now, peddled into what mere hours before had been the small but thriving community of Singleton, Missouri.

Keeping his eyes down on the pavement as he rode, Ken remained purposely unaware of the destruction and death surrounding him. He spotted his father's green Dodge pick-up and minutes later leaned his bike against the rear fender. Matthew was sitting in the bed of the truck tying ragged strips of a blanket around a makeshift splint, securing the obviously broken leg of a man unfamiliar to Ken. He was conscious, and his teeth chattered even though it was a mild morning. Matthew, or someone, had covered him in a grimy patchwork quilt with only the splint protruding. The man looked down at his leg and let out a low growling moan. Matthew shushed him and said he'd be okay, that as soon as they could they'd take him to the hospital. Ken saw his brother pour half a bottle of chewable children's aspirin in the man's mouth and hold a water bottle to his lips after he'd gnawed on the pills.

Seeing Ken, Matthew jumped down from the truck bed and hugged his younger brother. "Thank God we came through this untouched."

"Yes," was all he managed to respond.

"The ambulances are running relays to the hospital with the most seriously injured. Dad and I have driven some of the others who aren't hurt as bad. Mom's helping a woman with some injuries that aren't life threatening. Mark's going to carry her here, and then I'll drive her and this guy to the hospital."

"Matthew," Ken began and then broke down, unable to speak.

"It's okay. It'll be okay."

"No, Matthew. There's a little girl I found on my ride here," Ken pointed a finger over his shoulder in the direction he'd come and forced himself to continue, "She's dead. She's hanging in a tree with a branch stuck through her like a spear!"

"It's going to be okay. I know. It's horrible everywhere you look. We're going to concentrate on the living. The dead can wait."

"What can I do?"

"Search. Search wherever you can. Call out and listen for an answer. I think there are still people buried in the rubble. Mark and Dad pulled someone out a little while ago."

"Okay, I can do that."

"Good. Now get going. Some of them might not have much time. If you find anyone, yell for help. There are people searching all over town. Someone will come and help you."

As if in a panic he couldn't comprehend, Ken took off at an aimless run. He stopped when he heard Matthew call to him, "Ken! Slow down! Search, not run!"

And Ken did as instructed. He took a long breath and walked over a pile of brick, bent rebar and corrugated steel. "Hello!" he called again and again. "Is anybody here?" Nobody replied. He walked on, calling and searching, but all was still.

After five minutes – or was it twenty? – around the side of a fully exposed concrete foundation, Ken saw movement in the form of a two-by-four slightly rise and fall, rise and fall, rise and fall from a pile of lumber and roofing material. Rushing to the spot, Ken grabbed the piece of wood, hardly feeling the protruding nail he hadn't seen that thoroughly pierced the web of flesh between the thumb and index finger of his right hand. Pushing the plank to the side he saw the partially crushed wrist and hand that had created the movement.

"I'm here! I'm here!" he yelled down at the twisted mess at his feet. "I'll get you out!" Frantically he grabbed bricks and splintered lumber, throwing them aside as fast as he was able. Broken glass, tangled wires, powdery drywall sections – all grabbed and wrestled away. An arm appeared. Unthinking Ken grabbed the hand and felt the bones grate beneath his fingers. A muffled scream assaulted his ears. "Oh God! I'm so sorry! I'm so sorry! I didn't mean to hurt you! I'm going to get you out! I'm getting help! Oh, God, don't die! I'll be right back!"

Ken ran around the ruins of the building. "Help! Help! I need help! Quick! A man's alive!" he yelled as loud as he was able toward a small group of men about a hundred yards away. He saw them look up, and then three of the group ran toward Ken. Breathlessly one asked, "Where is he?"

"This way," and Ken was already running the short distance to the rubble pile. The three men had soot and dust on their faces, and Ken did not recognize them. He thought he saw blood on the gloves of one of the men who turned and said, "Nice job, Ken. You did good."

"Mr. Connor?"

"Of course." Picking up a long section of bent and rusted rebar, he added, "not exactly English class."

Ken thought it an odd thing to say, considering the circumstances, but replied, "No, I guess not."

With the four of them working tirelessly and almost methodically, more of the trapped man began to appear. First an upper arm and shoulder, then the man's head, his face turned to the side, his left cheek obviously crushed. Some kind of dust-encrusted matter oozed from the exposed, ruined eye socket. A large irregular section of wall covered the rest of the man's body. Quickly they lined up along a side and together heaved the heavy siding away. The man lay on his back, now fully exposed except for a broken wood beam that lay across his middle, slightly above his hips. Mr. Connor pointed a gloved finger at one end and said, "Ken, you and Ted are going to lift that end, and George and I will pull him out."

Mr. Connor and George positioned themselves on each side of the man, grabbing him firmly under his arms. "Okay, lift now!" he ordered. Ken and Ted did as they were told, lifting the beam, and clearing the man's body by two feet or more. "George, on the count of three, we pull. One, two, three…"

Ken dropped the beam and covered his mouth with his now bloody and splinter-filled hands. Mr. Connor and George had indeed pulled the man out, half the man. His torso slid from where he'd lain, while his hips and legs remained, connected only by a pinkish-white length of intestine. Nobody said a word as the man's head slowly turned to face directly at Ken. A calm settled over his countenance, and he smiled, blinked his remaining eye, and said in a surprisingly conversational tone, "Thank you, son," before letting out a long sigh and dying.

Mr. Connor and George released their hold on the man and sat down on either side of his head. Dumbfounded, Mr. Connor looked to Ken and muttered, "Jesus Christ… Jesus Fucking Christ."

Ken did not know exactly when, but at some point, Singleton was filled with firemen, police, emergency medical technicians and other first-responders. Even the Missouri National Guard arrived. Ken had another vague recollection of seeing his father holding hands and praying with a dying young woman. Ken had many such images imbedded in his mind, and all of them were terrible. He also had a memory of his mother washing and bandaging his hands before putting him to bed. Later, he was told, he slept fitfully for two and a half days.

The television stations showed non-stop coverage of the tornado and its aftermath. Newscasters from all networks invaded Singleton to show the disaster to the rest of America and interview the eyewitness victims of the storm. For the first day after his period of sleep, Ken watched these reporters and their interviews. He knew some of the people being questioned, but most he did not. He recognized Mr. Marker who owned a small hardware store in Singleton that was flattened. A CNN reporter on the scene where Marker's store once stood approached him with a microphone as a cameraman filmed the two.

He began by saying, "I'm standing in the ruins of what was once a Singleton, Missouri, hardware store. With me is its owner, Gary Marker."

Ken watched a seemingly confused Mr. Marker answer questions from the reporter. "Gary, this must be a terrible day for you."

"Yes, it is for me and everyone in Singleton."

"Will you tell our viewers what it feels like to go through a tragedy like this?"

"I don't know. I'm still pretty numb. My business is gone. Everything I've worked for my whole life is gone. Maybe my insurance will pay for some of it; I haven't had time to check on that."

"Gary, did your home survive the storm?"

"No, it's gone too."

"Where were you when the twister hit?"

"I heard the evacuation notice on the TV, and my wife and I went to the high school gym."

"What was that like?"

"It's a concrete block building with a reinforced steel roof. It can withstand about anything. There were a lot of people there, and all were glad to be safe and away from danger."

"How do you feel now?

"Thankful to be alive. My wife and I prayed together, and soon everyone in the gym started praying. It must have worked because the loss of life could have been a lot worse. I know a bunch of folks died, but more came through alive. I thank God for saving so many people and sparing our lives."

"Will you rebuild your business and house?"

"I haven't had time to even think of that kind of stuff. Like I said, I just thank the Lord my wife and I are alive."

"Do you think you'll stay in Singleton after this or will you move where there are no tornados?"

Mr. Marker thought a moment and answered, "This is our home. Our friends are here. Our church is here. God allowed us to live, so I expect he wants us to stay right where we are."

"Well, good luck to you, Gary." The reporter turned full face to the camera and concluded, "Jason Wainright in Singleton, Missouri. Back to you, Anderson."

Ken thought this interview was similar to all he'd heard. Everyone said they were thankful to be alive. Some lost more than others. Some lost loved ones and friends. All said they planned to stay in Singleton.

Immediately following the tornado Ken Melzer, an insightful fifteen-year-old high school sophomore, began thinking. He started thinking and questioning… and couldn't stop thinking and questioning. He flipped the TV off and went to his room to lie down, wide-eyed and wide awake.

Later Ken heard his mother call, "Ken, come for dinner."

He opened his door a few inches and called back, "Thanks Mom, but I'm not hungry." He closed the door and resumed his pondering.

Over the next few days Ken hardly left his room. He snacked and used the bathroom, but stayed mostly secluded. His brothers returned to college, and his parents thought it best to leave him alone, if that's what he needed.

On Sunday morning Ken's father knocked lightly on his door, opened it, and was surprised to see his son already dressed and sitting in his desk chair staring out the window. "Oh, I see you're up bright and early."

Ken turned to face his father, "Yes. I'm not sleeping too well. I guess I got more than my share after the-"

"You sure did. You know your mother and I are very proud of you. You were a big help to a lot of people after the tornado."

"I suppose."

"Anyway, better have some breakfast and get dressed for church. Always a full congregation after a tragedy, and I've worked on a special ser-"

"I won't be going, Dad."

Pastor Melzer stopped mid-sentence. "I see. Well, I think it might be good for you to attend, especially today. Church can be very comforting and can give you a boost of faith during difficult times."

"I don't think so, not for me."

"Well, I can't force you to go, even though I think you should. We can talk about this later."

"If it's all the same to you, I really don't want to talk about this. I don't think you'd understand."

Ken's father smiled warmly. "You'd be surprised at how much I'd understand. I've been a minister for a very long time. Part of my job is listening to my parishioners and *understanding.*"

"I'm not one of your parishioners."

"Of course you are. You're a member of my church, our church. And you're my son."

"I'm your son, but I'm not a member of your church."

"I don't understand?"

His agitation getting the best of him, Ken blurted, "I thought you just said it was your job to *understand.*"

Pastor Melzer locked eyes with his son. He was more befuddled than angry at this display of disrespect. "I know you're upset and probably a little confused right now. Are you sure you don't want to go with your mother and me to church?"

"Positive."

"Okay then. Perhaps later we can talk about whatever is troubling you."

"Perhaps, but I don't think so."

Isaiah Melzer had learned when to push and when to withdraw. He clearly sensed this was a time to withdraw. He did, and closed his son's bedroom door behind him.

Weeks passed. Ken felt he'd been living in a foggy daze. He went about his chores and did his schoolwork, but spoke little and refused to talk about the tornado. He tried to block it from his mind, but couldn't. It was now a part of Ken Melzer, a part he detested. He couldn't expunge the memories and images of what he'd seen and been a part of. He knew he'd done nothing wrong, yet he felt unclean, as if touched by something dirty, something evil he couldn't wash away. His lack of appetite left him feeling hollow and empty. Any attempt to eat more than a spoonful or two of anything induced waves of nausea and at times vomiting. Frequently he detected a bitter taste rise up in his mouth that lasted until he could force a little food into his body. His weight dropped a pound or two a week until finally his parents took him to their family doctor.

Dr. Simmons was a kindly physician in his sixties. He examined Ken, and aside from being underweight for his height and age, found nothing physically wrong with the fifteen year old. "I'd like to speak alone with Ken, if that's all right with you?" he said to Pastor and Mrs. Melzer.

"Yes, of course," they answered almost in unison and returned to the waiting room.

Alone now, Dr. Simons said, "Ken, I know you went through a tough time during the tornado. We all did. I know because I was there too."

Ken said nothing.

"Things happen in this world that can be downright ugly and horrible... like that night and the following days."

Ken nodded.

"But we don't, we can't, allow these things to spoil our lives. We have to recognize that we are the lucky ones. The people who died that night and those who survived in, well, *bad shape...* who will *never* be whole again... just keep in mind, they'd give anything to be like you and me. Healthy, and well, and in one complete piece."

Looking directly into Dr. Simmons' eyes Ken nodded again.

"As a doctor I've witnessed my share of horrors. The thing I've taken away from all of it is to cherish life and health... because it can be fleeting. I've learned to look to the future more than the past. I try to be optimistic. I also try to help whoever I can along the way." He gently placed his hand on Ken's shoulder and concluded, "And knowing your folks like I do, and knowing you since you were a baby, I believe you are like that, too."

Ken looked down at the floor and tears began to flow from his eyes. He tried to stop them by shutting his lids as tight as he could, but that only made his lips quiver and finally turn to sobs. Dr. Simmons wrapped his arms around Ken and pulled him tight.

"It's okay. It's going to be okay…" he said softly over and over until Ken regained control and pulled back.

Ken wiped his nose with his sleeve and brushed the tears from his cheeks. "Thank you. I think I'll be okay. I shouldn't be so selfish. I'm putting everyone I know through even more of a tough time than they deserve."

Dr. Simmons was not surprised at this statement and said with a slight chuckle, "See? I thought I had you pegged pretty well. You are more concerned with others than with yourself. Just like your ol' man."

Ken forced a smile and again said, "Thanks. That was a big help," and repeated, "I think I'll be okay now."

For five weeks Ken refused to attend church with his family. He also would not explain his reasons for this refusal. He said little and initiated no discussions. Aside from answering mundane questions from his parents, doing his schoolwork and chores around the house, Ken showed little in the way of emotion or enthusiasm. When he ate at all, he'd asked to be excused from the dining table as soon as he'd finished, avoiding the time he and his parents previously spent in pleasant conversation.

Finally, one evening when Ken had left the table after eating only a single dinner roll, his mother said, "Isaiah, I've had enough of this behavior. Talk to your son and find out what in the world has gotten into his head."

When the dishes had been cleared and the kitchen cleaned, she looked to her husband, nodded her head, and said, "Now. It's time. I have some sewing to do in the other room. You talk to Ken."

Standing at the foot of the stairs, Pastor Melzer called to Ken's closed bedroom door, "Ken, Son, would you come down here. I'd like to talk to you."

The bedroom door opened a crack, and Ken said, "Can we talk later, Dad. I'm kinda busy right now."

"What ever you're doing can wait. We need to talk now."

"Be right down." Ken had completed his homework soon after getting home from school that day. As usual he was either lying on his bed or looking out the window when his father called.

Knowing this conversation was overdue and dreading the thoughts of it, he finally braced himself for the inevitable and went downstairs.

"Ken, lets go to the living room where we can be more comfortable."

Ken followed his father and took a seat on an end of the sofa next to the armchair that was understood to be reserved for Pastor Melzer. Sitting on the edges of their seats, father and son turned to face each other.

"Ken, it's no secret you are troubled. The tornado affected all of us, but life must go on, and you need to move along too."

"I am *moving along*." The sarcasm came across more than Ken had intended.

"Son, are you angry? Have I done something wrong?"

"No, nothing. You are who you are."

"And what do you mean by that exactly."

"I don't mean anything by that."

"Are you afraid to say?"

"Afraid? No, I'm not afraid."

"Then tell me what you meant when you said 'I am who I am.'"

"Fine. You're a minister and a good Christian. That's what I meant."

"Is this not a good thing?"

"It's a good thing for you, I suppose."

"You suppose?"

"Yes."

"Do you think it wrong to be a minister and to try to be a good Christian?"

"Truthfully?"

"Yes, of course, truthfully."

"Okay then, I think it's a bunch of shit."

The spontaneous slap that stung the left side of Ken's cheek came so quickly he had no chance to flinch or dodge the open hand that came his way. It was the first time Pastor Melzer had struck his son. Even as children, he'd never used physical punishment, always believing kindness was the more powerful tool of persuasion than pain and force.

"I'm sorry for that, but I don't take it back," he said sternly to his son. "I won't have you offhandedly dismiss my life's work and relegate two thousand years of Christian philosophy to a single word relating to excrement."

"I'm sorry. You're right. I deserved that," Ken said to the floor.

"We are going to talk, but first we're going to set some ground rules," Pastor Melzer said, and didn't wait for his son to reply. "First, you will look at me when you speak to me." Ken brought his head up and faced his father again. "Second, you'll show respect for me, and I will show respect for you. Is that understood?"

"Yes."

"Third, if you are troubled or have doubts about... well, about anything, now is the time to air them out. Do you agree?"

Ken said nothing and started to shift his gaze back at the carpet, but caught himself, and again looked at his father. He noticed lines around his eyes and across his forehead that he hadn't seen before. "Yes, I agree."

"Good. Now, we're going to start again. It's obvious you are having, among other things, I think, a crisis of faith. Am I correct?"

"I guess you could call it that."

"A crisis of faith?"

"Yes."

"Would you explain why this is so?"

Ken hesitated. "Do we have to do this now?"

"Yes, we do. Right now."

Ken took a deep breath and let it out audibly. "Okay. I don't share your faith anymore. *I* have no faith anymore."

"I see. And why not?"

"Why do you think?"

This time it was the pastor who hesitated as if regaining his composure. "Rule number four: you will not answer my questions with another question. Is that understood, too?"

"Yes, I'm sorry."

"Continue with why you have lost your faith."

"The tornado took my faith, just like it took most of Singleton and all those lives."

"Explain, please."

"You saw those interviews on TV? All the people who lost everything? Well, every one of those idiots... sorry, this isn't easy for me either," Ken looked toward his father, who unknown to Ken, was thinking that he must remember that this conversation is about his son, not about him, not Pastor Isaiah Melzer.

"That's okay. Go on."

"All of those people, those victims who'd lost everything, *everything* Dad, they all praised God. They were actually thankful that they prayed to their God, who they think spared their lives – even though He destroyed everything about their lives."

"And this is why you have lost your faith?"

"Yes, of course it is."

"There is more going on in your mind. Tell me."

"Dad, I saw a little girl hanging in a tree. She was dead with a branch stuck through her chest. I saw a man still alive until he was pulled in half by my English teacher! So I've been asking myself what kind of god would allow this to happen... to happen to an innocent little girl and an ordinary man going about his life? And I come up with a couple of possibilities."

"I'm listening."

"Either God doesn't exist, or maybe if He does, He's ambivalent and doesn't really give a shit." Ken waited for the second slap that never arrived. "Or maybe it's not God who's in charge, maybe it's Satin or some evil force who would want things like this to happen."

"I can tell you've been doing a good deal of thinking and soul searching. Are you now an atheist?"

"I don't know what I am."

"Do you believe in anything?"

"I think all the talk and preaching..." catching himself once again he continued, "I mean no disrespect to you, but the whole idea of a caring, and especially of a merciful God... well, that seems ridiculous."

"Continue."

Ken wiped perspiration from his upper lip. "For the last month I've been thinking. Let's suppose for a minute that I go to someone's house, and I barge in with a gun. I tell the guy and his wife who live there that they have to get out and lie down in the front yard while I burn down their house – which they do. Then I burn down their house and confront them afterward still lying on the ground. I tell them to get up. And instead of shooting them I put my gun down and walk away. Then the police come and a reporter comes and puts them on TV so they can tell the world what just happened to them. So, Dad, what do you think they'd say?"

"It's your story. Finish it."

Ken couldn't help the smile forming on his lips. "I'm sorry, this isn't funny, and I don't want it to be insulting, but I can't get past this part without shaking my head in some kind of confusion."

"You don't have to apologize, Son. Finish your story."

"Okay. So this guy and his wife are in front of a camera and have a microphone stuck in their faces and, well, they are really pissed. They tell the world about the stranger who held them at gunpoint, burned down their house for no reason at all, and then just walked away. They tell about all the things they lost – their house, their photographs and furniture and TV and files and... everything. It's all gone. They demand the police find the guy who did this to them and put him in jail. Hell, if they could, they'd want to kill him." Ken looked incredulous at the tale he'd just told.

"And your point, Ken?"

"Dad, my point is so obvious! That's what God did! God took everything away from all those people for no reason at all. Yet because *God* chose not to *kill* them as well as destroy their lives, He gets a pass! They *thank* Him and *praise* Him for *not killing them!* Like, ruining their lives doesn't matter so long as they didn't get killed too! This is crazy thinking! This is so illogical, I can't even begin to explain it, yet this is what happened, and what the stupid people of Singleton actually said on TV... to the world!"

"And you think all the people who got hurt in one way or

another should blame God?"

"Of course I do. Who else should they blame?"

"Why blame anyone?"

Ken had trouble following this kind of logic, or illogic, or nonsense, or whatever it was. "*Why blame anyone*? Are you kidding? If God could have stopped the tornado and didn't, why not blame Him?"

"So, you want God to control every aspect of life? Wouldn't that make us mere puppets with no free will?"

"Free will has nothing to do with it. Nobody w*illed* the tornado. It was a part of nature, and if I were able to *I'd* have stopped it! Why didn't God?"

"Because God is nature. God is all things."

"And God's not held responsible for anything?"

"No, He's not."

"Why?"

"I can't answer that."

Ken glared at his father as if he were some moronic stranger. "You can't answer that?"

"That's what I said. There are many things I can't answer." Pastor Melzer looked kindly upon his son and allowed a short laugh to escape his mouth.

"I don't think this is funny."

"Nor do I, I assure you. Do you think you are the first person to have doubts? To doubt the existence of God? Do you think I don't have doubts?"

"No. I always assumed you have no doubts."

"Everyone should have doubts about everything. We are imperfect beings – imperfect in our actions and thoughts and knowledge and imperfect in our understanding of the universe. That is no reason to not have faith."

"Then how can you act so sure about believing in God?"

"Simply because I do believe in God."

"How can you be so sure?"

"I'm *not* sure in the sense of *certainty*, but I know my own heart, and I trust my heart."

"I don't understand."

"We think with our heads and feel with our hearts. Both are

equal in their importance to our lives. Some people have trouble keeping the two in balance. The brain helps us understand our world factually, scientifically, empirically, while our hearts help us to emotionally deal with these facts – or lack of facts."

"Lack of what facts."

"Facts that are beyond our knowing, at least at this time."

"Such as?"

"Such as the meaning of existence, the entirety of the universe, the origins of all life."

Ken had never heard his father speak like this. He seemed like someone else, someone he knew intimately, but never questioned or understood. Like a rush of warmth, in the last few minutes his respect for this man had grown immeasurably. "Dad, I've never heard you speak like this. I never knew you even thought like this."

Isaiah Melzer laughed again and put a hand on his son's arm. "Sometimes it is best to keep thoughts such as these private. Some people feel threatened by them. Just because something is inexplicable does not make it threatening. I believe, among other things I believe, that one needs to feel comfortable with not knowing everything, or having all the answers one might want to have."

"Yet, with all this unknown stuff, all these questions, you believe in God?"

"Yes. The more we learn and understand about the universe, the more wondrous the concept of God becomes. Science glorifies God; it doesn't deny God's existence."

"But praying, and knowing God might pay attention... or might not... How do you deal with that?"

"It can be a tricky balance. Perhaps prayers are *not* heard by God, but studies have shown that when people are sick and are prayed over, well, they seem to recover more completely and faster than those whom nobody prays for. Like I said, I don't have all the answers. But I do know that without belief and faith in God, our lives would be meaningless."

Ken thought about what his father had just said. "Why does faith give our lives meaning?"

"This is something you can feel with your heart more than

your brain. Think of it this way. When you work on a difficult math problem, and finally understand it, you've used your mind to deal with a situation. You know when you understand. Faith and belief have little to do with the brain, and more to do with the heart. You must trust your heart just like you trust your brain. You must understand what you can in life, and for the things you can't understand, you have to rely on your heart, to trust your heart. Does this make any sense to you?"

"Yes and no," Ken said somewhat perplexed. "I'm not ready to pray to God if he may, or may not, listen. I don't want to have anything to do with a god who could have saved a little girl's life, but chose not to. I'm okay with not knowing everything, but I don't want to use God as the answer to everything I don't know. Does that make sense to you, Dad?"

"Yes, it makes sense, but I have to warn you that this kind of thinking isn't enough to support your life, emotionally speaking. If you have no faith, no beliefs, you will have no hope."

"I can have hope without faith."

"Perhaps."

"I'm okay with not knowing. I'm not saying there's no God. I think after what I saw after the tornado, if there is a God like you insist, well, that's a god I don't trust or want anything to do with. Again, let me ask you something."

"Sure."

"Suppose I saw a little girl start to walk into traffic, and I didn't stop her, and she got hit by a car... what would you think of me?"

"You know the answer to that. And I know the direction of your argument. All I can say is that you are not God, and I am not God, and we cannot judge God by our human standards. God is not man."

"I thought man was made in God's image."

"This discussion is not about scripture. It's about you, and how you are going to manage in a life without faith."

"Well, maybe I have faith in mankind. Maybe I have faith in myself."

"Looking at the evil and corruption of the last few centuries, faith in mankind might be misplaced. Whether you know it or not, you are talking about Humanism. And," he added, "it can be a slippery slope."

"I could say the same for God."

The discussion was turning into a stalemate, and Isaiah Melzer knew if ever he was going to influence his son's thinking, this was a quagmire to be avoided at all costs.

"Ken, I want to end this talk for now, but I also want to reiterate something I said earlier. I want you to know how proud of you I am. My pride in you has nothing to do with your faith or lack of faith. It is based on your character alone. You have shown yourself to be a fine person in a Christian sense, as well as in a secular way. Faith has nothing to do with that."

Pastor Isaiah Melzer stood, and Ken Melzer stood. The father suddenly grabbed his son in an awkward embrace and held him tightly for a few moments before abruptly leaving the living room.

Neither father nor son referred to their discussion in the following weeks. Yet, day after day Ken wrestled with what his father had said. No matter how he twisted and turned the conversation in his mind, he couldn't grasp the idea of an educated, logical person embracing a belief system based on feelings and faith alone, with nothing factual to support the concept. It was not that he didn't *want* to believe. The entire subject was evolving into a conclusion that Ken *couldn't* believe. It might be comforting *to* believe, reassuring to believe, but for Ken it would also be insincere, even hypocritical, to *allow* himself to believe, to have faith, to *like* God and want to have a personal relationship with Him. After a while, Ken got tired of the whole intellectual exercise. He'd resolved to be, as his father had said, satisfied to not have all the answers, to accept a less than full understanding of the universe. Anyway, he concluded one night, if he spent too much time agonizing over all of this, life would pass him by. And life, he decided, was an adventure – full of pitfalls like the tornado – as well as excitement and fun. Taking Dr. Simmons' suggestion, he decided to spend more time looking toward the future with optimism and less time evaluating the past. He was done with church. If this hurt his father, he couldn't help that. He had his own life to lead. He'd already wasted enough time both in church and in pondering unanswerable questions. If a lack of faith made life more difficult, so be it. Bring it on, Ken thought. He could cope with whatever life threw at him! No crutches, no false hope of divine intervention. Ken would make his own way in life, and to hell with whatever anyone else thought! Maybe at death he'd find the answers and know the truth, but maybe not. That was both not knowable and not worth thinking about.

Ken felt suddenly drained from the last months of emotional and intellectual conflict. The tornado had come and gone. Time to put it out of his present thinking. An act of God? An act of nature? Who cared? It came out of nowhere, did its immense damage, and left just as quickly. That was all he needed to know. The question *why* had no answer. He couldn't know, and didn't try to know. It was what it was, and that was that. No more sulking, pondering, obsessing.

Ken went to sleep with this final resolution, and woke to find himself famished. He dressed and went to the kitchen where he polished off two bowls of cereal and four pieces of toast. To his delighted and surprised mom he declared, "Looks like a beautiful weekend! I'm going for a bike ride!" And before she could respond, he was off.

Throughout that summer the weight Ken had lost since the tornado came back as muscle and bulk. Still too young for a full time summer job, Ken did some work for neighbors and pocketed a little spending cash. His free days were spent exploring on his bike and perusing the used car lots. At the end of summer Ken would turn sixteen and get his driver's license. He planned on finding an after school job, saving his money, and buying his first set of wheels just as soon as he could. That was every small town mid-western boy's dream. He'd also found a girlfriend that summer, and on one especially warm night managed to lose his virginity, which also was every small town mid-western boy's dream. Life was good for Ken Melzer. And for certain it was an adventure!

The ambush came a few days before school resumed. Matthew and Mark had returned from Central America where they'd spent an incredibly hot, muggy summer with a church group helping to build a small hospital back in some god-forsaken jungle – the *hot, muggy* description was theirs, the *god-forsaken* part was Ken's. Unknown to the now sixteen-year-old soon-to-be junior in high school, his father and brothers had been in conference about the youngest member of their family. Underestimating the intellectual acuity and maturity in his youngest son, Pastor Melzer thought – wrongly as it turned out – that Ken's older brothers might be able to influence him and put him back on the track of the faithful. Matthew called Ken to the backyard where Mark and his father were already seated around their patio table. It was a bright afternoon and the striped umbrella secured from the center hole in the table offered some shade and relief from the sun. Each held a sweating, cold Diet Coke can. "Get you one?" Mark offered his younger brother.

"Sure."

Ken sat at the table, and in a minute Mark returned from the kitchen and handed him the Coke.

"So, how does it feel to be back in civilization?" Ken asked the two as they relaxed in their chairs.

Matthew answered first, "Downright cool by comparison."

"You got that right," Mark chimed in.

Pastor Melzer said, "You boys did good work down there. That hospital will save a lot of lives."

"And hopefully our influence on the locals will save a lot of souls, too."

Ken felt suddenly uncomfortable and out of place. He took a long swallow from his can. Changing the topic slightly he asked, "Pretty primitive down there, huh?"

"You have no idea, Little Brother." It was Mark who spoke. "They still practice some kinda Voodoo or something and have witch doctors, too. The ignorance is epidemic."

"Sounds charming," Ken laughed.

"No, actually it was alarming and awful, if you want to know the truth," Matthew interjected. "Unsanitary conditions, bad water, no sense of cleanliness," then he added "or Godliness."

Ken couldn't help saying, "C'mon, all societies and cultures, even the primitive ones... they all have religion of some kind."

"If you call dancing around camp fires and squirting themselves with chicken blood religion? These people are illiterate and totally ignorant. We did what we could for them with the hospital, and tried to teach them about hygiene, and I'm sure we converted a number of them to Christianity."

Ken kept his thoughts to himself. He began to understand why his company was required on the patio this afternoon, and he was determined not to take the bait. Gulping the remainder of his Coke and crushing the can he said, "I'm gonna go inside and grab another one of these. I'll be back a little later."

"Stay where you are. I'm getting another for myself," Mark said. "Be right back."

While Mark was getting the Cokes, Matthew asked, "So, ready for your junior year?"

"I suppose. Summer seems too short."

"It always seems that way, but I have to admit I'm glad to be back in the old U. S. of A. Going to the Third World really makes you appreciate what we have here."

"I'm sure."

Mark returned and put a fresh can in front of his brother. "To a good summer!" Matthew toasted and raised his can. The other three did the same, and Ken smiled to himself thinking of his girlfriend, Kathy, and that special night two weeks ago.

"So, Ken, Dad says you gave up church. Is that so?" Mark asked.

"If Dad says so, it must be true. I don't think he's turned into a liar since you two left to save souls." The obvious sarcasm wasn't lost on anyone.

"That doesn't sound like the Ken we left behind," Matthew said.

"It's not."

Pastor Melzer spoke calmly, "It seems Ken has had a change of heart since the tornado."

They were just getting started, Ken realized, but enough was enough, "This is between me and myself. It doesn't concern anyone else."

"Not so, Little Bro," Matthew again. "Our family sticks together and helps each other."

"I agree, but I don't need help. Not from you, or Mark, or Dad either. At least," he added, "not regarding whether or not I attend church."

"If you'll excuse me, Gentlemen, I have a sermon to work on," and their father left the three brothers sitting on the patio.

When he was in the house Mark snarled, "You little shit, don't you see what you're doing to him. His life is the church, and so for that matter is Matthew's and mine. You turn your back on that, and you'll destroy him."

"He's stronger and smarter than you know. And by the way, don't ever call me *a little shit* again."

"So you're a tough guy too, huh?"

"Maybe I have to be."

Matthew laughed and asked, "And why's that?"

"Dad might understand, but you two wouldn't. Maybe when you are as old and wise as him, you will too."

"Listen," began Matthew again, "this is going all wrong. Ken, we're on your side here. We're trying to help you because you seem a little lost."

"I'm not lost. I'm actually feeling like I finally found myself. Look, I know you two mean well, but this is my business and my life. If you both find happiness in a ministry, that's great. But it's not for me."

Mark said, "It's not having a ministry we're talking about. It's your soul and your well-being."

"My soul is just fine, thank you very much. And so for that matter is my life."

Matthew said, "Maybe you think so for now, but later in life you'll need guidance and a strong sense of right and wrong if you are to be any sort of decent person. Looks to me like you are headed down the wrong path."

Ken laughed at his older brothers. "You think I don't know right from wrong? You think I need guidance?"

Mark responded, "Sure. Everyone needs guidance. Without a belief in God you're lost, you're blind."

Still laughing Ken said mockingly, "Mark, why don't you just sing *Amazing Grace*. Maybe that would have a better effect, but I doubt it."

"You really are a little shit. And with your *new attitude* you are headed for trouble, big trouble."

"Well, thanks, Mark, for your assessment of me and my future."

Matthew tried to diffuse the acrimonious direction this was taking, "Ken, remember who you are talking to here. We're your family, and we're concerned for your well-being. Give us a chance to change your mind."

"Not even half a chance. Leave me alone. I'll do just fine on my own."

Mark interrupted, "Not without a moral compass, you won't."

"And what *moral compass* are you referring to?"

"The Bible, learning to be God-fearing and righteous in your deeds and endeavors."

"Sounds like the makings for a good sermon for a mindless flock of sheep who can't face the harsh realities of life without-"

"Enough!" Matthew was standing now. He crushed his Coke can and threw it aside. "Ken, you've turned into a wise-ass sixteen year old who thinks he's smarter than everyone else. So have it your way, but when you find out how terribly wrong you are, when you find how misguided and meaningless your tragic life has become, know that Mark and I will be there for you, and Dad too if he's still around by then. We'll forgive you and welcome you back with open arms."

Ken sat and couldn't believe what he was hearing. Fine, they can have it their way, he thought. Then without any forethought said, "I thank you both for your honesty and charity, but-"

"Stop the smart-ass stuff-" Mark began before Ken cut him off.

"Okay, Brothers. I'll get right to the point, no bullshit. Now listen up, and listen good because I'm only gonna say this once. Right now I make a solemn vow that I'll prove you two, and Dad also, wrong. I promise you, I vow to you, I'll find my own way in life and I'll have my own moral compass to guide me – not yours or Dad's or some god's – I'll have my own. I'll make my own success and help others along the way, too. And not because I'm

God-fearing, which by the way I'm not, but because like you and everyone else in this family, I too have a strong sense of right and wrong. I won't have to talk about it; I'll do it. My actions will speak louder than any words spoken in some sermon. And all of you, meaning Mom and Dad too, can hold me to what I just said."

Matthew and Mark listened to their brother, impressed, but not entirely convinced. Getting up from his chair Ken crumpled his Coke can, and in a dismissive gesture, tossed it as Matthew had thrown his. "And I'll tell you one more thing before this discussion ends," Ken leaned toward his brothers with both hands firmly on the table. He glared first at Mark and then at Matthew, "I saw what your God did last spring in Singleton. I saw what He did and what He *could have done*, *but didn't*. And I tell you now and forever," Ken squinted his eyes in the sunlight and concluded through clenched teeth, "I want no part of a God like that!"

In the years that followed – through high school, college and law school – Ken never once regretted that unplanned and spontaneously expressed vow.

TWENTY-FOUR

Roy Dillard sat on his bunk and calmly tried to take stock of his present situation. For the first time since being locked up, he felt on the verge of panic. He shut his eyes and slowly counted to five before opening them. It helped. He did it again, this time counting to ten. He slowed his breathing and forced himself to think rationally. He knew exactly how he'd gotten to this point, knew exactly what he had done, and had not done. Roy knew what he must do, and what he must not do. He was not shooting from the hip. Instead, his aim was true and well thought out. Yes, he was facing a capital charge of murder, enhanced by a hate-crime charge. True, the evidence was compelling, overwhelming, actually. But Roy Dillard knew this from the start, and he knew what he was doing. It was too late for doubts and second guessing or changing plans. He wasn't simply messing with Ken Melzer about believing in the justice system and the jury system. Roy Dillard was counting on both. And Roy Dillard believed in himself and in Ken Melzer's role in this case.

Again, he closed his eyes, silently counted to thirty, slowly breathed in and breathed out. He was ready to write the questions his attorney, Ken Melzer, would ask him on the stand – under oath, as a witness. Ken would ask the questions his client would write for him – tonight, from a jail cell, on a yellow legal pad – and not deviate from a single word, not ad lib a follow up question or skip a line. Roy Dillard had spent weeks putting this together in his mind, and now it was time to put it all in writing. At this realization, this self-actualization, Roy Dillard smiled to himself. That's it, he thought, let the old confidence return. This was okay; everything would turn out just fine. It was scary, sure, but the outcome would be exactly as he wanted.

Roy Dillard began to write. He didn't stumble for words or consider the order of the questions. Everything had been worked out in his mind. He had it down pat. And so, he wrote line after line, even placing in parenthesis the word *objection* when he was sure the Prosecution would object to a question. It was time for Ken Melzer to understand that Roy Dillard was in control now, and that he anticipated everything that was about to happen. His attorney might not believe in his innocence, might believe him insane, or perhaps not. None of it mattered anymore. What Ken Melzer thought, or didn't think, was immaterial and irrelevant at this stage of their relationship. They both had a part to play, and the show must go on!

TWENTY-FIVE

Until Hank Parnell and Ken Melzer realized what Winston Schneck was up to, they were surprised and baffled. Before jury selection was to begin, Hank and Ken had discussed whom they would like to see on their jury. "Ken, you might not like this, and I don't necessarily like this either, but trust me on this – I've been through this a number of times."

"I'm open to whatever you think best."

"Good, because this is the way these things need to be viewed. You have to try to be purely objective and although it may not sound very nice, what I'm going to say comes from years of experience with different juries."

"Like I said, I'll do whatever you advise."

Placing emphasis on certain words he wanted Ken to consider, Hank opined as if he were stating the obvious. "Okay then, black jurors are potentially the kiss of death for Roy Dillard. Black men might want to convict a white man for gunning down a *brother*. Black women might want to convict a white man for killing an innocent *black man* who might represent a *husband* or *son*. White men on a jury might harbor at least some unspoken bias against Blacks – perhaps from losing a job because of Affirmative Action, or maybe just feeling physically intimidated by large, imposing black males. Who knows? It could be a lot of things, but I believe *Caucasian males* might somehow show a little more compassion for an average-sized *white man* who killed a *hulking black guy*. White *women* might see the situation in a similar light as a white man, but many women frequently shy away from guns and the men that like them. Firearms are often viewed by some women as "masculine objects" that get their men in trouble more times than they get them out of trouble. Plus, women of either race don't like violent men. So, we need to agree that white men would be the most favorable jury candidates."

"You're right I don't like it, but I assumed as much."

Hank chuckled and said, "Yeah, I suppose you probably did."

At the beginning of the jury selection process, Schneck had only one question for potential jurors, and he asked it in an almost bored, matter-of-fact manner: "Do you understand that this is a capital murder case, and that the death penalty is in play; and if so, do you have any problem with finding a man guilty who might then be subjected to the death penalty?" Of the first ten possible jurors, only one seemed to have a problem with the death penalty. This individual, a black woman, was dismissed.

When Winston Schneck eliminated several black men from the jury pool and accepted several white men, Hank and Ken were taken aback, pleasantly so. The Defense eliminated several more black men and women without apparent concern from Schneck, who seemed amenable to more white men on the jury. It was then the *Eureka* moment struck Hank Parnell. Shaking his head, he smiled broadly, and was met by an equally wide grin from Winston Schneck.

"Hank, what's going on here?" Ken whispered. "Why are you smiling to Schneck, and why is he smiling back?"

Turning to Ken he quietly said, "Because Schneck is so confident in this case, he wants to give us the most generous jury he can."

"But why give us any advantage?"

"He doesn't think there is a snowball's chance in hell we can win, and he's covering his ass against future appeals. Any claim of biased jury selection that we might have asserted as a point on appeal has just been nullified."

"Is that a normal strategy?"

"No, of course not, but this case is anything but a normal case."

The following morning the fourteen white men of the jury, including two alternate jurors, took their seats at the side of the courtroom. They ranged in age from twenty-four to sixty-seven, and in educational background from a high school almost-grad to a master's degree in economics. They were dressed from T-shirts to ties.

Roy Dillard sat in the middle of the defense table sandwiched between Ken Melzer on his left and Hank Parnell on his right. He wore an inexpensive dark navy blue suit with a white shirt and a conservative blue tie. Roy had lost fifteen pounds while in jail, and his suit hung on his frame as if it were a hand-me-down from an older and larger sibling. It made him appear smaller than he was, and somehow less formidable, even frail. Ken liked the look and thought it might make him appear less threatening.

Across the main isle in the courtroom, Winston Schneck sat by himself at the prosecutor's table. Clearly, this was his case and his case alone. To his right were piled a few files and folders, but Schneck was staring down at notes on a legal pad in front of him. He had yet to make eye contact with Ken or Hank. In fact, he seemed oblivious to everything around him except for his yellow pad.

Charlene sat two rows directly behind her husband. Every seat in the room was occupied by reporters and courthouse junkies who waited in line for several hours to be sure of getting a seat for what might prove to be a fast, slam dunk murder trial. Mainly, these people wanted to see the evidence, especially the detailed and much publicized video of the horrific *Super Bowl Murder and Jewelry Heist*.

"All rise. The Circuit Court of the 17th Judicial Circuit is now in session, the Honorable Daniel Peters presiding," came the loud and clear baritone of the Bailiff.

The room fell to silence and instantly all were on their feet, everyone except Winston Schneck who remained sitting for a few seconds, still reviewing his notes. He was only half out of his seat when Judge Peters said, "Be seated."

Judge Daniel Peters was fifty-nine years old, white, and wore a friendly countenance. His gray hair was clipped short, and he was clean-shaven. Daniel Peters was known as a fair judge who was never considered friendlier to either the Defense or the Prosecution. He was a middle-of-the-roader, an impartial and consistent judge who lacked any flamboyance or showmanship. The people of Florida had entrusted him with a job to do, and for a dozen years that's what he had always done. It was known by all the Broward County bailiffs that the only thing Judge Peters required was a full carafe of coffee – cream and very lightly sugared – placed by his tall black mug at his bench.

Looking over his courtroom, Judge Peters began, "Good morning ladies and gentlemen. We are set for trial in the matter of the State of Florida versus Roy Dillard. Let the record reflect that all parties and counsel are present. Is the State ready for trial?"

Winston Schneck rose to his feet and responded, "The State is ready, Your Honor."

"Is the Defense ready for trial?"

Ken Melzer rose, and in as steady a voice as he could muster said, "The Defense is ready, Your Honor."

"Are there any matters to be heard before I bring in the jury?"

Both Winston Schneck and Ken Melzer rose and together replied, "No, Your Honor."

Judge Peters instructed the Bailiff to bring the jury into the courtroom. The jurors filed in and the Bailiff directed them to their seats.

"Will the Clerk please swear in the jury?"

The Clerk of the court stood before the jury box and said, "Will the jury please stand and raise your right hands." When they did, she continued, "Do each of you swear that you will fairly try the case before this court, and that you will return a true verdict according to the evidence and the instructions of the court, so help you God? Please say 'I do.'" In unison they did, and she concluded, "You may be seated."

Again Judge Peters said, "Very well." He looked to the single person sitting at the prosecution table for a moment, as if something or someone was missing, and stated, "Mr. Schneck, you may proceed with your opening statement."

"Thank you, Your Honor." Schneck walked around his table and stopped in the middle of the floor between the judge and the jury. Facing the box he glanced at the faces before him and smiled in a friendly manner. He was gratified to see several of the jurors nod slightly.

"Good morning gentlemen of the jury," he began. "My name is Winston Schneck, and I am the State's Attorney for the Florida jurisdiction that includes Broward County... and yes, I am very aware that my name is a little, shall we say... unusual?" He waited for most of the jurors to grin through a now diffused awkward beginning. "That's okay; really, I assure you I've been through this once or twice before." A few more smiles. "As State's Attorney, it's my job to prosecute individuals who have broken the law. And that's what I'm here to do today.

"I'd first like to thank you all for being here. I know you have busy lives, and taking time out for jury duty can be inconvenient, to say the least. So, let me first say I appreciate the fact that you all are here. I'd also like to remind you that we have a truly wonderful criminal justice system in the United States of America. In our great country a person is innocent until proven guilty. So, it's my job to supply evidence and prove to you all that this man," Schneck turned to the defense table and pointed, "the Defendant, Roy Dillard, is guilty of murder in the first degree with the additional charges of committing a hate crime, assault, and stealing well over a million dollars worth of fine jewelry and watches." Schneck waited as the jury looked at Dillard who, he was glad to see, glanced down at the table before him and did not look back at the jury.

"Yes, gentlemen, take a good look at him and remember, right now, at this time and place, Roy Dillard *is an innocent man!*" Schneck paused to let his surprising words sink in. "Any of you want to know why he's an innocent man? I'll tell you. He's an innocent man because our system says he is... that is, of course, until I start to present evidence to the contrary. Then, Gentlemen of the Jury, you'll begin to see him in a different light. The innocence this country, this system, affords him will peel away like the layers of an onion until all you'll be left with is a small little knot of wicked guilt!"

Schneck walked back to his table, grabbed his yellow legal pad and held it up over his head for the jury to see. "I have all kinds of notes written down here, all kinds of things I intended to say to you this morning. But I'm not going to waste your time with all of that! I could go on and on about the evidence I'm going to provide, and the witnesses who will testify to what happened on that evil day. Believe me, I could drag this case out with reams of stuff showing how guilty this man, this Roy Dillard character is, but I recognize and respect that your time is valuable. In fact, right now I want to apologize to every one of you for having to be here at all! I'm going to show this jury such an abundance of irrefutable evidence that I'd be surprised if you needed more than a few short minutes to deliberate and bring back a verdict of guilty to all charges." He walked back and tossed the pad on his table. Turning again he said, "I also apologize that you will have to see the horrendous nature of the crime in question." He paused again, "Yes, I did say *see* what happened last Super Bowl Sunday. I'm sure you're all thinking *how are we going to see something that happened in the past?* Well, I'll tell you how. Because four different cameras – and I'm talkin' the highest quality, most expensive security cameras – recorded the Defendant, Roy Dillard, brutally kill in cold blood an innocent delicatessen delivery man, strike a young woman across the face, and force her under fear for her life to fill a laundry bag with jewelry. Then you'll see him drive away – yes, all of this was filmed, right down to his license plate number. In a sense, you, the twelve men of this jury, will feel as though you are all eyewitnesses to this heinous crime. As I said, I'm sorry you'll have to suffer through the viewing of this murder, but I'm also glad for you. I'm glad for you because rendering a guilty verdict will be the right thing to do. You'll know for sure this man is guilty as charged because you will have seen his face and witnessed his actions. In the months and years to come, you'll have no doubts, no second thoughts, about the role you played on this jury. Your conscience will be one hundred percent clear. You'll sleep well at night and put this whole awful case behind you. And that's as it should be.

"And another thing: the Defense will claim Roy Dillard is not guilty because he's supposedly insane, that at the time of the crime he didn't know right from wrong. You know why they are claiming this?" Schneck glanced at the blank faces of the jurors. "It's because they couldn't come up with anything else! Roy Dillard is no crazier than any of you or I, and I'll prove that too. Trust me on this."

Judge Peters raised his eyebrows and looked over at Ken Melzer. Ken just sat there, and Judge Peters said nothing.

"Let me conclude by asking you once again to look at the

Defendant and think of him as a blank artist's canvas. Now look at me and think of me as the artist who is going to fill that empty canvas. Consider the evidence and witnesses as the paints and colors I'm going to use. Each piece of evidence and each witness will fill in a piece of the picture until ultimately what you will have is the portrait of a sinister, a hateful, and most importantly, a *guilty* man!"

For a long moment Schneck stood before the jury box as if he were going to say more. He peered at the individual faces, nodded his head, and quietly said, "Thank you," before returning to his seat, incredulous at the lack of strident objections from the Defense that he had expected throughout his opening statement. This is going to be a cakewalk, he thought to himself.

Ken Melzer listened to Schneck's tirade, and a subtle panic began to rise from his chest to his neck. He felt as if his throat was closing and he couldn't breathe. Quickly, he unscrewed the cap from the Evian water bottle in front of him and took two quick gulps. He stared down at his own empty, fresh legal pad and closed his eyes, pretending to study notes that were nonexistent. He heard Schneck finish and start to walk to the prosecution's table. He caught himself as he began to silently ask God for help, but quickly opened his eyes and took a deep breath.

Earlier he'd discussed his opening statement with Hank. The conversation had been short. Hank Parnell told him to try to ingratiate himself with the jury, make them like who he is. "Let them feel they are a part of your defense team, like they want you to succeed." Hank added that Winston Schneck might be an outstanding prick, but he certainly is a master at jury manipulation. "Watch, listen and learn from him," Hank suggested. Ken should represent his client the best he could and follow Dillard's instructions, if that's what Dillard wanted. Hank reassured Ken that he'd surely done all he could for Roy Dillard, but there were limits to the defense he could argue, much of which was limited by the cooperation and information provided by his client. "Sometimes," Hank said, "you do what you can and if that's enough, great; and if that's not enough, well, so be it. You do all you can, and afterward you move on to the next case. I think," Hank concluded, "this is probably one of those times."

Judge Peters looked to the defense table and said, "Does the Defense wish to present an opening statement?"

Ken stood and replied, "Yes, Your Honor." He was surprised to feel suddenly less nervous. Hank's words from the previous day had run through his head in the nick of time.

Ken Melzer, counsel for the Defense, stood and walked to the exact spot Schneck had occupied minutes before. "Ladies and gentlemen of the jury…" Ken stopped himself, smiled sheepishly, and began again. "*Gentlemen* of the jury, my name is Ken Melzer and I am counsel for Roy Dillard. I hope you'll indulge my nervousness. Unlike Mr. Schneck, who you just heard from, I haven't been at this job very long. In fact, this is my first major case, and my first jury trial." Melzer pointed to the defense table and continued, "The gentleman seated at the end of the table is Hank Parnell. He's sort of the head honcho in the office and has been my guiding light from the beginning of this case. This is a little unusual, because normally in a case of this seriousness, this magnitude, the most experienced attorney would take the case. However, in this instance, my client, Mr. Dillard, insisted I be his lawyer. And inevitably this is *his* case and *his* decision."

Winston Schneck had to force himself not to yield to the impulse to stand up and object. He realized that objecting might appear to be bullying an inexperienced attorney, and he didn't want to add a shred of empathy to what was flowing in the direction of Roy Dillard or his lawyers.

Ken let these words sink in, and as they did he saw exactly the surprised look from the jury box he'd wanted. Good, he thought, Schneck's sentiments might just start to fade from the forefront of their minds. "My job is to represent Roy Dillard and to make sure he receives a fair trial. I'm supposed to defend him, and in so doing demonstrate to you, the jury, that Roy is not guilty. Well, to be perfectly honest, I don't know if I can succeed in this." Ken paused once more and saw several jurors look to the person seated next to them with perplexed expressions on their faces. Two of them actually shrugged their shoulders before looking back at Melzer. *Now I've got their attention.*

"I know the evidence that Mr. Schneck intends to introduce against Roy looks pretty bad. And I know that my job is to refute that evidence. But I don't know how I'm going to do that." The jury was riveted on Ken as he began to pace back and forth in front of the jury box as if pondering what he was going to say next. He stopped and looked up as if he'd forgotten he was in a court of law giving an opening statement.

"You see Roy isn't very helpful to me. He's smart and quick, but totally confusing to have to deal with. In fact, when out of total exasperation with his lack of cooperation, I asked him how in the world I was going to offer an opening statement, he told me to, and this is a quote from him, 'Wing it, Ken.'" Melzer looked to the floor and shook his head from side to side. "Honestly, that was what he instructed me to do! And that brings me to the crux of this unusual opening statement. Through this trial I am going to follow Roy's instructions... because that's all I can do. Mr. Parnell and I represent him, and this is what he wants. I assure each of you on the jury that he's had excellent legal counsel and advice from Mr. Parnell over there," Ken gestured to the defense table a second time. "Yet, no matter what he's been advised, he's insisted on one thing and one thing only."

Winston Schneck was so taken aback, he didn't know whether to object or let Melzer dig Roy Dillard's grave deeper. Melzer had essentially blamed an anticipated guilty verdict on his client, and in so doing, waived attorney-client privilege for Schneck's probable cross-examination of Dillard. Failing to object was not in Schneck's nature, but he had to see how this was going to play out. He glanced at Judge Peters, and they exchanged an imperceptible expression of befuddlement.

Ken tried to look exasperated again before he said, "Roy tells me again and again... in fact, every time we've met, and that is a whole lot of times, you can be sure, that he has the utmost faith in the justice system, and that ultimately the jury... meaning you twelve fine people sitting before me right now, will find him *NOT GUILTY!*" Melzer lifted his arms, opened his hands to the seated jurors and said, "And you wanna hear the funny part of all this? I truly believe him." Again Ken watched the jurors look to each other bewildered. Good. Time to end this ridiculous opening statement. "I'll leave you with something Mr. Schneck said. Look at this man sitting at the defense table, and remember, he is innocent until you twelve jurors unanimously say otherwise." Ken turned abruptly as if to return to his seat, but he stopped and scratched his head before he turned back to the jury. "Oh, I almost forgot. The Prosecution said we are using the insanity defense; and that is true. However, Mr. Schneck said Roy isn't any crazier than any of you or him for that matter. I think those were his words, yet it's instructive to note that Mr. Schneck has never, ever, not even once, spoken to Roy! I'll let you all decide for yourselves if you think Roy is insane or not, but my bet is that you twelve would have to be crazy, to use Mr. Schneck's words again, to find Roy Dillard sane." Ken turned again as if to walk to his table and still once more stopped halfway there. "One last thing I also almost forgot to mention. The Prosecution said we were using the insanity defense because he said we didn't have anything else to use." Melzer walked back to the jury box and offered a conspiratorial smile before saying, "Don't be so sure of that."

He suddenly did an about-face, strutted to the defense table, and returned to his seat next to Roy Dillard.

Judge Peters stared at the three emotionless faces at the defense table. He tried not to appear incredulous for a few moments before saying, "The Prosecution may call its first witness."

Winston Schneck stood and announced, "The Prosecution calls Detective Robert Hanson."

The Bailiff left the courtroom and returned within a minute escorting a man wearing a brown suit to the witness stand. He was sworn in and took a seat behind a thin microphone.

Winston Schneck stood in front of his table and began, "Please state your full name and occupation."

"My name is Robert W. Hanson. I'm a detective with the Ft. Lauderdale Police Department."

"And how long have you been a detective?"

"Eleven years."

"In addition to your normal duties as a detective, do you have any special qualifications and training?"

"Yes. I have certifications in ballistics analysis and I have taught others seeking their certification in ballistics. I have published several articles in law enforcement journals and publications and have assisted, and at times overseen, the ballistics lab here in Broward County."

"Your Honor, I hereby tender Detective Hanson as an expert in ballistics analysis," Winston Schneck said confidently as he glanced first at the jury and then snidely at Ken Melzer.

"Does the Defense wish to question Detective Hanson on his credentials?" Judge Peters asked Ken.

"No, Your Honor."

"Very well. Detective Hanson is recognized and may testify as an expert in ballistics in addition to his factual testimony. You may proceed, Mr. Schneck."

"On February 1st of this year, were you called to the scene of a murder?"

"Yes. I was."

"Where and in what county did this occur?"

"Palm Drive in Ft. Lauderdale, Saltzman's Jewelry Store. That would be Broward County, Florida."

"Can you describe what you first saw when you arrived at Saltzman's?"

"Sure. I arrived just after the first responding officers got to the store and secured the scene-"

"Excuse me for interrupting, Detective, but could you explain what *securing the scene* means?"

"Oh, sure. Well, it means the officers went through the store and made sure there were no threats left in the building, that only people who should be there were there."

"And were there any people in the store who shouldn't have been there?"

"No. Just the old gentleman, Mr. Saltzman, and a young woman who worked there. I think she was his niece." Detective Hanson removed a small pad from his shirt pocket, flipped a few pages and said, "Her name was Laurie Silva, age thirty. And of course, the deceased, a Mr. Chester Bentley, age thirty-four."

"Please continue, Detective."

"So, as I said, I arrived soon after the store had been secured. The first thing I saw was a man lying on his back, apparently dead, on the floor."

"Before we get to him, what did you observe about the store itself when you entered?"

"The glass cases that I assume contained jewelry and watches were empty and the backs of the cases, you know, where the sales people reach in to get items to show customers, well, they were open."

"And the deceased man on the floor, please describe his condition."

"He was a black man in his thirties, big built, you know, muscular, and like I said, he was lying on his back."

"Continue, Detective."

"The first thing I saw was a big pool of blood around his head. And there was a large nickel plated revolver sticking out of his mouth."

"A large revolver sticking out of his mouth? Were you able to observe how that had occurred?"

"Yes. The front sight of the gun was imbedded in the roof of the deceased's mouth."

"I see. Continue please."

"The deceased man's cheeks were blown out, and his top front teeth were broken off. Also, the top of his head was pretty well gone, I mean, from the blast, and there was a baseball cap stuck to the ceiling of the store."

"Do you know how this cap managed to be stuck to the ceiling, Detective?"

"Well, obviously I didn't see it happen, but the exiting bullet blew the cap off the deceased's head, along with what appeared to be brains and blood... and it flew to the ceiling and stuck there by the blood and stuff from inside his head."

"Do you know why the bullet didn't just go through the hat?"

"My understanding is that the bullet was a high velocity hollow point that is made to expand on impact, so by the time the bullet entered and exited the skull, the bullet would have mushroomed-"

"Excuse me Detective, what does it mean when a bullet *mushrooms*?"

"That means that the hollow tip of the bullet expands and peels back from the hollow cavity so that it ends up looking like a mushroom."

"Is my understanding of your testimony correct that the bullet exits the gun barrel, and upon impact, expands so that the frontal diameter increases dramatically?"

"Yes. Exactly."

"By how much would this type of bullet expand?"

"Being at such close range, it would expand to approximately twice its diameter."

"So, in that case, after expansion, the bullet would look like the mushroom you described before?"

"Yes."

"Please describe to the jury the effect such expansion had on the victim in this case."

Detective Hanson's expression went grim as he turned to face the jury. "Because of this mushrooming effect, the bullet could not simply puncture the cap as it would have had it been a pointed, non-expanding projectile. Instead, it pushed the cap off the victim's head. And when the cap hit the ceiling, the mushroomed, or fully expanded, bullet then continued through the cap and into the ceiling material."

"And because of this mushrooming, the bullet would not be able to simply puncture the cap as if it were a pointed projectile?"

"That's right."

"Therefore, it would tend to push the cap to the ceiling?"

"I would think so, and only then, when it hit the ceiling, would the bullet go through the cap."

"Detective, do you have these hollow pointed bullets in your service weapon?"

"I do."

"Why is that?"

"Because they are the most lethal."

"Do all police use hollow pointed bullets?"

"Not all. Some departments don't allow their use for public relations reasons."

"Why is that?"

"Some departments think they are too deadly and give the police a bad image," Hanson replied matter-of-factly.

"Returning to the scene at the jewelry store, is what you observed common in your work as a detective?"

"You mean the cap stuck to the ceiling?"

"Yes, that and the gun sticking out of the deceased man's mouth."

"Nothing I've ever seen before – either the gun sticking out of his mouth or the cap stuck to the ceiling. In fact, I talked to a few of the officers who secured the scene, and they all seemed to think it pretty unusual as none of them had ever witnessed anything like it before."

"What would cause the front sight to lodge itself into the roof of Chester's mouth?"

"When a cartridge is fired, the barrel of the gun rises as the bullet exits the barrel. That is what occurred in this case. The recoil was powerful enough to cause the end of the barrel where the front sight is located to jerk upward with sufficient force to jam the sight into the roof of the victim's mouth."

"Do some guns recoil more than others?"

"Yes, the bigger the caliber, the more the recoil."

"Do you know the caliber of the gun protruding from the victim's mouth?"

"I do."

"How do you know this?"

"I read the ballistics report."

Melzer was instantly on his feet. "Objection, Your Honor. The ballistics report is hearsay. This witness cannot testify from it."

Schneck responded, "Your Honor, the Defense stipulated in the pretrial hearing to the admission of the ballistics report without the need for the ballistician to authenticate it."

Judge Peters replied, "I'll sustain the objection. The report has not been introduced into evidence at this point in time and it is hearsay."

Schneck said with a bit of irritation, "All right, Your Honor. At this time the State moves the ballistics report into evidence as State's Exhibit 1 pursuant to the pretrial stipulation."

The judge looked over at Ken, who was still on his feet. "No objection, Your Honor."

Judge Peters turned to his Clerk, "Please mark the ballistics report into evidence. You may continue, Mr. Schneck."

The Clerk placed a label on the ballistic report and handed it back to Schneck, while at the same time Roy Dillard chastised Ken Melzer with a glare not visible to the jury.

"May I approach the Witness?" Schneck asked, already halfway to the witness stand.

"You may," replied the judge.

Schneck handed the marked ballistics report to Detective Hanson. "Is this the ballistics report that you just referred to regarding the investigation of the murder that is the subject of this case, Detective?"

Detective Hanson briefly glanced through the pages. "Yes, it is."

"And is this the type of report or documentation that ballistics experts such as yourself rely upon in forming their opinions?"

"Yes. Just as doctors have to rely on medical records, we rely on reports generated by the crime scene investigators and lab technicians."

"Detective Hanson, based upon your knowledge and experience, were you able to identify the type of weapon you saw sticking out of the deceased's mouth?"

"Yes. It was a Smith and Wesson Model 57."

"Was your independent determination of the gun being a Smith and Wesson Model 57 consistent with the findings contained in the ballistics report?"

"Yes."

From a box under his table Schneck removed a plastic bag. "Your Honor, at this time I would like to introduce into evidence State's Exhibit 2, as stipulated by the Defense." The Clerk marked the exhibit and handed it back to Schneck. "May I approach the Witness, Your Honor?"

"You may."

Walking to the witness box, Schneck reached into the bag and with a fast motion pulled a large revolver, making sure as he did so that the long barrel swung past the jury box. He knew several jurors were familiar with firearms, and two were NRA members. Schneck was gratified to see these men involuntarily flinch as the gun barrel pointed their way. Opening the cylinder, Schneck held the revolver high and said, "I'd like to assure all in the courtroom that this immense weapon is fortunately unloaded." He took a few steps toward the Witness, handed the gun to Detective Hanson and resumed, "Detective, is this the revolver you saw protruding from Chester's mouth?"

"It appears to be, but I'd have to check the serial number with the one in the ballistic report."

Schneck handed back the ballistic report. "Please do. The serial number is listed near the bottom of page 1."

Hanson found it, then with the cylinder released to the side, he peered inside the frame of the gun. Looking up he said, "Yes, they match."

Schneck smiled broadly to the jury, "Well that's a relief!" He noticed a few returning smiles and also the beginnings of a frown from Judge Peters. "Detective, in your opinion, is this an unusual weapon to find at a crime scene?"

"It's the first one I've ever seen used in a crime."

"Based on your experience, how do you account for that?"

"Well, the Model 57 is a special revolver that is not only expensive to buy, but a gun you don't usually see in most gun shops."

"What is the primary use of this Smith and Wesson Model 57?"

"It's used mainly for hunting."

"Hunting, Detective? Hunting what?"

"Big game."

"You mean like deer and moose?"

"Yes. With a well placed shot, most big game animals could be brought down with a Model 57."

"Don't hunters use high-powered rifles to hunt big game?"

"As a hunter myself, I can say they usually do, but some hunters use handguns."

"Could you hunt with your service handgun?"

"Not really. I mean I could, but it's not powerful enough for humane kills on game."

"Not even with hollow pointed ammunition?"

"No, it lacks the power – you know, bullet diameter, bullet weight and velocity."

"But this Model 57 doesn't lack the power?"

"No, it has plenty of power."

"What caliber is the Model 57 Smith and Wesson revolver chambered for, Detective?"

"It's a .41 Magnum."

"Is that a normal handgun caliber?"

"Not for personal defense, but like I said, it's used more for hunting."

"Just how powerful is the .41 Magnum?"

"Well, it makes the 9mm cartridge in my service pistol look puny, and it packs a lot more punch than a .357 Magnum."

"Have you ever shot a .41 Magnum, Detective?"

"Yes. I've shot the .41 Magnum as well as the more common .357 Magnum."

"How would you compare the firing of a .41 Magnum with the more common .357 Magnum, just to give us a reasonable frame of reference?"

"The .357 is loud, and the recoil can be pretty substantial."

"What happens during the recoil of a .357 Magnum?"

"The gun pushes back in your hand sharply, and the muzzle-"

"Sorry to interrupt, but what's a muzzle?"

"That's the end of the barrel."

"Okay, thanks for clarifying that. You can continue explaining the recoil from a .357."

"Sure, so the gun comes back and then the muzzle, or front of the barrel, rises so that after each firing you have to lower the gun to realign your sights for the next shot."

"I see. How would the recoil from the .41 Magnum used in this crime compare to the recoil of a .357 Magnum?"

"It would have a significantly more violent recoil than a .357 Magnum."

"Enough that the recoil would raise the muzzle of the gun up, and imbed the front sight on the end of the barrel into the roof of Chester's mouth, and shatter his front teeth?"

"Well, that is exactly what happened, so yes. There is no other reasonable explanation."

"You stated a moment ago that you've never seen one of these .41 Magnum Smith and Wesson revolvers used in a crime. In your opinion, why is that."

Melzer was on his feet, "Objection, Your Honor. Relevancy and calls for speculation."

Judge Peters looked to the prosecutor, "Mr. Schneck, before I rule on this I'd like to hear the reasoning behind this line of questioning."

Schneck had baited that hook, and like an unwary bass, Melzer had swallowed it.

"Your Honor, I'm attempting to establish the state of mind of a killer who would choose this kind of weapon. It is indeed relevant to this case. Detective Hanson has been qualified as an expert in ballistics as well as in his capacity as a detective experienced in crimes involving firearms. His opinion as to the general use or lack of use of a particular weapon during the commission of violent crimes is not pure speculation and should be allowed."

"Overruled. Mr. Schneck you may proceed with this line of questioning, but only as to the Witness's opinion regarding the general use or lack of use of the weapon, and not specifically as to this defendant."

"Thank you, Your Honor." Schneck turned back to the witness stand, "Detective, I believe the question I asked was why, in your opinion, this type of Smith and Wesson revolver in .41 Magnum isn't generally used for criminal purposes?"

"Well, first of all, as you can see, this is a big gun, you know, one that would be hard to conceal, compared to the usual .38 Special or 9mm handgun. And second, like I said, it's expensive and hard to find. And third, well, let me put it to you in a way that was said to me when I first got started in hunting. I was going to buy a rifle in a really big caliber for hunting deer and wild hogs here in Florida. The guy who was teaching me about hunting rifles and calibers said the gun I chose would get the job done, but ammo would be more expensive than normal, recoil would hurt more and besides, he said, '*you can't kill 'em deader than dead.*' In other words, you don't need a .41 Magnum to kill someone at point blank range."

"Thank you Detective Hanson. Now I'd like to turn your attention to video evidence obtained from the crime scene. Did you gather the evidence?"

"Yes. Actually, the crime scene technicians gathered the video evidence, but I was present when they did. It was marked, placed into a protective container, and delivered to our crime lab for analysis."

"Have you seen the raw footage of the video evidence?"

"Yes, of course. Numerous times. The evidence came from several cameras."

Schneck asked, "Was any of the video evidence edited?"

Detective Hanson answered emphatically, "No, it was not. Because the cameras had been recording for quite some time before the event, I was only interested in the relevant portions of the videos surrounding the time frame of the crime, and none of that material has been edited in any manner whatsoever."

Schneck handed a plastic evidence bag containing several DVDs to Detective Hanson and asked, "Detective, is this the original video evidence taken from the crime scene?"

Detective Hanson examined the plastic bag's markings and looked at each DVD. "Yes, this is the original evidence gathered at the scene."

Schneck walked over to an easel assembled near the witness stand and flipped over a large blank page revealing a simple sketch of the entranceway and interior of Saltzman's Jewelry Store. He invited the detective to step down from the witness stand and handed him a pointer.

"Detective, would you agree that this is a rough sketch of the crime scene? It is not meant to be drawn to scale."

"Yes. It depicts the layout of the jewelry store."

"Without describing what is on these videos, please explain to the jury how the videos were shot." Schneck feigned quick embarrassment. "I'm sorry, that was an unfortunate choice of words. Please explain how the videos were recorded."

Using the pointer, Detective Hanson explained to the jury, "The videos were recorded from four different security cameras. Three of the cameras were located inside Saltzman's Jewelry

Store – one in the upper east corner, one on the upper west corner and one between the other two. All three were installed behind the glass display counters facing out to show the public section of the store's interior. The fourth camera was equipped with a wider-angled lens than the interior three. It was positioned by the single front entrance to record patrons entering and exiting the store as well as to capture a portion of the sidewalk and parking spaces directly in front of the entrance."

Detective Hanson handed the pointer back to Schneck. "Thank you, Detective. You may return to the witness stand."

Schneck turned to the Judge, "Your Honor, at this time I'd like to publish to the jury the composition of video tapes of the crime. The Defense has stipulated to their admissibility."

Within minutes a huge seventy-inch flat screen monitor was wheeled in on a stand and situated so that the jury, the Witness, and the defense team had a clear view from their seats. Judge Peters stepped down from the bench and stood off to the side so that he, too, would have an unobstructed view of the monitor.

While the video and monitor were being set up, Judge Peters instructed the jurors that they were to watch the video without commenting and reminded them not to draw any conclusions until all the evidence had been presented and final jury instructions given.

Winston Schneck plugged in the unit, and the screen went instantly bright white. He again faced the judge, "Your Honor, may I address the jury concerning the nature of this evidence?"

"Mr. Melzer, do you have any objection?"

"No, so long as Mr. Schneck keeps his remarks factual and in no way tries to lead the jury to conclusions."

Schneck smiled inwardly. What a pompous little fool, he thought. Everything I say and do is meant to *lead* the jury.

"Mr. Schneck you may proceed."

Walking to the jury box, but facing the whole courtroom, Schneck stated, "Considering the graphic nature of the evidence to be viewed, I have purposely waited to present this after Detective Hanson's testimony. In this way, I've tried to lessen the shock of the horrific scene of the crime –"

"Objection! Move to strike." Red-faced, Melzer was on his

feet.

Sternly Judge Peters growled, "Sustained. The jury will disregard Mr. Schneck's characterization of the evidence. Mr. Schneck, you will keep your remarks factual and your own personal views to yourself."

Trying to appear contrite, Schneck said, "I'm sorry, Your Honor. Perhaps it is best I simply explain the mechanics of the evidence, and play the footage." Schneck continued, "I will show the first film, the one from the outside camera, in two parts. The first will be that of the Defendant entering the-"

"Objection, Your Honor! Mr. Schneck is drawing a conclusion that is strictly within the province of the jury. The content of the video will speak for itself."

"Sustained!" Judge Peters took a quick sip from his ever-present black coffee mug and said, "Mr. Schneck, you have been around the block enough times for me to know you say very little, if anything, that you do not intend. I warn you not to try the patience of this court."

Schneck did not apologize this time. Instead he continued as if nothing had interrupted his comments. "The first part from the outside camera will show the... excuse me, it will show *a person* entering the store. I will then show separate viewings from each of the three inside-mounted cameras. When these have been viewed, I'll show the second part of the film from the outside camera which captures the individual in question leaving the store and driving away."

Schneck turned to Judge Peters, "I am ready to show the video. May the lights be dimmed?"

"Bailiff, please shut off the lights in the front section of the courtroom. You may proceed when you are ready, Mr. Schneck."

The viewing lasted less than ten minutes. The effect was obvious when the courtroom lights were turned back on. Not a sound could be heard in the entire room, and Schneck inwardly rejoiced at the pale, expressionless countenances of the twelve jurors and two alternates.

"Your Honor, I have one more related piece of evidence I'd

like introduced in conjunction with the video just played."
Schneck reached to a shelf on the wheeled stand under the TV
screen and produced a brown nine by twelve inch envelope. "I
have four photos. Each is made from one individual frame from
each of the four security cameras." Holding the envelope above
his head Schneck said, "I'd like to enter these as State's
composite Exhibit 4, and publish them to the jury."

Schneck handed the photos to Judge Peters who reviewed
them with an expressionless face and instructed the Clerk to mark
them into evidence as a composite exhibit.

Schneck walked to the jury box and paused as if he were about
to speak, but didn't. He used this simple tactic occasionally to
garner heightened attention from the jury, to build a bit of
suspense and anticipation of something exciting to come. He then
turned and stared directly at Roy Dillard sitting at the defense
table before slowly pulling the photos from the envelope.
Returning his attention to the jury box, he handed the four eight
by ten inch enlargements to the juror furthest to the left on the
front row. "Please examine these photos and pass them along," he
said while returning his stare at Dillard.

Each photo showed a clearly focused and enlarged image of
the face of Roy Dillard. One a left profile, one a right profile, and
one full face. The fourth showed a partial side view of Dillard
tossing an apparently full laundry bag into his car before entering
the vehicle himself. The license plate was clearly visible.

Ken Melzer watched Schneck's cheap theatrics, thinking they
were poorly choreographed and too obvious. Still, he thought in
annoyance, he, the judge, and perhaps Hank Parnell, were the
only ones critiquing it this way.

In a short time the photos were collected and handed back to
Schneck who spent a few moments in front of the jury box
looking at each photo as if he'd never seen them before. Ken
glanced surreptitiously toward Dillard as Schneck was
ruminating over the photos just collected back from the jury. He
couldn't believe he was smirking! Maybe he really is crazy, Ken
thought, he's gotta be!

Schneck turned his attention back to the Witness. "Detective,
the video compilation that we all just watched... do you consider

them to be typical security camera footage?"

"No, these are much better."

"Can you say why this is?"

"Sure, these were fairly new cameras and of the highest quality. The focus and clarity are the best I've seen in my career."

"When did you see the films?"

"Within an hour of the crime."

"How did you use the recordings in your investigation?"

"Well, we had a clear view of the car and license plate as well as images of the suspect."

"The license plate was checked and found to match the vehicle, which was registered to a Roy Dillard. A copy of his driver's license was procured from the DMV – Department of Motor Vehicles – and his photo on the license seemed to match the security film images. A SWAT team was sent to the address on the license, and the arrest was made."

"Approximately how much time passed from the commission of the crime to the arrest of the Defendant?"

"Maybe an hour and a half or so."

"Who was the arresting officer?"

"I was."

"Do you see the individual that you arrested in connection with this crime in the courtroom today?"

"Yes, I do."

"Please point him out for the record."

Detective Hanson stared directly at Roy Dillard and then fully extended his arm pointing in his direction. "The person I arrested is sitting at the defense table between his two lawyers."

"Let the record reflect that Detective Hanson has pointed to the Defendant, Roy Dillard, and identified him as the person he arrested for the murder of Chester Bentley," Schneck declared triumphantly.

"Thank you, Detective Hanson. No further questions."

Judge Peters looked to the defense table and said, "The Defense may cross-examine the Witness."

Ken Melzer approached the witness stand. "Detective," he began, "you were at Mr. Dillard's home when the SWAT team arrived and ordered him to come out of the house with his hands raised and lie on the ground?"

"Yes."

"From the security camera recordings that we all watched, can you briefly describe what the gunman was wearing?"

"He wore a leather jacket, gloves, and long pants – jeans, I think."

"And when you got to Mr. Dillard's house and arrested him, what was he wearing?"

"He was wearing a T-shirt, shorts, and flip-flops."

"And his car was parked in plain sight in his driveway?"

"Yes."

"You're sure it was the same car recorded by the security cameras?"

"It was the same car. Same license plate, and same broken tail light that was visible in the video."

"What was Mr. Dillard's demeanor, his reaction, to being surrounded by a SWAT team and ordered to lie on the ground?"

"Well, he seemed a bit confused. He wanted to know what this was all about. He didn't seem to know why he was being arrested."

"What conclusions did you draw from that observation?"

"Objection!" Schneck was standing. "Calls for speculation."

"Sustained."

"Let me ask this a different way. Detective Hanson, you have seen a lot of people arrested, right?"

"Sure."

"Was Mr. Dillard's reaction similar to, or typical of, reactions by other people you've seen arrested?"

Schneck was on his feet again, "Objection. Relevance."

Melzer responded, "Goes to state of mind, Your Honor."

"Overruled. You may answer the question.

"Well, sort of. Lots of suspects act surprised when they are arrested, you know, they ask why they are being cuffed, and say they didn't do anything. They say they are innocent."

"What about suspects who are apprehended red-handed, who are caught in the act of a crime?"

"If they are really caught in the act, they usually stay silent. I mean, what can they say at that point?"

"Detective, you saw the camera mounted in the doorway of Saltzman's?"

"Yes. Security cameras are usually mounted in obvious places because they are there for two reasons – the first is to record any criminal activity and the second is to be a deterrent, you know, so that anyone thinking about stealing will think twice if they know they are being filmed."

Ken Melzer couldn't believe his luck with this answer. He continued, "So, in your opinion, based on your years as a detective, if someone knew a security camera would film them, would you expect that person to cover his face or mask his identity?"

"Objection, Your Honor. This again calls for speculation."

"Overruled. You may answer this question."

Detective Hanson looked at the judge who nodded to him and repeated, "You may answer the question."

"Yeah, if someone knows there are cameras around, they usually hide their identity."

"Were the three additional cameras also obvious to anyone inside the store?"

"Yes, they were out in the open."

"From what you saw on the video, did the gunman try to hide his identity in any way?"

"No. Not at all."

"From your experience, and considering the magnitude of the crime, does this seem out of the ordinary for a man planning the burglary of a high-end jewelry store to *not* try to conceal his identity?"

"I suppose so, yes."

"Detective, assuming the suspect knew he and his car had been recorded by numerous cameras, from your experience, do you consider it odd that he left his car in plain sight in his driveway, and then acted totally oblivious of any wrongdoing when ordered from his house?"

"I guess, but who knows-"

"Detective, a simple yes or no answer would suffice."

Hanson pondered the question. "Yes, it does seem a little odd when put in that context."

"Let's move forward in time. Were you involved with the team who searched Mr. Dillard's house after the warrant was issued?"

"Yes."

"And in what part of Mr. Dillard's house did you find the stolen jewelry?"

"We didn't find the jewelry."

"None of it?"

"No."

"Did you find the laundry bag that we all saw on the video? The one that contained the jewelry from the robbery?"

"No. We didn't find that either."

"What about the leather jacket the man in the video was wearing?"

"Nope, didn't find that or the gloves either."

"Were you surprised to not find these items?"

"Not really. We figured he had enough time driving home to stash the stolen items."

"And stash the leather jacket, too?"

"Sure."

"If the individual on the video didn't bother to conceal his face, why would he care about stashing the leather jacket?"

"Objection! Your Honor, please..."

"Sustained. Mr. Melzer, this is another question calling for speculation on the part of the Witness. Let's not go on a fishing expedition here."

"I'm sorry, Your Honor."

Turning back to the Witness, Melzer concluded, "Detective Hanson you have testified that the man on the video didn't try to conceal his face or identity from cameras that were placed so as to be seen and meant to be a deterrent, that Mr. Dillard made no effort to park his car out of plain sight, that Mr. Dillard acted confused about why he was being arrested, and that upon searching Mr. Dillard's house no stolen goods or clothing worn by the man in the videos were found. Is that a fair synopsis of your testimony?"

"I guess that about sums it up. So yes, I suppose so."

"Thank you Detective. No further questions."

TWENTY-SIX

Waiting for Ken Melzer, Hank Parnell sat at a small table in Starbucks with two steaming cups of coffee. Ken had been following Hank until he drifted too far behind and got stuck at a red light. A few minutes later he arrived and hustled over to the table.

"Sorry, I should have stayed closer to you, but my mind was on the trial."

"Not a problem. We've got over an hour for lunch. Hungry?"

"Couldn't eat a thing. I'm almost nauseated as it is. I'll try some coffee though." Ken pried off the plastic lid and took a short sip. "At this point I think the jury thinks I'm the crazy one, not Dillard."

"Hank laughed, took a swallow from his own cup, and then laughed again. "I have to say; I don't think I've ever heard an opening statement quite like yours. But you did what you could, and I think the jury liked you."

"Or pitied me…"

"No. I don't think that. Look, you have little to work with here. Dillard gives you nothing except a blind faith in the justice system that is going to put him away for life… or worse. Our shrink isn't exactly Sigmund Freud. They've got a ton of the most damning evidence to introduce, and we've got almost nothing. As we've both discussed a million times, the insanity plea rarely works even under the most favorable conditions. And we don't have favorable conditions. If this were a poker game, I'd say we were all in with maybe a pair of deuces."

"Well, that's comforting."

Hank chuckled again, "No, it's not comforting, but it is reality, and it's what we have to work with." He sat back in his chair and said, "Listen, Dillard asked you to 'wing it' for your opening statement, and you did a fine job considering our position. You at least put a little doubt in the minds of the jury by stating that

Schneck had never spoken to Dillard even though he insisted he wasn't crazy. That was good. I think the best part was the end when you reminded the jury that Schneck said we are using the insanity defense because that's all we could come up with, and you said, 'don't be so sure of that.'" And I gotta say, the way you smiled at them when you said it, well, that isn't something taught in law school. That's natural stage presence and timing."

"Well, thanks. Thanks for the pep talk. I mean it. That helps a lot. But I've got a question for you. Why did Schneck go on and on about the kind of gun used, and the caliber, and bullets. What was the point of all that?"

"What do you think?

"I'm not sure. To shock the jury or something?"

"No. He's trying to show that the delivery guy could have been killed with a smaller gun, but Dillard used a cannon. He's trying to show malice and hatred. Dillard is white. Chester Bentley was black. Schneck wants the jury to believe Dillard was making a statement by using that kind of weapon."

Ken reflected a moment. "And I didn't pick up on it. I'm such an idiot! Why didn't you pass me a note or something when I missed it? I could have addressed that on cross."

"I wanted to see if you'd pick up on it without my help. But don't worry; you can still address the issue."

"I'll have to."

"You will, and you'll do fine. But keep in mind, it won't matter. Ultimately, whether Dillard used a BB gun or a Howitzer, Bentley is dead, and Dillard is on video killing him. Treat this like a learning experience. Like I said before, Schneck is good at what he does, and he's especially good with juries. He's an asshole of the first degree, but the members of the jury don't know that. They only know him for what they see in court. And in court he's a prince."

"I know all that, but I'm still emotionally involved in this case. I have trouble dealing with it on an impersonal level, you know, stepping back from it."

"That's as it should be for your first big case. But mark my words; you'll harden over time. You'll learn to separate your professional life from your personal life. After a while almost everyone does, but if not, if you can't do that, this job will eat you alive."

"Now there's something to look forward to!"

Both lawyers laughed. Hank said, "Good to see you smile. Ease up on yourself. I couldn't do any better than you are doing right now. I don't think anybody could. Try to relax, let your instincts take over when you cross-examine Schneck's witnesses. And don't let him provoke you into objecting when it's to his advantage."

"I think I already figured that one out."

"I promise you, after this case you'll be a better lawyer. You can't learn this stuff from law journals or studying transcripts. You gotta be in the arena for yourself. And trust me when I say you're doing a great job."

They finished their coffees, checked the time, and Ken stood up saying, "I'll see you back in court."

"I'm looking forward to it."

Ken smiled. "You know something Hank? I think I am, too."

TWENTY-SEVEN

After the lunch break court was called to session, the judge was seated, and the jurors were marched to the jury box. Judge Peters said, "The Prosecution may call its next witness."

"The Prosecution calls Laurie Silva."

The Bailiff exited the rear of the court and returned with the Witness. She was shown to the stand, sworn in, and Winston Schneck began his questioning.

"Please state your name and profession."

Laurie Silva was dressed in a conservative short-sleeved black dress that hung loosely at knee length. Her dark hair was pulled back into a tight bun. She wore minimal makeup.

"My name is Laurie Silva and I work at Saltzman's Fine Jewelry and Watch Store in Ft. Lauderdale, Florida."

"What is your position at the store?"

"My uncle owns the store. I've worked there for a number of years."

"Miss Silva, I know this is not easy for you, so I'll try to be as brief as possible."

"Thank you."

"Were you working in Saltzman's Jewelry Store on February 1st of this year, Super Bowl Sunday?"

"Yes."

"Can you tell me what, if anything, unusual happened that day?"

"Yes. A man entered the store with a gun. He walked up to Chester, the deli delivery man, and shot him."

"Do you see that man in this courtroom?"

"I do."

"Would you please point to him?"

Laurie Silva looked at the defense table and pointed directly at Roy Dillard sitting between Ken Melzer and Hank Parnell. Still pointing she dropped her eyes, but not her arm.

"Please describe what the man you are pointing to is wearing."

"He's wearing a dark blue suit with a white shirt and a blue tie."

Winston Schneck said to the judge, "Let the record reflect that the Witness has identified the Defendant, Roy Dillard."

"The record shall so reflect," said the judge. "You may continue, Mr. Schneck."

Schneck questioned Laurie in moment-by-moment timeline fashion as to the gruesome details that she witnessed of the murder of Chester Bentley. After the jury heard Laurie's testimony corroborating what they had just seen on the video, Schneck continued his questioning.

"What happened next?"

"He turned to me and told me to fill a laundry bag with the inventory from the display cases."

Schneck asked, "Did you comply with his request?"

"Not immediately. I was in shock from what I'd just seen... what had just occurred. I think I just stood there frozen, not knowing how to respond."

"And then what happened?"

"He hit me across the face." Laurie's eyes gazed downward and her left hand rose to the side of her face as she relived the memory. "He hit me hard with an open hand."

"Do you know why?" Schneck asked.

Ken thought of objecting, but there was nothing to gain by it and he did not want to further emphasize the testimony to the jury.

"Because I didn't do as he said," Laurie responded softly.

"What, if anything, did Roy Dillard say to you after he hit you across the face?"

"He told me he had another gun, and he'd use it unless I did as he said."

"What did you do then?"

"I emptied the trays from the display cases into the laundry bag."

Schneck paused a moment to allow the jury to absorb the testimony they had just heard, and then transitioned into another line of questioning.

"You testified earlier that the man you saw Roy Dillard shoot was named Chester. What was your relationship to Chester?"

"Chester worked for a deli not far from our store. My uncle and I often ordered sandwiches, and Chester was their delivery man."

"Can you describe your relationship with Chester Bentley?"

"I didn't know him personally. We only saw him when he made a delivery. He was always friendly. My uncle particularly liked him. Chester told him jokes and made him laugh."

"He was a jovial and friendly man?"

"Objection! Relevance. Your Honor, this is an obvious attempt by the Prosecution to garner improper sympathy for the deceased."

"Sustained."

"Miss Silva, before he pulled the trigger, what, if anything, did the Defendant say to Chester?"

"I was in shock because it all happened so fast, but I'm pretty sure he said something and then used N."

"N?"

"You know. The N-word. I don't like to say it."

"I don't like to say it either but, for the record, please say the word this one time, and I promise I won't ask you to say it again."

In a very quiet voice, almost a whisper, Laurie Silva said, "nigger."

"Miss Silva, how did Chester react when he was confronted by the gunman?"

"I'm not completely sure, but when he turned to face the man with the gun, I thought it looked like Chester recognized him... maybe knew him... I even think Chester was about to say something, but then the gun went off."

"Thank you, Miss Silva. I know that last part was especially difficult for you. No further questions."

Judge Peters looked to the defense table and said, "Does the Defense wish to cross-examine the Witness?"

"Yes, Your Honor." Ken stepped around the defense table and walked toward the witness stand. It was better to take control of a witness from a close proximity than from afar.

"Miss Silva, you said you were in a state of shock after the shooting, is this correct?"

"Yes. It was pretty upsetting to see, I mean, see what I saw…"

"I'm sure it was and I'm also sure testifying today is not easy, but I have to ask if you are certain, absolutely one hundred percent certain, you heard the word 'nigger' used?"

"I think so, yes."

"Miss Silva, I'm not trying to badger you, but saying you 'think so-'"

"Objection! Your Honor, *badger* is exactly what Mr. Melzer is doing. The Witness has answered the question!"

Judge Peters spoke to Ken, "I'm going to allow this question once, Mr. Melzer. But only once."

"Thank you, Your Honor." Facing the Witness again, Ken Melzer said in a kindly voice, "I'm only asking this of you because of the seriousness of the question, and because you said under oath you were in a state of shock. So to be perfectly clear, are you certain, without any doubt whatsoever, that you heard the word 'nigger' used?"

Laurie Silva looked deep into Ken's face, then tilted her face down and answered quietly, "I'm pretty sure that's what I heard."

"And being in shock while all this is unfolding in front of you, you can't be certain that Chester recognized the person who shot him, can you?" Ken asked gently but confidently.

"No, I can't be certain. He just looked like-"

"No further questions."

When Ken returned to his seat he found a small printed note on the table. *NICE JOB! GOT A LITTLE DOUBT INTRODUCED.*

Judge Peters said, "I think there is enough time for one more witness provided the Prosecution believes examination will be relatively brief. Mr. Schneck?"

"This shouldn't take too long, Your Honor."

"Fine. You may call your next witness."

"The Prosecution calls Joan Landers."

A short time later the Bailiff returned to the courtroom leading a middle-aged, dark-haired woman to the witness stand. She was sworn in and seated.

"Please state your name and profession."

"My name is Joan Landers. I am one of the founders of the South Florida Hearing Institute in Ft. Lauderdale, and I've been the director of the Institute for twelve years."

"I see. Ms. Landers what is your field of expertise with regard to dealing with the hearing impaired?"

"I teach signing as well as lip reading to those who are hearing challenged. I also train instructors in this field. And I've written two books on the topic as well as numerous articles related to the subject."

"Ms. Landers, what is your relationship with me?"

"We have no relationship. I've never seen you before today."

"Have we ever spoken on the phone?"

"No."

"Have I emailed you?"

"No."

"Texted?"

"No. I've had no communication with you personally."

"Then how is it that you find yourself in this courtroom today?" Schneck asked.

"Well, largely out of curiosity," Ms. Landers replied. "Some time ago I received a phone call from a secretary in your office who asked if I could be available this week to appear in court to testify as an expert witness. When I asked what I was going to testify about, I was told only that it would involve my field of expertise and that as long as my opinion was truthful, my cooperation would be appreciated."

Feigning confusion, Schneck asked, "Well, is such a request of an expert witness unusual?"

"Absolutely."

"Why is that?" Schneck persisted, the jury now becoming intrigued.

"Because when a person testifies as an expert witness, there are usually a number of face-to-face meetings or telephone conferences between the attorney and the expert. The expert must sometimes review voluminous records in order to form a well-reasoned and supported opinion. The line of questioning and the ultimate opinion sought are discussed at length before trial.

Depositions are taken. An expert witness doesn't just appear in court absent serious preparation for his or her testimony."

"Well, today it appears that one will, Ms. Landers," Schneck said affably. "Let's begin."

"Are you familiar with the Super Bowl Murder and Jewelry Heist?"

"Only what I read in the papers or heard on the news. That was months ago."

"Do you know who was killed or what was stolen?"

"I think it was a man, but I'm not sure. I assume jewelry was stolen because of the headlines, but I really don't know."

"Can you please state what you know about the man who was killed?"

"No, like I said, I'm not even sure if it was a man or a woman... or if there were more than one."

"So, Ms. Landers, is it accurate to say you know almost nothing about this case or why you have been called as a witness today?"

"That would be essentially accurate. I'm not familiar with the details of your case. I've testified as an expert witness numerous times, I received a check from our office this week for my standard expert witness fee, and I then received a subpoena to appear in court today. I don't think it would be a particularly great intellectual leap to conclude that you intend to ask my expert opinion on some matter today," Ms. Landers said with a hint of sarcasm in her voice. Schneck couldn't have been more pleased.

Schneck then turned to the judge and said, "Your Honor, you have heard Ms. Landers' testimony as to her qualifications. She has been qualified as an expert witness regarding communication skills involving the hearing impaired. I tender her to the Court as an expert in that field."

Judge Peters turned to the defense table. "Does the Defense wish to voir dire the Witness as to her qualifications?"

Ken turned toward Hank Parnell. "What do you think? Should I try to question her credentials?" Before Hank could reply, Roy leaned over and whispered to Ken, "Let her testify. She's not going to make a difference."

Ken stood and addressed Judge Peters. "The Defense has no objection to this witness testifying as an expert in her stated field."

"Ms. Landers, I don't doubt for an instant that you can read lips, but I'd like for you to demonstrate your skill for everyone here today. I'm going to stand by the prosecution table over there," Schneck said as he paced the few steps to the table. "Can you see my lips from this distance?"

"May I use my glasses?"

Schneck smiled, "Of course."

Joan Landers reached into the pocket of her gray pantsuit jacket, removed a pair of wire-rimmed glasses, and placed them on her face. "I'm ready now."

"Ms. Landers, I'm going to mouth a short sentence without making a sound. Then I'm going to ask you what I said. I have the sentence written in large letters on a piece of poster board face down on my table. After you read my lips and tell what I said, I'll hold up the poster, and we'll see how accurate you were. And just for the record, has anyone told you or even hinted at what my sentence is going to be?"

"No. I have no idea what you might say."

Ken Melzer was on his feet. "Objection! This courtroom demonstration has no relevance. The Witness has already been qualified as an expert. We stipulate that she can read lips-"

Roy tugged on Ken's jacket sleeve to get his attention. "I want to see this little demonstration. It might be entertaining. Let them go through with it. It's not going to hurt us."

Ken looked at Judge Peters and subtly rolled his eyes. "Objection withdrawn, Your Honor."

With a shrug of his shoulders, Judge Peters looked over to Schneck. "Okay, Mr. Schneck, you may proceed."

"Okay. Let's give this a try." Schneck faced the Witness and took a few seconds to mouth a sentence. When he was finished he said, "Do you need me to repeat it."

"No, once was sufficient."

"Good. Please tell the court what I said."

"You said, 'the men at the defense table appear to be worried and sweating.'"

Schneck was already holding the large poster board with those exact words for the jury and the courtroom to see.

"Objection! Objection! Your Honor, this is outrageous-"

"Sustained! Counsel, approach the bench!"

When Schneck, Ken and Hank were standing close together in front of the judge's bench, Judge Peters leaned forward, and in a growling whisper that the jury could not hear, addressed Winston Schneck. "Mr. Schneck, I will not tolerate this kind of inappropriate showmanship in my courtroom. You are too experienced an attorney not to understand boundaries that must not be crossed."

"Yes, Your Honor. I suppose that was a poor choice for a sentence..."

"You suppose correctly, Mr. Schneck. Let me be very clear about my position on such antics. Should they occur again, I have the power to hold you in contempt. I will also have the power to favorably consider a defense motion for mistrial, if made under appropriate circumstances. Do you have a comfortable understanding of my expectations for the behavior of attorneys appearing in my courtroom, Mr. Schneck?"

"I do. Please forgive me, Your Honor. I apologize to the Court for my poor judgment..."

"Step back, Counselors. You may proceed with your witness, Mr. Schneck."

Schneck's little ploy caused half-hidden smiles to emerge on all the jurors' faces. It was obvious they enjoyed his little touch of humor in the midst of a murder trial. How could they not appreciate his affability and sense of fun? More importantly, they liked him.

"Ms. Landers, I'm going to show you a video of someone saying something in a jewelry store. I want you to assume there were three cameras from three angles recording simultaneously. You'll view only a few seconds worth of video. In that short time one man says something to another man, and that is what I'd like for you to lip read for all of us. This, Ms. Landers, is why you've been called to testify today. And again, for the record, have you seen this video or have you even been told about it?"

"No. This is all a surprise to me."

Schneck requested the lights be dimmed as he wheeled the giant screen in front of the Witness. "First I'll show the left camera, then the right, and finally the footage from the center camera. Remember, each will only last a few seconds, and I promise the video is cut before you'd have to endure anything else that occurs. All I want you to do is ascertain what was said. Do you understand?"

"Of course."

"Good. I'll play the three videos now."

The viewing lasted less than a minute.

"Ms. Landers, would you like me to show you the video again?"

"That won't be necessary."

"Were you able to read the lips of the man speaking?"

"Yes."

"Ms. Landers, within a reasonable degree of certainty, do you have an opinion as to how many words and what words were spoken by the man who you observed on the video a moment ago?"

"Yes, I do," Ms. Landers said matter-of-factly.

"Good. Ms. Landers, how many words were spoken?"

"Only two words were spoken."

"In your opinion, what were those words?"

"Surprise, nigger."

"And once again, Ms. Landers, are those two opinions within a reasonable degree of certainty?"

"I would say more like absolute certainty, Mr. Schneck," Ms. Landers said looking directly into Schneck's eyes and then turning her head to the jury to confirm her testimony.

"Thank you Ms. Landers. No further questions."

A low murmur spread through the courtroom. It was abruptly cut off by a sharp gavel rap. "Does the Defense wish to cross-examine the Witness?"

Ken Melzer stood silently thinking for a moment before meekly responding, "No questions, Your Honor." When he sat down he noticed another scrap of paper before him. On it was scribbled, *SO MUCH FOR THE DOUBT. EASY COME, EASY GO...*

TWENTY-EIGHT

Ken Melzer waited until the courtroom had emptied for the day. Only then did he meet his wife in the nearly deserted hallway. She gave him a brief hug and said, "I'm very proud of you."

Surprised, Ken said "Really? I'm not sure what you could find to be proud of."

"Don't be so hard on yourself," she said taking his arm and leading him down the hall. "You showed great resourcefulness, and you were also very quick to recognize when you needed to object. You also demonstrated restraint when you could have objected, but didn't."

"Thanks, but I feel like the captain of a sinking ship."

"That's actually a pretty good analogy. Like the captain of the Titanic... it wasn't his fault the ship hit an iceberg. He wasn't even at the wheel when it happened. The guys on watch missed it. By the time he was called to the bridge, the damage had been done. All he could do was follow an honorable protocol, you know, getting as many people into life boats as he could before he went down with the ship."

Ken chuckled, "You've been hanging around the yacht club again, haven't you?"

"Ken darling, I'm serious. Dillard is the Titanic here, and you're the captain who got called after the damage had been done. You're going through the legal protocol our system affords. And you are doing a fine job. Nobody could fix the hole in the Titanic, and nobody can undo what your creepy client did either. He's going down just like the Titanic, and nothing is going to stop it. So again, I'm very proud of you."

Ken looked down and said, "Well, thanks. That means a lot."

"And I'll tell you something else too. That little weasel Schneck knows you're sharp. He may have this case slam dunked, but I'll bet in that oily brain of his he's storing away the knowledge that someday in the future, on a different case, he'll go head to head with you again. And he already knows when that day comes he'll have an adversary to be taken very seriously."

"I think he's already forgotten my name, and in a few days he won't give a second thought about this case, or about me."

"Wrong on both accounts. He took this case to further his career. It's a headliner, and he wants it all for himself. And don't think he's not sizing you up. He knows his people will face you again, and he wants to be ready when that time comes. I'm impressed with you, Hank's impressed with you, and you can be sure Schneck won't ever take you lightly."

Ken stopped walking. "Thanks for the positive strokes. I don't know how much of that is just a supportive wife consoling her husband before he gets his head handed to him, or whether maybe there is some truth in what you said."

"It's all truth. You just refuse to see it."

Either way, it's nice to have you on my team."

Charlene pulled him close. "Now and forever."

As he had for the last couple of weeks, Ken slept that night in the makeshift office in the spare room. At least he tried to sleep. A week ago he'd sworn to Charlene that once the trial was over, he'd move back to their bedroom and be normal again. Jokingly he'd commented, 'if nothing else, that's something to look forward to,' but Charlene had seen no humor in the comment. She'd responded, "I want my husband back. I want *you* back. It's fine to be a lawyer by day, but after this trial you better be my husband the rest of the time."

He couldn't help but laugh, which had only seemed to annoy her. "I will, Honey. This is my first big trial. Once it's over, I'll be okay. Next time, I'll know what to expect. I'll be able to deal with it... next time."

At last she had relaxed and smiled weakly, "You'd better."

"Or what?" Ken had said playfully.

"Or what? I'll tell you what, Buster. You stay in that office much longer, and I'll move your stuff in there and make it permanent!"

"I doubt that. You know you find me irresistible. Even now,

you probably hate yourself for even thinking of kicking me out."

It was at that point that Charlene had hurled a sofa pillow, hitting Ken squarely in the face. Taking advantage of the situation, Ken had thrown his hands to his face and dropped to the floor moaning, "My eye, my eye, ahh my eye..." It worked. Charlene was there in a flash, "Oh Honey, I'm so sorry. Oh God, are you okay? Baby, let me see, please, take your hands away, let me see..." Ken couldn't stifle the laugh that erupted through his fingers.

"You bastard!" Charlene had giggled, throwing herself on top of him. Ken grabbed his wife, tickling her ribs, and causing her to squeal.

The lovemaking that followed on the living room floor had been urgent and brief. The second lovemaking was more relaxed, longer – even languid – but just as satisfying and overdue.

Ken had then known that after the damn trial concluded he would never want to spend another solitary night in the guest room office.

TWENTY-NINE

Ken looked at the brass ship's wheel clock on his desk at the PD's office. Twenty minutes before show time. Day Two. He closed his eyes, took three deep breaths, and was just getting into a relaxing, empty, mind-clearing meditation when his cellphone vibrated on the desktop.

"Hello."

"Hey Little Brother..."

"Mark?"

"Try Matthew. You have been out of communication a long time. Can't even tell which of your brothers is which."

"Sorry. I was preoccupied and not paying attention. You surprised me."

"No problem. So, how's the big murder trial of the century going?"

"Hardly the trial of the century. I'm getting my clock cleaned but good."

"The guy's guilty, isn't he? What did you expect?"

"I won't answer the first, and I didn't know what to expect. This is my first big trial."

"Is this how you are living up to your *do-gooder vow*?"

"It's my career. It's what I do, vow or no vow."

"And you feel okay about trying to get a criminal, a murderer, off?"

Ken seethed, but held his tongue. Matthew spoke again, "Do you?"

Collecting himself, Ken replied, "Matthew, let me ask you something, and you gotta answer quick. I don't have much time. I have to be in court in a few minutes."

"Shoot."

"If you were given the chance, would you try to save my client's soul?"

"I'll answer quick. Yes, of course."

"Well, think of it this way. I'm trying to save his *life*. If I succeed, you can fly down here and work at saving his soul." Ken quickly added, "Out of time, gotta go." And ended the call.

Like the previous day, Ken Melzer sat at the defense table with Roy Dillard and Hank Parnell. And also like the previous day, Winston Schneck sat alone at the prosecutor's table reviewing notes on a yellow legal pad. The Bailiff announced the judge, all rose, then were seated, and it was off to the races. Ken smiled at this metaphor. He pictured a two-horse race with one thoroughbred stallion charging out of the gate while a sway-backed tired nag trotted far behind. Jeez, he thought, first I'm the captain of the Titanic, and now I'm dead last in a horse race.

Ken had been informed the Prosecution was going to call only four final witnesses – all would be brief – and he should be prepared to present his defense. He was surprised at first, but really, why prolong the inevitable? Schneck would prove his legal acumen by blasting through this trial in an incredibly short time, and with a minimum of witnesses. He'd grab the headlines, and Ken might be mentioned as an afterthought. Probably just as well, he rationalized. Not much glory in losing. The less he's associated with Roy Dillard, the better.

The first witness was called promptly at nine o'clock. Winston Schneck's voice sounded clear and rested. "Please state your name and occupation."

"My name is Nick Jillian and I own a franchise chain of several small restaurants in Florida."

"What is the name of the restaurant chain, Mr. Jillian?"

"Quick Chick."

"Oh, Quick Chick. I know that, great fried chicken," Schneck said with a friendly smile even though he'd never even consider entering a Quick Chick, and he didn't eat fried food. "How many restaurants do you own, Mr. Jillian?"

"Four, and soon we'll add our fifth."

"How long have you been an owner of Quick Chick restaurants?"

"Got my first one about eleven years ago, and have been

adding them since."

"Who runs each Quick Chick?"

"Each one has a staff of workers, but a manager oversees each individual restaurant."

"In what capacity did you employ Roy Dillard?"

"He was one of our managers."

"Was…?"

"Yes. Well, I mean he was until he left his position a few weeks before this… this unfortunate business that happened on Super Bowl Sunday."

"What was his reason for quitting?"

"He didn't give a reason. Just said it was time to try something new."

Schneck then asked, "Were you glad to see him go?"

"No, not at all. I wanted him to stay."

"In what way did you try to dissuade him from quitting?"

"The usual. Offered him a salary raise and some additional benefits – that sort of thing."

"Would you rehire him as manager after the trial?"

"If he's found not guilty, and wants his job back, he can certainly have it."

"How would you rate him compared to your other managers?"

"He was one of the best managers we ever had."

"How long was he in your employ?"

"I think about six years or so. I'd have to look it up if you want exact dates."

"No, that won't be necessary. In those six years, did Roy Dillard do anything to lead you to believe he was unbalanced or insane?"

"Objection! The Witness is not a psychologist or a psychiatrist."

"Sustained."

"Mr. Jillian, while employed by you for approximately six years, did Roy Dillard miss many days of work?"

"No. In fact, aside from his scheduled vacations each year, in all that time I don't recall him ever taking more than an occasional sick day."

"Would you consider him conscientious?"

"Extremely so."

"Punctual?"

"Yes."

"Reliable?"

"Always."

"Even tempered?"

"Yes."

"Polite?"

"Yes, that's one of his best qualities."

"While in your employ, did Mr. Dillard ever act in a way that was erratic or unprofessional with regard to managing his Quick Chick restaurant responsibilities?"

"No, nothing. I wish all my managers were as careful and professional as Roy."

"Before hiring someone for the important position Mr. Dillard held, how do you screen candidates for potential managerial positions?"

"That's pretty standard. We check backgrounds and references from previous employers."

"Were you alerted to any problems or red flags?"

"We found no past problems. Nothing at all."

"Typically, how long do most managers last in your restaurants?"

"Usually a couple of years. The job can be stressful and the hours can be fairly long, especially if employees fail to show up or problems arise – then the manager has to fill in wherever he is needed. Roy had been with us longer than anyone so far."

"You said the job can be stressful. To what degree?"

"Very stressful. We've had electrical outages, burst water lines, employees not show up – sometimes several at a time, equipment malfunctions; customers have had fist fights in the dining areas... That kind of thing. And it all falls back on the manager to handle."

"And Mr. Dillard was able to cope with all these stressful problems?"

"Yes."

"Always?"

"Objection! Your Honor, the Witness has already answered

this question.

"Sustained. Move along, Mr. Schneck."

"Certainly, Your Honor. Mr. Jillian, has Mr. Dillard given you any reason to think he is unbalanced mentally or-"

"Objection again! Your Honor, you have ruled before on this same line of questioning!"

"Sustained *again,* Mr. Schneck, once more will not be tolerated. The jury is instructed to disregard this question."

"No further questions, Your Honor."

Judge Peters turned to the defense table, "Your witness Mr. Melzer. Do you wish to cross?"

Ken Melzer didn't bother to answer the judge. He was on his feet, and asking his first question while walking to the witness box. "Mr. Jillian, how often did you see Roy socially?"

"I'm not sure what you mean by socially?"

"I mean outside of work. Did you have dinner together often?"

"No."

"Ever?"

"No. Mr. Dillard was an employee of mine, and a fine one at that, but we were not friends, if that's what you are getting at."

"I see. So you haven't gone to, say... a ball game with him?"

"No."

"Ever take him out to lunch?"

"No."

"Has he been to your home?"

"No."

"Ever gone fishing with-"

"Objection! For goodness sakes, Your Honor, *fishing?* The Witness has answered each of these redundant questions. Do we have to suffer through this litany of silly activities until we are reduced to learning if Mr. Jillian and the Defendant dig worms together?"

The courtroom erupted in laughter. Judge Peters gaveled twice and said, "Mr. Schneck, a simple objection would have been sufficient. Sustained. Mr. Melzer, you've made your point."

Ken turned back from the judge and continued, "Is it accurate to say you know Roy in a professional capacity *only?*"

"Yes, that is accurate."

"And just to be perfectly clear, you have never associated with Roy outside of Quick Chick?"

"That is accurate also."

"Therefore, what Roy does, or doesn't do, in his private life away from his Quick Chick restaurant, is unknown to you?"

"I suppose..."

"Do you check up on your managers when they are not working, during their own time?"

"No, of course not."

"So, to sum this up, you know Roy as a manager, but not in any other capacity?"

"Yes, that's what I've already said."

"Has he got any hobbies that you are aware of, Mr. Jillian?"

"Not that I am aware of. I really wouldn't know."

"Do you know his friends?"

"I don't."

"Do you know if Roy *has* any friends?"

"I wouldn't know. It's none of my business."

"Mr. Jillian, how many hours a day did Roy work?"

"Eight, unless there was an emergency or a problem, then it might have been more."

"Since there are twenty-four hours in a day, and you have knowledge of eight of those hours, or one third of a day, is it accurate to say you only know about one third of Roy's life, and the other two thirds are completely unknown to you?"

"I never looked at it that way before, but yes, I suppose that is true."

"What Roy does, or doesn't do, for two thirds of his life is a total mystery-"

"Objection! Asked and answered, repetitious, cumulative. Need I go on?" Schneck shouted toward the judge.

Judge Peters glared at Schneck and responded crisply, "Overruled. Continue, Mr. Melzer."

"That's good enough," Ken said flippantly. "No further questions, Your Honor."

The judge turned to the Witness, "Thank you, Mr. Jillian. You may step down."

The Prosecution called Mr. Saltzman to the witness stand. He was helped along the main aisle by the Bailiff on one side and his silver-headed cane on the other. After being sworn in, Schneck went to work.

"Please state your name and occupation, Sir."

"My name is Isaac Francis Saltzman, and I am the proprietor of Saltzman's Fine Jewelry and Watches on Palm Drive in Ft. Lauderdale, Florida."

"Mr. Saltzman, may I ask how old you are?"

"You may. I am proud to say I'll be eighty next month."

"And how long have you been the proprietor of your fine store, Sir?"

"Since 1973. When I opened my door for the first time, this city was little more than a stopping point between Palm Beach and Miami."

"I'm sure it was. That's very interesting, Mr. Saltzman. Tell me Sir, during all these years how many times has your establishment been robbed?"

"Exactly once."

Attempting to seem in friendly conversation with this witness, Schneck absently asked, "And why do you think that is?"

Ken was about to object, but thought better of it. He didn't want to seem like he was interrupting an old gentleman or delaying the obvious.

"Well, that's an interesting question. I'd say it's because I run an honest business, and I am respected by the community. Of course," he added, "I've always maintained excellent security measures."

Wrong question, Winston Schneck realized. From the corner of his eye he saw that punk Melzer smirk at the old codger's answer. Don't get cocky now. Stick to the notes on the pad. "Yes, of course. When was the one robbery you mentioned?"

"Why, you know very well when it was."

"Please, Mr. Saltzman, the question is for the benefit of the jury and court record."

"Oh, yes. Certainly. The robbery was on Super Bowl Sunday of this year."

"Did you witness a shooting connected with the robbery?"

"Yes, you know I did."

"Mr. Saltzman, please tell the court who you saw shot and killed."

"Why, it was that nice delivery man from the deli… Chester."

"Chester Bentley?"

"Isn't that what I said?"

"What was your relationship to Chester?"

"Certainly, we were not friends. I was fond of him, and always found him to be an acquiescent Negro."

At this archaic and awkward remark, the courtroom twittered with uncomfortable chuckles. Smiling, Judge Peters very lightly gaveled the courtroom to silence.

"Mr. Saltzman, what do you remember after the shooting?"

"Not much, I'm afraid."

"You don't remember anything after the shooting?"

"No. The next thing I remember was waking up in a hospital bed. That was the next day. At least that is what I was told by a very nice nurse."

"Why were you taken to the hospital after the shooting?"

"I'm not sure. That nice nurse I told you about… she said I fainted. Or maybe it was a heart attack… or a stroke… or something like that. I forget what she told me exactly."

"Thank you, Mr. Saltzman. No further questions."

Ken knew there was nothing he could ask the old gentleman that would help the Defense. Schneck was solidly in control. If the jury disliked Dillard before, they despised him now. Schneck was so far ahead in this horse race that Ken could barely see his dust. Ken declined to cross-examine. With a decided limp, the frail proprietor of Saltzman's Fine Jewelry and Watches was helped out of the courtroom.

The Prosecution's third witness was called and sworn in.

"Please state your name and occupation."

"My name is Clarence Ballantyne. I work as a profiler for the Federal Bureau of Investigation."

"How long have you held this position with the FBI?"

"Nine years."

"Mr. Ballantyne, what qualifies you to be a profiler?"

"I hold a Master's Degree in Criminal Justice and a Ph.D. in

Psychology."

"Those are very impressive credentials, *Doctor* Ballantyne. Could you briefly explain to the court what a profiler does?"

"Sure, the short answer is that I study crime scenes for clues to determine what kind of person committed the crime, what his or her state of mind might have been at the time. That sort of thing."

"And this helps solve crimes?"

"Very often, yes."

"Dr. Ballantyne, without mentioning any names, of course, could you give an actual example of a crime – a murder perhaps – you helped solve by profiling?"

"Sure." Clarence Ballantyne paused in thought a moment. "Within the past year, I was called to a crime scene in which a young, single woman was stabbed to death. Without being overly graphic, let me just say she was stabbed multiple times after she was dead. This all happened in her living room, which the killer trashed. Upon investigating the scene, I found that none of the doors had been forced, and all of the windows were closed and locked with the air conditioning running normally. The victim was wearing an engagement ring, but not a wedding ring. There seemed to be little indication of any struggle. I could go on and on, but suffice it to say, from these few clues I was able to determine the killer knew the victim, and unsuspectingly she had let him into her house. From the fact that she became engaged only two days earlier, and that her fiancé was out of town, I had the detectives question her friends about any recent boyfriends who might feel jilted. By the following day we had a confession and a jealous boyfriend in custody."

"Fascinating, Dr. Ballantyne. But what about the multiple stab wounds you mentioned? What did that tell you?"

"We call that *overkill*. It almost always means the killer was emotionally attached to the victim in some way, and simply killing – in this case stabbing the victim – wasn't enough. Usually in these overkill murders, the killer is both satisfying his own desire for revenge, or making a statement... or both."

"You mentioned something about making a statement. Could you elaborate on that?"

"Sure. As an example, back in the Civil War time when there

was a great deal of animosity in certain parts of this country toward Blacks, mobs were known to lynch people of color for the slightest infraction of some law. After the hanging, and before being cut down, the bodies were set on fire and left to burn. This was an obvious indication that the mob wanted it known that the victim wasn't merely hanged for committing a crime, but for being the object or a symbol of their hatred. It was another form of the *overkill* I mentioned before."

"Dr. Ballantyne, have you seen the videos of the murder we are concerned with today?"

"I have.'

"From what you could see, was there any indication of *overkill*, or possibility of that *making a statement* you told us about?"

Melzer jumped to his feet. "Objection, Your Honor. This witness is now being asked to express an expert opinion, but he has not been tendered or accepted by the court to be an expert. I question whether a profiler is even qualified to be an expert. The science is questionable and lacks precision."

Instead of Schneck immediately responding, Roy Dillard stood up and addressed the judge. "Your Honor, I'm finding this testimony very interesting and I would like to hear the rest of it."

"Mr. Dillard," Judge Peters snapped angrily, "If you have anything to say, address it to your counsel. Do not interrupt these proceedings again."

"I apologize, Your Honor. May I speak with my attorney for a minute?"

"You may," Judge Peters responded less angrily.

After a very brief conversation with Roy, Ken addressed the judge. "Your Honor, at this time I will stipulate to this witness's expertise as a profiler and a psychologist and withdraw my previous objection."

After the court reporter read the question aloud for the Witness, Dr. Ballantyne replied, "I would say there was every possibility of both overkill and making a statement."

"Would you explain this to the jury?"

"The fact that it appeared the victim was induced to turn around to face the attacker-"

"Excuse me, Dr. Ballantyne, you said *induced* to turn and face the attacker. How was he induced?"

"It appeared quite clearly on the video that the attacker tapped the victim on the shoulder while pulling his weapon. The attacker shot the victim after he had turned to face him."

"How is this indicative of overkill or making a statement?"

"The attacker clearly wanted the victim to see him, to know who was going to kill him, before he pulled the trigger."

"I see. From your perspective as an FBI profiler, did the way in which the attacker shot the victim suggest anything to you?"

"Yes. The attacker could have simply shot his victim in the back or in the chest after he'd turned, but the attacker chose to place the barrel of the gun in his mouth before shooting him."

"In your experience, is the placement of the barrel in the victim's mouth significant, and if so, how?"

"Yes it is very significant. We have to delve into psychology a little to analyze these possibilities..."

"Please do. I believe you said you hold a Ph.D. in Psychology?"

"Yes, I do."

"Sorry for the interruption, please continue, Dr. Ballantyne."

"In homicides, killers focusing on the mouth can reveal many possibilities. Throughout history, the slain have had their mouths mutilated or perhaps stuffed with various substances – I'll leave the details to the imagination. For example, it is a known fact that at different times in history, in some cultures, a victim's tongue might be cut out to indicate he or she was a liar, a traitor who told secrets, or perhaps just a gossip. It could also be done as a warning to others to not say a particular thing. Then there is the sexual possibility." Clarence Ballantyne paused, "Do you want me to delve into this?"

"Yes, but if possible, not in any great detail."

"The mouth can be associated with sex in different ways. It can be used to merely *speak* about the subject, which in some places is a punishable offense, or the mouth can obviously be used for kissing or other sexual acts."

Winston Schneck rubbed his chin in thought and paced before the Witness. "Dr. Ballantyne, in your experience can the weapon of choice be indicative of the killer's desire or intention to make a

228

statement?"

"Certainly."

"How are you familiar with weapons, Dr. Ballantyne? Handguns in particular?"

"It's an integral part of many crime scenes. I am familiar with most types of handguns and their calibers. I have also studied ballistics with the FBI lab."

"Have you read the ballistics report on this case?"

"I have."

"Do you recall the caliber and bullet style used in this murder?"

"Yes. The revolver was a Smith & Wesson in .41 Magnum caliber. The ammunition was hollow point."

"In your experience, is this a common or uncommon gun and caliber?"

"Uncommon. The .41 Magnum is more of a sporting caliber, better suited for hunting and some kinds of competitive long range target shooting. But, even in these circles, it is definitely not a common revolver and caliber."

"Could you relate this to your ideas about *overkill* and *making a statement* at a murder scene?"

"Yes. There are a number of lesser calibers one could use in a point blank shooting that would be just as lethal as the .41 Magnum – without the huge muzzle blast, recoil, and well, *overkill*. A person who chooses such a devastating weapon is probably making the statement that simply killing the victim isn't enough."

"Assuming the killer did not know the victim in this particular case, what might this tell you?"

"The obvious might be race. The killer is white and the victim was black. But that is not the only possibility, just the most obvious."

"Thank you, Dr. Ballantyne. No further questions."

Ken Melzer put down his pen, picked up his legal pad, and stood up.

Judge Peters looked at Ken and said, "Your witness, Mr. Melzer."

Ken Melzer walked up to the witness stand and stood for a moment before Clarence Ballantyne. "Mr. Ballantyne, is psychology an exact science?"

"No, of course not."

"I appreciate your skills in helping to solve crimes, but is *profiling* an exact science?"

"No, it is not."

"Ever make mistakes?"

"How do you mean?"

"I mean, had you ever thought you had a perfect profile only to find out you were wrong?"

"There never is a *perfect profile.*"

"I see. Well then, have you ever thought you had a pretty good idea of what a suspect would be like, and then find you missed the mark by a mile?"

"Actually, not in the way you are intimating. I've been wrong before, sure, but I've never *missed the mark by a mile.*"

"How have you been wrong? You gave an example before of how you were right, so how about an example of how you were wrong about a profile."

"I'd have to think about that one."

"Take your time, Mr. Ballantyne; I'm sure you can come up with something."

Clarence Ballantyne looked down from the witness stand at the young assistant public defender before him. Initially he was angry at his impertinence, but after a moment's reflection, he allowed a smile to creep across his face. "I have one for you, Counselor. About two or maybe three years ago I worked up the profile of a killer who strangled a prostitute in a cheap motel. I measured the size of the finger bruises on the victim's neck and determined there was considerable power in the hands that had crushed the victim's windpipe. I recognized a number of other clues left in the room and on the victim – who was clothed, by the way – and pieced together a pretty good profile on the man who committed the strangulation. But it turns out I was totally wrong." Clarence Ballantyne stopped there, waiting to be prodded for more information.

"Can you tell us where you went wrong, Mr. Ballantyne?"

"Yes. As it turned out, I was right about everything except one very important point. It seems the killer was not a man at all."

"That sounds like a huge mistake to me. I would think that was one of the most crucial and basic aspects of any profile, wouldn't you?"

"Yes, you are right. But how was I to know the *woman* who strangled the prostitute in the motel had previously had a sex change? She started life as a male, but a year before the murder became a woman. I guess that was one of my biggest mistakes as an FBI profiler," Ballantyne replied snidely.

Ken Melzer was caught off guard. He turned from the Witness as if in thought, trying desperately for a question to divert this embarrassment. Before he could, Clarence Ballantyne spoke again, "I should add that by using the balance of the analysis, conclusions, and recommendations contained in my profile report, the police were able to arrest the murderer within a week."

"Mr. Ballantyne, you stated you viewed the videos. Do you know how many cameras were used?"

"I believe there were four – one outside by the entrance and three inside the store."

"Are you aware the cameras were not hidden in any way?"

"Yes, that is my understanding."

"Do you know why most stores have their cameras in full view?"

"They are used as a deterrent."

"Given this, in your professional opinion as both a psychologist and a profiler, isn't it unusual for someone knowing he is being recorded on video to commit a robbery and murder?"

"Yes, it is unusual."

"Speaking as a profiler, what might this tell you about such an individual?"

"Well, the obvious is that the individual might want to be recognized."

"Given your experience in past cases, what reasons might an individual have for wanting to be recognized?"

"Several actually. The individual might wish to be known for a crime, to gain notoriety, if you will. Or, he might want to be easily recognized and apprehended for the purpose of being punished."

"Very interesting. Speaking now as a psychologist, would a person behaving in this manner be considered normal?"

"No, not *normal* in common layman usage of the term."

"Could he be considered insane?"

"Possibly, but not conclusively without additional evidence or actions."

"Please explain how someone sane, someone who knows right from wrong, would want to be identified committing this kind of act."

"Many people who are perfectly sane and rational commit suicide. In this case it is possible the person in question had a death wish at the time. Some people wish to commit suicide quietly in private while others wish to attain the same result with publicity and fanfare. Of course, the end result is the same. It is not indicative or conclusive of insanity. Not by a long shot."

"But it is a possibility?"

"Objection! Your Honor, the Witness has already answered this question."

"Sustained."

"Mr. Ballantyne, you testified that the choice of weapon can speak to the killer's motives and state of mind. Is this accurate?"

"Yes, basically that is what I said."

"So, a person's choice of a powerful weapon over a less powerful weapon can be revealing?"

"Yes."

"What if it is the only weapon available?"

"I'm not sure I understand the question."

"Mr. Ballantyne, you seem fairly familiar with this case. Have you read the police reports?"

"Yes."

"According to the reports, did Roy Dillard purchase the Smith & Wesson handgun in question?"

"No. I believe it was stolen."

"So, fair to say that this particular gun, this revolver that everyone is making such a hullabaloo over, was in actuality an item of opportunity rather than an item of choice?"

Winston Schneck couldn't help the smile that appeared on his face. He thought, *gotcha you little twerp! I purposely avoided this hoping you were stupid enough to bring it up on your own. You took the shovel; now dig your own grave!*

"Actually, it was indeed an item of choice."

Ken recognized his mistake, but it was too late now. The question had been asked and Ballantyne continued, "According to the police report I read – perhaps there was a different one you read?" Ken thought that was snide, but he deserved it for being such an idiot. "There were three stolen handguns found in the Defendant's house along with some expensive watches and jewelry from a previous burglary. The guns consisted of a small pocket size .38 Special revolver, a Colt Python revolver in .357 Magnum, and the big nickel-plated Smith & Wesson Model 57 .41 Magnum. So, according to the police report you referred to, I'd say he had three weapons of *opportunity* and it appears he *chose* the biggest and most powerful. I'd also like to add that according to the report, ammunition for each gun was also found. So there really was a choice among the three weapons."

Ken knew he could ask if the report stated that the ammunition was reported stolen with the guns, but what would be the point? The damage had been done and he looked like a fool for bringing the subject to light. Struggling for a way to derail the momentum of the Prosecution and this witness, Ken asked, "Mr. Ballantyne, you say the direction of the gunshot can give a clue to the motives and state of mind of the shooter, correct?"

"Yes, that is what I said."

"As a psychologist, in your professional opinion, is it possible shooting a person in the mouth could be a random, unplanned action taken in the moment?"

"I suppose that is always a possibility."

"Is that because psychology is an inexact science and human motives are subjective?"

"Of course, but-"

"Assuming the inexactness of your profession," Ken Melzer interrupted, "couldn't the shooter be acting irrationally out of insanity?"

"That's always a possibility, however-"

"And couldn't he just as easily have shot the victim in the

eye?"

"I suppose so."

"The ear?"

"Under this line of reasoning, yes."

"The nose?"

"Again, yes."

"The throat?"

"Objection!" Schneck affected a tired and frustrated tone to say, "The Witness has answered this ridiculous line of questioning. Must we suffer through the listing of every piece of Chester's anatomy?"

"Sustained. Mr. Melzer, you've made your point. Let's move along."

"According to the police report, what was the finish on the three guns?"

"The small .38 Special had a blue finish. The .357 Colt Python was also blue, and the .41 Magnum was nickel finished."

"Mr. Ballantyne, I saw a recent National Geographic show on TV about ravens – you know, the bird variety – and it's interesting to note they are attracted to shiny objects. In fact, their nesting areas are often littered with bits of colored glass, plastic or reflective metal. I raise this point because I'm wondering if a person with no knowledge of firearms might choose one because–"

"Objection! The question assumes Mr. Dillard has no prior knowledge of firearms, a fact that has not been ascertained-"

Melzer's quick response cut Schneck off, "I was speaking hypothetically. I believe I asked 'if a person with no knowledge...' I did not refer to Mr. Dillard specifically."

"Overruled, continue with your questioning."

"Thank you, Your Honor." Ken turned back to the Witness. "Mr. Ballantyne, I was asking if a person with no knowledge of firearms might choose one that stood out because of size, or perhaps because it had a flashy plated appearance. Might he be consciously or unconsciously attracted to it because of its bright finish, much like a raven is attracted to a shiny piece of aluminum foil?"

"I'm not sure I would make comparisons between ravens and

234

people-"

"Perhaps not," Ken broke in, "but a simple affirmative or negative response would be appreciated."

"Yes. People are attracted to objects for many reasons."

"In your opinion, would you say children are often attracted to objects because of their unusual appearances?"

"Children are attracted to things for many reasons…"

"Mr. Ballantyne, please answer the question as asked. If you need to qualify your answer with an explanation, you may do so after you have answered the question."

"Yes, children are often attracted to the unusual."

"Is it true that people considered psychotic or insane are often considered *childlike?*"

The Witness laughed before answering, "Yes, Mr. Melzer. Among many, many things, some psychotic individuals *might* be compared to children."

Before Ken could think of another question, Ballantyne added, "Was this the simple answer you were hoping for?"

Judge Peters admonished, "The Witness will speak only to answer questions directly asked of him."

Ken ignored Ballantyne's comment, but he was sure the jury wouldn't. "No further questions."

"Does the Prosecution wish to re-direct?"

"No, Your Honor. It seems the Defense has made that totally unnecessary."

Judge Peters digested this last remark before saying, "Does the Prosecution wish to call another witness?"

"Just one more, Your Honor."

"Call your last witness."

"The Prosecution calls Dr. Ivan Donahue."

As with the previous witnesses, he was led to the witness stand by the Bailiff, and sworn in.

Schneck stood before his final witness. "Please state your name and occupation."

"My name is Doctor Ivan Donahue. I teach psychiatry at the University of South Florida College Of Medicine in Tampa."

"Dr. Donahue, may I ask your age?"

"I am fifty-eight."

"Have you always taught psychiatry?"

"No. I was a practicing psychiatrist for twenty-eight years. I've been teaching for three years."

"Did you have a private practice?"

"No, I was on the staff at Johns Hopkins Medical Center in Baltimore."

"For twenty-eight years?"

"Yes."

"What is the national ranking of the psychiatric division of Johns Hopkins?"

"Johns Hopkins psychiatric division is consistently ranked in the top ten of all hospitals in the United States."

"That's very impressive, but now you teach?"

"Yes, at the USF College of Medicine."

"May I ask why you left Johns Hopkins?"

"I like warm weather, and I like to play golf."

"I understand completely," Schneck chuckled, "I'm sure you earned that privilege."

"That's what my wife says."

"Then she and I are in complete agreement." Schneck noticed the grins on the faces of the jury. "Let me ask you this, Dr. Donahue: During your long career at Johns Hopkins, how many patients did you examine and treat?"

"I couldn't give you an exact number."

"Hundreds?"

"Certainly."

"Thousands?"

"I would assume at least a few thousand over a twenty-eight year period."

"How many articles on psychiatry have you published?"

Ivan Donahue answered, "I've published over fifty articles in a number of medical journals. I've also authored three books on psychiatry. I might add that two of my books are currently required reading at several medical schools in this country and abroad."

"And how many times have you testified as an expert witness, that is, before this case?"

"A number of times." The Witness smiled confidently and

added, "When you write medical books that are well received and used as standard references, the legal community takes notice. To be more specific, I've probably testified as an expert witness in at least a couple dozen trials."

"I'm sure that is true, but tell me, have you ever testified as an expert witness for the *Defense*?"

"Yes."

"For the Prosecution?"

"Oh sure. I have testified numerous times for both sides."

"After examining and evaluating a defendant, have you ever determined the individual in question to be legally *sane* and *with the capacity to know right from wrong*?"

"Yes, on many occasions."

"After examining and evaluating a defendant, have you ever determined the individual in question to be legally *insane* and *without the capacity to know right from wrong?* "

"Yes, as before, this has also been my testimony in a number of trials."

"Doctor, have you examined the Defendant, Roy Dillard."

"I have."

"I'd like to save significant time by stating to you that the Defendant has entered a plea of not guilty and has asserted the affirmative defense of insanity. In simple layman terms, this means the accused cannot be considered guilty if at the time the crime was committed, he was mentally incapacitated to the point of not being able to discern right from wrong. So, Dr. Donahue, rather than having me ask you several hours worth of detailed questions about your examination of Roy Dillard, perhaps you could explain to the jury your final psychiatric evaluation of the Defendant with regard to the legitimacy of the Defense's plea of insanity."

Melzer was on his feet. "Your Honor, Dr. Donahue has not been tendered as an expert witness and should not be allowed to offer opinion evidence at this time. The Defense has offered no evidence regarding Mr. Dillard's sanity or lack of sanity yet. Dr. Donahue's testimony would be appropriate for rebuttal purposes, if Mr. Dillard presents evidence of his lack of sanity at the time of the crime."

As Judge Peters looked over at Schneck waiting for his response, Roy Dillard got Melzer's attention and whispered in not so soft a voice, "Let him testify to whatever he wants. There's no need to prolong this. It's not going to matter anyway."

As Schneck began to reply, Melzer addressed the judge, "Your Honor, I withdraw my objection to Dr. Donahue's testimony."

Judge Peters looked at Melzer both with surprise and a bit of confusion. "Then I assume, Mr. Melzer, that you are stipulating to Dr. Donahue as an expert in psychiatry?"

"Yes, Your Honor. We so stipulate."

"You may proceed, Mr. Schneck," Judge Peters said as he settled back into his swivel leather chair and poured coffee into his mug.

Schneck turned to his witness. "Dr. Donahue, please describe to the jury what your findings were regarding your evaluation of Roy Dillard."

"I can surely do that." Dr. Donahue shifted in his seat and leaned toward the microphone. "I thoroughly examined Mr. Dillard over several sessions. I can say with considerable confidence that in my opinion Mr. Dillard does not display characteristics of an individual who would be psychotic to the extent of not knowing right from wrong. I believe this to be accurate for the present, and within a reasonable degree of medical certainty, would hold true regarding the time of the criminal act for which he is charged – I believe that was only several months ago. I will also say again in my opinion, based on years of similar interviews and examinations, that Mr. Dillard tries to be manipulative through acting out behaviors with which he wishes to be identified. Regarding defendants in criminal cases, this is not that uncommon. Actually, it shows cognitive awareness and a clear sense of the *real* versus the *un*-real or fantasy."

Schneck paused for a moment and took a formal stance in front of Dr. Donahue, careful not to block the jury's view of his witness. "Dr. Donahue, although I believe your testimony has been clear, I must ask this question more formally. Given your years of experience practicing and teaching psychiatry, and having examined Roy Dillard personally, do you have an opinion within a reasonable degree of medical certainty as to whether Roy Dillard was capable of discerning right from wrong and understanding the consequences of his actions at the time of the murder of Chester Bentley?"

"Yes, I do."

"Please tell us what that opinion is."

Dr. Donahue looked over to the jury and spoke directly to the jurors. "It is my opinion that at the time of the murder of Chester Bentley, Roy Dillard understood the difference between right and wrong and could appreciate the consequences of his actions."

"Thank you Doctor." Schneck glanced toward the jury box and said, "No further questions," and returned to his table.

Hank Parnell was frantically scribbling on a piece of lined yellow paper torn from a legal pad. As the Judge was asking if the Defense wished to cross-examine the Witness, Hank pushed the scrap passed Dillard to Ken Melzer who was beginning to stand. Ken glanced down and read: *YOU'RE OVER YOUR HEAD HERE. NOTHING TO GAIN. LET THIS ONE GO!*

"No questions, Your Honor."

Winston Schneck rose to his feet. "If it pleases the court, the Prosecution feels calling more witnesses would be an exercise in redundancy. In respect for this court and for the jury's time and patience, the Prosecution rests."

Judge Peters looked at his watch and took a sip from his coffee mug. "In that case, we'll adjourn for the day. The Defense may call its first witness tomorrow morning at nine o'clock." He lightly struck his gavel, stood up, turned his back to the courtroom, and left.

THIRTY

With his elbows on the table and fists under his chin to support his head, Ken Melzer sat with eyes closed in his usual place at their small kitchen table.

"Honey, you really need to eat something."

"I know, but if I did, it would probably come right back up."

Charlene glanced across the table at her husband. He looked pale and gaunt. "You have to keep your strength up. You aren't sleeping much, and with so little food you won't be able to think straight."

As if in a daze, Ken looked down at the table. He mumbled to his wife, "Do you think I could use that as an excuse for my performance today? I could tell Hank it's really not my fault I screwed up so badly. You see, I'm not eating or sleeping enough these days-"

"Stop it! I won't have you talking this way!"

Ken broke his trancelike pose and stared back at Charlene. "How should I be talking?"

"For Christ's sake Ken! Get your tail out from between your legs and act like a goddamn man!"

"Char, please-"

"No, I'll talk any way I want and say anything I want! And I'll tell you something else. Your brother Matthew calling right before the start of today's proceedings sucked. What's wrong with him?"

"Char, he's my brother-"

"And that doesn't give him the right to interrupt your train of thought before you're to appear in court. His problem, and yours by proxy, is that he and his other brother, Mark, are both products of Midwest, provincial, small-town small-mindedness."

"That's not really fair."

"Fair or not, it's fact and you know it. At least you had the good sense, and balls I might add, to get the hell out of there before it smothered you to death."

"Can we change the subject please, Charlene?"

"Sure, I'll change the topic. Let me tell you something else. You need to pick your head up and stand proud."

Ken removed his elbows from the table and faced his angered wife. "Stand proud? Proud of what?"

"Look Ken, Darling, I come from a family of lawyers. You may have gone to law school, but I've been around attorneys and courthouses, heard details of about a billion cases, and watched trials my whole life. And one thing I know for damn sure is some cases are winners and some are the pits. But your job as a public defender doesn't afford you the privilege of picking and choosing what cases you'll take. In private practice, yeah sure, but not as a PD. So some cases you glide through, and some you stumble through. You do the best you can, and if that's good enough, great. And if it isn't, so what? You do what you can and that's it! That's what you're paid for and no more! Enough of this self-pity, and agonizing over some low-life, possibly psychotic, killer and thief as if he were some long lost cousin you are trying to save."

Ken sat up straighter, "And my blunders today? What about that?"

"I'll tell you about that. Listen Ken, there's an old expression, *when you got nothin', you got nothin' to lose.* You were grabbing at straws. That's all you can do at this stage. You were given nothing to work with by an uncooperative client, so you did what you could hoping to hit on something, maybe create some doubt in a juror's head. And you hit on a couple of ideas and missed on a couple."

Across their small table the Melzers stared at each other. "Do you really think I might have created some doubt?"

"Perhaps. The stuff about only a crazy person would do what Dillard did knowing he was being filmed by four cameras, that was good. It certainly makes me doubt his sanity. Is it enough to show, as the law requires, he didn't know right from wrong? I doubt it, but maybe he didn't. See, I just said *doubt.*" Charlene laughed and reached across the table taking her husband's cold hand. "C'mon Honey, lighten up. I think you showed tremendous resourcefulness today. You had to think fast on your feet, and that's not easy. I was impressed with the way you cross-examined that jerk, Ballantyne. What a pompous asshole he was!"

"Yeah, he was kind of an ass…"

"I also liked the way you called him *Mister* Ballantyne after that snake, Schneck, kept calling him *Doctor* as if he was an MD or we were on a college campus. I also thought you looked particularly sharp when you reinforced to the jury that both profiling and psychology are inexact sciences. That brought his intimidation factor down a few notches in the minds of the jurors – jurors who tend to be awed by supposed *expert* witnesses."

"Thank you, Char. You always know the right things to say. What would I do without you?"

"Without me, you'd probably be living out of the back seat of your Honda and drinking cheap wine from a paper bag."

Charlene was the first to leave her kitchen chair. They met somewhere between their previous seats and embraced. "I do need you so," Ken whispered in her ear while being aware of the faint citrus scent of her hair.

"I know you do, Darling. And I need you too."

For a full minute they stood tightly in each other's arms, perhaps swaying ever so slightly, until Charlene broke away. "Now sit and listen," she insisted kindly. "Tomorrow you are going to call your first witness. And he's not going to win this case for you. Then you are going to call the shrink, and he's not going to win this case for you either. Lastly, you'll call Dillard himself to the stand, and I have no idea what that will bring… and neither do you for that matter. But, I tell you this, Ken Melzer, by tomorrow night, the next day at the latest, your role in this awful business will be over. You'll have played your part to the best of your ability, because that's your job. And then it's in the hands of the jury. Whatever they decide, and whatever happens after that, is of little consequence to you or to *us*. Roy Dillard will leave our lives for good, thank God. And I don't want to hear his name spoken ever again. Hank Parnell gave you this case because that's what Dillard wanted, and he thought it would be a good learning experience for you. And Hank was right. It has been, but that's all it's been. So accept it at that, a learning experience. If there was even a rat's ass of a chance he was not guilty, you'd never have been allowed near this case. You got it mainly because it was a slam dunk for the Prosecution."

Ken stared at Charlene and wanted to smile, but didn't. "You're right. You're always right. When this is over in a day, maybe two, we move on. We concentrate on us and our lives, our life together."

Charlene reached her hand to him and stood. "It's getting late. You may be tired, but I'm not. So you better get in that bedroom and give me something to help me sleep. And then afterward, you can sneak out to the kitchen and grab a snack before you get some sleep too. Got that, Mister?"

"Got it," Ken said with a grin.

Charlene led her husband to their bedroom, unbuttoning her blouse along the way.

THIRTY-ONE

Ken Melzer and Hank Parnell shared their usual table at Starbucks. Hank looked at his watch, "Eight o'clock. One hour 'til fun time."

Ken let out a chuckle, "Yup, should be lots of fun."

"Don't worry. You'll call two witnesses this morning, we'll break for lunch, and after that you can put your pal Dillard on the stand. Then after a couple of closing arguments, say *sayonara* to this whole ridiculous trial."

"That last part sounds awfully good to me."

"To me too," Hank laughed. "And once the jury returns with its guilty verdict and they haul Dillard back to jail, you and Charlene can take a couple of well deserved weeks off together. I'll handle the penalty phase."

"I'm liking the sound of that already."

"I thought you would." Hank looked at his watch again. "We better head to the courthouse. And remember Ken, try to relax and just do what needs to be done. Don't expect any miracles today. Get this over with, and then put it behind you for good."

Standing, Ken agreed, "Count on it."

Every seat in the courtroom was filled. Ken spotted Charlene a few rows behind the defense table. She put two fingers to her lips then subtly pointed them at her husband.

He briefly smiled in return.

"All rise…"

Judge Peters addressed the three sitting at the defense table. "Is the Defense prepared to call its first witness?"

Ken stood, "Yes, Your Honor."

"You may proceed."

"Thank you. The Defense calls Jerome Cleaver."

A tall and thin African-American man sauntered down the aisle a few feet in front of the trailing bailiff. He wore a pullover black sweatshirt with the hood hanging freely behind his neck. His jeans were baggy and slung obviously low. If not for the loose fitting sweatshirt that extended below his belt, this new witness might have revealed to the courtroom his boxers... or worse. He also wore a cap with the brim turned backwards. Ken Melzer read the hastily scribbled note slid across the table to him from Hank Parnell. *So much for your jacket and tie suggestion.* The Bailiff motioned for Jerome Cleaver to take the seat in the witness stand, but before being sworn in Judge Peters said, "Sir, as a show of respect for this court, and as a personal favor to me, please remove your cap." Jerome did as he was asked. "Thank you. Bailiff, you may swear in this witness."

Once sworn, Ken Melzer approached the podium. "Please state your name and occupation."

"My name is J. Eldridge Cleaver and I work at Quick Chick." Before Ken could begin his examination, his witness added, "But you can call me Jerome."

Judge Peters stifled a smile and was about to tap the courtroom back to silence, but thought better of it, and let the hammer hang in midair for a few seconds before placing it back on his desk.

"Okay, Jerome. What is your age?"

"I'm twenty."

"And how long have you worked at the Quick Chick restaurant?"

"About a year and a half, maybe a little more."

"Jerome, can you tell me who the manager is that you work for at Quick Chick?"

"Yeah sure, that would be Mr. Hernandez."

Ken was aware of Schneck's grin as he shook his head in amusement. "Jerome, who was your boss *before* Mr. Hernandez took over."

"Oh yeah, that's him sitting right there at that table next to the other guy." J. Eldridge Cleaver pointed, and without thinking, Ken turned back to his table. Over his shoulder he heard, "Hey, Mr. Dillard."

This time Judge Peters did use his gavel. "The Witness will speak only when asked a question, and then only to answer the question."

"Thank you, Your Honor." Ken began again, "Jerome, for how long was Mr. Dillard your boss?"

"A year or maybe a little longer."

"During the time Roy Dillard was manager at the Quick Chick, what would you say was the racial makeup of the restaurant?"

"Hard to say as we had all kinds of people come in to eat."

"No, Jerome, I should have been more specific. I'm referring to the employees, you know, the people who worked there."

"Oh, right. Well there were some Cubans or Mexicans or something, there were a few Whites, and the rest were sisters and bros."

"By *sisters and bros*, do you mean African Americans?"

"Well yeah, what else could I mean?"

"Sorry, I should have known." Ken paused for a few seconds before asking, "Did Roy treat everyone who worked at Quick Chick equally?"

"Nope, he didn't."

Flustered, Ken had to continue, "Can you explain that?"

"Sure. The people who worked there the longest made more money than the new people, and the counter people made more money than the people who cleaned up. That ain't equal, but it makes sense, I guess."

"I suppose it does." Ken took a breath and was relieved to be able to ask, "Jerome, I'd like you to tell us how Roy treated everyone with regard to race."

"Oh, I see what you're getting at. Yeah, sure. I don't think he cared what color anyone was – employee or customer. Maybe except for once. Wanna know about that?"

Ken had no choice. "Sure, Jerome, you can tell us."

"There was this girl who worked the counter for a while. This bitch was fine!"

Judge Peters banged his gavel hard, "Mr. Cleaver, removing your cap was a favor to me, and I'd like to ask one more favor-"

"Sure," Jerome interrupted.

"Please refrain from the use of any profanity in this court."

"Sorry, I'll try to be careful."

"Thank you. Mr. Melzer, you may continue."

246

"Jerome, you were describing… excuse me, you were *telling* us about an instance where Roy behaved differently to one particular employee…"

"Right. Well this bi-, sorry, this girl, she named Amber or something, anyway she had long blonde hair and was… well she looked awfully young and fine, umm, umm, umm, you know?"

"Jerome, could you just explain how Roy behaved toward her that was different from the way he behaved toward the other workers?"

"Well, he was extra nice to her, you know, like kinda too polite, and always asking if there was maybe anything she needed help with. You know, I think he liked her, and maybe it showed too much. He didn't ask me if I needed extra help." Jerome let out a loud laugh. "I wouldn't want no extra help anyway."

"I see. Well, aside from Amber, did Roy Dillard treat anyone special or differently?"

"Nah, just her. And that didn't last very long, 'cause she got a job somewhere else."

"Because of Roy?"

"No, she just got a better job makin' more money."

"Jerome, I don't want to sound disrespectful, but I have to ask this. Did Roy ever use the 'N' word?"

Again Jerome laughed long and loud, "Hell no!" He quickly looked to Judge Peters, "Sorry, I mean, no he didn't ever use it. Only brothers can call each other 'Nigga.'"

"By *brothers* do you mean African-American men?"

"Yeah, course."

"Did you ever hear him say the word?"

"No."

"Jerome, did he allow the *brothers* to use the word?"

Jerome laughed again, "It sounds funny when you say *brothers,*" and he continued to laugh.

"Can you please just answer the question?"

"Oh yeah. No, Mr. Dillard told us we could say whatever we wanted on the street or in the hood, but in his restaurant we had to watch what we said. No bad words, and no calling no one 'Nigga' and such."

"How Did Roy treat the Hispanics with regard to how he

treated the Whites and the African-Americans?"

"He treated them just fine. He even spoke a little Spanish to them. They seemed to like that."

"Jerome, did your boss, Mr. Dillard... did he ever have an opportunity to help you outside of work?"

"Oh yeah, you mean what we talked about before?"

Judge Peters let the mirth die down on its own. Schneck turned to the jury, smiled and shrugged. He knew he could object to these leading questions, but this was too entertaining to interrupt.

Ken plodded on. "Can you answer the question, Jerome?"

"Yeah, once when I had to work late helping to clean up-"

"Sorry to stop you, but what was *late*?"

"After midnight, I guess."

"Fine, continue please."

"So this time, I'm mopping the floors and shit... I mean we had some *stuff* spill and I was mopping and cleaning. Anyway, it was late, and my ride never showed up, so Mr. Dillard said he'd drive me home. And like, I told him that might not be too cool, him being a white guy and all, 'cause where I live is all black, you know? I said it was late and he might not want to be driving around in my hood."

"What did Mr. Dillard say to that?"

"He said it was okay. He said he didn't care, that he'd drive me home anyway."

"And did he?"

"Yeah, he did."

"Anything happen when he got to your neighborhood and dropped you off?"

"Yeah, there were some bangers hangin' out near where I live, and they looked like they might cause trouble for Mr. Dillard when I got out of his car. But I told them he was cool, and they left him alone."

"Thank you, Jerome. No further questions."

"Mr. Schneck, your witness, if you wish to cross."

"Thank you, Your Honor."

Schneck walked in front of the Witness. "J. Eldridge Cleaver?"

"Yes, sir."

"Do you know where the Defendant lives?"

"Who?"

"Sorry. Mr. Dillard. Do you know where Mr. Dillard lives?"

"No. How would I know that?"

"I thought perhaps you hung out there with him. Am I wrong?"

"Yeah, you wrong. We never hung out."

"Ever see him with his friends?"

"No. I only saw him in Quick Chick, you know, when I was workin'."

"So you don't know if he called anyone 'Nigger' outside of the Quick Chick."

"Mr. Dillard? Nah," and Jerome laughed again. "He never call nobody Nigga."

"How would you know what he calls people outside Quick Chick if you only saw him while you were working in the restaurant?"

"'Cause Mr. Dillard, he never use that word."

"Do you mean he never used the word in the restaurant, but you don't really know if he called anyone 'Nigger' outside the Quick Chick-"

"Objection! The Witness has answered this."

"Overruled. The Witness will answer the question."

Jerome looked at the judge. "Me?"

"Yes, answer the question please."

"I guess I don't know how he talked outside of work, but Mr. Dillard, he never…"

Ken thought this was some kind of courtroom-witness déjà vu. First he does this to Schneck's witness, Nick Jillian, and now Schneck's doing it to the Defense's only character witness, Jerome Cleaver. So be it. *Touché,* Schneck.

"Mr. Cleaver, on the night Mr. Dillard drove you home, did he appear afraid to drive into your neighborhood?"

"No. He said it was a'right with him."

"Not afraid?"

"No."

"Apprehensive maybe?"

"I don't know what that mean."

"Was he tense or more cautious than usual?"

"Nah, he was cool."

"Were you surprised at him being so *cool*?"

"I guess."

"Do you think he was not fearful or *apprehensive* driving after midnight into a very dangerous black area because he might have had a gun in the car?"

"Objection! Objection! Your Honor, this is outrageous, the prosecution is-"

"I agree with you, Mr. Melzer. Sustained! The jury will disregard that last question."

"I'm sorry, Your Honor. No further questions for *Mr. J. Eldridge Cleaver.*"

The Defense called their last witness of the morning. Ken watched Dr. Conroy walk to the witness stand, and noticed for the first time he leaned slightly left, with one shoulder dipped lower than the other. He wore pale slacks and a navy jacket with a blue shirt and a yellow tie. After being sworn in, Ken went to work.

"State your name and occupation please."

"My name is Charles Conroy and I am a psychiatrist."

"*Doctor* Conroy?"

"Yes."

"And Dr. Conroy, how long have you been a practicing psychiatrist?"

"Not quite fifty years."

"That's a long time. Has this been your only occupation?"

"Yes. I've been enthralled with the whole subject of the brain and human behavior since... well since I was a young man."

"I'm sure it's been very rewarding on a number of levels."

"It has been indeed."

"Dr. Conroy, have you examined the Defendant, Roy Dillard?"

"Yes, I have, quite a number of times."

"Can you describe his attitude or demeanor during your examinations?"

Conroy smiled and thoughtfully replied, "Let's say he was not always cooperative."

"Could you explain what you mean by *not always?*"

"Sure. Mr. Dillard has mood swings. At times he was forthcoming and compliant, while at other times he was adversarial, even combative and uncommunicative. His responses to my questions were often inappropriate, not normal."

"Please explain *normal?*"

"Normal is a relative term. Let me put it this way. If you suddenly became my patient, Mr. Melzer, I believe your demeanor would be fairly predictable, with communication generally open. I think that is what most reasonable people mean by the term *normal.* With regard to Roy, I never knew how he would receive me. At times he was cooperative and openly revealing. At other times he seemed like a different person altogether – someone who was edgy and looking for an argument. So getting back to your original question concerning Roy's *normalcy,* I would have to conclude that compared to a well-adjusted and well-balanced personality, Roy was not normal."

"Dr. Conroy, did Roy relate anything to you regarding his past that might have a bearing on his present psychosis?"

"Objection!" Schneck was on his feet. "Your Honor, aside from yet another leading question, this calls for a conclusion; assumes facts not in evidence."

"Objection sustained."

Ken responded, "Your Honor, I would like to tender Dr. Conroy as an expert in the field of psychiatry. He has testified to being a practicing psychiatrist for nearly fifty years." Looking directly at Schneck, Ken continued, "Unless Mr. Schneck would care to voire dire Dr. Conroy as to his qualifications or for some reason challenge my calling Dr. Conroy to testify before this jury, perhaps Mr. Schneck would stipulate to Dr. Conroy's qualifications as an expert in psychiatry."

Schneck pointedly returned Ken's stare and turned smiling toward Judge Peters. A moment later he offered the same smile to the jury and replied, "I have no desire to keep any testimony that may shed light on this case from the jury. I'll stipulate to Dr.

Conroy testifying as an expert and let the jury decide for themselves as to his credibility." Schneck had to admire this kid Melzer for asking a leading question he knew would be objected to and sustained by the judge. The jury heard 'psychosis' and the suggestion had been aired. Perhaps Melzer had some potential brains and tenacity after all... but for now better pay attention to the old quack on the stand.

Ken began again, "Dr. Conroy, what, if anything, did Roy reveal to you that influenced and ultimately solidified your final determination of his mental condition?"

"Well, it seems Roy has a history of drug abuse which-"

"Excuse me, Doctor, what kind of drugs are we talking here? Marijuana? Cocaine?"

Conroy chuckled softly, "Not hardly. No, Roy was a frequent user of hallucinogenic drugs."

"Such as..."

For effect, Conroy paused by taking a breath between the words he spoke. "LSD. Peyote. Mescaline. Psilocybin mushrooms."

"When did this abuse occur, Doctor?"

"When he was in college. About a dozen or more years ago. I would have the exact time in my notes."

"That won't be necessary, unless you feel specific dates are important."

"No. Suffice it to say, he had a bad time of it, and that can have residual effects even this many years later."

"Let's start with college years. What effect did drugs have on Roy?"

"Roy used these hallucinogenic drugs with such frequency he was often overlapping them."

"Overlapping?"

"By *overlapping*, I mean taking a different drug before the previous one had worn off. This practice can be physically as well as mentally or psychologically dangerous, and potentially damaging."

"Was his drug usage damaging?"

"I believe Roy kept himself in a drug-induced state somewhere between reality and, well, somewhere else – somewhere unreal –

perhaps fantasy, perhaps hallucinatory, perhaps dreamlike."

"From your examination of Roy and his revelations about his past, do you believe during that time in his life that he was able to function as a normal and productive individual?"

"No, he was not able to function as you describe."

"What happened to him immediately after this time in his life?"

"Roy told me he dropped out of college temporarily. He gave up drugs completely, and after a while returned to college, and graduated some years later."

"You briefly stated something about *residual effects* from extended drug use. Have residual effects affected Roy over the years, and if so, can you explain how it has affected him?"

"Yes. Roy revealed that he suffered migraines and intense nightmares after he quit drugs. I believe they continue to the present time. He also has chronic mood swings."

"Yet, Dr. Conroy, he was able to hold a job requiring responsibility and punctuality?"

"Yes. This is a bit unusual, but not unheard of. Many people suffering severely from varied types of psychosis can function for long periods of time before showing signs of their illness."

"Can someone suffering from a psychosis, as you determined Roy Dillard clearly is, continue hiding his or her illness indefinitely?"

"It might be possible, but it is highly unlikely."

"In your nearly fifty years of practicing psychiatry, have you known anyone similarly ill to lead a normal life without at some point having, shall we say, issues?"

"*Issues* is another nebulous term that is overused. Let me state that I believe Roy holds back his symptoms. He actually has learned to control them and appear as sane as anyone, but deep down, he is a ticking time bomb that-"

"A time bomb?" Ken interrupted.

"For lack of a better term, yes. Not that he will necessarily explode in a violent way, but he would certainly have episodes of less than lucid reality."

"You're losing me there, Doctor. Can you explain what you mean when you state Roy *would certainly have episodes of less than lucid reality?*

"In simple terms it means that Roy will have, and has had, breaks with reality."

"As in not knowing where he is?"

"Yes, perhaps."

"As in not knowing who he is?"

"Yes, that too is possible."

"How about not being able to tell what is real from what is not... like a dream or fantasy?"

"Yes, this is exactly what I am referring to. It would be hard to predict, but any of those you mentioned are real possibilities, even probabilities."

"How 'bout not knowing right from wrong during a time when he has had a break from reality?"

"Yes. If the episode was severe enough, combined with the intense pain of a migraine headache, he could be functioning in a world of his own making."

"Like a fantasy or make-believe world?"

"Yes, exactly."

"You are certain of this?"

"As certain as I can be. *Certainty* is always difficult to define in dealing with the human mind. But I can tell you that I've seen many, many patients over the years that would fall into this same category. And I believe Roy Dillard would be one of them."

"Is there a name for Roy's illness?

"It would fall under the widely used general term schizophrenia."

"A split personality?"

"Ah, split personality..." Conroy smiled confidently and slightly shook his head slowly from side to side before speaking again. "Another overused term, a cliché actually. Let me address this by saying that I used *schizophrenia* and this is probably the term you mean." He quickly added, "And that is a misunderstood term too. It can mean multiple personalities, but that is actually an extremely rare situation. In its simplest definition, schizophrenia is a mental disorder in which a person breaks with reality. Usually the individual is unaware of when such an episode occurs, or even as a constant condition. The real and the unreal coalesce. It can be a chief cause of suicide actually. I've known schizophrenics to be so afraid of these episodes that in times of lucidity, they plan and carry out their own demise. It's tragic for them and their loved ones."

"Dr. Conroy, from your examination and evaluation of Roy Dillard would you conclude he is suicidal?"

"There is that distinct possibility. Roy is a very conflicted and complicated young man with personality disorders that..."

Ken Melzer kept Dr. Charles Conroy on the stand for an hour and fifty-three minutes. At the end of that time it had been established – or at least the possibility had been established – that Roy Dillard suffers migraines and insomnia, has past and present suicidal tendencies, shows manic depressive behavioral patterns, revealed a periodic bipolar personality, was severely damaged by past drug abuse which now induces episodic schizophrenia, deals with passive-aggressive mood swings, and at any given time may or may not know right from wrong.

Judge Peters asked Winston Schneck if he would prefer to break for an early lunch.

"This shouldn't take too long, Your Honor. I'm sure I can clear this up before lunch and we can dismiss the Witness."

A little surprised at the prosecutor's flippancy, Judge Peters replied, "Very well then, you may proceed with your cross."

Winston Schneck walked to the stand and looked directly at the Witness for an uncomfortably long moment. "Dr. Conroy, let's start with the Defendant's drug use in college. Can you state in which mental institution the Defendant was admitted?"

"I never said he was in a mental institution."

"Was he?"

"Not to my knowledge."

"Can you state how long the Defendant was under a psychiatrist's care?"

"I'm not sure he was under a psychiatrist's care."

"Maybe a *psychologist's* care?"

"I don't know that he saw a psychologist during this time. I do know he spoke with a counselor provided by the university."

"Didn't the billing records reveal names of psychiatrists or psychologists under whom the Defendant sought care?"

"There were no billing records. This was a free service provided by the university."

"From whom exactly did the Defendant receive psychiatric treatment during this time?"

"Counselors were provided by the university."

"Counselors?"

"Yes."

"With medical degrees like yours? Or perhaps counselors with advanced degrees in psychology?"

"I wouldn't know. Records were not kept. The counselors were volunteers."

"Typically, in your experience, Dr. Conroy, who are volunteer counselors on college campuses?"

Conroy shifted uneasily in his seat, "They can certainly be medical professionals or other concerned individuals."

"Other concerned individuals? Could I volunteer to be a counselor?"

"You seem to have a good deal of life's experience, so I suppose you would be accepted."

"I'm a lawyer, yet I could be a counselor?"

"Objection! The Witness has answered the question."

"Sustained."

"If there were no billing records, and the university didn't maintain files, how did you learn about the Defendant's drug use and *supposed* mental illness?"

"From Roy himself."

"The Defendant told you the information about this time in his life… to which you have testified?"

"Yes."

"And you believed him?"

"I had no reason not to."

"I've heard mental patients often lie and try to manipulate other people. Is this true?"

"That is a broad statement that could apply to anyone, not just a mental patient."

"Thank you, Dr. Conroy. My point exactly. Yet you believed what the Defendant told you?"

"Objection! Again the Witness has answered this question."

"Overruled. The Witness will answer the question."

"Yes, I believed what Roy told me because I based my evaluation-"

"You have answered my question," Schneck interrupted and quickly asked, "You stated the Defendant could be argumentative, even combative. Is that right?"

"Among a number of things, yes."

"Does that make him insane?"

"Of course not. But that combined with-"

"Did the Defendant appear to understand your intentions during your examinations and interviews?"

"Yes."

"And what were your intentions?"

"As a physician, my intent was to evaluate Roy, to ascertain his mental condition, his state of mind, as it relates to this case."

"As a physician are you also trying to treat or help the Defendant in any way?"

"Yes. As a physician it is always my desire to help people, but I was retained solely to examine and evaluate Roy, not to treat him. If my evaluation helps him, then so much the better."

"You agreed with the statement that you tried to help him… in any way you could?"

"Objection!"

"Sustained."

"Dr. Conroy, are you currently a practicing psychiatrist?"

"Yes."

"Do you run an active private practice, or are you practicing psychiatry through a hospital?"

"I no longer maintain an office, but I do see patients."

"How many patients do you have at the present time?"

"Only the few who I've been treating for a number of years."

"More than twenty?"

"No, less."

"Ten?"

"I still see three or four long-time patients. They rely on me, and I won't abandon them."

"So, you are retired?"

"Semi-retired."

"May I ask how old you are, Dr. Conroy?"

"A week from today I'll be seventy-seven."

"Under your semi-retirement, do you evaluate many defendants for courtroom testimony?"

"Yes, and obviously this is one of them."

"In the last four years, do you know how many examinations like this one you have performed?"

"A number, for sure."

"More than ten?"

"Yes."

"Twenty?"

"At least."

"How many of these were requested by the State's Attorney's office, the prosecutor's office?"

"I'm not sure."

"Half of them?"

"No."

"Less than half?"

"I'm not sure if any were requested by the prosecutor's office."

"Is it your testimony that you only testify on behalf of the Defense?"

"It is generally defense attorneys who have retained my services."

"So you have not testified for the Prosecution in the last couple of years. Is that accurate?"

"That office has not requested my services."

"So to be perfectly clear, you have never been hired by the State's Attorney's Office. Is that correct?"

"Yes."

"In those numerous cases in which you testified, how many of the defendants that you examined were, in your opinion, deemed mentally ill?"

"That is a very difficult question to answer using *mentally ill* as your stated parameter. That is far too general a layman's term to-"

"Dr. Conroy, please answer this. How many of the defendants that you examined for the Defense did you deem to be sane, and either fit to stand trial or be sane enough to be treated as normal defendants for their alleged crimes?"

"I'm not sure exactly. Each patient is a case study unto himself or herself-"

"Were there any?"

Dr. Conroy hesitated before answering, "Probably not."

"All crazy? All insane? None knowing right from wrong?"

"Those are again general terms-"

"Let me ask you this. Were you living in the state of Texas in 1972?"

Ken Melzer felt a sickening dread sink heavily to the pit of his stomach. He knew Conroy was a poor witness, but this could be a killing blow. He braced himself for the next inevitable questions.

"Yes, I lived in Texas for a number of years in the late 1960s and early 1970s."

"Were you a practicing psychiatrist at that time?"

"Yes."

"Did you belong to an organization called *Doctors Against the Death Penalty*?"

"Yes."

"Were you a founding member?"

"Yes."

"In 1972 were you the president of *Doctors Against the Death Penalty*?"

"Yes."

"On July 4th of 1972 did you personally organize a demonstration outside the courthouse in Houston?"

"I was not alone in organizing the demonstration."

"But you were the leader, the elected president of the organization?"

"Yes."

"Dr. Conroy, do you believe in the death penalty?"

"Objection! Your Honor, this has nothing to do with Dr. Conroy's professional evaluation of Mr. Dillard."

Melzer saw Schneck produce that annoying phony smile and respond, "Your Honor, it has everything to do with Dr. Conroy's evaluation of the Defendant. I'm simply trying to ascertain the credibility, or lack thereof, of this witness."

"Overruled. Continue, Mr. Schneck."

"Dr. Conroy, I'll ask again. Do you or do you not agree with the death penalty?"

"I do not."

"Under any circumstances?"

"No."

"You are aware, are you not, that this is potentially a death penalty case?"

"I am, yes."

"And yet, knowing this, you accepted the Defense's request to examine this defendant even though-" Schneck stopped himself mid-sentence and allowed his words to hang in the minds of the judge, jury and spectators. "Withdrawn. I have no further questions for this witness."

Judge Peters watched Schneck return to his seat at the prosecution table before asking, "Does the Defense wish to re-direct?"

"No, Your Honor."

"The Witness may step down." The judge looked at his watch, and took a swallow from his coffee mug. "Court will adjourn for lunch. We'll resume at one-thirty."

THIRTY-TWO

Hank Parnell returned from the Starbuck's counter with the usual two large coffees. He placed one in front of Ken Melzer, and sat down across from him. Ken took a sip and faced Hank.

"You know what I'm thinking about, Hank?"

"I haven't a clue, but I'm sure this will be good."

"I'm thinking about dinner tonight." He took another sip. "Wanna know why?"

"Sure. Like I said, I'm sure this will be good."

"Because when I'm eating dinner tonight, I'll know this whole god-awful ordeal will be over."

Hank laughed and drank from his cup. "That's an interesting way to anticipate dinner."

"It's all I've got to look forward to right now." He raised the cup to his lips, but didn't drink. "I'm dreading putting Dillard on the stand," he said over the brim.

"Ken, as I've said a million times before, do the best you can, and forget this when it's all over."

"You don't understand. This morning, just before I put *J. Eldridge Cleaver* on the stand, Dillard has me take three close-up photos of him – one from the front, one from the side and one from the rear – and gives me a phone number to text them to. Then he hands me some sheets of paper. A few contain the questions I'm supposed to ask him, and one page is a dopey little contract he made up that stated in ridiculous terms that I could only ask the questions he provided. He demanded I sign it."

Hank's smile turned into a full guffaw, "Welcome to life outside private practice."

"Hank, this is serious. I actually signed the paper, and promised to ask only the questions he wrote down. What else could I do? Maybe Dillard really is nuts. Can you believe this shit?"

Hank put his coffee cup down and the smile vanished. "For

you to use that kind of language, you must be serious."

"Yeah I know. I save it for dire situations only, so I guess this must be one."

"Probably not as bad as you think. This case is way beyond lost at this point. If that's what Dillard requires, so be it. Give him what he wants, and then walk away knowing you represented your client according to his wishes, and to the best of your ability. So you'll ask the questions he wants, Schneck will destroy him on cross, give a brief closing argument, and that's that. Your job's done and your conscience is clear. I'll do what I can for him at the sentencing phase."

"I suppose so. I really have little choice. I just want this over. Watching Schneck discredit the *good Dr. Conroy* was painful. It took me almost two hours to get him to diagnose Roy as a complete loony. I even think some on the jury may have had some reasonable doubt about Dillard's sanity, even if they didn't buy into all of his analysis. And then it took Schneck only a few minutes to blow him, and all our hope, out of the water."

"It's exactly what I expected. Schneck's one of the best at mutilating witnesses on cross. Look what he did to Cleaver. Too bad you couldn't have put Jerome on the stand *after* Conroy. At least then we'd have been treated to a little comic relief to end the morning session on."

Ken couldn't help but laugh along with Hank. "I'm going to head back, Hank. I want to review Dillard's questions again."

"Okay. I'll be there in a little while." Hank took another swallow as Ken started to walk toward the door and called after him, "Ken..."

He turned back to Hank, "Yeah?"

"Just wanted to remind you it's almost dinner time."

Ken Melzer did not remember *all rise* or hearing Roy Dillard being sworn in. He was only aware of being on his feet standing in front of the defense table. He held the sheets of paper in his hand that Dillard had given him earlier.

"State your name please."

"Roy Dillard."

"Mr. Dillard do you understand the charges against you?"

"Yes."

"And you fully understand my job as your lawyer is to represent you in this case?"

"Yes."

Ken stared down at the papers he was holding, and turned to the jury. He held his hands partly outstretched to his sides, his left hand held the single sheet contract, and his right hand held the pages of questions. Ken turned back to Dillard, "Roy, did you give me these papers this morning?"

"I did."

Once more Winston Schneck allowed the leading questions to pass without objection. He was quietly enjoying Ken Melzer's exasperation, even desperation. Let him run with these idiotic shenanigans. Either way, his head is going to be handed to him in the end.

Holding up his right hand Ken asked, "These are questions you want me to ask you, is that correct?'

"Yes."

Ken held up the other hand, "And this is the contract you wrote, and had me sign, that states I can only ask you the questions you submitted to me. Correct?"

"Yes, that's right."

"And you told me in no uncertain terms I can *only* ask the questions you provided. Is this correct?"

"Yes."

"Is it also true you instructed me to ask no follow-up questions or ask any questions of my own, even those that in my professional opinion might help you in this case?"

Roy Dillard smiled broadly. "Yes, Ken. Those were my instructions. And I might add I do understand the old adage that says *the person who represents himself in court has a fool for a lawyer.*"

There were sounds of light laughter in the courtroom. Ken noticed smiles on the faces of the jury. Schneck sat emotionless by himself at the prosecution table. He was amused by this courtroom abnormality, but revealed no emotion.

"You understand I now have my hands tied and cannot use my best judgment to help you in any way that I feel I can?"

"I fully understand that."

Ken took a deep breath and let it out audibly. He looked at the first question on his sheet. "Mr. Dillard, it has been established that the victim who was shot in Saltzman's Jewelry Store was named Chester Bentley. Did you know him?"

"No."

"Had you ever spoken to him?"

"No."

"Had you ever seen him before?"

"Never."

"Roy, have you worked steadily from the time you graduated from college?"

"Yes."

"Have you ever taken any vacations?"

"A few weekends out of town, once on a lark I spent several days in New York City. That's about it."

"Have you spent money on cars?"

"Just enough to get reliable transportation."

"Do you drink or smoke?"

"Neither."

"What do you do with the money you make?"

"I pay my mortgage and my bills. The rest I save or invest."

"What kind of investments have you made?"

"Objection! Your Honor this is wasting the court's time. Are we going to suffer through what he likes to eat and what color ties he prefers?"

"Overruled. Mr. Melzer I understand these are not your questions, but I hope this line of questioning has a point to it."

"I assure you, Your Honor, this all has a point." Melzer tried to sound confident, but doubted his assertion.

"Very well, continue."

"Mr. Dillard, about your investments…?"

"Stocks mostly. The market's been on a bullish trend for a few years now and I've been fortunate to have taken advantage of it."

"Would you please state your net worth?"

"I have about a hundred thirty thousand dollars equity in my house. I have no debt beyond my mortgage, and I have a stock portfolio combined with a money market account worth an additional two hundred sixty thousand. So, my net worth is approximately three hundred ninety thousand."

"What future plans did you have for your investment money?"

"As you know, I managed a Quick Chick restaurant. I planned on purchasing my own franchise, and over time acquiring more – like Nick Jillian did, you know, the owner of the restaurant I managed."

"Roy, there were guns and some jewelry stolen previously in a home break-in that were found in your garage. Please explain how they got there?"

"I don't know how they got there."

"Did you steal the Smith & Wesson .41 Magnum revolver used in the shooting?"

"No."

"You heard Dr. Conroy testify. Do you agree with the findings he presented to this court?"

"Yes."

"Mr. Dillard, you are under oath and must tell the truth. Do you understand this?"

"Yes."

"Dr. Conroy testified that you abused drugs in college. Do you agree with his testimony?"

"Yes."

"Do you remember the effects it had on you?"

"Vividly."

"Positive or negative?"

"Definitely negative. That time in my life is now a part of me I wish I could wash away, but I can't. I haven't been the same since."

"Dr. Conroy spoke of schizophrenia and split personalities. Does this mesh with your own-"

"Objection." Schneck tried to sound bored. "The Defense is once again leading the Witness, this time leading him to diagnose himself-"

Melzer turned abruptly and cut him off. "Are you kidding me, Schneck? I'm leading the Witness? These aren't even *my* questions! How could I be leading *anyone*?" Ken's fierce and defensive tone rose up from the depths from weeks of frustration.

It was so spontaneous and terse that he surprised both himself and the prosecutor. So be it, he thought, I'm sick of this whole charade.

Judge Peters tapped his gavel lightly. "Gentlemen, let's not forget ourselves here. Mr. Schneck, you objected before the question was fully asked, so I cannot rule on your objection until I hear the question in its entirety. Mr. Melzer, please ask the question of your witness. If Mr. Scheck still has an objection, he may raise it before the Witness answers. Please proceed and try to maintain an acceptable level of courtroom dignity.

Ken shuffled the papers in his hands pretending to find where he had left off, but was actually attempting to settle his own nerves. Hank Parnell sat with his arms folded across his chest. He wore an amused smile on his lips.

"Mr. Dillard, Dr. Conroy talked of split personalities and schizophrenia. Does this mesh with your own self-actualization?" Ken couldn't help adding, "I believe that is the exact wording of the question you submitted."

Not to appear to have accepted a scolding, Schneck was on his feet glaring first at Judge Peters and then turning his scowl to Ken. "Objection! Leading. Calls for an expert opinion. Lack of foundation. Calls for speculation. Not relevant!"

"Do you have any further grounds for your objection before I rule?" Judge Peters calmly asked Schneck. "I think that ought to about cover it, Your Honor," Scheck replied with a subtle hint of sarcasm in his voice.

"Your objections are overruled. The Witness may answer the question. Madam Court Reporter, please read back the last question," Judge Peters politely said while looking directly at Schneck.

After the Court Reporter read from the transcript, *Mr. Dillard, Dr. Conroy talked of split personalities and schizophrenia. Does this mesh with your own self-actualization? I believe that is the exact wording of the question you submitted*, Dillard answered, "Yes, Ken, that was my question. And my answer is in the affirmative. To use Dr. Conroy's word, I am completely *lucid* at the present, but there are times when I fight to control myself. Split personality? Well, I often feel there are two of me – one who is positive and successful, and one who has fallen through the cracks, one who has been handed the short end of the stick time and again."

Ken stared at the man on the witness stand. He glanced down at the pages in his hand, and then looked back at the Witness, the Defendant. "Mr. Dillard, Roy, I want to ask follow-up questions. I want to help you, but unless you rescind the restrictions placed on me, I have no choice but to continue with your stipulated questions."

"That is correct, Mr. Melzer, Ken." The mimicking sarcasm wasn't lost on anyone in the courtroom.

"Then I have no choice but to continue." Ken was clearly pissed.

"Yes, no choice at all."

"Mr. Dillard, you have told me over and over that you believe in the justice system; is this correct?"

"Schneck started to rise out of his seat to object, but caught the judge's eye before making a sound. He sat back down quietly. Better to sit down than get slapped down, he thought to himself.

"Yes."

"You have also stated on numerous occasions that you believe the jury will not find you guilty; is this also correct?"

"It is correct."

"On the grounds of insanity?"

"Yes, until Dr. Conroy performed poorly as a witness."

"Is this why you decided to testify yourself?"

"Precisely."

"And you think the answers you have given to the questions you provided will lead you to this end?"

"I do."

Ken folded the papers in his hands, looked to the Witness, glanced at the jury, and stated loudly, "No further questions. Your witness, Mr. Schneck."

Ken sat down at his usual seat. Schneck was already on his feet. Ken passed a note to Hank that read, *I forgot to say, "The Defense rests."*

A note came back saying, *No worries. When W.S. is done, Peters will ask if you want to redirect or call another witness.*

That's the proper time to rest.

Winston Schneck walked around the prosecution table and approached the Witness. Smiling he asked, "May I call you Roy?"

"Only if I can call you Winnie."

Laughter filled the courtroom. Judge Peters was forced to use his gavel. "Mr. Schneck, I believe it best if you refer to the Witness as Mr. Dillard."

Schneck couldn't hide the crimson that colored his cheeks. He thought, you're mine, asshole. "You stated the jury would find you not guilty; is that correct?"

"I stated I believed in the justice system."

"In this firm belief of yours, even after all the evidence presented against you, you believe the jury will find you not guilty?"

"I suppose we'll just have to wait and see; won't we?"

"Answer the question please."

"Look, I said I believed in the justice system. That's my answer."

Schneck smiled. "Fine by me, I'll accept that."

"Good."

Judge Peters glared at Roy Dillard and admonished, "Please speak only to answer questions presented to you. Is that clear?"

"Yes, sorry."

Schneck ignored this interruption. "You stated you did not steal the gun used in the murder of Chester Bentley. Is this correct?"

"Yes."

"And you testified you did not know how other stolen guns and jewelry wound up in your garage. Is this correct?"

"Yes."

"You do know the Smith & Wesson .41 Magnum revolver used in the murder was stolen, don't you?"

"That's what I understand, yes."

"So how did you come to have it in your possession on this past Super Bowl Sunday?"

Dillard paused and thought a moment before answering. "I

believe it is in my best interest to take advantage of the Fifth Amendment of the United States Constitution and not answer this question on the grounds that it might incriminate me."

Schneck turned to Hank Parnell and Ken Melzer. They both sat at the defense table – Parnell busy reviewing Dillard's pages of questions, Melzer with his head down scribbling notes, probably doodling to appear busy, Schneck thought. He again faced the Witness. "You do this on your own volition, without advice from counsel?"

"Yes. I can think for myself."

"Well, I sure do hope you are thinking for yourself and not acting on the advice of your attorneys. I would hope that at least they understand that once you have taken the stand voluntarily and have answered the first question, you have waived your right to take the Fifth. You do understand that, Mr. Dillard, don't you?" Schneck said with exaggerated incredulity.

Judge Peters tapped his gavel. "Okay, everyone. Bailiff, please escort the jury to the jury room while we get this sorted out. Probably a good time for a bathroom break anyway."

After the jury was removed from earshot of the courtroom proceedings, Judge Peters addressed those remaining in the courtroom. "Up to this point the legal theatrics and unique challenges presented in this trial have been somewhat amusing; however, we have come to a detour along that path that now directs us into the realm of serious legal issues. Let me address the Witness. Mr. Dillard, you are the Defendant in this action and have apparently tied the hands of your very capable attorneys. That, Sir, is your right and you do so at your own peril. You have made the decision to voluntarily take the stand in your own defense. You have every right not to do so, but once you've taken the stand and answered even the most basic question, you have then given up your right under the Fifth Amendment to refuse to answer questions that may tend to incriminate you. In other words, once you have voluntarily agreed to take the stand in your own defense, you cannot cherry-pick which questions you will answer and which you will not. Without stating what was discussed, I ask you if you have had the opportunity to discuss with your attorneys your decision to take the stand in your own defense and the consequences of that decision?"

Roy Dillard looked at Judge Peters and in the most vulnerable voice he could muster replied, "No one ever told me that I couldn't take the Fifth."

Judge Peters looked in astonishment not at Ken but at Hank. Before Judge Peters could say a word, both Hank and Ken said in unison, "We didn't know he was going to take the Fifth." Ken continued, "Your Honor, until this morning when Roy handed that list of questions to me, I didn't know he intended to take the stand. As you have observed, Roy is unequivocal in his instructions to us. He hasn't asked us to defend him in any unethical manner, so we are doing the best we can to give him the best defense under the circumstances."

Judge Peters frowned. "Well, here's the thing, Mr. Dillard. The law requires that you answer Mr. Schneck's questions now that you have testified in your own defense. If you attempt to take the Fifth, my only option will be to instruct you to answer the question or be held in contempt of court with all that attending unpleasantness, which your attorneys can explain to you."

Judge Peters spoke to everyone in the courtroom. "We will take a twenty minute recess so that Mr. Dillard may confer with counsel."

Schneck replied, "Your Honor, I'm in the middle of my cross-examination. I object to permitting the Witness to confer with his attorneys after I've begun my cross-examination."

Judge Peters looked hard at Schneck. "I'm rapidly losing my patience with your behavior given the circumstances of this unusual trial. Perhaps you might consider both the advantages and disadvantages of my rulings before you sound off with objections. Of course, I give that advice to all counsel present in this courtroom, not to just you, Mr. Schneck," Judge Peters said in a quick attempt to cover his own ass in the event either side might suggest on appeal that he was favoring one side over the other with his advice.

Hank, Ken and Roy returned to the defense table and huddled in conference as to how to disengage themselves from their respective dilemmas.

Schneck retreated to the State's table alone to consider his approach when court returned to session. His first thoughts were how he was going to stick it to Dillard, force him to answer questions that would undermine any defense he intended to assert, or watch him go down in flames as the judge held him in contempt for taking the Fifth. But then those thoughts were interrupted by the unsettling realization that given that scenario, an appeal on the grounds of ineffective assistance of counsel would inevitably reverse any guilty verdict, and the case would have to be retried. Holy shit! *That prick on the bench just unknowingly saved my ass from an impossible situation. There certainly are advantages and disadvantages that need to be considered. Fuck Dillard and his legal team,* Schneck thought to himself.

Twenty minutes later the jury was escorted back to their seats in the jury box and Judge Peters invited Scheck to resume his cross-examination of Roy Dillard.

The court reporter read back Schneck's last line of questioning to Roy. "'Mr. Schneck:' *You do know the Smith & Wesson 41 Magnum revolver used in the murder was stolen, don't you?* 'The Witness:' *That's what I understand, yes.* 'Mr. Schneck:' *So how did you come to have it in your possession on this past Super Bowl Sunday?*"

Schneck looked at Roy with an anticipatory smirk. Judge Peters looked at Roy and told him to answer the question.

"I take the Fifth," Roy replied.

Judge Peters looked at Roy in astonishment. "Do you wish to reconsider your answer given our previous discussion?"

"No, Your Honor."

Judge Peters looked toward the Bailiff. "Please escort the-"

Schneck interrupted the judge. "Excuse me, Your Honor. That's not going to be necessary."

"How so, Mr. Schneck?"

"Your Honor, may we have a side bar?" Schneck asked.

Judge Peters signaled Hank and Ken up to the bench along with Scheck and the court reporter so the jury would not overhear them. "Go ahead, Mr. Schneck."

Schneck said in a hushed tone, "Your Honor, I am not going to object to Mr. Dillard taking the Fifth. I understand that you can compel him to answer my questions, but that won't be necessary."

"Are you telling me that you are waiving your right to an objection to this witness's refusal to answer your questions?" Judge Peters asked.

"That's exactly what I'm doing, Your Honor."

"Judge Peters looked directly at Schneck. "Do you understand that if the Witness asserts his Fifth Amendment right that I will have to give an instruction to the jury that during their deliberations they are not to consider or give weight to the fact that the Witness asserted that right?"

"I fully understand that you will give that instruction, and I encourage you to do so," Schneck added with a sly smile that he directed at Ken.

"Okay. You may step back. Mr. Schneck you may resume your cross-examination."

While the court reporter was setting up again next to the witness stand, Schneck thought to himself, I've just taken away Dillard's best hope for an appeal. Any argument for ineffective assistance of counsel in now moot because I'm going to let the asshole take the Fifth on every question I ask him. Now there's no harm done to him by his lawyers. Let the judge tell the jury to disregard Dillard's taking the Fifth. It's the old cliché: you can't unring a bell. I'm going to ring that bell over and over, and let the jury try to deliberate about what they didn't hear!

"Mr. Dillard, let me repeat the last question. How did you come to have in your possession the stolen Smith & Wesson .41 Magnum revolver used in the murder this past Super Bowl Sunday?"

"I take the Fifth," Roy said confidently.

Judge Peters then instructed the jurors that they were not to draw any conclusions one way or the other from the Witness's taking the Fifth.

"Do you deny having this weapon in your possession on-"

"Objection. Witness has answered this question," Ken stammered, feeling things now were spiraling out of control.

"He never answered the question, Your Honor. He took the Fifth! In his own defense, as a witness for himself!" Schneck responded, grandstanding for the jury.

"Mr. Schneck," Judge Peters began, "I know this is, shall we say, irregular, but you have stipulated to wave your objection to the Witness taking the Fifth, so I am gong to accept the Witness's answer and sustain Mr. Melzer's objection. Ask your next question."

Schneck walked up to within a foot of the witness box and looked directly at Roy. He asked his next series of questions slowly and deliberately, changing his gaze from Roy to the jury each time Roy responded. "Mr. Dillard, were you at Saltzman's on Super Bowl Sunday of this year?"

"I take the Fifth."

"Do you know the whereabouts of the stolen jewelry from Saltzman's?"

"I take the Fifth."

"Did you know there were security cameras at Saltzman's?"

"I take the Fifth."

"Did you drive away from the scene of the robbery and murder on Super Bowl Sunday?"

"I take the Fifth."

"Were you acting as if you didn't know why you were being arrested when the police came to your home?"

"I take the Fifth."

"Okay then, on a different subject, records show you rent the house you live in, yet you testified under oath that you pay a mortgage on this house. How can this be?"

"The house is not in my name."

"You pay the mortgage on a house that is not in your name?"

"Yes."

"And you have a stock portfolio and money market account worth two hundred sixty thousand dollars?"

"Correct."

"If this is so, how could you qualify for a public defender?"

"You did the research. What do you think?" Before Schneck or the judge could respond, Dillard continued, "None of it is in my name. Not the house or the assets. Technically, I have no worth."

"Before we get further into this, let me remind you that you testified only minutes ago that you were completely lucid at the present time. Does that still hold true, Mr. Dillard? Are you in a lucid state of reality at this moment in time?"

"Yes, I am completely *lucid*."

"You're not suffering some kind of psycho-split-personality thing?"

"I always feel that at least in some way."

"Oh, I see. So you are trying to say half of you did something and half of you didn't." Schneck knew he sounded sarcastic and nasty, but fuck it, this guy is guilty as shit and deserves to take some heat.

"In a manner, yes."

"So by taking the Fifth, you are protecting the good half of you from the bad half of you?"

"Objection."

"Overruled. The Witness will answer the question."

"Yes, that is more accurate than you know."

"So who exactly are you protecting, Mr. Dillard?"

Roy Dillard shifted in his seat, but said nothing. Judge Peters turned his way, "The Witness will answer the question."

"I'm protecting my assets and my brother."

This was so unexpected Winston Schneck was at a loss for words. An inner voice warned him of impending danger, but he couldn't stop here. Schneck's research team hadn't mentioned a brother or any investments. "You are protecting your *assets* and your *brother*?"

"Yes, that's what I said."

"Is this a real brother and real assets, or fantasy assets and a make-believe brother?"

"Real, of course."

"Is he older or younger?"

"Younger."

"How much younger is this brother of yours?"

"Four minutes."

"You mean four years?"

"No four minutes. We're twins."

Alarms blared in Schneck's head, but he was unable to do anything to heed them. "And what is this supposed brother's name?"

"Doug Watson."

"Your twin brother has a different last name than yours?"

"He changed it years ago."

"Where is your brother?"

"He now lives in Ft. Lauderdale."

"And before that?" Schneck knew he was making amateur mistakes, but he plodded on in uncharted territory.

"He was in jail before that. He's been living in South Florida since last December."

"And you are protecting him?"

"I've been protecting him – or at least trying to protect him – since we were kids."

"And the house and assets you alluded to are in his name?"

"Yes, everything."

"Is he involved in this murder and robbery?"

"You'll have to ask him. I think it is in my best interest to take the Fifth from here on out."

Stop for Christ's sakes! Stop now! The voice in Schneck's head was shrill and insistent. Winston Schneck turned to the bench. "Your Honor, because of this unexpected revelation, I'd like to request a recess until tomorrow afternoon. I'd also like to reserve the right to recall Roy Dillard to the witness stand at that time."

Judge Peters directed his attention to the defense table. "Does the Defense object to a recess?"

So as not to reveal his total mystification at this unexpected turn of events, and taking a cue from the subtle shrug of his client's shoulder from the stand, Ken Melzer nonchalantly replied, "No objection, Your Honor."

The judge took a swallow of coffee from his mug and said, "The court will adjourn until two o'clock tomorrow afternoon."

A gavel sounded. Ken looked down at the new note pushed his way and read *Dinner might be a little late.*

Ken, Hank and Roy Dillard sat in a locked meeting room in the courthouse. Ken tried his best to control his anger and tone as he began the conversation. "Roy, you have a brother? A twin brother? And investments? And a house? And we only find this out now? What kind of crap are you trying to pull here?"

"I told you I believe in the justice system. Now watch it work."

"I... we... don't have time for games. Listen, man, this is the final hour, and your life is at stake. Come clean with us. Explain this Doug Watson brother thing."

Rather than me explain it to you, just get him in here and then put him on the stand tomorrow."

Ken looked at Hank who said nothing. "And just how do I get hold of him?"

"Call him, Ken. I gave you his number this morning. You sent him some very attractive snap shots of yours truly. Remember? I'm sure he's out of the barber shop by now."

"Good thing you forgot to inform the court that the *Defense rests*," Hank finally chimed in.

For the first time in Winston Schneck's career as State's Attorney, he violated the office's façade of decorum, respectability and restraint, and exploded on the three young Assistant State's Attorneys in his office. "I asked you to research this scumbag, and you give me nothing about a brother? A *twin* brother! And nothing about a house and investments! Christ on a crutch! Now I find out this guy, this con, this Doug Watson jerk, may have a record as long as King Kong's dick! Don't you get it? Dillard had no motive. He's as squeaky-clean as a Girl Scout's twat, but his brother is bad news, a fucking loser. Dillard was trying to save his brother's ass by taking the fall for him, but figured he'd get off on an insanity plea. Stupid little turd didn't realize that's nearly impossible, even if he was a raving loony. So when it gets too hot for him, when it looks like he's gonna actually take the real fall for his brother, he has no choice but to rat him out. I guess brotherly love only goes so far, huh? If you lame fucks had done your job in the beginning, I'd have had this Watson creep in the first inning, not in the bottom of the ninth!" Schneck looked down at his desk and studied the contents of its surface. He picked up a glass paperweight, bounced it in his right hand a few times, and then hurled it at his closed office door.

Shards of glass fell like splintered icicles across the floor. "Now get the fuck out of here! All three of you sorry-ass pieces of shit!"

Judge Peters addressed Winston Schneck, "Does the Prosecution wish to recall Roy Dillard to the witness stand?"

Schneck rose to his feet but maintained his gaze down at the legal pad resting on the tabletop. "Not at the present time, Your Honor." Schneck knew he sounded less than confident. It wasn't a feeling he was accustomed to, but nonetheless it was how he felt.

"Very well," the judge looked to the defense table, "Mr. Melzer, do you wish to call another witness?"

"Yes, Your Honor, the Defense calls Doug Watson."

Even though Winston Schneck braced himself for the arrival of this next witness, the shock of him walking down the aisle caused him to nearly choke. Doug Watson was a duplicate of Roy Dillard, a clone, a perfect double, right down to the slightly hooked nose, the close-cropped ginger hair, his height and weight... everything. All eyes in the courtroom went from Watson to Dillard and back to Watson again. A female reporter near the back audibly gasped, "Oh my God!" To make matters worse, Doug Watson wore a leather motorcycle jacket zipped down the front and zipped at the wrists. Upon recognizing the jacket and jeans, Schneck thought, *Oh shit! It's the same clothes from the murder!*

Doug Watson was sworn in and sat expectantly in the witness stand. Ken walked to within a few feet of him and abruptly stopped, as if he were afraid to get too close to this witness. His theatrics were not lost on Schneck. "Please state your name."

"Douglas Watson."

"Where do you reside, Mr. Watson."

"I don't have a permanent address. I was staying with this girl I met, but that didn't last. I stayed with my brother, Roy, from time to time."

"Does your brother allow you to drive his car?"

"Yeah, when he isn't using it for work and shit."

Judge Peters almost interrupted to request Watson watch his

language, but let it slide.

"Mr. Watson, would you please remove your leather jacket?"

Without saying a word, Watson unzipped the sleeves and the front. He stood and pulled the jacket from his lean torso revealing a tight-fitting, sleeveless white tank top. Removing the jacket also revealed multiple jailhouse tattoos. A bold red swastika was emblazoned on his left upper arm balanced with an identical black swastika on his right. A hangman's noose decorated one forearm with the words *LYNCH 'EM ALL* written along the rope. Watson's other forearm displayed a double-edged dagger dripping blood. Embossed over the blade was spelled in bold letters *Defender of the Aryan Nations*. There were other tattoos entwined with these larger ones that were too small to make out. No matter, Ken thought, these will do.

"Mr. Watson, did you know a man named Chester Bentley?"

"I knew him."

"Where did you know him from?"

"Prison. We were cellmates for a time."

"Friends?"

"Are you kidding?"

Judge Peters said, "The Witness will answer the question."

Watson turned to glare at the judge who seemed to cower back slightly. "No, we were *not* friends."

"How would you describe your relationship with Chester Bentley?"

"What difference does it make now? He's dead."

Before the judge could speak, Ken said, "Doug, I don't like this any more than you, but please tell the court about your relationship with the deceased."

Watson looked down to his lap and said in a soft voice, "He tried to make me his bitch."

"I believe that is a term used by inmates in prison, but could you be more specific as to its meaning?"

"What do you think it means? He wanted to make me his *girlfriend.* If you can't figure that out for yourself-"

"I know this is difficult for you, but did you... did you do as he wanted?"

"I did what I had to. The guy was huge. I had no choice.

That's why I joined the Aryan Nations. They protected me. I didn't have any trouble with them after that."

"Who are *them*?"

"The Ni... the Blacks. Who else?"

"How did you feel about Chester Bentley in particular?" Ken asked.

"After what he forced me to do, I hated the fucker! What would you expect?" Doug spat, his anger evident by the deep red color filling his face.

"Who got out of prison first, you or Bentley?"

"He did. Why?" Doug asked, but Ken ignored the question.

"Do you know where he moved to after he got out?"

"Yeah. I heard somewhere around Fort Lauderdale. Why?" Again, Ken ignored the question.

"Mr. Watson, let me see if I understand your testimony. Please correct me if I'm wrong about anything that you've said here in court today," Ken said to his witness, fully expecting an objection from Schneck that never came. Ken continued, "You were sent to prison and placed in a cell with Chester Bentley."

"Right," Doug agreed.

"Chester Bentley, your cellmate, was a large black man."

"Yeah."

"He forced himself on you against your will."

"Yeah." Doug squirmed in his seat and glanced over at Roy sitting at the defense table.

"How many times did he assault you?" Ken asked.

"I don't fuckin' know. A lot. What the hell difference does it make? He's dead."

"He gets out of prison. You're still in."

"Yeah."

"By the way, how did you find out where Chester Bentley lived?" Ken asked.

Doug hesitated a moment before answering. He again glanced over at Roy and then replied a bit less eagerly, "I'm not sure. I asked around and that's what I heard." He eyed Ken and asked, "What's going on here?" Again, Ken ignored his question.

"After you got out of prison, you had access to Roy's home and his car."

"Right. Unless he needed it for work," Doug replied.

"You knew where Chester Bentley lived because you made it a point to ask around while you were still inside."

"Yeah, I guess. So what?"

"You hated Chester Bentley for what he did to you."

"What do you want me to say? Hell yes, I hated him." Doug continued to shift his gaze between Roy and Ken.

"I don't have any other questions for this witness," Ken said and returned to the defense table.

"Would you like to cross this witness, Mr. Schneck?" Judge Peters asked.

"Oh, absolutely, Your Honor," Schneck replied as he eagerly came from around his table to confront Doug Watson.

"Mr. Watson, why are you here today?" Schneck began.

"Some guy handed me a subpoena that said I had to show up."

"No, I mean do you know for what purpose you're testifying today."

"I thought it was to help my brother somehow."

"And just how did you think you were going to help him?"

"I don't know. Just answer some questions to straighten things out. I know he's in a shitload of trouble."

"Did you meet with either of your brother's attorneys before testifying today?"

"Only for a couple of minutes this morning," Doug replied. "Why?"

"What did they tell you?" Schneck asked.

"That's attorney-client privilege," Doug replied smugly, trying to establish some control.

"But you're not their client, are you?" Schneck asked patiently, enjoying the hunt as much as the anticipated kill that inevitably would follow.

"No. They're my brother's lawyers."

"So, you don't have an attorney-client privilege to assert." Schneck looked toward Judge Peters.

"You have to answer the question, Mr. Watson," Judge Peters instructed.

"Okay. It don't matter much anyway. They said that if I wanted to help Roy that I should just tell the truth."

"And have you been telling the truth, Mr. Watson?"

"Yes, but I don't see how talking about what happened to me on the inside is going to help my brother."

Schneck thought to himself, what a fucking moron. This guy must have thought he was going to be asked alibi questions or something. He doesn't even know about the video. Well, let the good times roll.

"Mr. Watson, Chester Bentley raped you over and over again in prison. You hated him and all other Blacks. You joined the Aryan Nations to demonstrate that hatred. You made it your business to find out where Chester Bentley was going when he got out of prison. You let your hatred simmer until you got out. You followed Chester Bentley around so you knew where you could find him. You borrowed your brother's car, drove to the jewelry store, and when your hatred was at a full boil, you got your revenge by blowing Chester Bentley's brains all over the ceiling. You killed Chester Bentley on Super Bowl Sunday, didn't you?" Schneck sneered.

"What the fuck?" Doug yelled as he leapt to his feet, now standing in the witness box. "You're setting me up, you bastard!" he yelled at Roy. Enraged, Doug's face was beet red as spittle flew from his mouth as he spoke. "You're trying to save your own ass, you fucker!" Doug screamed. "I'm not answering any more questions. I'm taking the Fifth. I want a lawyer," he demanded, looking to Judge Peters.

Judge Peters banged his gavel as two courtroom bailiffs raced to restrain Doug Watson. Once handcuffed, he was unceremoniously removed from the courtroom and order was restored.

"No further questions, Your Honor," Schneck said quietly, having quickly composed himself. He turned to the horrified jury and smiled.

THIRTY-THREE

Ken walked through the front door, dropping his briefcase a few feet inside. Charlene came out of the kitchen wearing white running shorts and a yellow T-shirt.

"I thought this dinner would be a celebration of the end of the famed Super Bowl Murder Case," she said. Ken thought he detected weariness in her voice.

"It is the end of the Dillard case. I'm done."

"Really?"

"Really."

"What if the brother wants you to defend him?"

"I won't do it. Hank can assign someone else to deal with him, or he can take it himself. I'm finished. In fact, I doubt he even qualifies for the PD's office. Roy put everything in his name, so he has assets. And pretty sizeable ones at that."

Charlene slowly walked up to her husband and wrapped her arms around his neck. Ken was keenly aware of the warm contact from her knees on up. "You have no idea how glad I am to hear that."

Ken held his wife close, tight. He tilted his head down and breathed deeply of her scent. "Me too," he said softly. "I just need to wrap up a few details tomorrow morning and *it is over*. For good."

Charlene unraveled herself from Ken and said, "Come into the kitchen. I'm just finishing up – Chicken Marsala. I've got a glass of wine already poured for you."

Ken picked up his glass while Charlene removed a baking dish from the oven. Without looking at him she asked, "Are you sure Schneck will agree to dismiss the case against Dillard?"

Ken laughed, "Which one?"

Returning the laugh she said, "Roy, of course."

"He really has no choice. Schneck's between a rock and a hard place. If he allows the case to go to the jury, they won't convict because there's just too much reasonable doubt. How could they find him guilty after seeing and hearing his creepy brother? Roy had me establish he didn't know Chester Bentley, and that he had a net worth of almost four hundred grand. So, no motive to commit a murder, and no real need to steal when he was planning to buy a fast food franchise with his own investment money. In fact, we established that Roy got along well with his black co-workers, so there is really nothing to suggest he would commit a hate crime. And now it's obvious, he's innocent and his brother is the guilty one who knew Chester Bentley – intimately it seems – and had plenty of motive."

"And all this time we assumed Roy was guilty."

"Yeah. You, me, Hank, Schneck and everyone else who's been following the case. No one thought there was any possible way he was innocent."

Charlene put two steaming plates on their small table. She refilled the wine glasses, and lifting hers toasted, "To you… and me… and a future that does *not* include this *fucking* case!"

Ken hid his displeasure at Charlene's words, and quickly took a long swallow from his wine glass.

THIRTY-FOUR

"You're a free man, Roy."

"Never doubted it for a minute," he replied smiling confidently.

Ken, Roy and Hank were in the same conference room as the day before. Ken was incredulous at how much had changed in twenty-four hours. Schneck had announced that the State was dismissing the charges against Roy Dillard. He saw no point in pursuing the case against Roy with such overwhelming evidence supporting a different theory of the case. Not dismissing the case would make him look vindictive and weaken his argument that it was Roy's brother who had committed the murder of Chester Bentley. The jury had been dismissed. Judge Peters had left through the door to his chambers, headed for home or maybe a bar – if any were open this early. The courtroom had emptied, the reporters scrambling to call in on their phones. Ken Melzer still couldn't believe the outcome. This seemed more like a dream, or a scene from the theater of the absurd. But he was definitely awake, and this was not make-believe. Roy had been cleared of all charges, and under the rule of double jeopardy, could never again be tried for the same crime.

Roy Dillard continued, "Now all that's left is for you, Ken, to go downtown and get my brother out of jail."

Ken looked to Hank Parnell before saying, "Sorry, Roy. I'm finished with the Super Bowl Murder and Jewelry Heist case. He'll have to get his own lawyer. He as assets, remember?" I'm taking some time off."

Roy unexpectedly howled with laughter. Getting control of his speaking voice he said between escaped giggles, "Ken, Ken, Ken… You aren't done yet… almost, but not quite. I'm counting on you to reunite the Dillard brothers. This won't take long. Actually, you might enjoy it and you won't even have to represent anyone."

Annoyed and not trying to hide his feelings, Ken said, "I don't know what part of what I just said you don't understand, but let me be crystal clear. I'm done. I'm not your lawyer anymore, and I'm certainly not your brother's lawyer."

"I agree, just listen-"

"No! You listen Roy; you haven't been straight with me. Not from day one. You withheld important information; you used me, had me tied in knots. I gave you one hundred percent, and you know it, *knew* it all along and still-"

Roy burst forth with another round of that irritating laugh, "Calm down. You'll give yourself a heart attack! I've always been straight with you. You simply chose not to pay attention to me. I told you I believed in the justice system and that the jury would never convict me. And I was right. You *heard*, but you didn't *listen*."

"I don't care anymore. I did my job as best I could. You made me look like an idiot. You got what you wanted and I-"

Serious now, Roy interrupted, "Bullshit Ken! I made you look like the most brilliant fucking lawyer in the state of Florida, maybe the entire country. And when you go downtown and bring my brother back the whole world will know it!"

Roy turned to Hank, "You got that envelope my brother gave you?"

Hank reached into his briefcase and produced a padded manila envelope covered in packaging tape. On one side in bold black letters, and printed in permanent marker, was written *PROPERTY OF ROY DILLARD. DO NOT OPEN EXCEPT IN HIS PRESENCE!* Hank passed it to Roy who with some effort ripped it open. He extracted a cellphone and a small zip lock plastic bag containing a computer flash drive.

"The phone battery will be dead, but not to worry, everything you need is saved on this." He handed Ken the plastic bag. Play this, get my brother, and then you really are done with this case. I promise."

The secretary escorted Ken Melzer from the waiting room to Winston Schneck's office and closed the door behind him. Schneck was sitting behind his cluttered desk shuffling through piles of papers. He looked up and stared at Ken. Dropping the file he was holding, and pushing back in his swivel chair, he said, "So I suppose someone's going to represent Doug Dillard or Watson or whatever the fuck name he's going by. He's refused to answer any questions until he sees a lawyer."

"May I sit?"

Schneck waved to the sofa by the side of his desk. Before sitting Schneck said, "What are you trying to prove, Melzer? You waste my time, and the judge's time, and the jury's time... for what? So you can grandstand in some unethical way to make yourself look smart? I gotta admit, for a while I thought you were doing a pretty good job with a loser of a case. I was even a little impressed. But then you pull this shit out of your hat at the last minute... and all for what? You could have gotten him off any time you wanted. You had the key to your client's freedom all along. This was all a big fucking waste of time – an embarrassment for both of us. You have no reputation yet, but I have one, and it's a damn good one that's taken me a lot of years to earn." Raising his voice he concluded, "And I'll be goddamned if I'll allow some snot-nosed, wet-behind-the-ears, just-outa-law-school schmuck, working his first major case for the PD's office, to tarnish it!"

Expressionless, Ken sat for a few moments as if letting Schneck's words sink in. Then he spoke in a measured and soft tone, "I was only doing my job. None of this was planned out. I was as surprised as-"

"Don't piss in my face and call it rain! Now it's obvious why you didn't file for discovery. What lawyer doesn't file for discovery? I'll tell you. Only one with a surprise witness he's saving to drop as a bombshell, that's who. This was all planned from the beginning, wasn't it? Answer me that!"

"I'll tell you what kind of lawyer doesn't file for discovery – a lawyer who is following the explicit instructions of his client who told him not to file, even after he begged his client to let him do it. That's who."

Schneck was on his feet, "You are a lying sack of shit, Melzer!"

Ken did not react to this uncontrolled outburst. He uncrossed and re-crossed his legs, but said nothing.

Even more enraged by his lack of effect on this newbie assistant public defender, Schneck yelled, "I got nothing more to say to you. Get the fuck out of my office! I profoundly wished that the next time our paths crossed could have been in court with that low-life Watson freak, so I could have torn you a new asshole so big you'd have been able to eat beer bottles and shit glass without getting scratched!"

Ken made no effort to rise. Instead he said, "You have a wonderfully colorful way with words, Winston, and I hate to burst your bubble, but you won't be seeing me or anyone else in court representing Doug Watson."

"Don't fuck with me Melzer-"

Suddenly and unexpectedly Ken was on his feet moving toward Schneck. He pointed to the vacated desk chair and hissed, "Sit!"

Shocked and without thinking, Schneck did.

Ken leaned toward him, resting both hands on the front edge of his desk. "Now you listen to me, Schneck, and you listen good. This trial is concluded and nobody is going to represent Doug Watson."

"What's that supposed to mean?"

"It means," Ken said with a theatrical flair, "the famed *Super Bowl Murder and Jewelry Heist* case is over – caput... ended... finalized... history." Ken reached into his pocket and tossed the zip-lock bag on a haphazard pile of files before the seated State's Attorney. "Don't say a word! Just put this in your laptop and watch." Ken returned to the sofa and sat down as before.

Schneck's monitor transitioned to a scene in a crowded parking lot. The sun was shining, and judging by the shorts and T-shirts many were wearing, the day was warm. The video showed a stadium and gaudy signs of all kinds proclaiming welcome to the Super Bowl. A blur of unfocused movement was replaced with a close-up selfie of a smiling face. As he watched the lens go from close-up to wide-angle, Schneck let out a low, growling, "Jesus Fucking Christ." What at first Schneck thought was Roy Dillard morphed into the tattooed torso and head of

Doug Watson. He wore a gray tank top and tan camouflaged shorts. The image spoke, "Hi everyone, I'm Doug Watson and I'm here on a beautiful sunny day in Phoenix, Arizona ready for the start of the Super Bowl. But first, I need some souvenirs! So I'll just wander over here to this vendor, and buy a meaningful little keepsake." Schneck watched in disbelief as the unbroken footage showed Watson walking while obviously filming himself. A black man appeared at a tented booth. "Hi," Watson says to the vendor, "What's your name? Mind if I film this for everyone back home?" The man seemed keenly aware of Watson's offensive tattoos, but still said, "Name's Mac. You can take my picture if you want." Watson again, "Great, Mac. I really appreciate it. Let me buy one of those jerseys – size 'Large.'" Watson handed Mac a hundred dollar bill. "Keep the change, bro."

Ken saw the sweat forming on Schneck's upper lip and forehead. He almost felt sorry for him, but not quite. The video lasted another few minutes as Doug Watson buys Navajo Indian Fry Bread from a woman named Becky Spotted Horse and, after tossing it in a trash bin, bought a corndog from Julio Martinez's stand. "Well," Doug Watson says smiling, "I better get going. Man there sure are a lot of out-of-state cars here!" The camera again moves rapidly for a few seconds until it settles on a New Mexico license plate, then ones from Colorado, New York, Washington, Vermont, California and Wyoming. "My battery's starting to run a bit low, so I better end this. I hope everyone enjoys this Super Bowl! Bye for now!"

Schneck stared at the screen as it went blank. He continued to look into his monitor as if there might still be more, but there was not. Schneck looked up as Ken started to speak. "I was given this less than an hour ago. I knew nothing about it. Yesterday at this time," Ken looked at his watch, "I assumed by this day Roy Dillard would have been led away in cuffs, and I'd be planning a vacation with my wife."

The color still drained and absent from his face, Winston Schneck said nothing. Ken continued, "My office has been discharged from further responsibility for Roy Dillard, and we do not represent Doug Watson; however, as an officer of the court, I have just delivered to you substantial and irrefutable exculpatory evidence as to Doug Watson. I don't think you can continue to prosecute him in good faith. Now, make the call to release him. I want to get out of here." Still no response from Schneck. Ken concluded, "I was used just as you were. Justice was not served, and that was not my intent."

Ken Melzer slowly rose from the sofa and picked up his briefcase. He glanced at the still motionless man sitting behind his desk before he walked to the door and opened it. As Ken was leaving he heard Winston Schneck mumble, "I believe you."

As arranged, Ken Melzer and Doug Watson walked into the Pizza Hut where Hank Parnell and Roy Dillard were seated. On seeing his brother, Roy stood, and the two embraced for what seemed to Ken an awkwardly long time. A few other diners glanced at them, but only briefly – pizza being more interesting than two identical men hugging.

Ken made no move to take a seat as Roy said, "Got a Stuffed Crust Supreme coming in a few minutes." Reaching for the pitcher on the table he added, "Let me pour you a beer."

Ken replied, "No, I gotta go," and turned to leave.

"Wait. Ken, I need a word. Let's go outside."

Once in the parking lot, Ken leaned against his car and said, "Look, I got nothing to say to you."

"Well, I got something to say to *you*."

"Fine, but make it fast. I need to be somewhere."

"C'mon, Ken, don't look so down. You're a hero! Every lawyer in the country will think you are the most hot-shit attorney to ever grace a courtroom."

"I don't care about that. You played me. I was just a tool for you. You are guilty of murder, and burglary, and every other charge that was leveled against you. You should be in prison. You should be on death row-"

"Shut the fuck up, Ken! Get over yourself and listen to what I have to say!"

Eye to eye Ken spoke sternly, "Be quick."

"I said I believed in the justice system, and I do. And it *worked*."

"No, it *failed*. If it worked, you wouldn't be standing in this parking lot right now."

"Wrong. Maybe *your* justice system of lawyers, and judges, and juries, but not in *The Real* Justice System."

"What are you talking about?"

"You of all people should know, coming from a family of ministers-"

"How do you know that?" Ken interrupted. "I never told you anything about-"

"Oh, please. I think this has been the information age for a lot of years now. I know about you – have for a long time, one of the reasons I wanted you to represent me."

"Go on."

"Look, there's more to justice than evidence and witnesses. Life isn't two-dimensional. Life's not always black and white, good and evil. There's a lot of gray area between right and wrong. I'm telling you, Ken, justice was served."

"Yeah, sure. Whose justice?"

"Universal justice. Pure Justice. God's justice."

"I don't get it."

"Sure you do. Sometimes the decisions in courts serve dubious justice. How often do the rich and powerful land in jail, regardless of their crimes? Almost never! Compare that to the huge numbers of poverty stricken, uneducated masses that inhabit our penal system. I know they commit a disproportionate amount of crime, but you and I both know the right lawyers and the most money usually prevail. Follow me?"

"Make your point, I gotta go."

"My point is that real justice isn't meted out in court, it's saved for later. Why do you think we have the whole concept of heaven and hell? It's because the common man, the average schnook, needs to feel that when the bad guys get off, when the rich and powerful and evil ones walk away scot free, that their justice will eventually come. No high-paid lawyer is going to get Hitler, or Stalin, or even O. J. Simpson off the hook. Their justice comes from the Universe... from God. And He doesn't need evidence presented by lawyers. He doesn't need to be sweet-talked by a talented deceiver. No-siree, real justice will be swift and final. And that, Ken, *that* is what I have faith in."

"And therefore, God, or whoever, is going to judge you innocent?"

"We're all sinners, all guilty."

"Don't mince words with me. In your *unique system of final justice*, you are going to be acquitted, like you were today in the Broward County Courthouse?"

"Yes. Wanna know why?"

"Sure. Tell me, Roy."

"Because there is more to this than you think, than you know. You'll have to take my word on that." Roy smiled, "Something you have always refused to do. But trust me on this, and someday you'll understand."

Ken turned to unlock his Honda. "I doubt it."

As he got in he heard Roy say over his shoulder, "I don't."

THIRTY-FIVE

The local headlines read, **SUPER BOWL MURDER CASE DISMISSED, TWIN BROTHER ARRESTED!** Twenty-four hours later the same paper's front page proclaimed, **HOODWINKED! PROSECUTION EMBARRASSED! MURDERER FREED!** Other papers around the country carried similar headlines and stories. Most showed present or file photos of Winston Schneck; some had photos of Ken Melzer.

For days after the Super Bowl Murder and Jewelry Heist trial, CNN, FOX, MSNBC, and all the other network news programs had editorials and round table debates concerning the outcome of this unusual case. Typically, those from the political left agreed with one prominent Harvard law professor who said *it was better to have a few guilty people go free than allow even one innocent person to be wrongly convicted.* Many on the political right were so outraged by this failure of the justice system that they demanded new provisions be added to the rules of double jeopardy. *Surely*, they argued, *the letter of the law is important, but there needs to be a human element introduced to also represent the spirit of the law...*

The news cycle, being as rapidly changing as it is, combined with viewers' and readers' short attention spans, would eventually move this story further and further to the back of news programs and papers, until it disappeared altogether. For Winston Schneck, that couldn't be soon enough.

"Mr. Schneck, it's the Governor calling from Tallahassee on line One."

Winston Schneck lifted the heavy black landline phone and pushed the first button. Play it cool, he thought. Act as if this was no big deal, just an annoyance that would fade away. "Hello, Governor."

"Schneck, you fucked up big time. This was supposed to be a slam dunk. Now we've got every news broadcast and newspaper in the country looking at Florida like we're a bunch of backwoods hicks who can't even convict a murderer who's caught on tape! What the hell kind of show are you running down there?"

"Let's not get too carried away here, Governor. Nobody could see this coming. It's unfortunate, but I've seen this kind of thing before. Some people are upset right now, but in a week or two it'll all be forgotten."

"Nothing is forgotten with an election coming up. If I even admit I've met with you, my opponents will connect me to this case and bring it up every chance they get."

"Now Governor, I think that's a bit reactionary. You of all people know how these, shall we say, small hiccups fade quickly with time-"

"What's that supposed to mean, Schneck? Just what are you referring to?"

Fuck! Schneck admonished himself. *Don't piss him off more than he's already pissed. Change directions.* "I meant, like all people in the public eye for any length of time, there are always small... problems... that can arise. I didn't mean anything specific. I was speaking in generalities-"

"Bullshit, Schneck. My past problems are just that, *past* problems. I've dealt with them, and they are now history. One thing I know for sure is that I don't need any more problems. And I see this case, and any association with it, as a *major problem*. The kind of *problem* I don't want or need. Schneck, *you* are a problem I don't need."

Schneck could see his ship sinking before his eyes. "Look, we had a deal-"

"You're right, we did. But the deal hinged on you convicting Dillard. You didn't live up to your end. I was willing to appoint you Attorney General, but that option isn't on the table anymore."

"And what about the other little potential *problem* I can help you with?"

There followed an icy silence on the line. Schneck could hear the Governor breathing. *Let him chew on that,* Schneck thought. *I can wait him out.* "Look, Winston, you know I'm in a jam here. If I appoint you Attorney General of the State of Florida, I'm cooked with the black community, and just about anyone else literate enough to read a paper. You must know I can't help you out."

Schneck did not respond. *Let him stew.* More silence. "Mr. Schneck? Are you still there?"

"Yes."

"I tell you what. Let me win reelection. Then we can revisit this situation. Fair enough?"

Winston Schneck knew this was the best he could hope for. "I'll think about it," was all he said before abruptly hanging up on the Governor.

THIRTY-SIX

Driving home from the Pizza Hut, Ken Melzer felt a wave of relief unexpectedly wash over him. The Super Bowl Murder and Jewelry Heist trial was actually over. He was done with Roy Dillard and his convict brother. Dr. Conroy and J. Eldridge Cleaver were a memory. And as imposing and intimidating as Winston Schneck had been, he too was out of his immediate life. Ken hit the power button on the radio. The tuner had died a few months ago leaving Ken at the mercy of a single classic rock station that couldn't be changed. The soulful, southern whine of the Allman Brothers singing *Ramblin' Man* filled the Honda. It reminded Ken of how he felt years before, driving to the law school at the University Of Florida. It had been a trip filled with apprehension as well as optimism – a good feeling then and, Ken thought, a pretty good feeling now, too. He was done with his first big case and, through no brilliance or legal acumen of his own, had pulled off a not-guilty verdict that nobody imagined possible. The relief he felt was over the conclusion of the trial; however, the verdict remained troubling.

What was Roy talking about minutes before in the Pizza Hut parking lot? What was all that crap about some kind of *Universal Justice,* or *Pure Justice,* or *God's Justice?* Roy Dillard blew off the top of the head of an unarmed delivery guy, Chester Bentley, and then stole a fortune in high-end jewelry. So what if in prison his brother had trouble with Bentley. That doesn't give Roy or anyone the right to determine that Chester Bentley deserved execution, and then actually carry out the sentence. And the robbery… how could Roy justify that? No, Ken concluded, Roy belongs in prison, and as an accomplice, so does his brother, Doug. The fact they are both free is not his fault. Winston Schneck and his crack team of investigators can claim the credit for that. It was their case to lose. This was the slam dunk of the century. The evidence was damning in the extreme. Schneck simply wasn't able to tie it to the right person at the right time. Roy Dillard and his brother, Doug, outmaneuvered him. They had this entire scheme planned from Day One. Ken realized it was a masterful, if diabolical, plan. And to those who are convinced now, or who will be convinced in the future, that he, a fresh-out-of-law school assistant public defender, knew the truth and orchestrated this convoluted defense... well, Ken resigned himself into accepting, that was beyond his scope of influence. In fact, he also realized, if he did claim no knowledge of the real facts or strategy behind this trial, he'd be labeled a fool. Ken decided what was done was done, and nothing now or ever could change what had just happened in the Broward County Courthouse. He could either keep silent about the case and let people think what they want, or he could try to expound on the fact that his client kept him in the dark throughout the trial, which might make him look like the legal world's biggest stooge. Approaching his driveway, Ken came to the conclusion it didn't matter who had been Roy Dillard's defense attorney – whether it had been he, or Hank Parnell, or anyone else from the PD's office – the result of this trial would have been identical.

Ken Melzer walked through the front door, and absently placed his keys on the small hall table. "Char Honey, I'm home." There was no response. Ken saw the yellow sticky note on the kitchen table. *If you are reading this, I'm out for a run. Special dinner in the fridge – don't peek, it's a surprise! Congrats!!! Luv U Lots, C.*

Ken opened the refrigerator door. He was done with surprises, at least for the present. On a white oval platter covered with plastic wrap were two massive steamed and chilled lobster tails. Charlene must have gone to a special seafood market to find these monsters, he thought. She also must have spent a fortune. Next to the lobster tails was a matching round plate containing a half dozen large oysters on the half shell placed around a tiny crystal bowl of spicy red cocktail sauce. Ken still couldn't fathom how she could eat those slimy things that looked so unappetizing. The first time Ken had seen her eat raw oysters she'd laughingly told him it was an acquired taste, that she'd been eating, no, *slurping,* them since she was a little girl. He was glad to see there was also a wrapped package of smoked marlin. Now that was worth eating – and no slurping required. Cold, skinny asparagus and a bottle of French champagne would round out the meal. Again, Ken wondered about the cost.

"Hey, I specifically said no peeking!"

Ken hadn't heard Charlene enter the kitchen. She came up behind him and encircled his waist with her arms, pulling him close. "You don't take instructions very well, do you?"

"Guess not," he said leaning into her. He could feel the heat from her along his back and down his legs. She kissed the right side of his neck. "You're hot and sweaty."

"Guilty on both accounts," she giggled. "My sentence will be a long shower, and you've been appointed to guard me."

"And exactly who passed judgment and sentenced you?"

"Judge Charlene, who'd you think?"

"Then let's carry out the sentence," Ken whispered. "At least *someone's* getting sentenced."

Charlene took Ken's hand and led him toward their bathroom. "No shop-talk, Counselor. Just shampoo, soap and then lots of moisturizer."

Ken's shoes were already kicked off. "Whatever you say, Judge. It's your court."

Dinner ended up being late. Ken watched Charlene raise a shell to her lips, and with considerable wet slurping, suck an oyster into her mouth. As repugnant as the shellfish was to Ken, he found watching his wife eating in such a manner vaguely erotic.

Ken knew he shouldn't mention it, but didn't stop himself, "So how much did this little feast cost?"

Looking over an oyster shell she replied, "For a lawyer of your esteem... a mere pittance. Pocket change."

"Yeah, some esteem..."

"Well, you may not think so, but a lot of other people don't agree."

"What are you talking about?"

Charlene rose from the table and retrieved several note pages. "These were on the answer machine."

"From the home line?"

"Yup. I assume they didn't have your cell number."

"Who?" Ken asked in obvious confusion.

"Who do you think? Only CNN and a law firm in Tampa and another in Orlando, that's who."

"What do they want with me?"

"Ken, Darling, at least for now, you are the most famous defense lawyer in the country."

"I'm just a guy who got used by his client. I didn't do anything to-"

Holding the top message sheet she interrupted, "Not according to the McNeal, O'Brien and Driscol law firm in Orlando."

"Never heard of them. What do they want?"

"Well, I've heard of them, and they want you to call their office as soon as possible."

"For what?"

Charlene looked into her husband's eyes, "Honey, they want to hire you. You pulled off a miracle. You astounded the whole legal community. You're a star."

"But I had nothing to do with it!"

"They don't know that. Nobody knows that. And if you told them, they'd never believe it."

"But that's not the truth!"

"Doesn't matter. Trust me, they've studied every word of the transcript from this trial. In your opening statement you even hinted to the jury that you had something up your sleeve for them, a surprise. And you delivered. And Dillard's performance on the stand was so cleverly orchestrated with all that taking the Fifth crap; he could never be tried on perjury charges! But regardless, you *won,* Ken. And that's all that matters in this business."

"I never looked at it as a *business.*"

"Well, you need to because that's exactly what it is. And winning is all that matters."

"I thought justice mattered."

"It's a by-product of the business of law. If justice is served, that's fine, but lawyers are hired to win cases, not to seek justice."

"Sounds pretty cold, pretty cynical."

"Not cynical or anything else, just fact. Lawyers are like players in a high stakes poker game. No one cares about losers. The winners go home with the loot and," she thoughtfully added, "usually the girls, the expensive cars, and the fine clothes. And they take it all back to their big houses."

"And if they cheat to win?"

"If they don't get caught, they keep it all and wait to play another day."

Ken put down his fork and pushed away the half-eaten lobster tail. Charlene grinned at her husband and carefully continued, "Looking out for both of us, my father took it upon himself to give Jason Driscol a call in Orlando. They've known each other for years. Anyway, citing this case and your victory, he arranged an interview for you. Don't worry, Daddy assured me all you have to do is show up, act reasonably smart and the job will be yours. He'll help you, don't worry."

"I see... and the other calls on the machine?"

"Well, CNN apparently wants to hire you as a legal commentator or something. You're supposed to give them a call to find out more. There was a similar message from MSNBC. And then there was a call from a law firm I've never heard of in Tampa. They probably want to have you interview for them also. You should get more offers, but go with the one Daddy arranged in Orlando. The other firms probably aren't doing all that well and figure having your name on their letterhead will attract more clients and bring in more-"

"Charlene," Ken interrupted, "I'm happy where I am. I like working in the PD's office. I like Ft. Lauderdale. I don't want to live in Orlando or Tampa. I want to stay here. This is our home."

Charlene pushed her plate away, too. She glared at Ken, "And make no money. And live in this shithole of a house. And not be able to afford to put our future kids in pre-school, or pay for their college educations. And drive shit-cars. And wear last year's sale-rack clothes. And go out to eat maybe once every couple weeks, and order from the cheap side of the menu. And never make the right friends or join the right clubs. And-"

"Enough!" Ken yelled, surprising himself at the volume of his voice. He took two deep breaths and continued calmly, "What would you have me do, Char? What is it you so desperately want from me?"

"First, I can tell you what I didn't want. I didn't want this reaction to the calls we received today. Any other lawyer worth his salt would happily give his left nut for even one of those calls. You got several, and you'll probably get more." She stared at his complacent face and fought an urge to slap some sense into it. "I *so desperately want* you to be a *real* lawyer, a go-getter. I know how good you are in court. I've seen it with my own eyes. You could be great, but you'll never amount to anything even remotely resembling great if you stay in the public defender's office representing low life criminals, society's rejects, and misfit scum."

"You want me to take one of those job offers? You want to move?"

"Of course I want you to take an offer... the one my father arranged. Do I want to move? Sure, if that's what it takes, but I do know I'd like to move out of this crappy little house."

"I thought you liked this house-"

"Ken, you're talking like a small-minded fool." Instantly she regretted her choice of words and followed with, "But you most assuredly *are not* a fool. You just need to adjust your thinking. You need to forget the *foolish* notion that working for the PD's office is somehow more noble than working for *profit* in a private firm. Don't you want to provide for me, for us? Don't you want to better yourself, and our standard of living? C'mon, Ken. For Christ's sake, get real!"

As if he were suffering a migraine, Ken slowly stood and rubbed his temples. "I thought I knew what I wanted. Actually, I think I still do, and I've told you all that. But it's not what you want. I think you want me to sell out, to abandon my beliefs and values for money and status... money and status I don't even deserve. Listen, Char, Dillard and his psycho brother used me like a tool. They scammed the whole justice system. And now you want me to prosper by it? I know you're better than that."

"You sound like an idealistic, naïve little boy giving a school report on the Supreme Court or something. If you could see yourself through my eyes, you'd see a pathetic, frightened child lost and floundering in the complicated world of adults."

Ken sat heavily on the sofa and stared at the blank TV. A few minutes later Charlene reappeared in front of him. She wore a tank top and brief gym shorts. "I'm going for another run. Don't wait up for me. Daddy wanted to know your reaction to what he arranged with Driscol's firm. He had some suggestions for the interview. So I'll stop by his place later. And I gotta tell ya, I'm not looking forward to it!"

THIRTY-SEVEN

This time was different. Winston Schneck barely had a moment to take a seat and pick up an *Islands* magazine before a smiling receptionist approached him. "Mr. Schneck, the Governor will see you now. I'll show you the way."

When the solid oak door closed behind him, the Governor circled around his desk and greeted Schneck with an outstretched hand, "Mr. Schneck, good to see you."

"Good to see you too, Governor."

"And to what do I owe the pleasure of your visit?"

"Well," Schneck began, both men taking seats facing each other in front of the imposing desk, "I've made a major decision affecting us both."

"Really?" The Governor was instantly on his guard. "And what is that?"

"I've decided to be a part of your reelection team."

"Well, that's wonderful, Winston. I appreciate your support, but in exactly what capacity are you planning to be a member of my *team*?"

"Public relations." Schneck was enjoying the Governor's obvious discomfort and confusion by this unexpected visit.

"I see. Public relations. Hmm, interesting. And how do you expect to help with my reelection in this area?"

"I'm going to see to it that certain damaging information doesn't leak to the press; information that could potentially derail your bid for reelection."

The Governor absently wiped at the perspiration suddenly appearing on his forehead. "Mr. Schneck, I thought I made it clear I would do everything I could to help you once I am reelected... *if* I am reelected."

"Abundantly clear. That's why I'm going to do everything in my power to make sure you don't get damaging press during your campaign."

The Governor suddenly stood and spat, "Cut the shit, Schneck. What do you want from me?"

Schneck smiled and remained seated, "Like I said, I want to be part of your team."

"I don't have time for this Schneck-"

"Mr. Schneck, if you please."

"Fine, I don't have time for this *Mister* Schneck. Tell me what you want."

"Well, if I'm to put all my efforts into keeping negative press at bay, there will be expenses involved."

"I thought so. What kind of expenses?"

"Typical campaign expense-"

Raising his voice the Governor interrupted, "I said I'm busy, Schneck... Mr. Schneck... just get to the point. What do you want for these *services*?"

"Sit down, Governor. Relax."

Reluctantly, he did as instructed.

"Good, that's much better. Now, as we both know, campaigns are expensive." The Governor was starting to look annoyed, pissed actually. "For the crucial service I'll be providing, I'll need eight thousand dollars a month-"

"Are you out of your mind, Schneck-"

"Nine thousand-"

"You're fucking crazy-"

"Ten thousand... and I suggest you change your attitude. This isn't a negotiation, and your antagonism toward me isn't helping your case."

The Governor refrained from saying anything while he digested the last few moments. "Okay, so I pay you eight thousand dollars a-"

"Ten thousand."

The Governor was again silent for a few pounding heartbeats. "I pay you *ten* thousand for how long? For how many months?"

"What do you think is fair?" Schneck was enjoying this.

"Until reelection. That is if I am reelected."

"Oh, you'll be reelected. The polls show you solidly ahead."

"So I pay you until the polls close, and then you go away. Forever."

"Governor, please." Schneck said softly. "That's no way to treat an important member of your team. You pay me ten grand a month until you appoint me Attorney General for the great state of Florida."

"For God's sake, Mr. Schneck-"

"Pardon me, Governor, but I think it's time you call me Winston."

"Great. Look, Winston, you fucked up big time. The Dillard case made you a laughing stock. Besides, I already announced a new Attorney General to replace the idiot that's retiring."

"I know. But you only need her for the Hispanic votes she'll garner. After the election you'll find a reason to can her."

"And assuming I can do this, how-"

"You'll find a way."

"You of all people should know that I don't have the power to fire an Attorney General. She would have to be impeached through the legislative process. She hasn't committed an impeachable offense," the Governor said with growing exasperation.

Schneck looked at him with contempt. "I don't give a shit how you get rid of her. Use your fucking influence to find her a high-paying job that she can't refuse. Create either a situation or an opportunity… it doesn't matter which… so that she makes the right choice. Just get it done."

"Fine, but how can I possibly appoint *you* Attorney General?"

"Simple. Six months after you are safely ensconced in the Governor's Mansion… for the second time… you wait for a natural disaster – a flood or tsunami, an earthquake, a tornado – or maybe a plane crash or terrorist attack, anything to occupy the mainstream media. Then you appoint me. By that time, my name and the Dillard case will be old news, forgotten. Nobody will give a shit, and if they do, who cares? It'll make the news for a day and die immediately. Everyone will be focused on the real news story. If you can pull this off on a late Friday afternoon, that's even better. Nobody will take any notice."

"Got this all worked out, don't you Schneck-"

"Winston."

The Governor let out a long breath, a sigh actually and said,

"You'll get your money-"

"Cash. Delivered on the first of each month by courier."

"Yeah, sure."

"And my appointment?"

The Governor shut his eyes, and with them still closed, whispered with exasperation, "Yes, Winston, all that. Just as you planned."

When he finally opened his eyes, Schneck was gone, and the heavy office door was left open.

Winston Schneck sat on a green park bench at Ft. Lauderdale's George English Park. Normally at this hour of the morning he'd be in his office. But today was the first day of his vacation. The first he'd taken in years. Since the Dillard debacle, some local black leaders had been calling for his resignation. Better to be unavailable for comment. They'll get tired of looking for a dead horse to beat and move on to something else. He had plenty of vacation time built up. This will blow over, and he can get back to work whenever he chooses. It would all be temporary anyway. Every cloud has a silver lining he thought. Probably a politician came up with that old adage. With a little creative thinking most bad situations could be turned advantageous. The trouble was, most people took a defeatist attitude. Things go wrong, they give up. For Winston Schneck, when things went wrong, he got smart and got tough.

Carla Christianson's appearance interrupted his train of thought. The sight of her caused his breathing to become shallow and fast. She wore moderate length white shorts and flat sandals with a modest pink tank top. Always smart, never slutty or tartish he thought – a class act. The clothes were chosen to accentuate the tawny hue of her skin. Upon seeing Winston, she broke into a smile.

"Hey, Winston, what a beautiful morning!"

"Hello, Carla. It is a fine morning. I was just up in Tallahassee, a bit cooler there. And I might add, you look lovely as always."

Carla continued to smile. "Less muggy there. I've spent some time in Tallahassee."

"I'm sure you have. Take a seat. This won't take long."

"Sure. What's up, Winston? I was surprised to get your message."

"Well, we have a bit of a problem."

"Really? That's not like you."

"This is an unusual situation, but one I'm fairly certain won't last too long."

"You're getting me worried-"

"It's okay, Carla. I've got this thing under control. Let me explain." Winston made a show of looking over his shoulder as if making certain they were completely alone and out of hearing from anyone nearby. It was all an act, but Carla would buy it. "I'll get right to the point. The little escapade with you and that boy and the Governor... well, it seems that information leaked-"

"The video too?"

"Afraid so."

"But how could-"

"It doesn't matter how it happened, just know it did. Seems the people who got hold of the video in Tallahassee are threatening to expose it. If that happens, the Governor goes down, and you'd be identified. That might not sound like much, but you procured an underage boy and, well, that's pretty serious. Without mincing words, it'd mean jail time for you, and even I couldn't protect you if things got to that point. Plus, everyone in the country would know your face and connect you to this scandal. You'd never be able to live it down. It would ruin you and any plans you might have for the future."

"Oh shit, Winston, no-"

"Hold on now. It's going to be okay. I spoke with these people, and fortunately all they wanted was to make a deal. The Governor's reelection committee is paying them big time, but these are smart people who understand the law. They weren't satisfied with only the Governor. Apparently they know who you are, and figured you were of value to them, too."

"How much?"

"Two hundred thousand."

"Jesus Christ!"

"It's a bargain considering how much you make, and how

much tax free money you've socked away."

"I suppose it is, Winston. Still it's a shock."

"Listen, truth be told, they demanded a lot more than that. I'm going to pick up the balance. I mean, I'm the one that got you involved in this, at least partially."

"No, Winston, no. You can't do that for me. I'll pay it all. That's not fair on-"

"I insist. End of discussion about the money. You're safe and in the clear. That's what matters most to me."

Carla leaned over and lightly encircled his shoulders with her arms. "You've been so good to me these last years, and I've done so little for you. How can I repay you for all your kindness?"

Of course, it was meant rhetorically, but it was time for Schneck to pounce. "Carla, you must know how I feel about you..."

Surprised, Carla sat back and looked into his face. "No, Winston, I never thought about that. I mean, I never knew you felt *any* way about me."

"Well, then I hid my feelings pretty effectively. When I thought you might be in danger... I knew I had to do whatever I could to protect you. I mean... this isn't easy for me-"

"What can I do?"

"The two hundred grand is to be paid in weekly installments. I bargained with them to pay the balance, my part, in one lump sum – which I've already delivered. They want to be paid twenty-five hundred a week in cash. Someone will be meeting me every Thursday morning to collect. I thought you could deliver the money to me every Wednesday evening..."

"I can do that."

"And," Winston made a show of hesitating, "I thought maybe you'd like to stay for a short while..." Winston looked away as if embarrassed.

Carla allowed her earlier smile to return. "Winston," she purred softly and took his hand in hers, "after all you've done for me, it's the least I can do..."

Driving home, Winston Schneck thought, this puts a new and

literal meaning to the term hump day! Laughing out loud, a voice in his head said, the linings of some clouds aren't silver, they're pure gold.

THIRTY-EIGHT

After a nearly sleepless night in his cramped home office, the last thing Ken Melzer felt like doing was putting on a tie and going to his office. But he forced himself out of bed and into the bathroom. As he'd suspected, Charlene had not returned home that night, probably camped out at her father's place.

"Son of a bitch," he hissed loudly. In the empty house he alone heard his words and felt momentarily ashamed. What was he becoming? A failed lawyer everyone thinks is a courtroom genius? A failed husband who can't, or perhaps won't, provide for his wife? A miserable insomniac who stumbles around vocalizing obscenities to himself? "Fuck it," he grumbled, again feeling guilty for the language a second time.

Ken took a quick, cool shower, dressed, and headed to work. This was the first day in months he had an open schedule, nothing to prepare for, no one to see. He'd be on vacation soon anyway, so this was simply going through the motions of work. In this unassuming frame of mind, Ken was not expecting what awaited him.

It was exactly eight o'clock, the hour everyone working in the PD's office usually bustled and bottlenecked to arrive on time. Distracted by his own thoughts, Ken did not notice he was the only one arriving. Walking into the main reception area, he was met with a cacophony of party horns, balloons and multi-colored crepe paper streamers thrown his way. A banner had been strung across the hallway leading to the individual offices that spelled in glittered capital letters: *HORRAY KEN "HOBART FUDD" MELZER!* Beneath was written: *HIS Clients Never Do Time!*

Ken was too stunned to absorb the backslapping and comments of "Amazing job!" "I don't know how you pulled that one off!" "Great work!" "You're my hero!" "...An inspiration to us all..." Hank Parnell passed a huge box of donuts and said, "Listen up everyone! Quiet down! I think Ken is a bit overwhelmed by this little celebration. As we all know, he's a modest guy who does great things and considers them *just doing his job!"* Laughter and applause followed. "Have some donuts and coffee, but hearings, arraignments and calendar calls start in a few minutes, so don't piss off your judges by being late!"

Ken sat alone in his office with the door closed. He was still feeling the effects of little sleep and no breakfast. The intercom buzzed and Tina said, "Ken, you have a call on line One, a Mr. Alfonse Certino."

"I don't know who he is. Do you know what he wants?"

"He's pretty well known in legal circles – from New Jersey. You might want to take this."

Ken picked up the desk phone and pushed the line One button. "This is Ken Melzer."

"Yeah, this is Alfonse Certino calling from Jersey. Look, Mr. Melzer, I know you gotta be a busy guy, so I'll make this short and sweet. I liked what you did in court. Showed a lot of balls. I could use a guy like you."

"Ah, Mr. Certino, I'm not sure I understand the nature of this call-"

"Call me Al or Big Al, that's what my friends and associates call me."

"Okay, Al, how can I help you?"

"I got some legal issues I gotta deal with, you know, IRS stuff, some federal criminal shit. I need a guy like you. So, to answer your question about the nature of this call, I want you to move to Jersey. Don't sweat it, I'll give yous a nice home to live in, and you can be my private attorney, you know, like I'll be your one and only client. And don't worry; I can pay more than any of those other firms can offer you. Whaddaya say?"

Ken felt too shocked to say anything, but managed, "Mr. Certino, I mean Big Al, I'm uncertain about my future at the present, but leave your contact info with Tina, who you spoke with previously, and I'll try to get back to you when I'm prepared to make decisions. Thank you for the call. I'll transfer you back to Tina." Ken didn't wait for a reply. He counted slowly to twenty and then buzzed his secretary. "No more calls, Tina.

Anyone wants me, I'm unavailable."

"You got it. No problem."

Before he could calm his mind and take a bite of the frosted donut he'd brought back from his *little celebration*, there was a knock on Ken's door.

"It's open."

Hank Parnell entered. "I hope you were okay with the party. Kind of a tradition when the unexpected occurs."

"Sure, I understand. No worries."

Hank took a seat in front of Ken's desk. He noticed the total lack of clutter on the desktop. "Nice not having a pile of cases waiting for your attention, huh?"

"Yes. It's been a rough few months. I need to clear my head a little."

"I completely understand – been there, done that."

"I'm sure you have."

Hank shifted in his chair. "Look, Ken, I hope I'm not out of line here, but I think I know what you're going through."

"That I doubt."

"I'll get right to it. I got a call from your father-in-law."

"Well, that's just wonderful-"

"He told me about the... well, let's just say he's concerned about the... to use his words, *lack of singular purpose with Charlene,* concerning the future of your legal career."

"Go on."

"Not much more to say. You and Charlene, and I suppose her father, don't want the same thing."

"And how is this any of your business?"

"It's none of my business. I'm only trying to help."

Ken leaned back in his chair and closed his eyes. "I didn't sleep much last night. I'm sorry for snapping at you like that. I know you're trying to help."

"I take it Charlene wants you to capitalize on the Dillard case and land a high-paying job in a big firm. And I take it you like it here in the PD's office."

"In a nutshell, yeah."

"What are you going to do?"

"I don't know. I like my job here, but I don't want to lose my wife. If I do what will make her happy, I'll feel like I'm selling out. If I stay here, I'm letting her down." Ken sat forward and said, "I'm not in a happy place, Hank."

"I can see that."

Neither said anything for a brief time. Finally Ken said, "What would you do?"

"Doesn't matter what I'd do. What are *you* going to do?"

"Help me here. I'm stuck between the proverbial rock and a hard place. I'm screwed either way. But there is one thing that really bothers me, something I can't get a handle on no matter how hard I try."

"What's that?"

"It's that Charlene won't support me on this. I mean, we've been married a short time, and I've only been with the PD's office a matter of months. I could understand her feelings better if we'd been married a long time and I'd been working here for years... but months? I don't know. Does she want me, or does she only want my career?"

"I can't answer that one."

"I know you can't. But it has me more than a little bothered. Frankly, I'm damn disappointed in her, and it's got me tied up in knots."

"You want a little advice?"

"Of course."

"Take some time and don't come to any decisions for a while. You've just come off an intense few months with the Dillard case. Let things settle."

"I suppose that's smart..."

"But don't take too long. You're a hot commodity right now, but that has a short lifespan. If you're going to accept an offer to join a firm, you'll need to do it pretty soon... while you have the name recognition, while you're in demand, while the case is still on the news and being discussed. This won't last indefinitely. Fame is fleeting."

Ken considered what he'd heard. "That makes a lot of sense..."

"I know it does."

"Okay, so now tell me what you'd really do if you were me."

Hank hesitated and shifted again. "If I were you? Well, I'd take the advice I just gave you and think things over... alone. I'd go away for a while by myself. Someplace where I could reevaluate why I went to law school in the first place – what I expected to happen once I passed the bar. I'd question my motives and try to figure out if I want to serve only the downtrodden or if I want to be self-serving... or maybe find some kind of balance between the two. Then I'd consider Charlene and both her role in my life and in my career."

"I don't think you're telling me anything I didn't already know."

"That's probably good. It shows you're thinking logically, but I can tell you one thing you don't know."

"What's that?"

"Charlene is going to be staying in one of the condos her father's firm maintains – you know, for witnesses or visiting guests. A lot of the bigger firms have them."

"Charlene's father told you that?"

"Yes."

"For how long is she going to stay there?"

"Indefinitely."

"Then it looks like I really do have some soul-searching to do."

"I'd say so. And one more thing. You need to meet with Roy Dillard later today. He wants to see you before he leaves."

"Before he leaves? I didn't know he was going anywhere, not that I really care. And I've got nothing to say to him."

"Maybe you don't, but he has something to say to you."

"I'm done with the case, and I'm done with him-"

"I've spoken with him, and you really do need to see him. To answer your first question, he's leaving the country."

"Alone?"

"No. With his brother."

"And you're sure I need to see him?"

"Yes, absolutely sure. Starbuck's, two o'clock this afternoon."

Roy Dillard was already seated in a back corner table with a large coffee in front of him, and an identical covered cup across the small table. Ken took the seat opposite Roy without shaking hands or saying a word. He pulled the plastic cover from his paper cup and took a sip.

"Okay, I'm here. What do you want to tell me?"

"Look, I'm leaving later today, and you'll never hear from me or see me again – my brother, too."

"That part I like."

"I know you're upset with the way our trial played out and-"

"You got that right."

"But you recall I told you there was more to this than you knew? I said someday you might understand. Remember?"

"Go on."

"Well, I appreciate how upset you've been since finding out the truth. I know you feel used and even betrayed." Roy stopped and looked directly into Ken's eyes. "I couldn't let you continue to feel this way, to let your conscience eat you up over this whole thing, this whole situation that was out of your control from the beginning. So now I'm going to explain what I meant... that there was more than you know."

"I hope this isn't going to take long-"

In a surprising outburst of anger, Roy spoke louder than he'd wanted, "This may take a while. Now shut the fuck up and listen! I'm doing this for you!"

Ken fought the urge to walk out, but something deep in his gut told him to stay. "I'm listening."

"I'm sorry for that, Ken. I'm pretty stressed out myself – got a lot on my plate right now. Let's both calm down a little." Roy reached in his pocket and pulled out a coin. Laying it on the table he said, "I found this old nickel in the bottom of a box the other day. It was from a collection Doug was getting rid of... must have slipped out of a coin book or something. Anyway, it's not worth anything, just a worn 1927 Buffalo nickel." He slid it across the table to Ken and continued. "This is for you. Consider it a legal fee for the next little while, just until we part ways. That way you can consider yourself my legal counsel and anything I say to you will be privileged and won't go any further than this table."

Ken picked up the nickel. "It's got a hole in it."

"I told you it isn't worth anything. I suppose someone had it on a necklace or a key chain or something. Nineteen twenty-seven. Know what happened in that year?"

"Tell me."

"Charles Lindbergh made the first trans-Atlantic flight. Nothing's been the same since."

"I suppose."

"Anyway, do you accept the nickel and agree to be my lawyer until we leave this place?"

"Sure. Let's just get this over with."

Roy Dillard took a long swallow of coffee. He stared briefly at Ken, put his cup down and began to speak.

THIRTY-NINE

Without removing his head from the pillow, eight-year-old Douglas Dillard turned to the left. In dim orange numbers, the digital clock showed 3:04 AM. Turning to his right, from the other single bed in the room, he heard the steady, sleep-breathing of his twin brother, Roy. This was what he'd been waiting for. All kids find it hard to get to sleep on Christmas Eve, but to Douglas, it seemed his brother would take forever. He turned again and looked a second time at the clock. While he watched the last number change to 5, slowly and noiselessly he pulled the covers aside, grasped the tiny flashlight from under his pillow, and left their bedroom.

The house was dark, and he noticed the door to his parents' bedroom was closed with no light coming from underneath. So far so good. Turning on the flashlight Douglas made his way down the short staircase to the living room. Next to the decorated Christmas tree were the four lumpy and full stockings hanging from the windowsill. He paid no attention to the wrapped presents under the tree. It was the stockings he focused on. Each had been painstakingly knitted by their mother. Fabricated from green, white and red yarn, they were nearly as long as a man's arm. Each had a name across the top: *ROY, DOUGLAS, MOTHER, FATHER.*

Ever so slowly Douglas pulled his father's Christmas stocking from its hook. Careful to not make a sound, he walked across the room with it to the coat closet. Silently he opened the door and withdrew a cardboard box from under a pile of folded rain ponchos. In its place he put the contents of his father's stocking that had been so lovingly packed by his mother – candies, a tube of toothpaste, a can of the smoked oysters he liked so much, a package of two red bandanas, a jar of pickled onions, a pair of leather work gloves, a three-pack of chewing gum, and of course, the traditional orange from the toe of the stocking. Out of the cardboard box he withdrew an assortment of rocks that he'd collected from the yard. He placed each of them in the stocking, and re-hung it below the window as before. Smiling to himself in the dark, Douglas returned to bed. *Mission accomplished!* was the last thing he thought before being overtaken by sleep.

Jack Dillard's laughter could be heard all the way to the sidewalk in front of their small Indiana home. "You must have been pretty bad this year for Santa to leave you rocks in your stocking, Dad!" exclaimed Douglas gleefully.

"You must be right, Douglas!" Jack laughed long and loud again.

"Honey, I don't know how-"

"Were you really bad this year, Dad?" Roy asked.

Jack slumped in his upholstered chair, his bathrobe pulling tight against his flannel pajamas. Laughing so hard, he could barely catch his breath to say, "I must have been. I guess Santa really does make a list and checks it twice."

Rocks in the stocking became a family story told each year during the holiday season. That Christmas Jack finally got his stocking goodies, but only after Douglas admitted to doing Santa's bidding. He swore Santa made him substitute the rocks. It was clever, and funny, and well beyond the scope of most eight year old imaginations. Jack Dillard loved both his sons, but Douglas's wit and charm made him seem almost enchanting.

In school both Dillard boys were popular. Roy worked hard at his studies and took them seriously. Douglas seemed to take little seriously, yet managed top grades with minimal effort. Once before a seventh grade history test Roy asked his brother, "Aren't you going to study?"

"Why? I heard what Mrs. Jalstrom said in class. I skimmed the info from the text. What's there to study?"

Roy didn't answer. He reviewed hard and pulled a 92 on the test. Douglas got a 100. Roy never bothered to ask such a stupid question of his brother again.

Jack and Ruth Dillard were simple folks. After the eleventh

grade, Jack had dropped out of high school to work in his father's appliance repair shop. Four years later, when his father died of a sudden heart attack, Jack took over the business. He was an independent man who liked the idea of being his own boss. It was a one-man operation that barely paid the bills. Ruth graduated high school and married Jack soon after. Her skill was sewing, and she took in alteration work. A third bedroom in their home was known as the *sewing room*. It was here Ruth spent most of her days. Together they pooled their earnings, paid the mortgage, car payments, bills, and managed to save a little for the rainy day that never seemed to arrive. Honest and meticulous, every cent the Dillards brought in was entered in an inexpensive ledger. Cash that could have been pocketed and forgotten was entered in the ledger to the penny just as were checks or credit card payments. Income tax was paid as a duty, as part of being an honest citizen. Not a single dollar was omitted from the record. Jack and Ruth were proud of their honesty and never lost an opportunity to stress this value on their two sons.

Jack liked one-liners and clichés. He got them from movies, song lyrics, TV shows, or the famous punch lines of old jokes. Each day when the boys left for school he'd say, now pay attention *and don't sully the family name.* As Roy and Douglas got older they'd often beat the Ol' Man to the punch and tell him to not *sully the family name* before he could throw it at them. It became a running joke used so often it became a common expression like *see you later* or *goodnight.*

High school found both Dillard boys excelling in their studies. They spoke of college as a given, not a possibility. It was understood that Jack and Ruth couldn't afford college tuition, so loans or scholarships would be needed. Roy studied hard and maintained a 3.87 grade point average. Douglas kept his studies to a minimum and maintained a 4.0 average, although it irked Jack that his son didn't apply himself to his work. "Just because school comes easy to you, Douglas," his father would say, "is no excuse to sit on your backside and not do anything."

The reply was always the same; "But, Dad, if I ace the tests, why bother to study? I already know this stuff."

And Jack's answer to his son was also always the same;

"Because sitting around isn't productive. And it's important to be productive. If you know everything your teachers expect you to know, then study something else."

"Sure, Dad. Whatever you say," usually ended the discussion between this father and his headstrong son.

During the summer between their junior and senior years, both Dillard boys found jobs. Roy opened a savings account and put nearly all the money he earned safely away. He knew he'd need it for college even though he felt he could get at least a partial scholarship. Douglas cashed his paychecks and put the bills in an old cigar box. When he had a few hundred dollars saved, he began to scan the local trade papers and want ads. He first bought a washing machine and a refrigerator from a family who were renovating their house. Within a week he had run his own ad and resold both items for a fifty percent profit. As he worked he invested his earnings in used bikes, appliances, tools and household items. He managed to resell most of them in a matter of days. At the end of the summer Roy had saved a little over fourteen hundred dollars in his college account. Douglas could count nearly thirty-nine hundred, which he kept as cash in two cigar boxes. Jack Dillard didn't consider his son's buying and selling to be honest work befitting a high school kid saving money for college. And he let Douglas know it.

"But, Dad. Why work for small pay when I can buy and sell stuff and make more money... with less effort?" Douglas would answer his annoyed father.

"Because like I've been trying to pound into that thick skull of yours, you're not being productive! You're always looking for the easy way to accomplish what you're after. And the easy way isn't always the best way."

"You're missing the point here. The money will pay for college and-"

"No, son. You're missing the point. It's not always about the money. It's about you gaining a sense of satisfaction in working hard for something you want. Like I always say, it's about being a *productive* member of society. In all seriousness," Jack once concluded, "with your attitude, it's only a matter of time before you start to truly *sully the family name*." But Jack's words had little effect, and he never left these discussions feeling anything but anger and disappointment toward his brilliant, if rebellious, son.

A week before the beginning of their senior year, Douglas emptied twenty-two hundred dollars from one of his cigar boxes and purchased his first car – a thirteen year old Chevy Impala. Black with red interior, it had chrome dual exhaust pipes that a previous owner had installed for a better exterior sound, fair tires on aftermarket mag wheels, and *only* one hundred and seventy-eight thousand miles on the odometer.

Douglas drove his brother to school each day in the Impala, and within the first week of school it became known as the *Dillardmobile.* Roy was usually too busy studying to date, but Douglas pursued girls with enthusiasm. Jack and Ruth didn't mind the late night hours he spent on weekends, so long as he kept his grades up – as if they were seriously concerned about that – but on weekdays they wanted him safely at home by nine o'clock. This was fine with Douglas; most girls could only go out on the weekends anyway.

With near perfect SAT sores, by late January and soon after his eighteenth birthday, Douglas was offered his first of several full-ride academic scholarships for the following year. He had an aptitude for business, and it was understood that would be his chosen field. Jack's response was an unenthusiastic, "So, now you won't need to spend any of the money you saved for college tuition. I guess you can blow it all on fast cars or girls or something."

"Thanks for your vote of confidence, Dad," Douglas sarcastically replied. It was from this exchange that Douglas suddenly made a decision that, unknown to him at the time, would change his life forever. Without telling anyone, the following day Douglas went to the courthouse and filed papers to legally change his name from Douglas Dillard to Doug Watson. In eight short weeks the paperwork would be complete, and he'd be able to tell his father with complete honesty that he'd never again have to worry about one of his two sons *sullying the family name!*

Replies to Roy's college applications had not yet been

received, but it was still early. If nothing else, he'd have no trouble securing student loans. He was used to working, and was more than willing to pay them off after college when he found a career.

One of Jack Dillard's favorite sayings began with *...but that can all change in a New York minute!* And so did their lives. Valentine's Day began as any other day might. Roy and Douglas left for school in the Dillardmobile, Jack drove the pickup truck to his shop, and Ruth drove her compact Ford to a local dress store to gather skirts and dresses in need of alterations.

It was during this brief abandonment of their home that the fire began. The local fire inspector and the insurance adjuster later concluded it originated in a wall by an additional outlet that Jack had installed himself a few months before. The house was originally built during the boom years immediately after World War II. When purchased by Jack and Ruth, it was in need of work. Ruth was good at decorating, and Jack was good with tools. Between the two they kept their home a work in progress, making improvements as money allowed.

By the time a neighbor had called the fire department and the trucks had arrived, the simple frame home was already a total loss. That night the Dillard family moved to a furnished two-bedroom apartment.

"We were outgrowing that house anyway," Jack told his family. "We need to be optimistic during times like this. *Tomorrow is another day and I'm sure the sun will shine brighter on us then.* Boys," he added turning to Roy and Douglas, "let this be a lesson for both of you. Always buy good and full insurance. Murphy's Law tells us that anything that can go wrong will go wrong, and usually at the worst possible and least expected time. Insurance might be the only thing standing between you and catastrophe."

But some insurance companies pay claims only when forced to do so. When it was discovered the wiring that caused the fire was installed by Jack instead of a licensed electrician, they denied the claim on the grounds the fire was caused by faulty electrical work not done to code. Jack probably could have fought the insurance company, but it would have taken the time, money, and lawyers that Jack could not afford. He was a man who respected authority, and if a big insurance company said the claim was invalid, than the claim must be invalid. End of story. Ashamed that he was the cause of them losing their home, Jack refused to discuss the matter.

A week later, after selling Ruth's Ford, Jack was driving her to look at a used sewing machine advertised in the paper. Since the fire, Jack had not slept much, and it must have taken a toll on his reflexes because a stop sign he'd obeyed for years suddenly loomed in front of the pickup. Jack was too slow hitting the brakes, and he T-boned a garbage truck moving through the intersection.

Jack, a fanatic about seatbelts, along with his wife somehow neglected to buckle up on that day. The old pickup had no airbags, and Jack's momentum was stopped by the hard steering wheel. Ruth's trajectory left her sprawled and unconscious on the hood. After surgeries, both were taken to intensive care. With their medical insurance maxed out after three weeks, they were forced to return to the apartment.

Roy and Douglas left school to care for their parents. Jack was recovering well. His broken ribs were still taped, and fortunately his lungs had not been permanently damaged. A friend would give him a lift to his shop where he could manage some light work. They needed the money. Ruth's injuries were more severe, and the doctors insisted she stay as calm and still as possible in bed. But after Jack said he needed to return to work, Ruth felt she could not endure the idea of her sons emptying her bedpan or sponge bathing her – they were still teenagers for goodness sake! "Go back to school," she admonished them. "Neither of you can afford to miss this much of the school year. I'm doing much better now. I'm okay to be alone." But she wasn't.

Roy was staying after school to work on a paper in the library. Douglas said he'd pick him up later. When he didn't show up, Roy finally walked to the apartment. Arriving home he found his brother and father sitting in the unlit kitchen. "What's gong on? How's Mom?"

Jack started to speak, but couldn't. Visibly shaking, he stifled a sob, and walked from the room. Roy looked to Douglas who choked, "She's gone, Roy. Died while we were in school."

"Oh my God... how?"

Douglas could not talk. Each time he tried his words were cut off by sobs. Finally he was able to say, "They think internal bleeding, but they won't know for sure until the autopsy."

"But I thought she was doing better..." Now it was Roy who couldn't finish his sentence.

"She should have never been let out of the hospital."

"Then why was she?" He nearly yelled through his tears.

"Fucking insurance money ran out. For all Dad's talk about having insurance, his wasn't enough. He told me they always figured there was enough for one of them to be sick. They never thought they might both be in the hospital at the same time."

"Oh my God..."

"This sucks, Roy! First we lose our house, and the insurance pays nothing, and now Mom's dead because the coverage ran out. It's not right. Dad paid them for years, never missed a payment. And this is what he gets. I hate those fucking people..."

"What are we going to do? Oh my God, I can't believe Mom's gone."

"I don't know. Dad can hardly talk, and he's still in a bad way from the accident. I can't believe two months ago we were back in our old house living as we always had."

"*In a New York minute everything can change.* He had that right."

"Yeah, no shit."

But another *New York minute* was about to occur, and *everything was about to change* yet again.

Jennifer Lehrner, Debbie Collins and Barb Stanton were best friends. All three were cheerleaders and hung with the *populars* at school. They came from affluent families, and all three drove the new cars their parents bought them for their sixteenth birthdays. Their clothes were expensive, and their hair and makeup were perfect. Everything about them gave off an air of snobbery. Douglas Dillard had known all three of them since entering high school, yet none had ever spoken to him. He came from the wrong neighborhood, drove the wrong kind of car. Once Douglas tried to strike up a conversation after school with Jennifer, but she was unreceptive. Later he overheard her say to Barb Stanton and Debbie Collins, "Can you believe that lowlife, Douglas Dillard, tried to put the make on me…"

For days afterward the encounter and what he had overheard annoyed him, pissed him off actually. He, Douglas Dillard, kept a 4.0 G.P.A., had secured a full-ride scholarship, had tripled his summer job earnings by using his business smarts, drove a car he bought himself, and was destined for big things. Those three had only looks and wealthy families to brag about. In the years to come, his accomplishments would dwarf their shallow and indifferent lives. He looked forward to the ten-year class reunion he pictured in his mind. He'd show up driving a Mercedes and make the rounds with a super model wife on his arm…

Indiana winters could last long. The night of March 27th and the morning after were cold and snowy. Seven inches of wet spring snow covered the ground. By the end of the school day, though, the temperature had risen to the mid-forties and the streets were wet with melt water. Again Roy was working in the library, so Douglas was alone driving back to the apartment. He was playing a favorite CD and was in a good mood, at least as good as seemed possible since the accident. He had a date lined up for Friday night with a girl he liked. She was smart, and pretty, and had a fun sense of humor, too. He was thinking about her when he spotted Jennifer, Debbie and Barb walking together down a sidewalk. They were just about to walk past a deep muddy puddle by the bike lane of the street. Douglas saw the opportunity – perhaps a once in a lifetime opportunity like this – and took it.

Looking in his rear view mirror, he saw no other cars close by. He was laughing out loud as he approached the puddle to his right. Splashing the three most popular and snobby girls in school could become legend. This was going to be great!

Douglas hit the accelerator as he swerved into the bike lane puddle. He was aware something felt wrong, but was unable to correct it. The car seemed to have a direction all its own, as if there was no driver, no one in control. Later, the police determined what appeared to be a puddle was actually a skim of melted water over sheer ice. When the Impala swerved onto this ice, all traction was lost, and the heavy car slid sideways until the curb caught the mag wheels, flipping the car instantly.

Douglas was wearing his seatbelt and was able to disentangle himself from the overturned Chevy. Debbie, Jennifer and Barb were reduced to unrecognizable fleshy smears conjoined to each other by a chilling pool of thick coagulating blood. In shock and disbelief, Douglas stood over the three until his knees buckled and he fell to the ground.

On the night of the tragedy, Jack Dillard told his son, Douglas, he had indeed *sullied* the family name and promptly disowned him. The following day he wrote a concise note to Roy stating plainly that losing their house was his fault, that Ruth's death was his fault, that not raising Douglas with proper values was his fault, and that he was worth more to Roy dead than alive. He placed his modest life insurance policy – changed that day to list Roy as the sole beneficiary – next to the note, and using a well secured light fixture and a length of electrical cord, hanged himself.

Douglas had been waiting for the right opportunity to inform his father of his recent name change. He'd been waiting for just the right moment. Now, that moment would never arrive. His father was wrong. There had been no sullying of the family name.

Douglas Watson was tried as an adult for vehicular homicide and given fifteen years. He would serve twelve.

Roy Dillard graduated high school. He did not attend the graduation ceremony. At eighteen he was entirely alone. His grandparents on both sides were dead. Neither of his parents had siblings, so there were no aunts, uncles or cousins. Doug, of course, was in prison. The two wrote letters frequently, and Roy visited his brother as often as allowed until he went away to college.

There was no life insurance money for tuition. Roy's dad, Jack, had increased the insurance amount of his policy a year before, and unknown to him, this started the two-year suicide exemption clock back to zero. If he'd left the policy alone, the two-year suicide rule would have been surpassed. Changing the policy restored the two-year exclusion clause for suicide, and no benefits were paid out. Jack died for nothing.

Roy knew college was his only chance to get ahead in life. He got a partial scholarship, and the balance was paid by the student loans he secured. He took college seriously, leaving only temporarily to work for additional money needed for a car and living expenses. Upon graduation, he worked in the food industry. Hell, he thought, people are always going to need food. I'll never have trouble finding a job connected with food. And he was right. He relocated to South Florida where the weather was warm and the streets were free of ice.

The administrators of the correctional facility that contained Doug took an interest in him. He was not the usual prisoner. Doug had no prior juvenile record, had been a straight A student until his incarceration, and was always cooperative, even helpful. He'd been selected as one of the few who might be used as a model for other inmates, especially the younger ones. It was feared that if Doug weren't protected in some way from the general population, he would be corrupted and turn his obvious potential into criminal activity upon his release. For this reason, he was assigned a classroom of his own for helping other inmates earn their high school equivalency diplomas.

Twelve years later, Doug Watson was released.

Being identical twins, Roy could not hire Doug in the restaurant he managed. Even with different names, they both understood it could never work. Doug took whatever jobs he could secure, often for minimal wages. Roy tried to help him financially, but Doug refused, saying, "You've worked too hard to get where you are to have to sacrifice for me." Roy disagreed, but there was nothing he could do.

Doug remembered his earlier high school success with buying and selling used items through the paper. Twelve years later he tried the same thing using online classified ads. He had success, but working jobs, in addition to finding items to sell from garage sales and flea markets, took too much time and effort for the profits realized. Through a contact he'd met in prison, Doug was able to find a buying and selling operation that paid substantially better. The only hitch in the business was that the flow of marijuana he needed was never constant. He had no trouble selling the product for a nice profit. It was finding the supply that was always difficult. He got a lead about a person who might be able to help with the problem. Doug met the man, negotiated an amount he would buy on a weekly basis, paid for his first delivery, and was immediately arrested by the DEA agent who'd taken his money.

Doug Watson was sentenced to three years. He was sent upstate to Florida's Raiford Prison. This time he was not singled out for special privileges or given a classroom in which to teach other inmates. This was hard time, and on his first day he was assigned living quarters with a muscular black man as his cellmate.

After the steel door locked shut, Doug stood before this man, looked him in the face, held out his hand and said, "Hey. Name's Doug Watson."

The open hand across Doug's face was so fierce and unexpected that he was instantly brought to his knees. "Don't you ever look me in the eye again, boy! My name is Che Bantu. You call me *Mister Bantu.* And you do whatever I say or you won't last a week. Got that?"

Still on his knees Doug managed, "Yeah, whatever..." before a kick to his side sent him prostrate.

"Not *yeah whatever* you little white piece of shit! It's *Yes, Mr. Bantu.* Now you say it!"

Doug groaned, "Yes, Mr. Bantu."

"That's better. I'm glad we understand each other. Right?"

"Yes, Mr. Bantu."

"You my bitch, right?"

Doug said nothing until a boot to his stomach induced him to gasp, "Yes, Mr. Bantu."

The brutality imposed on Doug Watson lasted over two months. The attacks were often violent, sometimes painful, and always humiliating. The first time Doug resisted Che Bantu, the resultant assault was so explosive that he knew he had no choice but to submit.

His reprieve came after being approached in the yard by members of the Aryan Nations gang. They knew his plight and offered to help. Within days he was emblazoned with his first raw and swollen fresh tattoos, a signal to all he was a protected man. Doug was transferred to a different cell and associated only with fellow Aryan gang members until he was again released into civilized society.

FORTY

Ken sat across from Roy Dillard, his half-full coffee cup long since cold and abandoned. The two men stared at each other. Ken was still too stunned to speak. Finally, Roy smiled at him and said, "I told you there was more to this case than you knew."

Ken stuttered, "I... I had no idea..."

"It's too bad you never got to know Doug. He's a good guy. You'd like him."

Again, lost for words, Ken mumbled, "I had no idea..."

Laughing now, Roy said, "You've already said that."

"But Roy, you can't feel okay about all this?"

"Do *you* feel okay about this?"

Ken thought a moment, "I honestly don't know. My mind is reeling."

"You had a right to know..."

"But, but what about the stolen guns and jewelry the cops found in your garage? Didn't Doug steal all that stuff? That's not right."

"You're right, it's not. And Doug *didn't* steal any of it. He bought it on the street. Sure, he assumed it was stolen. He, no we, needed it to be stolen, but Doug didn't break into anyone's home or steal anything."

"But what about all the jewelry from Saltzman's? You stole well over a million bucks worth-"

"And their insurance paid for all of it except for a small deductible – which, by the way, they've been nicely compensated for."

"How so?"

"Trust me. Some time ago they received a package in the mail. No need to say any more."

Ken was about to ask a follow-up question, but hesitated and didn't. Roy continued, "Doug and I, and my folks too, lost our home and the damn insurance company withheld what they owed us. Then my mother died because the insurance money ran out and she got released from the hospital instead of getting the care she needed. Finally, out of the deepest kind of desperation, my dad killed himself for the small life insurance money I'd get for college, and because of the two-year exemption in the policy, they never had to pay it. So, no Ken, I don't feel bad about some unimaginably rich and huge insurance company paying a claim to Saltzman's."

"It's still a theft."

"Fine. I can't deny that, but I can justify it."

Digesting what Roy was saying, Ken remained silent.

"Look Ken, I wanted you to understand where Doug and I are coming from."

"I think I get a better picture of it now."

"Good. You need to know we never set out to hurt anyone... well, anyone who didn't deserve it."

"Chester Bentley?"

"Yeah, Chester Bentley, Che Bantu... whatever. That guy deserved to-" Roy checked himself. "Let's just say, the planet's a better place without him."

"I don't know how to respond to that. You can't just go around killing people you think deserve to die."

"Not people in general. Che Bantu in particular, Che Bantu specifically. What he did deserves the death penalty... period. And I stand by that. I feel good about that. He was a monster!"

"It's not up to you to judge-"

"If not me, then who? The courts? The prison system?" Roy let out a disgusted chuckle, "He did what he did to Doug and God only knows how many others in prison, and probably out of prison too. He was free. He acted with impunity." Roy's eyes appeared suddenly fierce. "He got what he deserved, what was righteous, and I stand by that. I sleep well at night knowing this. If I acted as judge, jury and executioner, so be it. Sometimes, in your heart of hearts when you know you are right, it becomes your responsibility to take action. Most people go through their entire lives never having to face that kind of situation, but for those who do come face-to-face with this sort of evil, well... they need to act or know for the rest of their lives they are cowards."

"That's a powerful proclamation."

"It is. And I'd bet if you were placed in that kind of eye-to-eye with evil situation, you'd do something about it too."

Ken shifted in his seat uncomfortably. Changing topics he asked, "Hank said you were leaving, going somewhere."

Roy glanced at his watch, "Yeah, got a flight out of Lauderdale in four hours."

"Where are you going?"

"Doesn't matter where, just so long as they have some first-rate doctors who can remove tattoos and maybe do skin grafts."

"When will you be coming back?"

"We're not."

Incredulous, Ken stammered, "You're leaving for good?"

"Yes. It's been decided for a long time. There's always a chance of a civil suit brought by Saltzman's insurance company." Roy looked at Ken as if deciding whether to continue, and then said, "Okay, here's the deal. Most of this was Doug's plan. He figured it out over the last couple of years while in prison. He's a smart guy, as you now know."

"Seems that way."

"Right. Well, all the jewelry got traded piece by piece or in small lots. Doug cultivated a ton of contacts while doing time in Raiford. He swapped the Saltzman proceeds for marijuana and cocaine. Through other connections he'd made, that product got sold to distributors. Doug learned his lesson the hard way about being a street pusher himself. Regardless, he knew everyone he dealt with. By the time all the jewelry was disposed of, Doug had increased the total worth of the heist by at least three or four times. I don't even know the final figures, but I do know Doug has non-interest bearing accounts in nearly every bank in South Florida. He opened them with small amounts of cash and then added to each with more cash and postal money orders he bought. He kept his deposits light, and to conceal any suspicion, never deposited to the same bank on consecutive days. It became almost a full-time occupation! But now he's closing the accounts by wiring the funds to new overseas banks-"

Ken interrupted, "What about your house?"

Roy smiled again, "Technically, Doug's house. It was in his

name. While I was waiting for trial Doug lined up a cash buyer who wanted a good deal on a house he could flip. It's already sold."

"You thought of everything…"

"Doug thought of most of it. It seemed like a foolproof plan. I suppose something could have gone wrong, but the odds were in our favor, and it went off without a hitch."

Roy suddenly stood. "Look, Ken, I am truly sorry to have put you through what I did. You are a stand-up guy, and I'd like to leave considering you a friend."

Ken thought a moment before standing and showing the Buffalo nickel he'd been paid, "I'm your hired lawyer, Roy, not your friend… at least until you walk out of this place. I don't know what I am then."

Roy unexpectedly approached Ken and gave him a full bear-hug embrace. Releasing him he said, "Thank you. It's been a pleasure knowing you, Counselor." He stepped back, allowed a short chuckle, and gave Ken a quick pat on the back as he headed for the door.

Ken sat down and absently took a sip of the Starbuck's coffee. Lost in thought, he was unaware of its cold and bitter taste. Minutes passed. So, he thought, this is what Roy meant by Universal Justice, Pure Justice, God's Justice… He was suddenly jolted back to reality by the vibrations of his phone. Fishing it out of his pocket he answered, "Hello."

"Well, congratulations, Brother. You must be awfully proud of yourself."

"Matthew?"

"Mark."

Ken felt lost for words. "I haven't talked to you for a while-"

"No, you haven't. You haven't talked to Dad in a while either."

"Yeah, I know, I've been pretty busy with-"

"We know what you've been busy with. You've been busy freeing a killer and a jewel thief."

"Is that what you called for? To give me shit?"

"Nice language-"

"What do you want, Mark?"

"Do you know what this trial of yours has done to our father? I want to know if this is your idea of *doing good for humanity.* I think that was an approximation of the words you used in your solemn vow to the family."

"You don't know what you're talking about, Mark. There's more to this case than you can possibly understand-"

"Good. Then why don't you explain it to me?"

"Can't."

"Why not, Little Brother?"

"Attorney-client privilege."

"That's bullshit-"

Ken snarled, "Nice language, Big Brother," before clicking off the call.

FORTY-ONE

Ken Melzer woke alone. For the briefest of moments he was surprised Charlene was not in the bed next to him. He sighed a long "fuck," glanced at the clock on his nightstand, and rolled out of bed. After a quick shower and no shave, he dressed – purposely leaving off a tie. It was strange seeing only his clothes in the closet. Last day in the office for a while, he thought as he pulled out of the driveway. He hadn't bothered to make the bed.

Ken sat behind his desk. He glanced around the office. Charlene had hung a few pictures and made sure there were books on the shelves. Not much personality in here, he realized. The brass ship's wheel clock sitting prominently on his desktop showed 8:13. Ken opened a deep, empty bottom drawer, grabbed the clock, and unceremoniously dropped it in. "Never liked that fucking thing," he said aloud as he slammed the drawer shut. *I gotta stop saying that word...* He pushed back in his chair, and stared at the ceiling.

A knock on the door brought him back to the present. "It's open."

Hank Parnell walked in. "Mind if I sit for a minute?"

"I got nothing but time..."

"How'd your meeting go with Roy yesterday?"

"I'm still trying to digest it all." Ken looked to Hank for a moment and asked, "Did he have the same discussion with you?"

"Yes."

"Well, I can tell you I still don't know how to process what he said."

"I'm not surprised," Hank responded calmly.

"How are you dealing with it?"

"I'm not, Ken."

"What do you mean, *you're not?*"

"Exactly what I said. I'm putting it out of my mind. I mean, of course, I thought about it for a while, and then I did the only wise thing I could do. I dismissed it."

"Why? How can you do that?" Ken asked incredulously.

"Look, this trial was an anomaly. It's a once in a lifetime event – if even that. A case like this undermines everything the justice system stands for. If defendants like Roy Dillard, or maybe I should say *the Dillard Brothers,* were common, our whole legal apparatus would break down. But fortunately, it's not common. In fact, cases like this are so rare it's best to discount them altogether, pretend they never happened."

Ken said nothing. He waited for Hank to say more, but he didn't. Finally Ken asked, "Did Roy talk to you about some kind of Universal Justice or Pure Justice?"

"Or God's Justice?"

"Yeah, that too."

"Yes," Hank said.

"And…?"

"Made a lot of sense, but aside from this particular case, it's almost always hypothetical."

"But not in this case, Hank?"

"No, not in this case."

"And you can just blow it off and forget about it?"

"I'm going to try." Hank hesitated, collecting his thoughts as if what he wanted to communicate had to be said correctly. "As attorneys, we deal with laws created and written by man. And man is fallible. Man is not perfect – not by a long shot. It takes a Roy and a Doug Dillard to remind us of that fact." Hank closed his eyes for a few seconds, opened them and concluded, "It's humbling actually, but in a good way."

"How is it good?"

"Because it keeps us mortals from getting too big for our britches, keeps us from thinking we have all the answers. The Dillards represent that gray area that often exists between right and wrong. I can't sit in judgment on this case, and neither can you or anyone else. I think Roy was right when he said in the end only God can."

"And if there is no God?"

Hank paused – thinking, then shrugged. "I honestly don't

know how to respond to that…"

Ken's cellphone vibrated on the desk in front of him. Looking down he recognized the illuminated number. "It's Charlene. I better take this."

Rising, Hank said, "Yeah, you probably should."

"Mind closing the door?"

Ken let the phone vibrate for a while before answering. "Charlene…"

"Hello, Ken."

"Nice of you to let me know you were moving out of-"

"I didn't call to get into that," she said interrupting him. "I made up my mind after you hesitated to take one of the offers that came in-"

"Just like that," Now it was Ken who interrupted, "I don't accept an offer, and you're gone, history…"

"I didn't want to make a scene out of it. I knew I was going to leave, so I did. I wasn't going to have a fight with you over it. I made up my mind, and I have no regrets."

"So that's it then. Just like that. One minute we're married, and the next we're not."

"I didn't say that."

"You didn't need to say anything. I think your actions speak louder than any words."

"Look, Ken, I don't know where we stand right now. I don't know how our marriage stands."

"All because I didn't jump at a position with a big law firm? Is that all you want from me and our marriage?"

"Rather than tell you what I *do want,* let me tell you what I *don't want.*"

"Great, Charlene. That would be helpful."

"I'm going to ignore your sarcasm because that is *not helpful.* What I don't want is to live in near poverty when it's not necessary. You could be an attorney with a fine law firm in Orlando right now, and ask for a great starting salary and benefit package, but the window of opportunity is short. You know this, yet you aren't going to do anything about it-"

"I never said that."

"Then I'm wrong? You'll accept their offer?"

An uncomfortable silence followed. "Thought so." Charlene continued, "I don't want to see the husband I love – and I do love you, Ken – agonizing over two-bit cases involving low-life clients. I saw what the Dillard trial did to you, and frankly, it was pathetic. I watched you sleepless and falling to pieces… and all for what? For a couple of scammers who got away with murder and a ton of jewelry? I know full well how tough that case was on you, but let me tell you; it was a bitch for me also. I stood on the sidelines helplessly watching it destroy you… no, watching you destroy yourself. And there was no compensation for you. And why? Because you're on salary, a small salary. You busted your hump and got nothing out of it. At least if you were in private practice you'd have a huge fee to bank. But you did the same work for nothing. Nothing! And I can't, and I won't, go through that again."

Weakly, Ken said, "So, it's all about you?"

"Don't give me that crap. No, it's not all about *me*. It's about *us*. It's about future children. It's about the friends we will or won't develop. It's about your career. It's about our financial future. We've been through this before. For Christ's sakes, Ken, wise up! Wake up!"

"So now what?"

"I don't know. For the immediate future I need to be away from you and the PD's office. I need to step back. I don't think you are going to change, and I need to decide how I'm going to deal with that."

"Sounds more like your father speaking than-"

"Leave him out of this. Sure, I talk to him. He's a smart guy with a lot of good advice to give, but this is my decision. It was my decision to move out. And any other decisions are also going to be mine."

"And what am I supposed to do while you're making decisions?"

"Same as me. Whatever you need to. You've got vacation time. I'd suggest you use it to reevaluate your life and career."

"Like you are doing?"

"Exactly like I am doing."

"Let me get this straight. I either take a position in a big firm making lots of money, or you're gone. Is that it, Char?"

"That sounds pretty cold, but I suppose it is. I want us to have a successful life together, and that's not going to happen if you stay at the PD's office doing basically pro bono work. I love you, Ken, but that's not enough to sustain me for the rest of my life. I don't want to start resenting you."

"Sounds like you already do."

"Perhaps."

"Nothing more to say, Charlene?"

"The ball's in your court."

"How much time do I have to convince myself to sell out everything I believe in and bend to your will?"

"From that I think I know where we both stand. I have nothing else to say."

Ken was about to speak more, but the call had ended.

Ken leaned forward and folded his arms on his desk. A moment later he closed his eyes and placed his head on his arms. He didn't know whether to feel anger or betrayal or disappointment. He always knew this day would happen – maybe after a few years – he just didn't think it would be so soon after starting with the PD's office. No point lamenting the timing. It was here and now, and he had to deal with it.

Okay, Ken calmly rationalized, she wants me to reevaluate my life and career, wants me to take a vacation – I can do that. Maybe she's right. Maybe it's time to take a hard look at reality. Am I in this position because it's what I truly want, or is it because I needed to make a point – to prove something to my father and brothers? There, he'd thought it at last! Charlene's forced the issue. Angry with Charlene, betrayed by Charlene, disappointed with Charlene? I don't know. Maybe in time I'll thank her!

Ken left his office and walked to the reception desk. "Tina, any calls for me?"

She held out a neat pile of message slips, "Only four law firms wanting you to call them as soon as possible."

"I'm going out to get a bite to eat. Would you mind putting those on my desk?"

Ken bought a sandwich and a Coke at a convenience store. Sitting on a park bench by a pond, he found that thinking about his situation killed his desire for food. Only the flock of ducks surrounding him benefited. His lunch lasted about a half minute with the aggressive, squabbling birds. And then they were gone.

Arriving back an hour later, Ken was stopped by Tina on the way to his office. "This package got delivered for you a few minutes after you left."

"Who's it from?"

"I don't know. There's no return address."

"Well, let's see what it is."

Tina handed him her keychain containing an attached tiny red Swiss Army knife. "This ought to work."

Ken opened the blade and slit the packaging tape. Peeling back the box flaps he was surprised to see a second box inside with a label across the top. Printed in heavy block letters, it read: **KEN, OPEN PRIVATELY WHEN YOU ARE ALONE.** Nonchalantly, Ken said, "Oh, I know what this is. Almost forgot I ordered this stuff – fabric and paint samples that Charlene wanted." Ken quickly re-folded the box tabs.

"And here I thought this might be something exciting…"

Walking back to his office he laughed, "Slim chance of that."

Ken closed and locked his office door before placing the box on his desk. He pulled the second box out from the first, and using a letter opener struggled to cut the heavy strapping tape securing this smaller container. Upon opening it he found a sheet of paper taped to a flat piece of cardboard covering the contents. The paper was printed in the same block letters as the warning label. The two large words covering the paper said: **WELL EARNED!** Ken lifted the cardboard and stared into the box. At first he was almost afraid to handle the contents. He was unsure if the bundles were in one thin layer or went deeper.

They went deeper, all the way to the bottom of the box.

Hundred dollar bills, wrapped with a holding strap twenty to a bundle, two thousand dollars each. Ken walked to the door and tried the knob – still locked. He returned to his desk and began removing the packets. He counted one hundred and twenty-five of them – two hundred and fifty thousand, a quarter of a million dollars.

As if he were a child about to be caught eating candy before dinner, Ken quickly replaced the cash in the two boxes. His immediate thought was that there must be some mistake, this wasn't his, he had to find the rightful owner and return it. But he knew who sent it, and from where it had originated. Ken felt his breathing quicken and sweat form on his forehead. Placing the box on the floor, he sat at his desk. *Calm yourself and think.* He wiped his face with a tissue, and took a few slow, deep breaths.

Ken realized he had few options. He couldn't return the cash to the Dillards as they were already out of the country. Roy told him the Saltzman Jewelry Store people received *a package*… no mystery what was in theirs. Giving them the money would be redundant. He could call the police… and say what? *I just received a box with a quarter-mil in it and I want to give it to you…* Give cash to the police? That's a joke. It'd never make it to the station. Tell Hank? Hell, maybe he got a package too. Maybe the words said it all… **WELL EARNED!** Maybe Charlene was right about *busting my hump for no compensation* especially in a case Hank categorized as *an anomaly.* Dillard and his brother were anomalies, the trial was an anomaly, the outcome was an anomaly, his role was an anomaly, and now this box of cash is an anomaly! What to do or think about the trial? Hank said he was going to forget about it. Perhaps that's what Ken needed to do. And the box of cash? It can't be returned. It can't be declared for income tax. It can't be given away. Can't forget about it. But Ken could forget about where it came from. Tell Charlene? She moved out and hung up on him, told him to take a vacation and reevaluate.

Ken pulled his top desk drawer and removed the 1927 Buffalo nickel Roy had given him. *Lindbergh,* the name briefly passed through his mind. As Dillard had said, *nothing's been the same since.* Noting the hole drilled in the top of the coin, Ken opened the ring on his keys and slid the nickel into place. Lifting the box from the floor, Ken strolled through the PD's office and took the elevator to the main entrance. From there he walked to his Honda parked below a sign that read:

RESERVED PARKING
PUBLIC DEFENDER'S OFFICE

AFTERWORD

LUNDEN, ARIZONA

Ken Melzer saw the bright warning light shining below the gas gauge in the Honda. From experience, he knew he had at least two gallons left. He also knew he could drive at least fifty to sixty miles before he'd be in trouble. Normally he'd have stopped for gas when the tank was about a quarter full – better to be safe than sorry – but he'd been lost in thought for the last hundred or more miles.

He'd found driving relaxing, and a good time to sort things out in his mind. He'd driven north on I-75 through Florida, then picked up I-10 going west. Somewhere in New Mexico the red engine light began to glow in the dashboard display. But the Honda seemed to run fine and sound fine. He'd deal with it later.

Cruising alone, with only a few old and stale CDs to play in the tuner-jammed stereo, afforded Ken some much needed time to think. And think he did, hour upon hour. Yet, he could reach no solid conclusions. Desperately, he wanted resolution to the situation in Ft. Lauderdale, but the further he drove, the more distant his problems in Florida seemed. *Out of sight, out of mind* might be a worn-out old cliché, but Ken realized there might be truth in it. Finally, somewhere in West Texas, Ken decided for now he was glad to be on his own, seeing a part of the country he'd only read about, and having time *and money* for himself. No office to check in with, no wife to call at home – at least for now, that is. Ken was so conflicted about Charlene that sometimes he longed for her with such intensity it felt almost physically painful, while other times he was glad to be alone, independent, and cruising the highway.

Closing in on Phoenix, Ken decided for no particular reason it was time to head north. A sign for I-17, NORTH, FLAGSTAFF showed an exit in two miles, and Ken took it. The Phoenix traffic lessened the further north he drove until the cars thinned to a scattered few, all traveling well beyond the speed limit. The countryside too changed to dramatic cactus-cluttered desert vistas, cliffs, and distant mountains. Because he was destination-less, and simply because *he could,* Ken exited I-17, and took a secondary two lane highway heading northeast through scenery totally vacant, yet spectacular.

It was forty minutes on this deserted road that Ken noticed the gas gauge warning light flash. A bullet hole riddled sign read *LUNDEN, 19 MILES.* Ken looked at his watch – 5:21. Good timing, he thought. I can fill up and grab a bite to eat. Maybe crash for the night if there's a motel around. Ken bought gas at the highway turnoff and asked the teenage girl behind the counter where he might get something to eat.

"Want cheap or expensive?" she asked seriously.

"What are my choices?"

"Cheap, well, there's a diner serves mainly truckers twenty-four seven. Expensive, we got Chuck's Desert Oasis."

Playing the concerned out-of-stater, Ken asked, "How expensive?"

"Well, it's a little out of my budget, so I don't eat there much, but you better be prepared to spend at least fifteen bucks for a dinner."

"I see. Well, maybe I'll splurge tonight. Where is this place?"

"Stay on this road about two miles. Chuck's is pretty much in the center of Lunden. You can't miss it."

Ken started the Honda and noticed a noise coming from under the hood. Probably time to see to that engine light. As the girl at the gas station had directed, Ken drove exactly two miles and pulled into the dirt parking lot under a sign proclaiming *CHUCK'S DESERT OASIS, FINE DINING, FULL BAR.* But it was something in the corner of the parking lot that caught his attention, and Ken parked the Honda next to it.

The car looked out of place in this one-horse Arizona town in the middle of nowhere. Ken walked around it and was surprised to see New York plates mounted front and back. *Porsche Boxster S* he read off the low and wide rear of the black sports car. A

FOR SALE sign behind the windshield listed the name *TOM* and a phone number. For a moment Ken was mesmerized by this German masterpiece of engineering.

He walked through the door and took a seat at a table with two chairs near the bar. A middle aged, balding man approached. "You look tired and hungry. What can I get you?"

"Got a specialty?"

"My steaks are the best around."

Ken immediately thought that might not mean much as there didn't seem to be any competition in the culinary world *around here*, but he said, "I'll take you up on one of those, medium."

"Ribeye or New York?"

"Surprise me."

"Comes with potatoes – baked or fried – and veggies."

"Great, baked sounds good."

"Something to drink?"

"Coors Light on tap?"

"You got it…"

Ken looked around the place. A few obvious locals in boots and western hats sat hunched over their beers at the bar. Several people occupied tables eating dinner. Ken figured that for a Wednesday this was probably typical. He noticed some deer and antelope heads mounted on the walls along with some aged and yellowed prints of Indians and teepees. He felt out of place in his polo shirt, khakis and sneakers, but he also felt strangely comfortable here.

The man brought the plate to Ken and asked, "Need any steak sauce or anything else?"

"Nope, I'm good." Then before the man left he added, "Are you Chuck?"

"At your service."

"I noticed that car for sale in your parking lot. Know anything about it?"

"I know it belongs to a guy name of Tom Sloan."

"Know why he's selling it?"

"Sure. He's leaving town. Heading for Montana. That's not the best car for the snow and ice they have up there. Far as I know, it's in good shape."

"Know what he wants for it?"

"I better let you talk to him. Finish your steak, and I'll call him. He doesn't live far from here."

The ribeye was huge, and it was all Ken could do to finish it. Chuck brought the check to the table. The bill came to twenty-one fifty including the second Coors Light Ken had ordered. He threw a twenty and a ten on the table and walked to the bar.

Leaning toward Ken, Chuck said, "I already called Tom. He'll be here directly. Another beer?"

"No, I'm good, but thanks for calling Tom for me."

Ken did eventually have a third beer with Tom Sloan and his friend, Mae Hollis. They confirmed Chuck's assertion they were leaving for Montana in about a week or so. Ken thought they seemed like good and interesting people. Their meeting did start awkwardly though, Ken thought. Tom and Mae introduced themselves and each shook Ken's hand. When he said his name was Ken Melzer, he wasn't sure if he detected recognition in Tom's eyes.

He asked, "So Ken, what brings you to Lunden, Arizona?"

"Actually, I'm just passing through."

"Really? Where are you headed, if you don't mind me asking?"

"No, I don't mind. I really don't know where I'm headed. I'm on vacation and thought I'd see some of the West."

Mae asked, "How long have you been on the road?"

"I guess about five or six days."

"Where's home?" she prodded.

"Ft. Lauderdale, Florida."

Tom said, "That's a long way from Lunden. What do you do there?"

Ken hesitated slightly before responding, "I'm an attorney."

Tom smiled. "Thought so. You must be the gentleman who represented the Super Bowl Killer."

"I can't deny it," Ken tried to sound glib.

"Interesting case." Ken thought Tom was about to ask more questions, but held back. Ken appreciated that. "Been on all the news shows and discussion panels."

"So I understand. There was more to that trial than the news people know."

Mae said, "I wouldn't doubt that for a minute." She glanced to Tom and said, "Ken must be beat from all the driving. Let's get a table where we can relax a bit. I could use a Coke."

Over the next two and a half hours, Ken had test-driven the Porsche – wow, what a ride! – settled with Tom on a cash price, and found out there was a motel a short ways down the highway. He also enjoyed the company of Mae and Tom. Instinctively, Ken knew they were decent people, and he liked them from the time he shook their hands.

Ken asked, "New York plates? You're a long way from home, too."

"Not home anymore. This was home for a while, but it's time to move on."

Mae said, "Tom was an English professor in Kingston, New York. At least he was in a past life."

Tom shot back, "And Mae was a lost and lonely singer and accountant from Tennessee until she met me and, fortuitously for her, I led her from the wilderness..."

Mae laughed, placed her hand on Tom's and turned to Ken, "You'll have to excuse Professor Sloan. He's always been full of shit!"

The three laughed and Ken said, "I thought I detected a little Southern twang there, Mae..."

Tom said, "By the lilt of her linguistic inflection, one can ascertain she hails from below the Mason-Dixon Line."

Again Mae turned to Ken, "That sort of eastern officiousness is only one part of Tom's many charms."

"Reminds me of an English prof I had my freshman year at Tulane."

Mae chuckled, "See, Tom, another kindred spirit from Dixie. Now I don't feel so alone..."

They chatted and cajoled each other until Ken said, "How 'bout we meet here tomorrow morning... say, nine o'clock. I can pay you for the car, and we can get a temporary tag put on it. Maybe I can find a place to sell the old Honda. I'll probably have to stick around here for a while until I do."

Mae looked to Tom who said, "Mae's been renting a house down the street from here. Nice little place. She's already moved out, and I'm sure you could rent it month-to-month, or even week-to-week. There's enough furniture there to get you by."

"I might just do that. The Honda needs a little work before I can sell it."

Mae jotted on a napkin. "This is the number of the people I rented from. You might want to give them a call. And this is our number – we're down to one phone for now. We'll be here about a week, and then it's off to Montana. If we can do anything for you while we're here, or if you ever get to Montana, give us a call."

"Thank you, Mae. That's very kind of you." Without thinking he added, "You might just hear from me sometime."

The three rose from their seats and Ken said, "I've got this," and threw another twenty and a ten on the table.

They walked to the door and stepped outside to the still-warm Arizona evening. Mae said, "At least you're used to the heat, Ken."

"Yeah, but this is nice. No humidity like in Florida."

Tom stopped abruptly a few feet out of the restaurant. Taking Mae's arm he pointed with his other hand and said, "Now that's certainly unusual."

Mae followed his gesture with her eyes. "You don't usually see ravens out this late in the day."

Three of the huge black birds stood on the roof of the Boxster. In unison they turned as if staring at Tom, Mae and Ken. Then suddenly, with loud raucous cries, the three took off simultaneously.

Ken said, "Ravens are intelligent creatures."

Tom mumbled, "Mysterious and spiritual too... at least to some of the Indians around here..."

Mae moved closer to Tom, but remained silent.

Ken broke from Mae and Tom. Walking toward his Honda he said, "See you tomorrow morning at nine."

On their short drive home Mae said, "I like Ken."

"I do too," Tom agreed.

"He reminds me of someone."

"Really? Who?"

"You – when you first came to Lunden."

"Why does he remind you of me back then?"

"I think there's a lot to him. I don't know if he's running away from something, or maybe running toward something new. But he's far from settled in his mind, I can tell that."

"You've always had good instincts. I'd never doubt them."

"See that you don't." And smiling broadly, Mae lightly punched Tom's upper arm.

348

ABOUT THE AUTHOR

William Goodman resides with his wife, Marion, in Bozeman, Montana and part of the winter months in Cave Creek, Arizona. An experienced outdoorsman, he is equally at home in the Rocky Mountains as in the Sonoran Desert. Both of their sons live in Montana.

Contact William Goodman at goodman.williamt@gmail.com